OF CRIME

AND HUMANITY

OF

CRIME

AND

HUMANITY

A Novel

MA'ON SHAN

Matador
9 Priory Business Park,
Wistow Road, Kibworth Beauchamp,
Leicestershire, LE8 0RX
Tel: 0116 279 2299
Email: books@troubador.co.uk
Web: www.troubador.co.uk/matador
Twitter: @matadorbooks

First UK Edition

ISBN 978 1789017 045

British Library Cataloguing in Publication Data.
A catalogue record for this book is available from the British Library.

Printed and bound in Great Britain by 4edge Limited
Typeset in 10.5pt Adobe Garamond Pro by Troubador Publishing Ltd, Leicester, UK

Matador is an imprint of Troubador Publishing Ltd

"I know, I'm a spoiled brat."
"But I like to spoil you, dear."

A PRAYER

By this my gift
I would build a causeway sheer athwart
The river of Samsara, and all folk
Would speed across thereby
Until they reach the blessed city.
I myself would cross
And drag the drowning over.
Aye, myself
Tamed, I would tame the wilful;
Comforted, comfort the timid;
Wakened, wake the asleep;
Cooled, cool the burning;
Freed, set free the bound.

(A PRAYER OFFERED FOR
BUDDHAHOOD BY A KING
OF THE BAGAN DYNASTY
IN THE 12TH CENTURY)

PART ONE

THE BANGKOK MADNESS

"Seriously, the Burmese girls are very pretty."

Rudyard Kipling

1

A . H . M . A . N .

―――∕∕∕―――

I finished the beer and ordered another one. I sank back in the plastic chair, basking in the warmth of Bangkok's afternoon sun.

People walking past the pavement café didn't take much notice of me. Even if they should accidentally glance at the row of tables lining the pavement, they would only find an ordinary young man who looked perfectly tranquil. A tourist, probably, carefree and with time and money to fritter away, had got himself drunk on the streets of Khao San; mundane and uninteresting; they turned their eyes away.

Truth be told, I was careworn instead of carefree, half-drunk rather than totally inebriated. I was taking a snooze, but peered through squinted eyelids every now and then at the movement of people in the surrounding area, looking for signs of danger. I knew they were coming to get me, any second now. I should have left Khao San before it was too late. I didn't know why I was still here. I must be terribly lost in the chaos of my mind and of the city. Never knew it would come to this.

I didn't travel to Bangkok unaccompanied. Kaya, a Thai girl, brought me here. It is a fast-paced city where things move quickly. It is a city to explore – for all its glory and beauty – and to ponder; as I came to discover, anything can happen here. For instance, sometime before my arrival, a mad man had destroyed the city's most revered statue of Great Brahma, the Hindu god of creation. The man was beaten to death by a group of angry bystanders outside the shrine. Then, within months of my arrival, the international airport changed name and location; and there was also a strange rumour about a *coup d'état* in the offing. Yes indeed, a coup. People who know enough of the metropolis – of its madness and eccentricities as well as all manner of sins and pleasure – know coups have occurred in the past, and know too, that coups will occur without fail in the future. It is only a matter of when. But coup or no coup was not my present concern, unless I had the misfortune of walking into one. And as I emptied my glass of beer and ordered another one, I pondered for the ten thousandth time how everything had started in the first place which had left me like a dog abandoned on an unknown street.

Ever since the first day Kaya and I landed in Bangkok and took up lodgings in a sultry, toasty apartment round the corner from the Khao San strip in Banglampoo a month ago, we'd been expecting encounters with some rough and unpleasant people who, when they turned up, might identify themselves as being from Interpol or the Royal Thai Police. We wouldn't be too surprised either if it were a bunch of sleazy characters belonging to the gangs of Bangkok, because the underworld was enraged. A money collector working for an underground banker had died mysteriously in a Thai-style massage parlour in Macao, and a million dollars were stolen. It wasn't hard to imagine that both the law enforcement agencies and criminal fraternities were on the move to hunt down those responsible.

I confess that I had a problem thinking straight recently, particularly after a rather unfortunate incident. Hours before I flew out to Bangkok I was involved in a close scuffle in very scary circumstances. My head was wounded as a result. Two days after we had checked ourselves in at Khao San, blood was found dripping quietly from my right ear. Simultaneously I also had severe toothache. Kaya decided that I should deal with the teeth first and took me to a dental clinic which was only a short walk from our apartment.

Inside the clinic, I was struck by a collection of academic certifications etched on aluminium plaques lining the walls. A degree in dentistry at Chulalongkorn University of Thailand. A master's degree from New York University in Buffalo, USA. Others engraved in languages beyond my comprehension all looked very respectable.

"I'm impressed," I said, looking at the qualifications.

"These things come in ridiculously handy on Khao San Road," said Kaya dryly. "Five dollars for an MBA, ten for a Doctorate. In this place, anyone can hang up a shingle and call himself a professional."

"If you're so sceptical, why bring me here?"

"No, I'm not sceptical. I only have reservations about these glossy certificates," she said, with a shrug of her bare shoulders. "But while we're here, let's give the guy a chance to amaze us with his ability."

And to our great amazement, the guy did.

The dentist – a small, bespectacled man in his late forties – asked me to lie down on the reclining chair for a check of my teeth. Afterwards, he stood scanning our faces quietly for a while.

"Anything wrong?" I asked.

"I can't tell yet," answered the dentist. "Do you mind if I take a look at your right ear?"

"Go ahead," said Kaya. "Tell us if it is the real cause of his complaint."

Minutes later, the dentist observed with eyes narrowing, "Did someone hit you over the head with a crowbar?"

This guy is brilliant, I thought, *he must have studied forensic science in addition to dentistry*. I muttered, pointing a finger at Kaya, "The real culprit…"

"Relax, let me do the talking," said Kaya decidedly, placing her hand on my mouth. Turning to the dentist, she explained, "One night I ran into some bad guys who attempted to rape me. My boyfriend came to my rescue and got hit."

"Did you call the police?" asked the dentist.

"No. For personal reasons, we don't want to go to the police or seek help at government facilities," answered Kaya, with an astonishing degree of perfect innocence despite having completely misrepresented the circumstances in which I had been inflicted with the injury.

Fixing the Thai girl with a long, suspicious stare, the dentist said, "I'm only a medical practitioner in a private practice. Don't tell me anything you don't want to; keep it to yourself. Tell you what, your friend needs an immediate operation to remove a blood clot in his head. If left untreated, it can cause severe headaches resulting in confusion or dizziness, as well as other problems like slurred speech, blurred vision, loss of physical coordination and balance; worst comes to worst, his face may become asymmetrical and one side of his mouth may drop…"

"Please help," I cried, on the verge of tears, as my handsome face had been the pride of my life.

But he apologised, saying that was something he could not do. He was only a dentist, and the best he could do to help was to find me a good hospital, contact a surgeon, and make all the necessary arrangements for the operation… if we'd trust him.

"Why should we trust you?" asked Kaya.

"The wound on your boyfriend's head will invite questions at the hospital, and the authorities will be interested to know if foul play was involved. Make me your agent, and I can prepare an excellent medical report for use by the hospital on completely believable grounds," answered the dentist.

I asked him how much it would cost.

"How much are you prepared to pay?" he asked back, forcefully.

"I don't know," I said, finding his question weird.

"I'll take a percentage," he advised, with a grin and a vicious curl of the lips.

Kaya and I blurted out virtually together, "What percentage?"

He gave us a wink; a quick and dirty kind of wink. His expression said something like, "Don't think I don't know what you've done," without actually saying it.

"What?" Kaya glared at him with a fierce scowl.

Drawing a deep breath, he said, "Do you want me to discuss the bank heist two days ago at Bangkok Bank's airport branch? A man and a woman have netted over three million baht from the bank vault.

The news said the man was hit on the head by a security guard in the scuffle before they made good their escape…"

Kaya exchanged glances with me, before asking, "Did you say three million baht?"

The guy folded his arms across his chest in a defensive posture and spoke nervously, "I didn't say it. It's in the news, all over the radio and TV channels." Under Kaya's intense gaze, he was faltering. "Perhaps I heard it wrong… maybe it was more, maybe less…"

Kaya was so amused by this guy who believed we were the bank robbers that she burst into explosive laughter. Then she held her breath and said to the dentist, "Thank you for being discreet. But listen, we are not the bank robbers, and I don't envy them for just a few million baht. My idea of striking it rich would have to be something mega. Or it isn't worth my time!"

She can be quite honest sometimes, I thought.

"Yet I don't mind discussing your fee based on three million baht," continued Kaya. "What about something like one percent?"

"*Ha*," replied the dentist.

I didn't understand the language, but could sense that he had made a counter offer.

"*Song*?" said Kaya.

The dentist shook his head. "No, *Ha*."

"*Sam*?" pressed Kaya. "No? *Si*?"

The dentist refused to back down and kept repeating, "*Ha*."

"Okay, okay, *Ha*." Kaya gave in and explained to me, "That means five percent."

The dentist, who had stuck to his original fee throughout the entire negotiation, was happy to reach an agreement and warmly shook hands with Kaya. I thought, if he could choose, he would have preferred to hug the scantily clad body of the Thai girl who was wearing only a pink vest-top and white beach shorts.

Later the same evening, I was checked into the Mission Hospital on Phitsanulok Road, and had the operation to remove the blood clot in my head the next morning. The surgery was deemed a success. I woke up ten hours later after a deep sleep. First I was confused and very drowsy, but slowly came round to realise that I had returned to the mess of my conscious life when I saw the pretty face of Kaya hovering above me.

A week later, our dear dentist friend arranged for my early release from the hospital, as my case was getting some undue attention. Kaya picked me up on the day of discharge. On our way back to our apartment in Khao San, Bangkok was hit by the first monsoon storm of the season. The storm slowed Bangkok traffic to a crawl; roads and lanes were inundated by heavy rain.

The downpour continued on and off for several days before the weather finally improved, with a hot, scorching sun reappearing to reign over a cloudless sky. Kaya took the opportunity to go downtown to do some shopping and pick up my medicine, while I remained indoors to convalesce. Then much to my dismay, blood was found oozing from my right ear again.

In retrospect my early discharge from the hospital had probably been premature, as my progress to full recovery turned out to be painfully slow. Not only had the operation failed to put me out of trouble, it had also led to some horrible after-effects: my neck stiffened like a rock, my right eye became smaller, with blurred vision, and my cheeks sagged. Initially I had difficulty recognising my once-handsome, princely-looking face in the mirror. It was only a month later that I began to regain some of my past charms as my hair grew back, my vision returned and the swelling subsided. But my somewhat misshapen face continued to feel like dead meat, and a line of ugly stitch marks behind the ear was still all too visible.

Kaya sometimes failed to hide her impatience over the snail-like speed of my recovery, as if she had a plan she was waiting to execute. Every time she was quizzed, she would say something like, "No, I don't have one. We'll know what to do next after you've completely recovered – hey, stop it! Don't be so grabby!" she screamed, blocking my hand that had got between her thighs.

I thought she was unreasonable. As a young man it is normal to wish to be gratified from time to time, as my senses – both sensual and sensuous – had never left me despite the intermittent bleeding from my ear and occasional headaches. But she was determined not to yield to my whims easily. She crossed her legs against my advancing hand, yelling, "Goodness me, you're a saint as well as a cheap little bastard! No, not now, not just now!"

One morning when I woke up after a long night of heavy rain, barely remembering another fight with Kaya before I went to sleep, I felt that all my pains, which had seemed so vivid here, there and everywhere for so long, appeared to have gone, like intruders who had finally retreated for good. There were no more headaches; even the bleeding from my ear had ceased completely. Elated, and realising I had fully recovered from the operation, I couldn't wait to wake up Kaya with the good news. As I rolled over to curl myself around her, I was astonished to find I was all alone in the entire bed. In the space usually occupied by her shapely, curvaceous body, there was only a dirty towel stained with probably my own vomit.

I whipped my head around and noticed she wasn't in the room, either. There was a note folded like an origami flower on the table under the window. I opened it and read it with utter horror. In the note she said she confessed she indeed had a plan and had now gone on to pursue it, without me. She said she would come back. That was how I understood it. Not exactly her words, but, to be precise, she didn't say she wouldn't. I could only hope that she would come back once she had finished her business, whatever it was.

I SPENT MY TIME WAITING for her return at a pavement café on Khao San Road, sipping coffee in the morning and drinking Guinness in the afternoon. This was already the fourth day since Kaya's sudden departure.

Peering into the open space from where I sat sluggishly in my chair, what came into view was pretty much the same all around Khao Shan. There was always a bustling, continuous flow of holiday backpackers, mostly young people sporting colourful T-shirts and wearing sandals or flip flops. They marched down the streets, huddled around food stalls and little souvenir shops, meeting some interesting characters on the way, like the funny little old man selling balloons, or some Akha tribeswomen dressed in full tribal costume hawking silver bracelets, before disappearing into bars and restaurants, henna tattoo shops or guesthouses. Watching the throngs come and go, I drank my beers quietly and retired for a little snooze.

I woke up with a start at hearing someone nearby whisper alarmingly, "What are they doing here? It's the age of information technology and we now pay our protection fee via direct debit. Is the online banking system down again?"

I opened my eyes and found it was the pavement café manager talking to his assistant. They were anxiously watching a bunch of thugs on the opposite side of the street. Two musclemen with tattoos on their arms and shoulders were guarding the entrance to a cheap guesthouse and training their eyes on the faces of people walking past them, as if everyone on the street were guilty of something.

A bald, stout man donning a military leather jacket and a pair of Ray-Ban sunglasses walked out of the guesthouse, followed by a tiny chap who was hopping like a sparrow. They had a chat with the tattooed men, glancing occasionally across the street at the pavement café where I was having my siesta.

The café manager, a pale-faced man in his fifties, his hair greying at the sideburns, murmured to his assistant, "It's Somchai, the right-hand man of Big Brother Wichit. The leather jacket is his brand, rain or shine, like his own skin. Why, he's coming over to us!"

On a hunch, I sank even lower in my chair and put a magazine on my face like I was fast sleep. Footsteps were heard approaching, and people pulled out chairs to sit down not far from my table.

"Good afternoon, Somchai," said the café manager. "I hope it is not about the protection fee…"

"Don't worry," answered a hoarse voice. "If we don't get the protection fee on time, we'll send you an electronic debit note with a twenty-nine percent surcharge. Same as credit cards."

"Then what brings you here, sir?" asked the café manager courteously. From a narrow gap under the magazine, I could see him serving the thugs cans of beer.

"We are looking for a Hong Kong man and a Thai woman," said Somchai. "Sushi, show him the picture."

The sparrow-like man spread out a mini-poster on the table for the café manager who, after browsing it for a second, shrugged to say, "Don't seem to have ever shown up at my place. Handsome man and pretty woman, though. What have they done?"

"Everything from drug trafficking to money laundering, prostitution, extortion, murder for hire and hijacking…" announced Sushi in a goose-like voice, as if reading from a menu of crimes for order.

"No, Sushi, there are only two of them, and they could not have done so much," sighed Somchai. "Though I am not your mentor, nor wish to be, at least I have a right to require that you only speak the truth that you know."

"They kill, they rob, they murder…" Sushi paused when he had exhausted his inventory. "Somchai, what else?"

"Sushi, you're my most trusted man because you don't know a thing," lamented Somchai. Turning to the café manager, he said, "They killed a money collector in Macao, and are understood to have escaped to Bangkok. We've been asked to track them down by our Macao partners and associates. We don't know if it was the same couple who struck again in last month's bank robbery at the airport."

"Wow, it's like a *Bonnie and Clyde* in modern times," remarked the café manager.

"Who are *Bonnie and Clyde*?" asked Sushi, scratching his head. "Do you mean *Mr and Mrs Smith*?"

Somchai told the manager, "You may keep the poster, and give me a ring if you notice anything suspicious." Suddenly he became peculiarly quiet, as though puzzled by something he saw. "What's that? A junkie? Sushi, go check him out."

When Sushi came over to remove the magazine from my face and help me sit up in my chair, I knew in all probability that what I had been waiting for had finally arrived.

"I don't know what to say. This guy looks like he's had a facelift," observed Sushi, eyeing my somewhat misshapen face.

Somchai laughed, not taking Sushi's words seriously. He said, "Show him the poster. Ask him if he knows anything."

My heart fluttered anxiously as the poster was unfolded before me. The images on the poster were not photos, only an artist's impressions. One had to applaud the artist for the remarkable likeness to the real people. The girl in the poster, young, alluring, with bright, round eyes, was unmistakably a true copy of Kaya, although I knew she looked better in the flesh. Her male companion was depicted as having wavy hair, full lips and intense, ink-black eyes that stared out of the poster at me, who was awestruck by the amazingly close resemblance. I yawned to hide my rising consternation, and mumbled, as if a little drunk, "Never met."

"What happened to your face?" inquired Somchai, with prying eyes.

"Traffic accident, in Beijing," I answered casually. "You know Beijing?"

"I know Beijing," interrupted Sushi. "Tiananmen Square? Right?"

"Very good," I intoned with admiration.

At that moment, a young man strolling past the pavement café caught my attention. He had a smart face, wavy hair and a build similar to mine, except that he looked kind of intellectual with a pair of rimless glasses. He was wearing denim jeans and a FCUK T-shirt with a picture of a rooster printed on the chest and there was the line "*Magnificent Cock*" tagged to the claws. What struck me as rather incredulous was that I had a similar T-shirt, also by FCUK, except my cock was larger and much more magnificent.

He's my saviour, I thought. With an outstretched arm I brought Somchai's attention to the young man who had stopped by a roadside stall where a Eurasian girl was being treated to a hair-braiding. "I guess that's your bird," I said. "No, not the girl. I mean the boy standing next to her…"

Somchai plonked his right knuckle-duster-clad fist on the table. That was the cue to act. The two tattooed musclemen plunged into the street, rushed to the side of the young man, and in the twinkling of an eye, grabbed him by the arms and carried him back inside the café as if he were only a small child.

Sushi made him sit down on a chair and asked with an air of importance, "Do you know me?"

"What nonsense!" grumbled Somchai at his most trusted assistant. "Let me do the questioning." Turning to the young man, he said, "Lad, I promise you everything will be over very quickly if you speak to the best of your knowledge."

"What right do you have to question me? Are you plainclothes policemen?" asked the young man furiously.

"You are half-right. Plainclothes, yes; policemen, no. But we are friends of the police, who trust us more than their own people, so you can trust me, too," said Somchai, very firmly. "Now listen, you smartass. I've got some questions, and you'd better be truthful with the answers. Where are you from?"

The young man, after pondering somewhat, decided to cooperate and answered, "Hong Kong."

"Were you in Macao three months ago?"

"Three months ago? I don't remember. I can only tell you I visit the place occasionally."

Somchai nodded to Sushi approvingly, apparently pleased with the answer. "Do you go to the casinos?" he pressed on.

"Of course. That's the only thing to do in Macao, like Las Vegas," replied the young man.

"What are your favourite games?"

The young man shrugged. "I play poker, blackjack and baccarat, anything that requires a sharp and analytical mind."

"And you win most of the time?"

"No, I don't make a living from gambling. I go there just to have fun."

"We know you lost heavily last time you were there…"

"No, I deny that…" cried the young man.

"And you borrowed money from an underground banker…"

"That's not true…" protested the young man.

I probably would have remained in my chair longer if the young man had continued to keep his captors happy with the right answers. However, as the cross-examination grew intense, I knew the young man would frustrate Somchai sooner or later because, in reality, he had nothing in common with me except as a replica of the original wandering in the streets of Bangkok, and a disappointingly remote one looking at close range.

Alas! What a poor lad for being a distant lookalike of me. Somchai was now slapping him in the face for wasting his time with irrelevant and ridiculous answers. The tattooed musclemen had jumped on him and started beating him up for not telling the truth.

I rose slowly to my feet, knowing it was high time to leave the scene as long as the young man was presumed guilty as charged, and retreated noiselessly from the gangsters, who took turns grilling their prey. As I walked out of the café, I took one last glance at the people behind me, and was shocked to find Sushi following me with a curious gaze. He met my eyes, put on a stupid grin, and waved goodbye. I waved back and slunk away.

I could have returned to my apartment, to pick up a few things and be gone forever. But I wasn't sure if my hideout had already become a trap when I saw several thugs talking and smoking outside the cul-de-sac that led to the apartment. I decided it was better to stay away for a few days until it was safe to return.

I walked out of Khao San without knowing exactly where to go. Bangkok was a strange city to me. Because of the need to stay indoors to nurse my wound, I had rarely been anyplace, except a stroll with Kaya along the riverside during an impending storm one night, and a trip to the monastery that houses the world's largest reclining Buddha.

After an hour traipsing around the city, I was lost and tired. Leaning against a lamppost, I suddenly heard a wave of thunderous sounds roaring above my head. I looked up and saw a long chain of connected silver-coloured boxes travelling in mid-air. Then I realised I was standing underneath the aerial tracks of the Bangkok Mass Transit Skytrain, and the Chidlom Station was just round the corner.

Chidlom, as described in a tourist guidebook I picked up from Starbucks, is the area with the famous Erawan Shrine. I remembered Kaya had once explained to me the significance of Erawan and the deity inside. The all-powerful, four-faced deity worshipped at Erawan is renowned for making wishes come true. Kaya said she had made it a habit to stop by Erawan to pray for protection and happiness whenever she was in the area.

Just then a brilliant idea dawned upon me that Erawan was the place to go. I thought that I should pop in at the shrine for a short rest as my legs were heavy and sore, and say a prayer too, in the hope that the almighty deity would be kind enough to listen to my wish, shine a light upon my thoughts and point me to a way out of my personal mess.

2

A.H.M.A.N.

—◈◈◈—

"Wish-making, or thanksgiving?" shouted a shrine attendant at Erawan, who approached me with a yawn.

He was a skinny, dark-complexioned Thai man, in his late twenties. When he yawned, two rows of teeth dyed with a thin tint of yellow stains were put on some kind of display in a careless fashion. I offered him a cigarette. The instant I lit the cigarette for him, his small eyes enlarged, his sleepiness gone. And, as though he had had a shot in the arm, he became galvanised.

"My name is Taksin Sintawichai, part-time shrine attendant," he said. "Welcome to Erawan."

I had a quick snoop around the shrine and saw that there were not many visitors at the time. A plump Chinese woman was paying with a wad of cash for a performance of Thai traditional dance.

"This is a thanksgiving gesture to show appreciation to Great Brahma for a wish come true," explained Taksin, glancing askance at the Chinese woman whose face was decorated with heavy makeup. "She must have found a rich husband."

A group of teenage girls dressed in shiny traditional Thai costumes stepped into position, and started spinning their bodies elegantly to the blaring music.

"Your first time here? Make a wish! Whatever it is, it will come true," said Taksin positively. "What's your trouble? Family matters? Money problems?"

I shook my head, as my present trouble was to do with money in its abundance instead of scarcity.

"Wives, girlfriends, Sex and the City issues?"

The attendant spoke with style, and I was impressed. But I shook my head again. There wasn't much to say about girls, as I was still single, with a lacklustre love life.

When he seemed to have exhausted his suggestions, he surprised me with more lofty subjects, which seemed odd coming from a shrine attendant.

"I hope it's not political. Freedom of speech? Human rights? We have it all in our country," said he, almost with a haughty air, "but you don't?"

I looked at him, wide-eyed with admiration. What a place! What a country! And what a people, who must have enjoyed a great deal of liberal democracy for a denizen to be able to speak with such pride and confidence. Feeling a sense of mental inferiority, I replied, somewhat superciliously, "To be honest, none of the above. I guess it's probably an existential angst I've been suffering since the day I was born."

He gave me a funny look and grinned good-naturedly. "That's okay. I know what you mean. I have come across many kinds of people at the shrine: from the grumpy and the freaky, the loud and angry, the cultivated and intelligent, to the bunch of lazy good-for-nothings," he said, adding with a drawl, "I think I know your type."

"My type? What about my type?" His eloquence irked me and I challenged him. "Anything you would suggest to do with my type?"

"Well, if you ask me, then please listen," he said. "My friend, you have not come to the shrine by accident. You must have made a divine appointment with Great Brahma..." His eyes were filled with a strange reverence as he went on, "Have a conversation with Him. Tell Him everything by going through all the major events in your life which have contributed in big and small ways to bring you here at this very point in time."

I was baffled. "How am I supposed to talk to Great Brahma about my life journey?"

"You see the bench over there? It's under the shade of a tree which will give you a little breeze. You go sit there, and look back at the past to derive great benefit from your historical reminiscences," he said. "In the meantime, while you're picking your brain or having a conversation with Great Brahma, I'll get you some flowers and incense for the offering later."

I welcomed the idea, as my legs badly needed a rest. Taksin walked me over to a bench in a corner of the shrine, and left me after I gave him 500 baht for the perfect offering.

As I sat down I found I was looking straight ahead at one of the four faces of the deity seated on a lotus in the centre of the shrine. Kaya once told me that Great Brahma, the god of creation, represents kindness, mercy, sympathy and impartiality. As I kept my gaze fixed upon Him, I felt none of those virtues except immense grace radiating from the eyes of the golden statue behind a film of incense smoke. It was both surreal and relaxing. I told myself not to doze off because if I was about to receive from Great Brahma some useful celestial guidance, I must be careful to include, as I reminisced, the most important episodes of my life. Thus I installed myself properly on the bench with a straight back and began to reflect upon my short life of twenty-something years as if it were a day of reckoning.

OH MY GOD! WHERE DO I BEGIN?

Okay, let me start with my name, which is Ah Man, and perhaps something of my lineage.

Mother told me this story of the family when I was small. It began with my great-grandfather, who was the governor of Nam Hai, a province in Southern China, of the Qing Dynasty, in the last decade of the twentieth century. My great-grandfather had a great palace, where flags embroidered with the stunning coloured insignia of his royal title fluttered on the turreted walls, and servants in gorgeous livery trimmed with gold braid and silver epaulets guarded the entrance gates. But sadly the glories of my great-grandfather and his king's dynasty were short-lived. At the turn of the century warlords battled each other for domination, and foreign powers invaded the coastal cities. The Qing Dynasty was toppled as a result. My great-grandfather, a loyalist, on hearing of the abdication of the king, vomited a bucket of blood and died. His only son, my grandfather, went into business with the fortune he inherited, making good money by investing in textile manufacturing. But the Second World War and the invasion by Japan, which had literally destroyed the economy, had cost him dearly. He had to leave the country, abandoning his production plants in Shanghai. When he died some years later in Hong Kong, his personal fortune was reduced to only a fraction of the original legacy. But it wasn't as small as it sounds when it was in fact a very sizable collection of imperial porcelain that was passed down to my father. With the imperial collection as a start-up, my father succeeded in building an antiques trading enterprise. Along with the business success, he would also have made his ancestors very proud with the acquisition of a drove of wives and concubines.

My mother was married to my father as wife number four. This was achieved after she had successfully ousted her predecessors and, more importantly, borne the only son of the family. I had very little recollection of my father; when he died at the age of sixty-five, I was still an infant. My uncle succeeded him in the family's antiques business. He, a widower with three daughters, became my stepfather by marrying my young mother. And I, as the only male heir of the combined family, was widely regarded the future successor to the family business.

Wrapping up her story, my mother said, "It's not because of a woman's frailty that I married your uncle a month after the death of your father. It was for our survival in the long term, if you know what that means." As a matter of fact I didn't; I was only ten when the story was first told.

As I grew up, the concept of survival had never really taken shape in me, probably because of my mother's over-protection. I didn't have her assertiveness or willpower. Some people considered me generally meek in disposition. I didn't mind, knowing that meekness is not weakness. I believed I could be brave should the situation require it.

As a young man, I was neither too clever nor too dumb, just average. I wasn't particularly hard-working in my studies, but with a bit of luck, I earned a place to study at Hong Kong's most prestigious university. My undergraduate education ended in disaster when I failed half of the subjects in the final year. The university, considering it a waste of taxpayers' money if I were asked to repeat the course, got rid of me by awarding me an ordinary degree in History and Cultural Arts without honours.

My poor results did not come as a total surprise. As a victim of unrequited love I was even kind of expecting it. In my final year I had a crush on a pretty English tutor. At the same time, I was also a little in love with a distant cousin living in a small town renowned for its beautiful scenery in Southern China. My English tutor and my distant cousin had a lot in common, with similar good looks and an unaffected elegance. I met my cousin for the first time in her hometown during a trip to pick up an antique vase at the request of my stepfather. I had never come across anyone of such unparalleled beauty, and I was smitten. On my second visit, I brazenly made my declaration of love, but my cousin was unimpressed. She thanked me for my kind attention and informed me, regrettably, that she was already engaged to a local schoolteacher.

My English tutor's response to my romantic endeavours was similarly discouraging. She ended her tutorship abruptly in mid-term and was never seen again on campus. It was only from the university bulletin that I learned she had left for England to pursue her studies in political science.

The repercussion of falling out of love took its toll. I fell into drinking, and in my depression let my studies slide beyond rescue. I blamed no one for my poor results, which were, after all, inconsequential as far as my career was concerned. No matter what, I would be working in the antiques trading business as per my mother's wish.

"As heir apparent, all the treasures will be yours after your stepfather has gone," she said.

I didn't see a reason to object to her plan when I was yet to discover my purpose in life. But my uncle, still going strong at a few years over sixty, didn't look as if he were to exit the stage anytime soon. He even had his own plan regarding succession. Because of my mother's failure to give him an offspring, he had decided to turn to a young waitress for help, promising her an official title and a large sum of money if she could bring him a male heir. A year later my stepbrother was born, posing a serious threat to my mother's ambition of controlling the family business for eternity. She was undeterred, however, and went on to set me up working in my stepfather's antiques shop after my graduation.

As assistant to my stepfather, I was regularly sent on errands to various parts of China to pick up antiques. I was therefore a collector of sorts, like the money collector I was about to meet later. Unlike he who collected debts – new and bad – I collected things old and lost-and-found.

A year after I started working in the antiques business, my mother made the unexpected manoeuvre of fortifying our position in the family. It was arranged that I would enter into wedlock with the daughter of an antique furniture shop owner who ran a much bigger business than my family. My mother spelt out to me the merits of arranged marriages: value-added, no hassle of two strangers beating around the bush, and with ready approval from the higher authorities.

I needed no persuasion. Like my dog, pampered and without a big ego, I didn't see why I should object to something which seemed to make a lot of sense and without sweat. I agreed right away and asked, "When?"

"Don't be impatient," she advised. "Your future wife is still underage. She will turn seventeen in the spring, and the wedding will take place immediately thereafter."

A month before the wedding, I received a phone call from my fiancée, whom I had never met. Her name was Apple. She wanted to see me. "It's urgent," she said on the phone, with a touch of melancholy in her tone.

On a chilly Sunday afternoon, I drove my father's Mercedes Benz to pick her up outside the Central Library. She was in her school uniform: a white shirt with a red ribbon tie; a short grey woollen skirt grazing her thighs; long grey woollen stockings; and a heavy, dark blue jacket with a gold lace-embroidered school badge at the upper-left chest pocket. She was carrying some heavy books and folders. I noticed there were some pimples on her cheeks, covered by a thin base of white powder that made her face more pale than white, almost bloodless in the freezing cold air. She had donned a black sports cap; at its rear, a ponytail tied with a rubber band wagged casually between her shoulders as she moved. She got into the car all smiles and charm. Only her eyes, tremblingly sensitive, betrayed a streak of sadness.

We quickly warmed to each other within a short time. While I was stupidly youthful at my age, she was disarmingly adolescent at hers. We burst into unstoppable laughter at almost anything, from a garbage bin blown from the street corner by a strong gust to helpless pedestrians struggling with umbrellas turned upside down like satellite dishes in the wind. But when the subject of our families was brought up, as is only natural for two people who were about to wed, she became mute and pensive.

She was already heating her small hands inside mine when we had our first dinner together. While I was meeting her in a social and courteous capacity, without ulterior motive, it was afterwards that I found she had come to see me with a plan. In retrospect, her plan was innocent and ingenuous, albeit a costly one, the way it turned out.

After our desserts and coffee, she asked me to take her to the lakeside. In our city we have no natural lakes, only man-made ones called reservoirs. All the same, they make good outing places for local citizens in the summertime; but this was winter, and the place was freezing. I asked why the lakeside. She said she wanted to look at the stars. I was not sure about it on a wintry night. She was, however, looking a little desperate and desperately unhappy, so I went ahead just to please her.

I drove to the Plover Cove Reservoir and parked the car at the end of a secluded road shielded by pine trees on two sides. To my surprise the sky was clearer than expected. The clouds were pinned to the sides, leaving a large empty space to the moon and the stars. But the night felt a little unsettling. The moon, only a pale half-moon, was like a thing dead and disembodied being washed up to its present spot. And the smattering of stars was like a pinch of white ashes scattering far and wide across the bitter cold sky.

Then all of a sudden, she asked me to kiss her. I kissed her. She untied her school ribbon tie and unbuttoned her white school shirt. Her breasts were young and firm; her nipples, erect and tilting slightly upward, were unspeakably girlish. We climbed into the back seat of the car to make love. She was, however, an apple too green and unripe for the taking, and we were also too clumsy to find the angle and position for our intercourse, given the narrow space in the back.

But she was determined, with undiminishing enthusiasm to get things going. Eventually I rose to the occasion when I was seized by a brutal and pitiless sensation in my groin, and I began to behave more like an animal than a man. I tore her underskirt to pieces and stripped our bodies to nothing but stark nakedness. She had also quickly learned to collaborate like a true woman. Her soft lips flushed crimson, shivering like a flower in the rain. A mysterious smell of flesh crept into my nostrils, causing my heart to pound violently. I entered her, and when I was only halfway into the little passage of her clam-tight vagina, she let out a sharp, earsplitting scream in a violent struggle that made the car rock like a boat on the waves. Birds were startled in their sleep; some began to engage in long, twittering conversations, as if to understand why the disquiet.

When it was all over, I asked her why the haste, as we were getting married in a month's time. Sucking in a deep breath with her arms crossed over her breasts, she said, "You must claim me now or never. It will be too late next month when I reach the age of consent."

Perplexed, I didn't know what to make of her disclosure.

"You know my dad is not my real dad, only my stepdad. He has been making ugly advances on me since my mum died," she said quietly. "And those ugly advances have escalated recently. I fear that he is waiting for the day when rape is a lesser crime on a seventeen-year-old, and most likely the crime will never be reported because it could wreck my future happiness." With a triumphant smile on her face, she continued, "Now he can stop his dirty imaginations and go to hell."

The next morning I woke up to find our car windows sprayed all over with a thin coating of ice. Apple was sleeping in my arms. Miraculously, her pimples had disappeared, and her cheeks were flushed with an aura of redness. I felt her forehead with my hand and found it was burning feverishly. I woke her up. We kissed each other good morning. After we got dressed, I drove her home.

In the days that ensued I was first struck down by pneumonia, followed by Apple. Hospitalised, I lay in a state of semi-consciousness for two weeks. Afterwards, I regained my senses and energy, and was discharged on New Year's Eve. My mother drove the Mercedes Benz to pick me up at the hospital – the same vehicle Apple and I had used as our motel exactly a month ago on the coldest night of the year. I wondered a little why my mother wasn't driving her black Porsche. But knowing her to be a reckless and aggressive driver who'd had her licence suspended twice for drunk driving and speeding, I quickly realised she might have crashed her car again. As soon as I got into the car, sat down and buckled up, my mother turned to me and announced that the wedding would not take place. Apple had been sent to intensive care when her pneumonia developed complications. She had died three days later.

I WAS QUITE HAPPY ABOUT going away on errands, as the household was becoming severely political, with my mother and her rival fighting for dominance. I went to China regularly, almost once a month, sometimes in a matter of weeks. And it had become a habit of mine that on my return from China to Hong Kong, I would stop over at Macao for a night or two, just to give my body and mind a nice treat.

Macao, the city of dreams, will never disappoint for its non-stop excitement at the casinos and chance encounters with girls from all over the world, some from places as remote as Ukraine. After two years in the antiques trade, I had made friends with some croupier girls and bodyguards, and built a good reputation as an antiques collector who would meet his deadlines on repaying loans using underground bankers to cover his losses in casinos.

Things went well for some time until a twist of fate struck.

My uncle was tipped off by a contact in China of a find by a gravedigger. The man had accidentally stumbled upon the tomb of a Ming Dynasty general, and made off with some extremely fine imperial wares before the site was boarded up by the authority. My uncle was offered a chance to buy up some wine cups at only one-tenth of the assumed market value. As such, I was tasked to go to Nanjing to pick them up.

Once in Nanjing, the deal was delayed because the gravedigger had gone into hiding. After a week, when the prospect of closing the deal still looked fairly grim, I had a call from my mother's maid. She told me that my mother had had a traffic accident and was hospitalised. Her condition was serious. I called my stepfather and told him I was coming back. He said no, insisting that I stay as long as necessary until I had acquired the wine cups.

I was furious, shouting into the telephone, "But what about my mother?"

He said there was nothing to worry about: she was only unconscious, and should wake up in a few days. Although I was annoyed by his cold and indifferent tone, I had no choice but to stay.

Finally, I met the gravedigger and the contact guy in a drab guesthouse, with the opportunity to examine the very precious wine cups. I spent an hour checking all four wine cups and the verdict was positive; everything about them, from shape and design to glaze and reign marks, was perfect. But, since being completely flawless was itself a cause for suspicion, I told the guys I needed more time.

The contact guy, a likeable and humble peasant-looking man wearing a Mao cap, seemed bored by the proceedings of my inspection. He asked if he could help speed things up. He opened a small box to take out a multicoloured wine cup, which immediately captured my attention for its extraordinary beauty. It was decorated with a design of dragons painted in delicate shades of blue, green, red and yellow with over-glazed hues matching the under-glazed outlines perfectly. As I admired the cup, the contact guy suggested giving it to me as my "fee" if we could close the deal within the next five minutes, because he had to catch the last train back to Shanghai. Overwhelmed by his friendliness I accepted his kind offer and completed the deal with convenient speed.

I thought I could make a fortune in the region of some two hundred grand with the extra wine cup. But there was no time to rejoice when, on leaving Nanjing, I received the news of the death of my mother who had never woken from her coma.

Now, without the urgent need to go home, I landed in Macao carrying the precious wine cups. I went to the casino in the belief that gambling was the best cure for grief, played a few hands, and won handsomely. I felt I had the blessing of my dead mother for the good fortune. Emboldened, I placed the multicoloured cup on loan for the necessary cash to play in the VIP room. It ran well at first, but my luck didn't sustain and I suffered heavy losses in a few games of poker.

Now I really hated my stepfather for my dismal situation and everything else. I went to the underground banker, and gave him all the wine cups as collateral for a new credit line in order to recover my losses. When I returned to the VIP room I was escorted by a man sent by the underground banker for my "protection". Five hours later, when I left the VIP room, completely penniless, the man had turned into my transporter, responsible for delivering me to Hong Kong for the loan repayment. His name was Tony, he himself a debt collector. He was a big man with a stocky frame similar to that of a polar bear, and all who knew him called him by his nickname Tony Bear.

Tony could have locked me up in a dark room before he was ready to deliver me to Hong Kong, but he trusted me because we knew each other from previous small loans, and also because of my reputation as a collector of ancient vases, plates, cups and saucers. He was kind to me; took me to the restaurant in the Sands Casino and fed me nicely. In return I only had to carry his briefcase as if I were his messenger as he went around the city collecting debts. I was grateful for his kindness and had no real complaints. And as it transpired, I carried his briefcase all the way from Macao to Bangkok.

Tony was very happy at the end of the day when he told me he had finished his job "above target". He explained to me that in his business there were three classifications of debts: new debts, old debts and bad debts. For new debts he succeeded in collecting, he was paid a service fee. For old debts, he would have a cut of ten percent. For bad debts, which his boss had either given up collecting or forgotten ever existed, the return to him was total.

"You're my lucky boy," he said with an enormous grin when he counted the piles of notes and placed them carefully in the briefcase. "I've won the jackpot with bad debts," he cackled unabashedly.

Tony suggested a good break before we were to catch the jetfoil scheduled to depart in two hours. He said he was tired after a long day's hard work of collecting money from debtors; several of them had required the use of force. He needed a massage, to be followed by a nap. He knew a place – a massage parlour serviced by a Thai girl rumoured to be a former beauty queen, with "the unforgettable face of an angel".

Sitting inside the taxi on our way to the parlour, Tony told me more of his "angel". Her name was Kaya. She had started working in Macao several years ago, selling her body to prospective customers by sitting on display behind the glass of an imitation fish tank like all other girls. Because of her great beauty, it didn't take too much time for her to become a hot commodity. Her boss was kind enough to offer her the opportunity to run her own massage parlour on a profit-sharing basis, and she was soon to command a clientele from powerful gang men to influential government officials. Then bad luck struck. Implicated in the casino city's biggest corruption case connected to a government minister, she was arrested and her massage parlour was ransacked. Although she was eventually released without being listed as one of the dozen defendants, the demand for her services had fallen sharply. It was from then on that she resumed making cold calls to some of her old customers (Tony Bear among them) whom she had turned away after her rapid rise to eminence.

I listened with suitable interest. Whatever Tony said, I understood he meant he was going to have sex.

"How about I wait for you in the coffee shop at Casino Royale?" I asked, with nothing but good intentions.

"Don't be silly. You come with me and take care of my briefcase," insisted Tony.

The massage parlour was on the top floor of a high-rise near the beach. When we walked out of the lift, a girl was already waiting outside the door. She was petite, slender and very pretty. Clad in a green hibiscus-print chiffon dress and standing against a burnished backlight from the interior, her legs and thighs were visible in silhouette through the gauzy fabric. She had a heart-shaped face, with big and intensely clear eyes. Batting her heavy eyelashes, she welcomed Tony with a kiss before she glanced at me with a funny look in her eyes and asked my brawny transporter, "Your pawn?"

"Yeah, but he is a good lad," answered Tony. "He is in the antiques business."

"Welcome to my place. My name is Kaya," said the girl extending her hand to me.

I took it; it felt soft and warm. Her striking beauty made me feel asphyxiated. I blushed with embarrassment, partly because I was somebody's captive and partly because I noticed that she wore no brassiere beneath her green chiffon dress.

Tony explained to Kaya our captor-captive relationship. "He has deposited with us some antique teacups. Very ancient, and very expensive, if they're not fakes."

Once inside the apartment Tony put down his briefcase and took off his jacket with Kaya's help. Then he continued, "He lost hundreds of thousands in a mere two hours playing baccarat – some record! My boss doesn't want the cups; he wants the money back instead, with interest. Hey, you sit here."

At Tony's gesticulation, I obediently put my bum on a chocolate-brown leather three-seater sofa next to his briefcase.

"Can you do something for me?" asked Tony with a vicious grin.

"What's that?" I said, with sickly dread.

"Put your hand on the handle of my briefcase and hold it really tight."

At his command I grasped the handle of the black leather briefcase.

"No, you have to hold it like you're squeezing a sponge. That's right, but tighter, tighter still."

I strained the muscles of my hand so hard that the blue veins beneath the skin bulged horribly. Kaya was looking inquisitively at the briefcase with a curious frown between her eyebrows. Finally Tony was satisfied and said laughing, "Now you can relax."

I loosened my grip, confused and troubled, not knowing why he should cause me the humiliation. And Tony explained, "Now listen, my lad. From this moment on, I've made you the sole custodian of the briefcase. You're now the owner, and I therefore expect you to take extremely good care of it and everything inside when I go off with my sweetheart for some sleep. Can you do that?"

Carefully I replied, "Yes, of course."

"Will you run away when I'm busy with Kaya?" he asked, with a positively villainous expression on his face.

"Of course not," I answered meekly.

"Good, very good," he commented with a thuggish laugh. "You should know that even if you try, you won't go very far. You will be dead before you even reach the end of the street."

"I know," I said abjectly. "Thank you for reminding me."

"Excellent," he said. "Now you can sit back and enjoy the time as the sole custodian of all the money inside the briefcase while I enjoy humping my girl. See you later."

Without a backward glance, he turned to Kaya and said, "Same old price? I won't stay long. I have to deliver him to be collected before eight in Hong Kong." Then he entered the bedroom, followed by Kaya.

From where I sat glued to the briefcase, I caught the unexpected vista of the bedroom with a king-size bed in the centre and further down an en-suite bathroom with frosted glass panels. I thought there was also a television set on a cupboard by the wall with a VCR attached to it. And that was all I saw before Kaya turned around to close the door.

Then something queer occurred. Kaya didn't seem to be in a hurry to join the big man in bed. She closed the door almost in slow motion. As the door narrowed to a gap and was within an inch of completely shutting, she startled me by popping her face up at the crack and sticking out her tongue at me in a naughty grimace. It was cute, and very sexy too. If I hadn't been made to sit on the sofa like a piece of shit, I would have turned on my charm in response, accepting her tongue in my mouth. Instead, I dropped my eyes with shame before hearing the sound of the door that shut with a click.

I sat back to relax, as I reckoned it would be at least an hour before I saw them emerge from the bedroom again. But to my surprise, the wait was over sooner than expected. In less than ten minutes after the door was closed upon me, Kaya burst out of the room, entirely naked, crying for help.

"Come with me, please!" she shouted and stormed back into the room.

I ran after her, leaving the briefcase behind. I entered the bedroom, but didn't find her, just an empty bed with her chiffon dress spread elegantly near the pillows. Then I heard her voice calling out from the en-suite bathroom, "Over here!"

I made straight for the bathroom, which was triangular in shape with a classic bathtub filled with green-coloured water and flower petals on the left, like a standard set-up in some spa advertisement. On the right was a glass cubicle for a standing shower.

Kaya was kneeling in front of the tub with hands clasped above her breasts as though she was praying. Tony lay beside her on the floor, his massive body unclothed, face paled to a sickly white, eyes shut, with piled-up masses of foam gushing at the mouth.

Kaya cried, with great pity in her voice, "Please, do something to make him stand up again and walk out of this door."

"What's his problem?" I inquired.

"I guess it's the erection pill he took a few minutes ago. He probably had a heart attack when we were about to share a bath," she said. "Wake him up and get him out of here! Then he can die anywhere he chooses. I have enough trouble with the police. I can't afford the death of a man of his status in my place. Help me. I'll give you anything you ask."

She stood up, as if to show what she could give me. She was in the flower of her youth – her breasts were full and firm, her legs long and pink-hued, and her shiny black pubic hair was bushy and curly.

I was, however, not in the mood to be aroused, as Tony's body lying in a pool of his own puke made me feel sick.

"Do you know how to apply mouth-to-mouth resuscitation?" asked Kaya. Leaning close, she opened her mouth, showing once again her tongue, the same shiny, slippery tongue I'd noticed earlier when she grimaced at me. She held me round the waist with her manicured hands and stuck her tongue in my mouth, engaging and chewing mine.

"Like that," she withdrew her tongue and said encouragingly.

Despite her VIP treatment, I still baulked at the horrible sight and the stench.

As soon as she realised the cause of my reluctance, she said, "Okay, let me try to make your job easier."

She entered the shower cubicle, and came out with a bucket of water filled to the brim. In two portions, she poured the water over Tony Bear's head. The first flush was weaker, just enough to wash the vomit off his face. The second flush struck with a force so great that Tony's head shook as though he was turning it by himself.

"He's still alive!" exclaimed Kaya. "Now go! Go!"

Her command was clear: I had to apply artificial respiration to Tony like I had learned it in my first-aid training back in my school days.

"You're sure it's going to work?" I asked uncertainly.

"Yes," she said with an affirmative nod. "But you probably should take off your clothes first."

The floor was flooding with water, and she helped me take off my T-shirt and jeans.

"Can I keep my briefs at least?" I asked.

"Up to you," she said. "Make yourself at home."

"Can you get me a towel?" I spoke with an artificial confidence as I was about to kick-start the rescue operation.

"Yes, of course." Kaya went to the shower cabinet and threw me a white towel.

Sitting astride Tony's thick, round torso, I wiped his mouth clean with the towel, and started pumping fresh air into his large lungs.

"You are very sweet, thank you," said Kaya. Then she, looking confident that everything would be fine, turned on the sprinkler to take a shower as if she had been waiting an insufferably long time for the break to wash the dirty stains off her body.

Although Kaya was a constant distraction as she washed her body, with her shapely legs separated so wide that even an ocean liner could pass through, I concentrated hard on my mouth-to-mouth resuscitation efforts, knowing it was a serious matter of life and death.

Yet after a certain lapse of time, Tony seemed to be drifting even further away. When Kaya stepped out of the glass chamber, draping a long towel around her shoulders, she said, "I think Tony is going to be okay. Am I right or am I wrong?"

I sat up from my crawling position to allow her a better glimpse of Tony's face.

"Holy shit! He's blacker than a black man!" she cried. "Can we try something different? For example, a little kung fu I watched on TV some time ago?"

She moved her hands up and down like two choppers to demonstrate what she was talking about. I sensed she meant CPR (cardiopulmonary resuscitation). I had watched a videotape on the subject during my first-aid training, but never practised. But I welcomed the opportunity to leave my mouth exercise behind for something different. So I changed my position slightly and started pounding Tony on the chest.

"That's exactly what I meant. I bet you my life that he'll stand on his feet again after you count one to a hundred," said Kaya, retreating to the door. "I'll be right back."

She left the room. I didn't know where she had gone. As I afterwards learned, she was already contemplating an escape strategy at the time.

"One, two, three, four…" I counted audibly at each and every pounding. After some fifty counts, Tony was still unresponsive, and the exercise was becoming monotonous. As the tedium becoming unbearable, I began to wonder if I could turn on the VCR for a sex tape.

Just then, unexpectedly, Tony bounced back to life. He sprang up like an automaton, sitting bolt upright and facing me with the look of a zombie. In his brief moment of partially restored consciousness, he might think I was attacking him. He grasped me by the neck, squeezing it and strangling me as if I were a doll. Although his discoloured eyes suggested that he was more revenant than living thing, what strength remained in him was still of tremendous power.

I fought back but couldn't get his hands off my neck. It was at this moment I caught a glimpse of Kaya at the door. "Murder! Murder!" I croaked.

Horrified by what she saw, she quickly slipped away to my great despair. The paw-like hands of Tony pressed deeper and deeper into the veins of my neck. When I thought I was about to die from suffocation, Kaya returned just in time, with a crowbar. Raising it high, she was, however, undecided where to hit as our two bodies were entangled with one another and rocking back and forth. In what I believed to be my last breath, I uttered my final words, "Just hit. You won't miss!"

Kaya, after another wee moment of indecision, closed her eyes in a display of blind determination and hit out with the crowbar. To my astonishment, it hit Tony right on the head and he immediately slumped to one side. But Kaya didn't stop there and went on hitting out blindly with the crowbar. With frightful precision, and to my complete disbelief, the crowbar hit me on the skull. I saw blood literally jetting straight out of my right ear before I passed out in a dead faint.

Without knowing how much time had elapsed, I woke up with the return of consciousness. I opened my eyes and found myself lying on Kaya's lap. She was sitting in a pool of blood.

"What happened?" I asked her.

"Tony's dead," she said quietly.

"My God, what've we done?" I cried.

"Tony's dead, and we're doomed," she said, with a beaten-down look in her eyes.

I felt a piercing pain in my skull. "I thought you were also trying to get rid of me," I accused her.

"No, it was a pure accident," she said. "I didn't mean to hurt you. I was only trying to save you. But the crowbar is heavy, and it went out of my control."

I rubbed my head where there was a lump forming, wet with dripping blood. "It's easy to call it an accident," I said.

"Forgive me. I didn't mean to hurt you, but I have hurt you. Let me make amends," she said softly.

Lying feebly on her lap, I didn't know how she was going to make amends for injuring me.

She said, "Tony has left his briefcase behind, of which he has made you the sole custodian. I've taken a peep inside. I think there's enough to buy us anything in our circumstances. Let's go to a quiet place and lie low until, one way or another, the dust settles."

Not a bad idea in my situation, I thought. I was in deep shit: my staggering debts, my family in turmoil, my role in the death of Tony Bear. It was as if she had handed me a second opportunity on a silver platter to start life anew.

Anyhow, from then on, our paths entwined. She gave my wound a quick fix with alcohol for the cleaning and a bandage for cover-up, helped me to my feet, and put me on a plane like I was her master and she my slave. That night, we took the last flight to Bangkok. With our new riches safely locked in the overhead compartment, we sat comfortably in our seats, drinking champagne and looking out of the Boeing 747's window to appreciate a large, lustrous moon in the starry sky.

"What are we supposed to do in Bangkok?" I asked her.

"As I said, we'll stay put and wait for the dust to settle. When the time is right, we will run again to a safe haven," she said with a confident smile on her face, as if she knew what she was talking about. "What do you think?"

I gazed at the moon's surface with shadows shaped like mountains and creeks, and said thoughtfully, "I don't know. I've never been a fugitive. I'll follow your plan."

"Then wish me luck!" she said. "As a matter of fact, I am not very good at planning. I know only to follow my heart to wherever it takes me."

"Well, I'm okay with or without a plan, as long as you know what we're probably going to do next," I said. "I'm an alien in Bangkok, and I've only you to depend on."

"Don't worry. You must have faith in me. You've lifted me from the hell of my miserable life. Will I abandon you who has pledged to share his life and all his wealth with me?" she said, with a meaningful glance at the overhead compartment. "Relax. Let's forget about any plan and play it by ear."

I was not sure if I had said anything about "sharing my life and wealth" with her. But my doubts were quickly smothered when she turned on a sweet smile and covered my mouth with her passionate lips.

We landed in Bangkok, found an apartment and lived together like newlyweds. The place we called home during our hiding was an unremarkable two-storey structure behind a cheap guesthouse among an untidy cluster of buildings in various shapes and styles on Khao San Road. On our first visit, we didn't know what to expect when the caretaker took us inside a cul-de-sac whose entrance was half-concealed by some roadworks on the main road. But we fell in love with the place straightaway for its seclusion. It was at the blind end of the cul-de-sac, accessible through a wrought-iron gate and a front courtyard paved with brick. Its plain interior, equipped with only a small bedroom on the upper floor and a bathroom in the basement, seemed just right for our purpose, even in its dilapidated state. The streetlamp outside the gate had been burnt out since time immemorial, the caretaker told us. I gave him a handsome tip for the orientation. He was so grateful, that he thought we might be interested to know that in the basement toilet there was a sealed passage which could get us to the front block in case of emergency.

"What kind of emergency?" I asked him.

"A fire, for example, or a police raid," he said. He went on to explain that the passage had been secretly built by a former tenant, a drug dealer, who had stayed there briefly. But the secret passage didn't take him too far – he was gunned down on Khao San Road outside the Silk Café.

"What a tiny bed! We'll have to lie really close to fit into it." These were the first words Kaya uttered when we stepped into the bedroom of our apartment, which aptly described both the flaws and merits of the place.

First the flaws: the place wasn't only small and minimal; it was also hot like a stove. But in the scorching conditions, it had the perceived merits of watching Kaya move around parading her beautiful body, sometimes skimpily clad, other times completely bare. Her fine, sand-smooth skin, her body aroma like the scent of lotus and her soft chanting at dawn, beautiful and hypnotic, left me constantly burning with a choking, spluttering fire. But owing to the need for surgery to remove a blood clot in my head and time to recuperate, we were "sexless" for the first couple of weeks after we moved into the apartment. Eventually I became fit again, and it was then that I discovered we were horribly split on a number of issues, with the "joy of sex" topping the list.

One night, the monsoon came and the rain poured down from the sky in torrents. We cuddled each other in bed, listening to the rain pelting against the windowpane like thrashing drum rolls. She had been putting up resistance to my advances for some time now. The harder the rain fell, the stronger her resistance had become.

"Do you know the rain is more generous than you?" I said insinuatingly.

"What do you mean by that? Have I not been generous to you?" She disengaged herself from my arms to sit on the edge of the bed. "We have quarrelled over the same issue already a thousand times. I don't think you should bring it up again."

Perhaps she was right that she was generous, but only to an extent. I could kiss her, touch her, or chart the contours of her body landscape with my eyes, toes and fingers. If she was in the mood, she would be kind enough to bare her breasts for me, which I would gladly chew and bite upon presentation. Sometimes she went so far as to lend me a hand, and I was thankful. Occasionally she would even allow me to melt in her mouth. But there was a limit to her generosity. She would never let me cross the barrier for some real sex.

"I am sorry to have dragged you into this," she said. "I am grateful for everything we have been together. You saved me from hell and I am all yours now. But please understand: my days as a whore are over."

"It has nothing to do with whether you're a whore or not," I said very clearly.

"That means you don't understand me," she cried. "I love you, and I want to make love to you, but not when I am still carrying the old baggage of a whore…"

I waited with mute rage for her to finish. And she continued, with tears cascading down her cheeks, "I need to become a new woman again. I will be a hundred percent yours when I am ready."

"When will that be?" I groaned. Burning with exasperation, I grabbed her shoulders and gave her a hard push. She fell backwards, lying squarely on the mattress. I forced open her legs. She made no resistance. She just said, with a superb calm which was oddly in contrast to my abrasiveness, "Do whatever you like. Rape me as if I were your whore and pay me after you've finished. Cash or credit card is welcome. I can even give you a discount as a friend of Tony Bear."

The chillness in her words was enough to deter me from advancing further. I gave up and kissed my flower goodbye. "Very well," I said. "Tell me. When will you be ready to sleep with me for real?"

"By the time I have thoroughly cleansed my body and purified my soul," she declared, in a no-nonsense tone.

The rain had stopped. Then, after a brief recess, it started all over again, pouring harder than before. The dreadful rain made hearing her vague, non-committal avowal more insufferable. With a cruelty that I would regret for a long time, I said, "To cleanse and purify? I think nothing would suit you better than getting outside to stand in the rain for a heavenly shower!"

To my rude suggestion, she reacted with extraordinary calmness and obedience. Quietly she crept off the bed and slipped out of the door. I heard her footsteps walking down the staircase to the courtyard. I thought I also heard the sound of rain lashing her body furiously from all sides, "Crack, crack, crack!"

As I listened on, I pondered and deliberated whether I should apologise and ask her to come back inside. But I chose to wait and see if she would learn anything from the punishment while I had a drink or two.

"Crack, crack, crack!"

As the sound became monotonous and soporific, I fell asleep. I woke up the next morning only to discover that she was gone, leaving behind a farewell note.

Thereafter, my lone wandering about the capital city began.

I BRIEFLY EXPLAINED TO TAKSIN, the shrine attendant, what had been replayed in my mind.

"Very good." He nodded appreciatively. "You're quite special, unlike those people who just come here and beg like leprous mendicants without knowing the importance of opening their hearts completely to Great Brahma."

He asked me to follow him to pray at each side of the four-faced Great Brahma, making offerings of the incense, candles, camphor elephants and flowers he had bought with my 500 baht.

Then he asked me to pray for people I cared for. Tony Bear first came to my mind. He had been a constant haunting presence in my dreams since I arrived in Bangkok. So I prayed for his soul, thinking that, if he were still knocking at the door of heaven and awaiting permission to enter, I would elevate my prayer to Great Brahma to admit the man, considering he had been nice and generous to me on the last day of his life.

When I was about to make a wish for Kaya, I felt a pat on my shoulder and turned to find that Taksin had sidled up with a bamboo cage of sparrows.

"Let go, at only one hundred baht," said Taksin. "Free the birds and they will carry away your troubles with them. You can accumulate heavenly merits by saving the birds from dying in captivity."

I paid him one hundred baht as we strode to the open square where a few boys and girls had similar bamboo cages with sparrows waiting to be let go at a price.

"Remember this," Taksin gave his last piece of instruction before I was allowed to open the cage door. "When you release the birds, say your prayer as though you are wishing upon a star." He again impressed me by speaking poetically.

I pushed back the small rod of the bamboo cage at the count of three. As the door of the cage swung open, a volley of sparrows jumped out and flew away in all directions.

"The birds have gone and all your troubles are no more," said Taksin, smiling with reassurance. "By the way, what's your name?"

"Please call me Ah Man."

I suspected Taksin might think it a stupid name, but he responded most positively, as if we had known each other for ages. "Ah Man, my friend, no more worries. Great Brahma will be with you and protect you," he said. "Don't forget to fetch me next time you come here – to thank Great Brahma when all your wishes have come true."

Affected by his warmth, I began to take him seriously as a friend. "Taksin, did you say you're a part-time shrine attendant?" I asked. "What's your formal profession?"

"Other than a full-time human being, I am also a self-serious poet," he said.

"That's very respectable," I praised him. "What kind of stuff do you write?"

"I compose verses by putting feelings into words," he said modestly. "I've just written something this morning. The piece is called *Breakfast at Café Democ*. Would you like to hear it?"

I didn't think I had the taste for poetry, but it would be rude to say no. So he went ahead. After a minute or so, I politely asked him to stop because I didn't understand a thing. I said, "Your poem sounds like a puzzle to me. Can you just tell me what you're trying to say?"

"All right." He looked a bit frustrated, but maintained his good spirit. "It is like this: every morning I go to work via Rajadamnoen Boulevard; I stop by Café Democ for breakfast. Outside the café stands the splendid stately Democracy Monument; it represents the rights and freedom of the Thai people. The sight of the monument always makes me weep. Do you know why? Because it is almost like you're having a daily supply of democracy at only the cost of a coffee and bread. I feel so blessed... I feel so blessed... I feel so blessed..."

"What a beautiful idea!" I said, thinking the guy must be some sort of idealist. He laughed heartily at my compliment. I praised him again for his noble spirit before I bade him farewell.

Taksin said, "Ah Man, it's such a pleasure talking to you. Next time you come, I'll buy you a drink and tell you more about how the brave Bangkokians have fought to preserve their hard-earned democracy through the years. Goodbye."

I boarded a tuk-tuk that parked outside the shrine. As the tuk-tuk was about to start off, I suddenly remembered I had yet to say a prayer for Kaya. I told Taksin I was going back inside the shrine. After Taksin learned of my intention, he said, "It's not necessary. Great Brahma understands everything that has gone through your mind. But if you want to feel positively assured, you can make your prayer on your way by the Chao Phraya."

"Do you mean the river?"

"Yes. Chao Phraya – the River of Kings," said Taksin meditatively. "It is a token of perpetuity and a world of timeliness. As the legend told, prayers spoken by the river are like heavenly music to the ears of the gods and will be taken with special importance."

"I like the idea," I said.

"Then I'll tell the driver to give you a shout when he sees the river," said Taksin.

The driver listened to Taksin for instruction and responded with a most benign smile, "*Maenam Chao Phraya*! No problem."

The tuk-tuk started and we waved goodbye until Taksin disappeared from my view behind the multitudes of people on the busy street.

Riding inside the tuk-tuk, I felt I was in a placid state of mind unknown and unexperienced ever since Kaya had disappeared from my life. As if I could finally relax a little, I lounged comfortably in my seat and fell into a sound sleep.

3

A.H.M.A.N.

———❦———

"**M**aenam Chao Phraya!"

The driver boomed next to my ear, startling me out of my slumber. I woke up and saw the tuk-tuk had pulled over on the side of the Chao Phraya River. Night had already descended. Vessels of variegated sizes, some with dim masts and others with illuminated roofs and flanks, chugged busily up and down the dark waterway, carrying loads of cargo or late commuters and tourists. Curiously I had the faint impression of having been here before.

I paid the driver and took a stroll. As I walked down the riverbank, I caught a glimpse of a monstrosity of steel and bricks lurking in the darkness on the opposite side of the river, which confirmed that I was right about my memory.

It was on one evening a month ago when Kaya and I were both feeling rather shitty for different reasons. Bangkok was under the threat of a gathering storm. Our apartment was hot like a stove. The pain in my battered skull after surgery kept me under constant torment. Kaya had found it more difficult to conceal her impatience over my slow recovery. Whatever the reasons, the effect was a sense of impending calamity over us. We thought we needed some fresh air, and she suggested taking me for a walk by the Chao Phraya River.

Strolling along the riverbank, she brought my attention to some strange buildings on both sides of the river: some with a fairly complete façade whereas others were no more than foundation pilings in various stages of completion.

"Abandoned and tenantless, there are hundreds of such sites in Bangkok with their construction suspended years ago, when the country's economy collapsed during the Asian Economic Crisis," she said, pointing to a cluster of forsaken structures visible only by their skeletal outlines in the distance. "People call them 'ghost' buildings."

"Ghost... buildings? Why?"

"It was after a mysterious fire on the top floor in one of those buildings that people began referring to them as 'ghost' buildings, because they couldn't explain how the fire started when no one lived there," she said.

"But is it true that no one lives in the buildings?"

"Speaking from my experience, the answer is no. While some buildings have been abandoned, with their foundations barely laid out, others are fairly complete. Some of those near completion come with fully furnished units or professionally designed mid-level gardens, which are intended for demonstration purposes during the property sale," she explained. "As a matter of fact, I spent a week in the one with a severed head."

She pointed to a decrepit monument-like high-rise on the other side of the river with a half-finished dome on top. "I stayed there briefly when I came to Bangkok some years ago. I had no place to go, running and hiding, like now. My father knew a lot about the construction sites in Bangkok and he gave me the idea that I could find temporary shelter in them."

It struck me as odd that she suddenly opened up to me about her darkest days. It wasn't that she had been particularly secretive of her past. It was only I never asked, because it was enough knowing that she was a Thai girl from the northern part of Thailand, a whore in Macao and a wanted person for the death of Tony Bear. But there were things I learned without asking. For example, on one occasion when she was depressed and rather drunk, she confessed that there was a guy who had not merely taken her virginity but had also buggered her. I didn't know if it was true. But I didn't ask her about it because I didn't want to embarrass her. However, on that evening, as we sat huddled under a large umbrella on the bank of Chao Phraya in the driving rain, she seemed suddenly eager to spit out everything once and for all. And without prompting, she began recounting to me what she had undergone during her country's worst economic crisis when she was a nubile young girl of only sixteen.

K.A.Y.A.

I WAS CROWNED MISS TEEN at only fourteen in a beauty contest run by a US consumer products company. It was to promote a new brand of sanitary towel for teens. The first prize was a sewing machine, plus unlimited use of the towels for a year commencing from the date of my first period. I never had the chance to lay my hands on the prize, which was sold straightaway for a few thousand baht to cover my mother's medical expenses for a chronic back problem. With what I had achieved at such a tender age, I naturally aspired to something bigger, which could help my family put poverty behind them. I craved that someday I would wear a larger crown, of provincial or national scale, a crown made not of paper and plastic but real jewels, and a prize worth not a few thousand baht but millions of dollars. Sadly, my lucky break never came, or it came too late to deter me from treading the path of becoming another piece of meat in the market of human flesh.

About two weeks after I turned sixteen, on one fresh, cool autumn evening with a shining silver moon in the sky, my father suddenly returned to our home village in San Mei. He, an excavator operator for a construction company in Bangkok, usually came home only on important occasions such as Songkran (Water Festival) or His Majesty the King's birthday, which are public holidays. If there were exceptions, it would be for something bad; for example, not long before he'd had to rush home with money for my mother's medical expenses after she had accidentally fallen down a slope and broken her hip. Although it was a little strange to see him show up at a time when he was supposed to be busy working in Bangkok, I and my younger brother, who was about thirteen, were ecstatic by his homecoming, and didn't probe. He had brought me a belated birthday cake, and a toy gun for my brother who thought of becoming a soldier someday. This was my father's last homecoming, because he never left again.

Two days after his return he was found hanging from a poplar tree on the hillside. In his suicide note, he said all construction sites in Bangkok had been closed and abandoned because the government had done something terribly wrong, which he did not quite comprehend. He confessed that he was too tired to continue with the endless struggles with poverty. He was, however, rather positive about his own departure because he, as a Buddhist, believed the curse of the poor family would be lifted after he was gone. He sounded only slightly apologetic for leaving us behind. He didn't even ask me or my brother to "be good in his absence"; perhaps he was in a hurry. He concluded by reminding my mother to use less expensive drugs for her back pain.

I had a dream about him forty-eight days after he died. His soul was colourless, his apparition faint. He looked very sad. He said his death hadn't been enough to lift the curse of the family because an unthinkable calamity was about to occur, with the fate of the country at stake.

"Today is my last day in this world. My time now remains in minutes and seconds. Therefore, listen carefully to what I have to say before I am completely gone. Your brother is the only hope of the family. You must protect him and do everything possible to help him grow up to become a useful man," he sobbed. "Got to stop now. I can see the gate opening and it is my turn to enter. Goodbye." Then from apparition to shadow, from shadow to emptiness, he disappeared as my dream went blank.

With my father's departure, the livelihood of the family, consisting of a sick mother and a kid brother, fell onto my shoulders. Despite the pressure, I resisted the call to become a bar girl – at least not before I had exhausted all other options. I still believed in the dignity of man; even when life was becoming an impossible daily struggle, I clung heroically to the honour of a former Miss Teen by turning down the more lucrative work of a bar girl. Instead, I got myself a job in a massage parlour, where you could still have the choice of feeling up meaty bodies for a living without having to put yours up for sale.

Nonetheless, a girl of my age and beauty didn't have to wait for very long to be discovered for purposes other than stroking the excess meat of living bodies. I was offered some very attractive deals, but I defended the pride of a former Miss Teen vigorously and resisted all attempts to trade my body at any price.

One day I was summoned to see the Madame of our massage parlour. Her name was Supang. She had large, strong hands, which were a little out of proportion with her small body frame. Legend had it that her palms could spawn a multitude of sensations that men could never achieve by masturbating themselves. But to the disappointment of her customers, she had retired those magical hands about ten years previously when the joints of her fingers started tormenting her with arthritis. Then she opened her own massage parlour, which had become very successful by combining sex and health therapy. She met me in her small office on the second floor of the massage parlour's three-storey building. As I entered, I noticed she was flipping through my personal file. She motioned me to sit down and said haughtily, "Sixteen and a virgin! It is rather funny, isn't it?"

"It is not funny if it is true," I retorted.

"Where have all the boys in your village gone?" she said, turning the pages of my file. "Oh, San Mei, poor place of widows and orphans. No wonder." Glancing at my body from head to toe, she continued, "What a sweet sixteen! You sure it has never been touched?"

"I don't know what you are talking about," I said, slightly agitated. "Can I go back to work now? A customer is waiting."

"It doesn't matter. He can wait," she said. "Your customer, who lost his wife last year, has made an offer for your first night."

She snatched the pair of gold-rimmed spectacles off her face and threw them on top of the file. Rubbing her small, tired eyes, she exclaimed, "You know we all need money to survive. Your family, my operation."

"My body is not for sale," I stressed. It was a line I had rehearsed many times in my private time, knowing that I would have to use it one day.

But like words falling on deaf ears, Madame Supang maintained her aloof expression and said, after scribbling a number on a scrap piece of paper, "Like to know how much you are worth today?"

Peering at it, I was a little taken aback, because it was a hell of a lot of money, more than an ordinary massage girl earned in a year. I was not to be tempted, however, and said, "Please stop insulting me."

"Well, it is really up to you." She crossed out a few digits with a pencil, reducing the number to a tenth of its original. "You might wonder where all the money has gone. You could have been robbed, but more likely you could have been ruined by an unfortunate incident of sexual assault."

"Please don't threaten me," I said.

"This is not a threat, only friendly advice," she said. "Beware of the many dark corners and dangerous back alleys in our cities. If possible leave your virginity at home and lock it up in a safe. Otherwise you'll be at risk of losing it when you're walking alone on a quiet, dimly lit street. And there's someone behind you, who jumps on your back and robs it from you, like it is a purse waiting to be pried open. In the blink of an eye it's gone. And the sad thing is that you don't even have the opportunity to give or deny consent."

I hated her callous tone, but knew that she was right about our trade. I had already had the experience of a few attempts by force in the massage parlour from customers who saw no difference between a massage therapist and a whore.

"You know, it's called rape. Should it happen to you, you'd be no more than useless rags," she said, moving her hands to push up her drooping breasts. "Therefore, hear and believe, make some money while you still can. You know, everything is for sale, including my tits. What a pity that I am not getting offers now as in the good old days."

As I had already made up my mind, I just said, "Can I leave now, if you don't mind?"

"That's okay if you can't decide now,' she said, glancing at her Rolex. "But I have arrangements to make, and I want an answer from you before six this evening."

I was speechless, dreadfully shaken by the fact that someone could set a deadline for the sale of the pearl which had been preciously preserved in uncontaminated waters for sixteen years in such an open and blatant manner.

Before she let me go, she pressed with more persuasive arguments, "Remember how your family has always been struggling? Can you imagine that now you have the chance to build a stylish grave for your father so that he can spend his time like a rich man in heaven or hell? Pay your mother's medical expenses, or for her drugs? Make way for your younger brother to leave the hills to study in the city? Afterwards, many doors will be opened to how you can use your body, for money or pleasure."

Seeing that I was beyond persuasion, she finished with a sneer on her lips and gestured for me to leave.

I said no to Madame Supang in the evening and again the next morning. But after a succession of sweet talk, threats and intimidation, I finally gave up fighting her and agreed to proceed, so long as she could meet my own terms and conditions.

"That's a good start," said Madame Supang in a pleasantly approving voice. "As long as it is within my capabilities, I'll do anything you ask."

In a firm and unequivocal tone, I stated, "First, it has to be an absolute stranger outside the group of customers I know. I would cringe or throw up simply imagining myself undressing before those ugly men."

To my surprise, Madame Supang responded positively by saying, "Fair enough. I don't think we have a shortage of decent applicants."

She turned on her computer and said, "I already sent out invitations last week, and the responses are overwhelming. I don't know how, but some people have got the idea that you are a former beauty queen and made enquiries. I didn't say yes or no. I want to keep them guessing." She chuckled with irrepressible glee.

"Secondly," I told her, "I could only do it in a room with all lights switched off."

Madame Supang looked unsure, and said after some hesitation, "I'll try my best, if that is what you ask. But that will certainly exclude those men who are more excited by pornography. I would like to know why it is necessary."

I explained that I had never had previous experience of coupling. I knew I would have to cope with what was to come, but was afraid of freaking out under a bright light and the gaze of a stranger.

"What a silly girl!" Madame Supang burst out laughing. "Don't worry. I'll take you through the process before your big day. Actually, you don't really have to do anything except spread your legs apart."

But there was something else, I told her. I wanted absolute zero recall of the man who had bought the right of my first night. I hoped that I would suffer less for the rest of my life if the guy remained forever incognito and faceless in my memory.

I thought Madame Supang would admonish me for being unreasonable. But she just said, "It is difficult, but not impossible. I'm sure there would be men willing to do anything for a virgin queen like you."

Two days later, Madame Supang came back with what she described as "a dream deal". "Everything in strict compliance to all your demands. Someone you've never met, in a room without lights. He merely asks to smoke a cigarette afterwards, which I think is only fair."

I trembled all over, knowing my fate was invariably and inevitably sealed.

She calmed me down by telling me that she had planned to set up my "wedding" on the top floor in the room with a large circular bed. "I'll make sure all lights in the room are switched off, which can only be turned on from outside, if it will give you some peace of mind."

Knowing that there was no turning back, I signed the contract, received the first payment, and gave it to my mother for settlement of the family debts that had accumulated since the death of my father.

On my "wedding" night, I was placed in an unlit room with my body draped only by a silk robe, without undies. Sitting cross-legged on the large circular bed with my eyes fixed on my maiden purse, I was a little mystified to find it looked somewhat similar to the "third eye" in the myths, and wondered if it would awaken me with a mysterious transformation. As I was waiting, I heard the sound of a temple bell sent forth from a distant monastery. I mentally counted after each strike. At number thirty-three, I saw a shadow slip through the door into the room. Though it was dark inside, I instinctively put my hands over my eyes to avoid catching a glimpse of the man who stealthily crawled onto the bed.

He touched me, removed my robe, and went on to undress himself. I lay on my back, stiff and nervous. I tried to keep my mind preoccupied with memories that would help me endure what was to follow, by remembering a day I went swimming with my kid brother. On the beach I saw all kinds of men staring with greedy eyes at my bare young body in my scanty, homespun swimsuit. The sky was blue, the water crystal-clear and cool, and we leisurely let our bodies drift on the undulating waves. Living then was effortless and free. We didn't turn back until we heard our mother cry from the shore, "Don't go too far. Beware of the sharks!"

It was at this moment I felt a sharp pain between my legs, as if I were being stabbed and pierced in the middle and all the way up my stomach. The pain was intense and excruciating. As I lay in darkness, I was aghast to realise that I had finally parted company with my virginity. Something had died violently inside me, and I was transformed forever. But to my great dismay, I felt no pleasure in the transformation, no tenderness or esteem, just endless mortification. And a lot of pain, too, that kept rising until I could not bear any more and passed out.

But my faint was only brief, and I quickly came back to consciousness when a light was shone upon my face. I opened my eyes and saw the light source was a cigarette lighter held in the man's hand. This made me at once fume with rage. I pushed away the lighter and the light went out in an instant.

"I think we've agreed to have no light in the room," I uttered in disgust.

"I need a cigarette," said the man quietly, clicking on the lighter.

"You don't need to burn your lighter over my face to have a cigarette," I cried, giving the lighter another slap and putting out the flame.

"Madame says I can have a post-coital smoke," argued the man. He clicked on his lighter again and brought the flame down from my face to my body. "You're very beautiful," he remarked.

Enraged, I lashed out, knocking the lighter from his hand. As the flame went out, I took the opportunity to jump off the bed and run to the other side of the room. I reached the end wall, bumping into what I believed to be a table, whereas things on top of it collapsed noisily into each other, while some items fell to the floor.

It appeared that the guy, who had recovered the lighter from between the sheets, never meant to use it just for a smoke. He flicked it on and turned the small flame to a taller glow as he got off the bed. He held the lighter near his abdomen. His face was still a blur, but anything below his waist, including his unsightly sex dangling between his legs, was fairly evident, to my horror and disgust.

He drew near, pressing his body against mine. I tried to push him away. He caught my right hand, twisting it and making me yell with pain. As he had to hold onto the lighter he could not at the same time restrain both my hands. My left hand, which was free, made a desperate dip into the objects on the table and felt something in the shape of a glass bottle with liquid inside. I grabbed the bottle and told him to stop. But as fate would have it, he wouldn't stop. He held the lighter above his head, laughing, as though we were playing a game. I raised the bottle, aiming at the lighter, only intending to put out the flame. After a few misses, I finally succeeded in hitting my target with a quick swing of my left hand. The lighter was thrown up in the air. I had probably overstretched myself because my left hand didn't stop there but went on to hit the guy on the head with the bottle. As a result, the bottle broke, spilling liquid with the strong smell of kerosene. As the lighter fell, the kerosene started burning in an instant. All at once the guy was on fire and he let go his grasp of me. In the burning light, I found the door and ran out of the room.

There was an open yard outside the room. As I was figuring out where I could go to hide my naked body, I heard the sound of quick steps behind me. I turned and saw the guy emerge from the door. He had already put out the fire on his body, although a slender plume of smoke was still visible coming from his tousled hair as well as soot stains on his cheeks and shoulders. As he approached I thought he was going to kill me, and I was so frightened that I froze to the spot.

He paused before me, looked me in the eyes and said, in a tone that was wounded and spiteful, "You'll be punished for this." He walked past me and disappeared into the little garden behind the yard.

While I was still recovering from my fright after he had gone, I was also somewhat astonished to find that the man who had slept with me was in fact an extraordinarily handsome young man in his late twenties. He had a sharply outlined nose and chin, sculpted cheekbones and sprightly eyes. With a broad chest and athletic shoulders, he walked across the yard like a male model pacing the catwalk, wearing nothing on his suntanned body but a self-important nakedness. His black hair, dyed with a patch of gold, was wet and unruly, steaming faintly from the fire.

I found it incredulous that it was a young man who had outbid many others to win my body. Although I was still angry with him for breaking the agreement, I found I had already forgiven his behaviour as only playful. I was even feeling kind of blessed, as if he had saved me from a disastrous experience for my first time. Thanks to him, I would never have to remember for the rest of my life that it was some ugly old man who had deflowered me. Now I began to blame myself for being ungrateful towards someone who had come as my saviour, and felt he was right that I should be punished for what I had done to him.

Two days later, I received a call from my mother. She said that my brother Kiet had been beaten up by a gang of thugs on his way to school. He had bruises all over his body and face. Worst of all, he was made to drink the piss of the lead guy before he was released. The humiliation was so great that my brother had vowed to have revenge at all costs.

I suspected what had happened to my brother might have something to do with me. I went to see Madame Supang, who had not spoken to me since the small fire that took place on the top floor of her parlour.

"I should not have insisted on a room in darkness. I'm sorry," I said.

"Not entirely your fault. Your customer wanted it too. He preferred to remain incognito because he is also famous in his own way." Madame Supang's sunken cheeks rose up and down while she was talking. "But why hit him with the kerosene lamp?"

"I didn't know it was a lamp. I felt it was glassy and cold in the dark and I thought it was a bottle of water," I explained, with tears in my eyes. "I was only trying to defend myself."

"Well, I don't know how this is going to end," sighed Madame Supang. She then gave me an account of the young man who I now regarded as my saviour.

His name was Martchu. As the youngest member of a gang behind a bank robbery, he had been arrested and sentenced to twenty years' imprisonment at the age of seventeen. He received parole after ten years in prison. Released only last month, he became a rich man overnight when he was given his due (reputably a part of the loot from the bank robbery which the police had failed to recover).

Madame Supang said that when she made the initial public offering of my first night, he came to see her and said he would take it at any price, because he was himself a virgin before he went to prison and remained one after the years spent behind bars. When she explained to him my terms and conditions, he said he had no problem with that, as he felt darkness might help alleviate his own awkwardness and inexperience too.

"He asked me if you were the Miss Teen of the PG Beauty Contest," said Madame Supang. "I confirmed it after he had signed the deal. He must have been curious to have a good look at your face even though he had agreed to the rules. It is, of course, naughty of him, but that is no excuse for setting him on fire, huh?"

I didn't know what to say. But what could I have done differently when it was unbeknown to me that my defiler was actually a young, handsome bank robber instead of some dirty old man?

I said, "I suspect he has beaten up my brother and insulted him in vengeance. What can I do now to appease him?"

Madame Supang shook her head and let her body sink into her large armchair as if drowning in despair. "I don't know. Perhaps you can call him and ask for his forgiveness," she said.

"You think it is okay that I call him?" I asked uncertainly.

"Of course," she said in a firm voice as she quickly sat up straight. "Do it now, before it is too late."

She picked up a spare mobile phone on her desk, pushed a few buttons and passed the phone to me. She said, "Talk to him. Promise him anything as long as he agrees to stop hurting your brother."

I took the phone and waited nervously, listening to the ringing tone screaming like a siren on the other side. But there was no answer after a minute. I closed the flap of the phone, handing it back. "No one there. Perhaps I'll try later," I said.

"No, you keep the mobile," said Madame Supang. "I don't want you to queue up at the public phone with other girls. You should keep trying every five minutes until you find him."

"That's very kind of you," I said, bursting in tears.

"No trouble," she said. "I just want you to know this is urgent and important. If we don't fix it in time, Martchu and his gang members could kill your brother today and burn down my shop tomorrow."

Acting on the gravity of the situation, I never stopped calling Martchu for the remainder of the day until I finally got someone to answer the phone sometime before midnight.

"Can I speak to Martchu, please?" I said, with apprehension.

"Who's calling?" It was the voice of a man.

"This is Kaya," I answered.

There was dead silence at the end of the line, as if the man had suddenly disappeared. But I could tell that he had not hung up and I promptly said, "Martchu, I am sorry, terribly sorry. Please forgive me."

The man stayed on the line without making a sound.

"Forgive me or punish me. Do whatever you like. But please don't hurt my brother again," I implored. Then I heard a click on the other end and the line went dead.

I dropped my head in despair, sensing things from bad to worse that might happen to my little brother. In desperation, I decided to go to see him. I planned to turn up on his doorstep and present him with my body as a sacrifice, which would leave him no choice except to either kill me or forgive me.

I put on my jeans and T-shirt, and, when I was about to go out, my mobile phone vibrated.

"Kaya speaking," I said into the mouthpiece.

The long silence at the other end told me that it was Martchu. Afraid the line would go dead again, I quickly said, "Last time you said you would punish me. Then please punish me, but leave my brother alone."

After another long silence he finally said, "Do you really know what punishment is?"

There was no good way for me to answer that question, but to keep the dialogue open I ventured with a comment, "I hope you are not thinking of the death penalty."

He broke into a ripple of laughter, then held his breath and said, "No. We are still too young to die, aren't we?"

"But I can die for you, if you ask me," I said, and genuinely meant it since I felt kind of indebted to him.

"Well, there's no need," he said. "Perhaps we should meet again. I'll use the opportunity to teach you a thing or two, in particular what real punishment is about."

"By all means, please," I said very firmly.

"What about meeting tomorrow night at the same place? I don't think a dark room is necessary any longer, as we have nothing to hide from each other now," he said.

"That's fine. But if you don't mind me asking, what are you planning to do?" I was already thinking about torture of the worst kind.

"Well, the punishment I know of is very simple. What you have to do is…" he cleared his throat as if to make himself perfectly well aware of what he was going to say, "… don't forget to clean your asshole an hour before we meet."

He hung up, and I was left in shock.

I told Madame Supang about the exchange between me and Martchu in our telephone conversation. She didn't look in the least bit surprised.

"Imagine a seventeen-year-old boy in our prisons – he is like a lamb in a pack of wolves. The worst kind of punishment he has known since he was seventeen is probably what he is going to apply to you in his vengeance. But you don't have a choice, do you?" she said. Not expecting a response from me, she breathed a long, miserable sigh and turned her eyes away.

Like a rerun, I waited in the room with the large circular bed at the appointed time. The only difference was that, on the previous occasion, I was led into a dark room almost as if I were blindfolded. But tonight the room was brightened by a garish crystal chandelier hanging from the ceiling, with glaring reflections bouncing off the four walls mounted with full-height mirrors. To my mild interest, the table from which I'd grabbed what I mistook to be a bottle of water happened to be a dressing table, with creams and lotions in big and small containers and a box of paper tissues, but the "bottle of water", which was in reality a kerosene lamp, had been removed.

When Martchu appeared at the door, I immediately buried myself under the sheets with eyes closed. I waited in suspense, thinking he was in the process of undressing himself. But after a full minute or so, nothing happened; not even a voice was raised.

I took a peep between my fingers and saw Martchu, standing against the wall and completely naked, was staring at me with a cold, stern expression.

Although I was prepared for the worst, I still hoped for something less torturous than the particular punishment he had in mind. Spreading my legs in a friendly gesture, I pleaded with him, "Martchu, please don't hurt me. Love me, and let me love you."

He ignored what I said, and cruelly replied, "I don't think I have to tell you what to do."

Madame Supang had warned me that I didn't have a choice. It was good advice, as I didn't feel particularly disappointed when I understood Martchu was serious about his punishment. In a display of deference, I turned my body round, kneeling on all fours on the bed, my spine to the ceiling, my head buried in the pillows and my buttocks raised high in the air like a bitch, waiting with the piece of flesh I had exposed to the cool air in the room. "I'm all yours now. Go get it," I said.

He was still not making a move.

Afraid that he would change his mind and walk away from the room like a telephone line that goes dead at the other end, I cried, "Punish me, Martchu, if that will make you feel better," and repeated as though I was reciting a mantra, "punish me, please punish me…"

The longer he made me wait, the more urgent I felt the need to persuade him into action. Initially I said my words only as if trying to reason with him. As he lingered, I became so desperate that I began to yell at him. This was probably how he finally became excited. All of a sudden I yelled no longer. I only screamed when I was, without warning, penetrated from behind by something thick and strong which felt as sharp as a knife. I should be pleased that it was finally happening. But the pain was killing me, and I found I was screaming as a way to forget about it.

As my screams heightened into a chain of hysterical squawking, he slowed down and asked, "Shall I stop?"

"No! Please don't," I wailed. "Thank you for punishing me!"

"You're welcome," he said, and continued with greater intensity.

It felt like he was cutting me up with a chainsaw and the torture seemed to last forever, until he eventually reached the point of climax. In his last struggle he let out a loud roar like that of a wounded animal, and his body hit upon mine so hard it was as if my posterior was designed to withstand the impact of a car crash. Then it took another long minute for his tumescent penis to deflate inside my rectum before he reluctantly withdrew, to my huge relief. It was at that moment I felt a streak of cool air escaping through the vacated space, and I timidly let go of a hissing fart.

"How dare you break wind before me!" he growled.

"I'm sorry," I at once apologised.

"No problem. You're forgiven," he chuckled.

I was relieved that he wasn't really offended. He turned my exhausted body to face him, wiped the tears from my face, and planted a gentle kiss on my lips. Then he buried his face between my breasts like a child who wants to feed on his mother's milk. He didn't suck; he only yawned instead, and was already snoring in the next moment. And I dozed off too, as the tremendous exertion had completely worn me out.

I woke up half an hour later and found he had already awoken. He clicked on his lighter, adding a flame to the room which was already brightened by the crystal chandelier. I blew out the small flame with my mouth and he clicked it up again immediately. When I tried to blow it out again, he pressed his body against mine and sealed my lips with his. This was lovely, I thought, realising that his lighter, when no intimidation was intended, could be very romantic.

At the end of a long, suffocating kiss, he sat up and said, "Bring your brother to see me."

Studying the patches of burns on his shoulders, I said, "Be careful. My brother has vowed to have revenge on you."

"How old is your brother?"

"Kiet is thirteen."

"Don't worry, he's still a child," he said, with scorn at the corners of his lips. "When I see him, I'll tell him that he will be placed under my protection from now on, and he will never have to drink anyone's piss again."

He pulled me close and let my head rest on his chest while gently stroking my hair. Then he went back to sleep.

At midnight, the inimitable temple bell from a distant monastery unfailingly chimed. I felt a peace never known before, and I felt love too, as I breathed in his body odour. It seemed things were finally taking a turn for the better, and I wondered if this was only a dream. "If it is, please don't wake me up," I muttered to myself, and fell peacefully asleep.

4

K.A.Y.A.

~~~

When I awoke to a room of broad daylight the next morning, Martchu was already gone.

Returning to my living quarters, I rang home and found out from my mother that Kiet had gone to Mae Sai. I had to wait for two days before I was able to speak to him over the phone. I was confused as to what a thirteen-year-old boy was doing in Mae Sai – a town on the borders of Thailand and Burma, and many miles from home. I couldn't wait to confront him when he returned my call.

To my query, he replied, "I went there to see Tai Lo."

"Who's Tai Lo?" I asked, puzzled.

"A friend," he said. "He used to live in our village. That's okay if you don't remember."

"But I still don't get it – why Mae Sai?" I asked.

"Tai Lo is now operating from there," he said. "He'll find me a job."

"Operating from there? What kind of language is that?" I exclaimed. "It's news to me that you're looking for a job. What about school?"

"School is useless. It couldn't even protect me when I was beaten up and insulted on the street," he said grudgingly.

"Kiet, I'm sorry," I said. "I think it's only a terrible misunderstanding between you and Martchu. He wants to make it up to you."

Kiet was silent for a moment and then said, "Can we not talk about it?"

"Of course not," I said. "You're my kid brother. I worry about you."

"I've grown up now," he said adamantly. "You don't have to worry about my business anymore."

"Don't be ridiculous. You're only thirteen, still a child. You should be studying in school at your age, as there's no job for a child like you," I said, trying to rationalise with him.

"Kaya, please stop patronising me!" he said, irritated. "We haven't seen each other since you went to work in Chiang Mai. You don't know how much I've grown in the past twelve months."

I felt guilty for being unable to visit home more frequently; I was not allowed holidays during my first year working in the massage parlour.

"I can tell that you've got a thicker voice," I said tenderly. "It's nice to hear you speaking like a man."

"No, not just a man, but a better man," he said, raising his voice. "Tai Lo said a child is a much better man if he is brave and fearless, and there are some really good jobs for a child like that. I'm going to prove to Tai Lo that I am someone who's brave and fearless."

Mystified, I asked, "How are you going to do that?"

"By meeting Martchu and making him apologise, or else," he said, adding after a pause, "I've already spoken to Martchu. He's coming to see me at Mae Sai."

This was a huge surprise. "Are you sure? It's Martchu who asked me… to bring you over to see him," I stammered. "Has he agreed to meet you?"

"No. He said he'd consider it," he answered. "I don't know if he's afraid. But he's a bank robber, and what's there to be afraid of? Even if it is a nose for a nose—"

"Kiet, what has the school taught you? It's an eye for an eye, a tooth for a tooth…" I said. "But you confuse me. First you talk about an apology, and now you're saying something about vengeance. What is actually brewing in your little head?"

"A piss for a piss... or there will be blood if he should chicken out. But no, I mean no harm to him. I will only ask him to sit down for a friendly chat with me. That's all," he said.

"But Kiet..."

"What the fuck!" suddenly he swore loudly. "Kaya, this is none of your fucking business, and if I were you I would keep myself out of this shit..."

"Kiet, stop it! You don't say fuck to your own sister!" I shouted down the phone, but he had already hung up.

I sighed and forgave him for his rudeness because there was something he probably didn't know, which was that all this shit had everything to do with my fucking business.

I took some time mulling over the matter and concluded that, as things stood, the meeting in Mae Sai would be vital in mending the relationship between the guys. I, however, wasn't confident that Martchu could be persuaded to participate. As I was contemplating what I could do to make things happen, my mobile phone beeped. To my amazement, it was Martchu.

He said, "Kaya, I must speak to you."

"Is it about my brother?" I asked hastily.

"Yes, your brother has called. But there's something else I want to talk to you about," he said.

"No, first things first. Are you going to Mae Sai or not?" I demanded.

"I've not decided yet. I don't know why your brother can't meet me in Chiang Mai," he said. "I probably would have told him to fuck off if it weren't for you."

"Thanks for not turning him down. I guess he might find it safe to meet you in neutral territory, considering what your people have done to him," I said. "He only asks for a friendly chat with you. I hope you're not afraid."

"Me afraid? Of course not. Your brother is only a kid," he said. "But it is a long way from Chiang Mai to Mae Sai. You can imagine how boring it is going to be on a bus for several hours."

"That's true. I'd like to go with you if I didn't have to work," I said.

"Work? What work are you talking about?" he asked uncomfortably.

"A whore's work, of course," I replied plainly.

"Are you already… whoring around?" he said, in a voice which was both harsh and disapproving.

"Well, not yet. I'm having a day off as my anus still hurts, thanks to you," I said. "But Madame Supang is already getting a little impatient, as there's quite a queue building up for my body as a secondhand virgin."

He heaved a sigh of relief. "Thank God, you're still not a whore!"

"I don't know what there is to be thankful for. As a matter of fact, I'm a doomed woman who is bound to be whoring around sooner rather than later. It's inevitable," I said bitterly.

"No, it isn't," he said. "I won't allow it, if you'll let me. I'll save you. That's the reason for this call."

"To save me… from whoring?" I asked incredulously. "Why should you do that?"

In a slightly jittery tone, he said, "Because of overwhelming emotions that have been tormenting me since we last slept together."

"That was two days ago," I said. "When I woke up you were already gone. Something happened?"

"Yes, something happened, but something good," he explained. "It was like this: I woke up at dawn, feeling blissful with you lying in my arms. I kissed you and you smiled, still soundly asleep with eyes shut. I touched you, and you suddenly turned around, clutching the pillow like it was your stuffed toy…"

"That's embarrassing. I must have been dead tired," I said.

"Yes, you were," he said softly. "But the amazing thing was that you looked completely at home, as if you were sleeping in your own bed. You seemed to trust me a great deal in spite of what I had done to you. You are sixteen, but you were sleeping next to me like some innocent child, with your bare body flopped out on the sheets, bottom upturned, legs wide apart. Under the circumstances, I wonder if any sane man would have passed up the chance of screwing you from behind for your absolute defencelessness. But I wasn't the same animal as the night before. I was flushed with emotions, which I still have difficulty finding the exact words to describe. Your innocence, that of a child, has touched me deeply, and made me feel sorry for what I did to you in the name of some ridiculous punishment. I vowed to myself on the spot that I would never hurt you again. Instead, I will only protect you and love you…"

"Martchu, you aren't serious, are you?" I asked, on the verge of crying.

"How could you doubt my seriousness?" he said. "I've waited two full days to observe whether my feelings are only some sudden, wild fancy that would subside in the passage of time. Nothing like that has happened. Let me tell you this: my heart is still burning fiercely like a red-hot iron. I am serious – deadly serious!"

I was beginning to sob uncontrollably.

"You still don't believe me?" he asked. "You can put me to the test, as there's nothing I won't do to prove my love towards you."

I didn't know how love could be tested – should I quiz him? Then I remembered something which was perhaps more pressing than romantic love, and I said, "Will you go to Mae Sai to meet my brother? Nothing would please me more."

His reply was ready and prompt. "If it pleases you, I don't see why not, although Mae Sai is way off my turf," he answered. "What about this: I'll go if you go too. We'll go to Mae Sai together to give your brother a surprise."

"I'd love to. It's been a long time since I last saw him," I said. "But I'm afraid Madame Supang would not let me…"

"Kaya, you still don't get it, do you? When I said I love you, it means you don't work for Madame Supang anymore," he exclaimed impetuously. "Tomorrow you'll go with me to Mae Sai, and you're not coming back. I'll meet you at Chiang Mai Bus Station in the morning and we'll catch the first bus to Mae Sai. I think you should start packing now."

He sounded reassuring enough, and I didn't know whether I should feel excited or alarmed. "It's as if I'm running away with you. How will this work?" I asked.

"Don't worry. It's going to be fine," he said boldly. "We'll make Mae Sai our first stop. After my business with your brother, we can continue our journey by crossing the border into Burma. Then we can travel to Sri Lanka, Nepal and the Himalayas. We can settle down in the mountains, if the idea appeals to you."

I felt a sudden fit of giddiness, rendering me temporarily speechless. Finally I came around to say, "I like the idea, although I think it's crazy. It could only happen in fairytales. But what the hell? I'm going with you to Mae Sai!"

He was ecstatic, and cried like a madman over the phone. He told me he wanted to tell me what he had been thinking for the long term. I asked him to leave it for another day, as I had already too much to stomach. But he continued talking feverishly for a few more minutes before he said goodnight and hung up reluctantly.

I sat collapsed in my chair, and as my giddiness persisted, I bit my finger until it bled. At the evidence of blood and the consciousness of pain, I thought this thing called love was probably real. Then I went to sleep.

I left the massage parlour early in the morning before Madame Supang came to work. I took a tuk-tuk to the Arcade Bus Station on Kaew Nawarat Road, arriving there before seven. The bus station was already crowded with tourists. I didn't know where to find Martchu. But he found me first, and hugged me from behind. He was surprised that I carried only a small bag. "You don't seem to have packed much. You're not coming back, are you?" he asked.

"This is all I have," I replied. But I lied. I had not cleared out everything from my locker in the massage parlour because I wasn't sure if I was leaving for good. I was faithless, I knew.

Our bus left the station for Mae Sai at around eight. We had two first-class seats, with me sitting next to the window and him by the aisle. I was nervous, and kept looking out of the window, as it was the first time I'd met him in broad daylight and fully dressed.

Amused by my shyness, he took my hand and squeezed it. "Can I kiss you?" he whispered. I pretended not to hear and withdrew my hand.

Without protest he put on a big smile and lay back for a nap. It was then that I had time to take a good look at him. He was indeed a very handsome man, with a fine face, strong cheekbones and thin lips. He seemed to be pretty relaxed taking a nap with his wavy hair dropping on his forehead.

Suddenly he opened his eyes, startling me with a grimace. "I'd almost forgotten," he said, sitting up and reaching for his knapsack on the floor. After some rummaging he took out a red rose. "I picked it in my front garden when I left home this morning," he said.

The flower looked withered and crumpled as a result of being stored in the knapsack. I said, "I don't want it if it's for me."

"No. The flowers in my front garden are all yours except this one," he said, fixing the red rose through a buttonhole on the lapel of his blue jacket.

I didn't know what it meant and he explained, "I confirmed to your brother that I'd be coming to Mae Sai. He asked me to wear a red flower for identification. Someone will pick us up at Mae Sai Bus Station."

The bus attendant distributed complimentary drinks and snacks. Sipping my sweet soy milk, I began to relax and feel less awkward sitting beside Martchu. I asked him if he had had a good chat with my brother on the phone.

"No. He never answered my questions without first consulting someone behind him. Even the red rose didn't seem to be his idea," replied Martchu.

It was at this moment that the name of Tai Lo flashed across my mind, but I didn't say anything, as I still had no recollection of Tai Lo as someone I knew.

I looked out the window and found we were already in the countryside. It was a beautiful day, warm and hazy, with a thin morning mist. The views were gorgeous, with a scattering of rural houses here and there on either side of the road, unending rice paddies stretching into the distance, and lush valleys and green hills further back.

I began to feel unwell when the bus started going uphill. I'd slept badly the night before, as I wasn't without apprehension about the trip to Mae Sai. I felt I needed a solid nap to make up for the lost sleep, and dozed off almost as soon as I rested my head on his shoulder.

He woke me up with a kiss when the bus made a stop midway between Chiang Mai and Mae Sai. He said he wanted to stretch his legs, and perhaps also grab a bite to eat. I chose to stay on the bus instead of moving around in the oppressive heat outside under a very hot sun. He asked me to keep an eye on his knapsack before he walked away.

After he got off the bus, I suddenly noticed that his knapsack was not fully closed. As I bent down to zip it back up, my hand came into contact with something inside, which was heavy and cold, like a piece of metal. However, the idea of checking with him what the object was just came and went, and I had completely forgotten about it when he returned to the bus with two large ice creams.

As the bus continued its way to Mae Sai, I dozed on and off for the rest of the journey. Martchu, on the contrary, was full of zest and vitality. He kept himself busy by working on his mobile phone with a small knife. I was curious but didn't ask him what he was doing, because I didn't want to be taken as a nosy girl.

The bus stopped at a mid-station for a thirty-minute break. We took the opportunity to have a quick bowl of instant noodles at a convenience store. When we returned to our seats as the bus resumed the journey, he showed me what he had done to his phone. Names had been carved out on its back that read: *Kaya and Martchu*, encircled by the endearing symbol of two hearts pierced through with an arrow. It was very sweet.

Finally we arrived in Mae Sai in the afternoon at about 2.00pm. As soon as we got off the bus we were met by a very strange boy.

He was about Kiet's age, between thirteen and fourteen. He had very small eyes, crew-cut hair and a dark complexion. Clad in some kind of uniform consisting a green khaki shirt, a pair of green close-fitting trousers and black boots, he looked to me like an undersized soldier. He took a while to scrutinise Martchu from head to toe before saying, "You're the only one here with a red rose. You must be Martchu."

"Yes, I am," said Martchu. "And you?"

"My name is Song," answered the boy politely.

"You mean 'Song' for 'Songthaew' the pick-up truck?" asked Martchu, with a glance at the cluster of red Songthaews waiting for customers in the bus station.

"That's right," said Song, with a childish grin. "My dad wanted me to become a Songthaew driver, therefore the stupid name."

He looked rather cute to me and I took my turn to greet him.

"Song, are you a friend of Kiet?" I asked.

He might have mistaken me for one of the passengers shuffling around Martchu. He said, "I have the strict order that I can only speak to the one with a red flower. It's none of your business whether I'm a friend of Kiet or not."

"Song, don't be alarmed," I explained. "I'm Kiet's sister, Kaya."

"You're Kaya?" he said, and started sizing me up with his small eyes. "Kiet told me his sister works in a massage parlour in Chiang Mai. That's some kind of whore business. But you're too pretty to be a…"

"Hey, kid, stop talking like that," snapped Martchu, in a hurry to protect me. "I can assure you Kaya is the sister of Kiet. And, more importantly, she is not a whore."

"I know why Kiet hates you, because you think we're all just kids," said Song in a bitter tone. "But you're wrong. We're men, and much better men than you."

He spoke just like Kiet, who had also described himself as a better man, and I wondered what these inflated kids were doing in Mae Sai when they should be studying in school.

Martchu looked a little taken aback by Song's reaction. But he refused to be drawn into a war of words. Instead he apologised, in a humble voice, for the presumed slight. "I'm sorry if I called you, rightly or wrongly, a kid," he said. "The thing is: we're very busy, and we don't have time to waste. Do you think you could take us to see Kiet now?"

I looked at Martchu with admiration. He was really attempting reconciliation by being careful not to spark another row, and seemed determined to move on with our lives by leaving behind his trouble with Kiet as quickly as possible. *This is a good start*, I thought.

Song jumped onto a pick-up truck, sitting on the bench on one side while we clambered after him and took the opposite bench.

"These trucks go to the border. Is that where we are going?" observed Martchu, as the truck pulled out of the bus station.

"All these red Songthaews drop passengers at the border control," said Song, without actually answering the question. In the meantime, he was eyeing me with disapproval, as if I should not have also come on board.

"I'm not sure Kiet wants to see you," he said.

"Of course he wants to see me, he's my little brother," I said.

"But he's not going back to school. You can't force him," said Song.

As I didn't want to discuss Kiet with him, I said, "What about you? Why are you running around as if you had nothing better to do?"

"Better things than what?" he retorted.

The truck made a turn into what appeared to be the main road, with an abundance of shops and hawkers. Song's eyes suddenly lit up as if he had seen something interesting. Pointing at the drove of beggars on the street, mostly children, he said with a mocking grin, "Not long ago I was one of them. But not anymore. Do you still think I have nothing better to do?"

"But what are you actually doing?" I asked. "Has it anything to do with the green shirt and trousers you're wearing?"

"It's for a special purpose," he answered, matter-of-factly. "Military training."

"Are you under some government programme or what?" I was curious.

"Government or governments. Call them employers, if you like," he said. "They need good soldiers like us who are brave and fearless."

He spoke with a certain feigned maturity that made me feel uneasy, and I said, "Who taught you all this nonsense?"

"Tai Lo," he replied. "But Tai Lo is not nonsense."

Tai Lo again, I thought grimly. I was a little incensed by the thought that I still had no recollection of the man.

Song pressed a button and the truck stopped outside a pharmacy at the corner of the street. We all got off. Song asked us to wait while he had to make a phone call.

Minutes later he came out of the pharmacy and said, "Now this is the instruction: I'll take Martchu, and Martchu only, to the border control. Kaya, you are not going, and if you like, you can wait here. I'm sorry."

"How long do you expect me to wait?" I asked him.

He reached out his arm, pointing at a tower building a few hundred metres away at the end of the road. "That's the border control," he said.

He had really exasperated me. "Song, for goodness' sake, please answer my question properly, which is not about where, but when and how long," I demanded.

"Not long. We're not going to the Burma side. The meeting between Martchu and Kiet will finish in no time, before you even know it," he said, again vague and evasive.

Martchu, who must have noticed I was about to explode for a reply as ridiculous as that, said hurriedly, "Song, it is okay. I'll go with you. But can I help Kaya settle down first, if you don't mind?"

"Go ahead," Song said, adding, in a mean-spirited way, "Time to say goodbye."

Martchu took my hand and brought me into the teahouse next door to the pharmacy. We sat down at a table near the window with an open view of the road.

"Song doesn't look like some normal kid to me. I think you have to be very careful with him," I said.

"Don't think I've come to Mae Sai unprepared," he said, with a meaningful pat on the knapsack. "I'm ready for all situations, and to use a little violence if necessary. So, why don't you enjoy having a cup of coffee while you wait here and stop worrying about me?"

"Do you think I can see Kiet before leaving Mae Sai?" I asked.

"I'll ask Kiet to call you after I'm done with him, then you can arrange the time and place to meet. How about that?" he said.

I nodded reluctantly. He gave me a kiss on the lips and took his leave.

He rejoined Song on the street and they started walking towards the tower building. Pausing at a pedestrian crossing, he turned around to wave cheerily at me. As if everything was under control, he looked bold and full of confidence. By then I was beginning to calm down.

The waiter brought me coffee, momentarily distracting my attention. When I looked out the window again, I had difficulty locating them in the bustle of the street. It was quite a while before I found them again. They were waiting and chatting on the pavement near the tower building. I told myself to be focused, because it was easy to lose sight of them with the train of people going to and fro past the window.

When I was wondering if Kiet would soon appear, I saw a blue Songthaew emerge from nowhere to stop on the curbside near Martchu and Song, and some people dressed in green scrambled out of the truck… It was at this moment my view was blocked by a big guy who paused outside the window. When it became obvious he had no intention of leaving the spot anytime soon, I couldn't help but call out impatiently, "Excuse me!"

The guy, instead of stepping aside, drew himself even closer. Now the tower building was completely blocked from my view. I thought I must tell the guy to move aside even though it might sound a little rude, as the street is a public place.

But before I opened my mouth, the guy suddenly said, "I got a call from Song, who said you've come to Mae Sai. Kaya, it's me, Tai Lo!"

I was stunned.

Standing in front of me like a wall, the guy was well built with broad shoulders and strong limbs. He had the features of a military man, with short, spiky hair, a weathered face with hard lines on his forehead, and sharp eyes with a frightening ruthlessness. He wore a green shirt, khaki trousers and boots, just like Song. But the clothes fitted him, because he looked like a real soldier to me whereas, for Song, they were merely costumes suitable for a kids' birthday party.

Seeing him at close range I found him familiar. Then all of a sudden a childhood memory returned, and I remembered him as a remote acquaintance. When I was small, there was a couple living with their only son in a decrepit wooden hut near the hillside in our village. But the name of the son was Thamchai, not Tai Lo.

"You are Thamchai, are you not?" I asked hesitantly, because Thamchai had been presumed dead some years before.

He grinned uneasily, his complexion turning ghostly, as if he were embarrassed by my good memory. "When I left the village, you were only a little girl. I'm surprised that you still remember me," he said. "I don't use the name Thamchai anymore. You can call me Tai Lo."

Now I understood why I had zero recall of Tai Lo when his real name was Thamchai, the illegitimate son of a Thai woman in our village and a Shan man from Burma. He was about ten years my senior. Due to his bull-like build and a readiness to bully and harass, all the boys in the village spoke of him with fear. My mother told us to avoid him because of his reputation as a rogue. We were fortunate to have never got into trouble with him, because he paid little attention to small children like us. The story was that he left the village after he had turned twenty-one, joining his father in Shan to fight the independence war against the junta. Nothing more was heard about him afterwards, until one day rumours spread in the village that he had been killed in a government raid in the jungle of Shan.

"People said you had died in the war. I'm glad it's not true," I said.

"No, I didn't die. I was only seriously injured and lost a bit of my leg," he replied.

So much for the preliminary courtesies. I hurried to say, "I was just watching the guys down the border control. I thought I saw a blue Songthaew and some men in green, but now I don't see them anymore."

He half-turned his body with a glance at the tower building in the distance, and said, "Is it about Kiet? Don't worry, he is in good hands."

"What do you mean by that?" I asked.

"Not long ago Kiet came to me for help with a situation," he said. "He has impressed me as a brave child who puts honour and pride before his own life. I have mobilised everyone available to help him."

Just then, a blue Songthaew came from afar on the main road, driving past the teahouse. I recognised it as the same truck that had earlier stopped near Martchu and Song. And I asked Tai Lo, "Do you know where the truck is going?"

He waited until the blue Songthaew had sped away and disappeared at the end of the road before saying, "To the village. They are going to talk things over in the village. I believe it is going to take some time. The boys will let me know when it's over. While we wait, what if I join you for a cup of tea?"

He didn't expect me to say no, and turned towards the door of the teahouse, moving with a noticeable limp, which was probably the result of what he referred to as "lost a bit of my leg".

He entered the teahouse, sat down on the seat opposite me and said, "Kaya, we all know Martchu is a bad guy, a bank robber and all that. He insulted Kiet, and it has been circulated that he has done some ugly things to you, too. Now you have delivered him to us, all by yourself. That is very brave and respectable."

I was a little taken aback at how he saw my presence in Mae Sai, but I didn't want to explain, especially not to somebody like him. "It's not exactly how you think," I simply said, and changed the subject. "There's something I don't understand. Why has Kiet chosen to come to you, of all people, for help?"

He grinned an ugly grin, putting his really bad teeth on display, and answered, "I think he's lucky to have found me. Nowadays I operate chiefly along the Thai-Burmese border, but rarely stay in one place for too long. It was last week I was having dinner with someone from our village in Mae Sai. He told me the story of your brother and how badly he wanted revenge. I therefore asked your brother to be brought to see me, and you know what? I liked him instantly."

What bad luck! I thought ominously.

In his eagerness to talk, Tai Lo did not seem to notice the distress on my face and went on, "He is such a fine boy, who has taken a keen interest in the battlefields. I, of course, can teach him a few things about killing from my vast experience of fighting in the jungle—"

It pained me to hear how Kiet had got himself involved with this guy, and I just couldn't resist making a somewhat stinging remark: "Tai Lo, can you still fight with your limp?"

He didn't appear to mind talking about his limp. On the contrary, he was quite proud of it as he carried on enthusiastically, "Thanks to the limp, I don't have to fight anymore. To begin with, early in my career as a soldier, I fought in the jungle for a couple of years. Then I was seriously hurt… didn't die, obviously. My commander sent me back to the frontline when I was only half-recovered, owing to the shortage of good soldiers. I was hurt a second time by stepping on a landmine and lost a bit of a limb. While I was recovering, I overheard my commander discussing with his people how soon I could be sent to the frontline again. I was deeply shocked. Then I had the sudden realisation that in modern warfare, replenishment of human stock, in the military lingo, is the most important thing, much more important than just fighting and getting killed. Therefore, after I had recovered but with a much shorter leg, I quit fighting and invented a new career for myself in the military business, which is the recruitment of boys and young men who could be deployed to fight…for a cause…"

He paused to take a gulp from my cup of coffee.

"Perhaps this is the most interesting part about our wars," he continued. "You know, in this world there is no lack of causes which people find worth fighting for. Say, for instance, to the reigning government, the cause is control over its stupid people who always want to have a better government; as to the opposition, it is the overthrow of the incumbent government which, if not already evil and corrupt, will certainly degenerate in time to become evil and corrupt; as to the junta, it is normal people being brainwashed by the fairytale of western democracy and becoming subversive; and to the people who think they are oppressed and persecuted, it is, of course, self-determination and independence…"

I yawned, not knowing what he was getting at.

"Well, if you still don't get it, let me try this: say, if it is men, the cause is always and undeniably women, and if it is women, it is who is sleeping with their husband. But listen to this…"

He paused for a hacking cough as if he had choked himself by his own turgid eloquence. Then with renewed energy, he resumed, "While there is no lack of causes worth fighting or dying for, there is always a constant shortage of good soldiers – soldiers who are young, soldiers who are daring and not afraid of dying. And as I've discovered in my newfound profession, boys – yes, boys – always make the best soldiers, because they are braver than you believe, stronger than they normally seem, and smarter than most think. I simply love boys."

I didn't know where his talking, so pointless and absurd, would lead. And if his purpose was to sell me on the idea of making my brother a child soldier, then I'd better tell him now to forget about it. And I said, "Tai Lo, I don't care what kind of recruitment business you are running. But let me tell you this: Kiet is only thirteen; he needs to get a proper education in school before anything."

"I meant no disrespect to what you have planned for Kiet," uttered Tai Lo with a deep voice as intended for an apology, but it wasn't so, as he said haughtily: "Your brother came to me for help, to have revenge at all costs on a bank robber who has humiliated him. With that sort of guts, I have little doubt that he would make a good soldier someday."

I wanted to tell him he was wrong, but just then his mobile phone rang.

He looked at the display panel of his phone for a while before pushing a button to take the call. "Who's this?" he said, then snorted, "Song, is it the phone I gave you guys? Now what the fuck is the matter?" As he listened, he began to scowl at nothing specifically for half a minute before finally uttering an almost insufferable sigh. "Song, I don't know what you're talking about. Can you stop shouting into the phone because it hurts my ear?"

He turned sideways to tell me, "Song said there has been an accident. But for all his gabble and babble I can't figure out what has actually happened!"

I was shocked. "Is he… all right?" I asked anxiously.

"Kaya would like to know if Kiet is all right," he said to Song over the phone, and a moment later duly informed me, "Thank God, Kiet's not been hurt in the accident, he is safe."

I wanted to know if Martchu was all right too, but never had the chance. Song must have said something grotesquely stupid, and Tai Lo was so mad that he began jumping up and down as he bombarded his phone with a mix of questions, rebukes and swearwords.

"Oh, for fuck's sake, did you say a gun? The man with a gun? And you guys with guns too! Say that again! You sure as fuck the guns are not loaded? How do you know they aren't loaded? Of course not! The guns you guys play with are not all toy guns. Some real, some automatic, some semi-automatic, some are toys just for show, but some are no fuckin' replicas. Don't fuck with them, as they can fuckin' kill you. As your commander, I have told you guys thousands of times you don't shoot each other except when your country is invaded by the US or Russia. This has been the highest military directive given to you since day one. Don't tell me you fuckin' don't know what a military directive is? A military directive is if you fuck up, you're dead. You're fucking dead, you know! Speak louder, will you? Who? Who the fuck is dead? Hey, speak up, I can't fuckin' hear you!"

He tossed his phone on the table with a slam, and said angrily, "He dropped my call! The son of a bitch dropped my call!"

Although I had heard only half of the conversation on this side, it was more than enough to shock me into thinking that something dreadful had happened. "What's wrong? What did Song tell you?" I asked.

"What would he have told me with his mouth full of shit? And he stopped talking to me as if he'd suddenly dropped dead. Maybe it's his phone battery," said Tai Lo, whose face was still flushed with anger. "It seems something has gone haywire. I think we should go down to the village to check it out."

His phone rang again. He picked it up and said, "Song, I'll fuckin' kill you if you ever drop my call again without prior permission. Okay, I hear you, it's the SIM card. But you're still responsible, because I can't fuckin' kill the telephone company. Now tell me what has made Chatchai wet his pants."

He sat down again, drank my coffee, and listened quietly without a running commentary.

After a minute or so of concentrated listening with his phone clamped to his ear, he said, in a much more relaxed voice, "Song, it doesn't sound too bad for the kind of mess you guys fuckin' made. Good job. You deserve a medal… no, no Purple Heart, not before you've done enough murders. I'll get you the Olympic, bronze or silver, if possible. Now, you little fucker, listen to me very carefully. You tell the guys to stay put in their positions; in the meantime, do nothing, touch nothing and move nothing until I get there. Yes, I'm coming over straightaway. I'll be no more than ten minutes, and I want you to meet me outside the village. You copy that?"

He closed the flap of his phone and said, tossing some baht notes on the table for the coffee, "Let's get out of here."

He walked very fast in spite of his limp. I followed him out of the restaurant and couldn't wait to ask him, "Can you tell me what happened?"

"You know it is Song I was talking to," answered Tai Lo, as he hobbled ahead without pausing. "He's a genius. Like all geniuses, they are so difficult to understand. So we're going down there to see it with our own eyes."

He turned into a side street where there were motorbikes lined up on both sides. After a few stealthy glances around, he began limping up and down the street along the rows of motorbikes as if he were reviewing a parade. At last he stopped before a black one with a skinny frame. He reached down to the engine box with his hand, and after some twisting here and tapping there, pulled hard, and the bike was startled into life. He mounted the bike, grabbed the handles and twisted them. The bike grunted alarmingly. He told me to get on the bike. I looked unsure.

"Trust me. It's safe," he said.

He was the last person I'd trust, I thought, but climbed on the bike nonetheless. I muttered, "Safety aside, this is theft, isn't it?"

"Again, in the military lingo, this is confiscation of private property in a time of crisis," he said, steering the bike down the street. "You might argue we live in a free society, with the protection of decent laws, but that's only in times of peace. For us career militaries, we live in wartime every day, and no laws are too sacrosanct to be left untouched."

I said nothing in retort, as I didn't want to argue with him. I dreaded that something awful had happened, and at present there was nothing more important than getting over to the scene as soon as possible. Practically, though, I could not open my mouth even if I wanted to, as the bike had now turned into the open road, roaring off at full throttle through the traffic. I put my arms around his waist to keep my body firmly on my seat, and closed my eyes to the whipping wind. At the same time I kept a mental count of the time in my mind.

About ten minutes later, the bike slowed down and gradually came to a halt. I opened my eyes and saw Song squatting with his back against the trunk of a large tree. He clumsily climbed to his feet and pulled the pair of sunglasses off his face as he staggered towards us with a sloppy salute.

Tai Lo returned the salute and snapped immediately, "Where did you steal those lousy sunglasses?"

"Martchu gave them to me," answered Song.

I frowned, finding it hard to believe that Martchu would give away his sunglasses, even if he wanted to be friendly with the boys.

"Did he give you his mobile phone, too?" asked Tai Lo again.

Song wasn't holding a phone in his hand and I was intrigued. He shook his head without giving a specific answer. I felt there was something sorely amiss. Tai Lo, however, did not press the issue of the mobile phone. He just said, as he limped ahead, "Song, you know I hate surprises. I need to know everything before I get down to the site. You understand that?"

"Yes I do," Song murmured timidly.

"Then what are you waiting for?" snapped Tai Lo.

And Song began, "Martchu has been telling jokes all the way to the village. They were very funny jokes. We laughed and laughed, and we just couldn't stop laughing…"

Tai Lo groaned impatiently. "Song, I'm warning you: we don't have time for chitchat."

"Sorry. No more chitchat. What if I fast-forward to the football field in the village…" said Song hurriedly. "… Martchu didn't find Kiet at the football field and asked where he was. We told him Kiet would not talk to him until he'd first met our demands, which was the plan, right?"

Tai Lo said nothing.

Song went on, "Martchu asked us what sort of demands. We told him to creep on all fours like a dog, and bark three times. Martchu frowned and said he didn't find our demand very nice. He asked instead to share some sweets with us. He opened his knapsack and took out a large bag of candies. He said, 'I want to be friendly with you guys.' It was at this moment that Chatchai spotted something spooky inside his knapsack, and yelled, 'There's a gun! The man has come with a big gun!' Martchu's face turned dark. He took out a handgun, pointing it at Chatchai. Some of our guys, like Min Myint and Timon, quickly dashed into the woods and returned with their assault rifles. But they were only to brandish them because we all thought they were replicas.

"Chatchai begged Martchu not to shoot. Martchu said nothing. He kept his finger on the trigger, as if he were ready to shoot any moment. I thought we didn't stand a chance and told our men to drop the weapons. I said, 'Give it up. We can't fight him with toy guns.' Martchu looked relieved at hearing what I said. He said, 'Don't worry. My gun is only intended as a gift for Kiet. Besides, it's not loaded. Almost a toy, like yours.'

"Chatchai, who was shaking with fear, said, 'I don't believe you.' Martchu said, 'You don't have to believe me. You only have to believe my gun.' He raised his gun, now with the muzzle aimed at Chatchai's head, and tightened his finger to shoot. At the sound of a click, Chatchai dropped to his knees with a terrible cry as if he had been hit. But he quickly stood up again. He was unhurt, except he had wet his pants. Martchu said, 'You see? I've meant to be friendly all along with you guys.'

"Timon said, 'We can be friendly to you, too.' He aimed his rifle at Martchu who, totally unafraid, did not even move sideways to dodge the imaginary bullet. Overpowered by Martchu's boldness, Timon lowered his gun. Everyone laughed. Martchu too, threw his head back laughing out loud. He even sniffed and barked like a dog without further request. I thought he had met most of our demand except creeping on all fours. Timon reminded him that he still had to get down on his knees. When Martchu hesitated, Timon said, 'Do it, or I'll kill you.'

"Martchu said laughing, 'Go ahead.'

"Timon, somewhat taken aback by Martchu's fearlessness, didn't know how to react. Perhaps just to save face, he raised his gun and pulled the trigger with his big thumb, firing at point-blank range at Martchu.

"Martchu was shot, and he fell, almost in slow motion like in a movie. Everyone was stunned. We thought it was only a game because we had only played with our toy guns. But Martchu dropped like a dead pig, and there was blood…" said Song whose voice had become hoarse and strained as if deeply affected by what had happened.

Tai Lo said, "I've told you not all of our guns are toys or fuckin' replicas. What have you done now? You've fucked up, as simple as that. But that's okay. This is the reality of war and you're not to blame."

"I've fucked up. I'm sorry," Song sniffled.

I sensed the coming of hell, and I howled at him, "Is that all? Have you finished all you want to say?!"

Song took a moment to compose himself, and said, with a shrug, "Well, there's not much to add. A replica gun, a real shot. At the sound of a loud bang that made the ground shake, Martchu was a goner."

I stumbled and fell in the mud.

Tai Lo picked me up. "What's the matter with you? It's only a bank robber. Don't be sentimental. You wanted him dead as much as your brother does," he lamented.

"That's not true. I never want anyone dead," I cried. "Was it always your plan to kill Martchu?"

"No. We only wanted to punish him, with Kiet to perform his part…" stammered Song. "Now Martchu is dead. What shall we do now?"

Tai Lo looked up at the sky, and said, after a moment of pondering, "Let's go ahead with our plan… probably with a little ceremony as appropriate."

"What kind of ceremony are you talking about?" I asked.

"A ceremony for both the dead and the living, for Martchu and Kiet, to settle the scores, to let bygones be bygones…" answered Tai Lo. "Come and join us. It will be a big moment for Kiet."

I didn't think I should object to it if the ceremony was intended to help the dead move on and heal the living. But I was filled with mixed emotions and I wanted to have some time for myself to mourn Martchu in private. So I said, "I'm feeling a little dizzy. Why don't you go ahead first? I'll have a little rest and catch up with you later."

"Very well. Take your time. You can find us at the football field at the end of the lane," said Tai Lo, limping off.

After they had wandered out of sight, I dragged myself into the woods, curled up under a tree and cried. Overwhelmed by a sense of loss, I cried unstoppably. But it was only after a short time that my tears dried up and my sadness was over, much sooner than I imagined. Perhaps I had come to terms with reality much quicker after the initial shock when I suddenly realised I wasn't that familiar with Martchu. We had only just begun to progress from a relationship in which he was the buyer and I the seller. Everything was still a kind of blur to me, as I wasn't even clear if he was a lover or a mere suitor. He'd made his declaration of love to me the night before and I was besotted. But this morning I wasn't so sure, remembering many a girl to have been sold to brothels by their boyfriends after they had made their incredibly important declarations of love. I didn't mean to be faithless. I just wanted to wait and see if we would travel to Mae Sai and back without mishap, as I was in no great hurry to jump from the frying pan into the fire. But too late now. A young life was cut short, a great romance came to an abrupt end. I thought I loved him, and genuinely felt sorry for him… he was handsome, he was funny, he even bought me ice cream… but all of this had become terribly irrelevant now.

I heard the sound of distant military shouts and singing in the air. It appeared that the ceremony was about to begin. Pulling myself together, I wiped my tears, brushed my hair and smoothed down my skirt, in order to look perfectly normal when I saw Kiet again. As I walked down the lane, I was both perplexed and apprehensive about what kind of ceremony it would be for both the living and the dead.

At the end of the lane was the football field, which was only a piece of deserted land of dirty mud and sand, surrounded by trees on all sides and with woodwork erected at both ends as goal posts. There was a group of people assembled in the centre of the field, all dressed similarly in green uniforms. They stood shoulder to shoulder, with arms linked like a wall. They didn't see me coming as they were facing the other way.

As I got near, the singing came to an end and Tai Lo called out, "Let the ceremony begin!"

Some team members echoed after Tai Lo. But there were others who were shouting, "Piss on him. His body a potty, piss on him!"

I was appalled, and started running towards the crowd.

It must have been the sound of my footsteps that caused the human wall to split in the middle as the people turned around to look at me. A skinny boy came forward to stop me from getting near. But there was no need, as I was already immobilised by the sight of a stiff, rigid body laid on the centre spot. By the blue-coloured jacket I recognised it as the dead body of Martchu, who was lying on his back, eyes projecting, arms stretched out, and one hand still wielding a gun. There was a large, gaping wound in his chest, with blood coagulated around the area. Kiet was standing next to the corpse, with hands at his crotch as if he were about to unbutton his trousers for a piss.

I now had a rough idea of what Kiet's part in the ceremony was about, and I yelled, "Kiet, what do you think you're doing?"

Kiet looked embarrassed and frightened by my presence, but he kept his hands on his crotch area. Physically he was thin and small. Other than a slight increase in height, there was a lack of strong evidence to suggest his coming of maturity of which he had boasted on the phone.

Tai Lo said, in the solemn voice of a priest presiding over the ceremony, "Kiet has pledged to exact his revenge at all costs. This is the moment, made possible by me, your commander, and his team of brave soldiers."

And the team of brave soldiers, all looking about the same age and wearing similar green uniforms, were chanting again, "Piss on him. His body a potty, piss on him!"

Tai Lo said to Kiet, "Go ahead. This is your sister's revenge, too."

Astonished, I said, "I beg your pardon? I would never do such a thing to a dead man."

"You're a girl and that's understandable," said Tai Lo. "What you can't do or won't do, Kiet will do for you."

"Piss on him. His body a potty, piss on him!" The boy soldiers caroled away like a chorus.

As Kiet hesitated, Tai Lo urged, "Kiet, remember how this man urinated on you, and remember how the same man has shagged your sister and buggered her ass. Go ahead and do it now, this is an order!"

Kiet procrastinated no longer. He pulled down his trousers and took out his penis, which, to my surprise, was decorated with a small amount of young pubic hair, like stubble on an unshaven face. A blush briefly passed over my face as I came to realise my kid brother was becoming a man. But there was still something childish about him when his uncircumcised penis looked more skin than bone. In order to perform, Kiet pulled back the prepuce, allowing a walnut-like penis-head flushed with a faint redness to emerge.

Everyone waited quietly without a sound, even the choristers. But as nothing was forthcoming, his chums thought Kiet might need a boost, and pressed on with their pure, innocent voices: "Piss on him. His body a potty, piss on him!"

Finally Kiet seemed to find himself galvanised into action. Short bursts of fluid began to emit from the narrow cleavage at the crown of his penis. As he got more confident, an uninterrupted stream of light yellow liquid was discharged from a swollen hose which now looked kind of manly and less boyish. As the yellow rain washed down on Martchu's body, it filled up the hollow of the chest wound before overflowing to the side to form a small pool of blood and urine on the ground.

I felt this was completely and absolutely insane and must stop. I said to Kiet, "You asked Martchu to come to Mae Sai for a friendly chat. What would you say to him now if he were still alive?"

Kiet pondered the question and his piss was interrupted. Not knowing the answer, he turned his eyes to his commander for help.

Tai Lo, grinning with an unholy glee, said, "Kiet, what have I taught you about forgive and forget?"

Kiet tried hard to think with a wrinkled nose, and said, after Song had whispered something in his ear, "It's easy to forgive and forget when your enemies are goners."

"So what will you say to Martchu now?" asked Tai Lo.

"I'll forgive him," said Kiet.

"No, you don't talk to me, you talk to Martchu," said Tai Lo. "And like your sister said, talk to him as if he were still alive, and finish what is unfinished."

With an obedient and serious nod, Kiet withdrew his eyes from Tai Lo and said, peering down at the body of Martchu, "I forgive you. Yes I do."

He then gave his penis a hard squeeze, and his piss, as if forced out of a little spray-dispenser, squirted forward almost immediately like a summer downpour. And the chanting picked up again: "I'll forgive you, yes I do. I'll pee on you, yes I do…"

I watched in disgust as my kid brother fired away relentlessly. The whole thing filled me with sorrow and pain. I suddenly felt so weak that I couldn't stand on my feet any longer and sat slumped on the ground.

As Kiet was coming to the end of emptying his bladder, his piss began to dwindle. The original rushing gush turned to drips, and the drops, gathered at the tip of his penis like morning moisture, disappeared after a few flicks. He put his penis back, rebuttoned his trousers, and stood licking his finger as if not knowing what to do next.

I gave him a wave, and he hopped over the dead body of Martchu and came to sit by my side. I held him in my arms, and cried, "What have you done to Martchu?"

He cried too, muttering innocently, "I've forgiven him. But will he forgive me too?"

"What do you think?" I asked.

"I don't know. I guess he would. Forgive and forget seem to be the only thing to do now," he said. "It is for the best, as no one will remember anything tomorrow, or the day after tomorrow."

"Hear, hear, you brother is really something," chuckled Tai Lo. "Have you ever heard that we human beings are a species of amnesia? We are so good at 'forgive and forget', almost as if it is part of our DNA. I imagine we just can't do without it, otherwise how are we supposed to handle the vast amount of crimes committed by and against humanity since time immemorial?"

No one knew what he was trying to say, and no one seemed to care. As the ceremony came to an end, the boys began to dig a pit underneath a rhododendron bush for the burial. Martchu's body was placed inside the makeshift grave, which was then refilled with mud and smoothed with sand and dry leaves. All the young soldiers, including Kiet, lined up and paid a last tribute to the dead man with a solemn salute.

Then the boys came back to the centre of the football field. Tai Lo said to Kiet, "Time to go. Say goodbye to your sister."

Kiet came over to kiss me on both cheeks. I asked if he was coming home. He shook his head and ran back to the company of the boys.

To my surprise, Song also came up to say goodbye. He handed me a mobile phone, which I recognised to be Martchu's Nokia.

"I saw the names of you and Martchu on the back of the phone," said Song quietly. "Please keep it." Before I knew what to say to thank him, he had already dashed back to his buddies.

At the prompt of a military command from Tai Lo, the gaggle of boys in formation made an about turn and marched off the football field in single file, disappearing behind the rhododendron bush.

Tai Lo must still have had something on his mind, as he didn't go off immediately after the boys.

"It's been quite some afternoon, don't you think?" he said dryly.

"So Kiet is a soldier now?" I asked him. "Is he not too young for the role?"

"Maybe a little early," said Tai Lo. "But he's not going to fight anytime soon. He'll first get some training back at the boot camp before he's ready."

"When he's ready… for whom is he going to fight?"

"Well, as I said earlier, there's no lack of causes people find worth fighting for." Immediately he started to lecture me again. "The same is true about the wide array of employers, which include, obviously, the government and governments on our borders and beyond, as well as the corresponding rebel factions against those governments. My able soldiers will sometimes fight directly for a single host, but many times indirectly for a combination of interests. Don't worry. Your brother is in hot demand. As you know, in our world, there are as many battlefields as there are ideologies. Trust me. I can promise you that I'll find him a good client and a worthy cause to fight for."

This was all bluffing, I thought with frustration. I said, "Tai Lo, I don't want Kiet going to the killing fields. He's still a child, and I want him to stay at home."

He heaved a pained sigh as if he had an acute headache. He said, "Kaya, you know it is not up to me or you to decide on Kiet's future. Remember the bravery he has demonstrated to us. He is not a child anymore. And becoming a soldier is his own wish, not mine."

"Tai Lo, stop this nonsense right now!" I said, raising my voice. "Let's talk business."

"Kaya, you're a smart girl," said Tai Lo, chuckling to himself with slight embarrassment. "Very well, let's talk business. You can buy your brother back if it's what you want. I only doubt if he'd welcome the idea, even if you had the money."

"How much are we talking about?" I asked.

"I don't know. I have to check with my boss and get back to you later," he replied, his voice non-committal. "For now, all I can say is: child soldiers are precious commodities in modern warfare, and Kiet is not cheap. All I can promise is: once I know the price, I'll give you a call as soon as possible."

He asked if he could find me a taxi to take me to the bus station for getting back to Chiang Mai. I told him I wanted to spend some time with Martchu. He said he understood, gave me a goodbye salute and limped off the field.

I stayed for about an hour sitting by Martchu's grave, mourning his sudden demise. I played with his mobile phone, caressing the grooves on the back where our names were etched with hearts and arrow. Finally, as the afternoon sun waned and dusk fell, I collected myself and left.

Back in Chiang Mai, I told Madame Supang all that had happened in Mae Sai. She was terribly alarmed. She asked me to leave the parlour immediately, for fear that Martchu's gang might come after me in retaliation.

But Madame Supang was, after all, not a bad woman. She knew I needed to survive and helped me find employment outside the country, as no sane establishments would give me refuge for my connection to the death of a bank robber. She sent me to Bangkok, where I stayed in a ghost building on the banks of Chao Phraya, waiting for her to complete arrangements for me to be sold to a nightclub chain in a small Asian city called Macao.

While still in Bangkok, Tai Lo called me back regarding the price for Kiet, which happened to be a considerable amount of money. I told him I had nowhere near enough. To be completely honest with him, I disclosed how much I had made from selling my first night to Martchu and also the kind of money I received from Madame Supang as the transfer fee to the Macao nightclub. Tai Lo seemed to be more reasonable than imagined. After some haggling he agreed reluctantly to take all that I had as the final price. As I had left all the money with my mother, Tai Lo was asked to contact her direct to make arrangement for Kiet's release.

After a week staying in Bangkok, I was set to depart. At the time, when I was hiding in a fish boat to be smuggled out of the Gulf of Thailand to Macao, my mother, who was tasked to see to Kiet's return, was also on her way across the Thai-Burmese border to a place called Shan where Kiet was having training in a boot camp. That was the last I knew of them.

During the time I stayed in Macao, I tried numerous times to reach them by long-distance call. But there was no one to pick up the phone at our home in San Mei. I kept calling them, initially a call a day. As time dragged on and without getting a response, my calls became less frequent. It was after six months when I called again that I got a recorded message that the number was no longer available. Later still, even the telephone company had gone out of business.

Despite the breakdown in communication, I kept faith that all was well. I held on to the belief that they had come back to Thailand but had moved to a new house; or they had not come back but had settled down in Burma in some faraway mountainous area called Shan, alive and well. I imagined them leading a happy life wherever they were. Such thoughts always gave me the strength to persist and persevere in my struggle for survival in Macao. I never doubted that one day we would meet again.

5

A.H.M.A.N.

———⁓⁓⁓———

Tears welled up in her eyes as her tremulous voice tailed off at the end of her story. I listened with awe at how she had got her boyfriend killed before she escaped to Macao and how she was involved in another man's death eventuating her return to Bangkok. As I remembered then, it was one midnight when the storm clouds were gathering in the sky above the Chao Phraya River. And as I remembered now, squatting all alone on the edge of the riverbank, I had come here with the purpose of praying for the wellbeing of Kaya who had vanished from my life four days ago. So I fell to my knees and prayed, trusting that prayers by the river, like heavenly music to the ears of the gods above, would be heard with supreme favour.

Afterwards I sat down there for a long time, wondering where to spend the night as I couldn't possibly go back to the apartment in Khao Shan which had become too dangerous for me. Gazing at the other side of the river, I suddenly became fascinated by a building with a half-finished dome on top. It was a high-rise of about forty storeys, fairly complete, and as I recalled, it was what Kaya described as the "five-star hotel with a severed head" where she had a brief stay when she was in Bangkok waiting to be smuggled out of the country to Macao.

On the spur of the moment, I decided to go and check it out. I thought it was not unlikely that Kaya might, after she had walked out on me, have gone into hiding in the building where she had been an erstwhile resident. I would probably find her there; if not, it still looked someplace to spend the night. Although I was somewhat intimidated by the dark, mysterious appearance of the building, I encouraged myself with the thought that if Kaya as a sixteen-year-old girl could have stayed there for a week, I didn't see why I couldn't.

Down the riverbank at the pier there were some water taxis waiting to take tourists for a ride along the river. A broad-shouldered man of about fifty tried to sell me the package including river cruise with food and drink. I told him I only wanted to get to the other side of the river. As this was a quiet night and he had nothing better to do he decided to give me a lift for 200 baht. Still disappointed with me for not taking up his better offer, he said grudgingly, "Don't see what you're up to over there. Not much to see except old houses, poor people, dirty streets, mini food stalls and some ghost buildings."

Bingo! I told him it was exactly the place I had in mind. I lied to him that I was a writer by profession, doing research in Bangkok for a ghost story.

"That makes sense," he replied sourly.

Without another word, he kick-started the engine and steered the boat toward the opposite shore. Five minutes later, I landed on a rundown pier enclosed by a low wall of wooden planks. Outside the pier I found myself on a backstreet on the border of a shanty town of small, crumbling box-like houses. Strolling down the street, I stopped briefly at a food stall for a bowl of noodles, and left with a takeaway bag of fish balls and fried chicken wings for my nighttime snack.

I found my way through a cobweb of narrow streets until I had walked out of the shanty area and entered, after a sharp turn, into a zone with monument-like structures looming black and forbidding in the distance. As I drew near, the clouds split to reveal a half-naked moon, which in turn graphically lit up the place. The zone, completely sealed off by a high wire fence, seemed to be frozen in time and left in ruins. Mounds of mud and small sand hills huddled like a crowd in the open space, chattering in silence. Scattered all over the place were shovels, jackhammers, hard hats, flags, wooden boards and signs of

"*Danger*" and "*Enter at your own risk*" in discoloured red paints. There were even outfits which appeared to have been cast off hurriedly, as if the workers had been ordered to leave the site in an emergency. The sense of flight was also strongly imparted by the sight of a bulldozer that had crashed into a half-collapsed barricade, with its compartment door thrown wide open. Hundreds of pieces of scrap paper, swept by a night breeze, flew in the air like a swarm of black butterflies that had escaped from hell.

Unceremoniously, I climbed over the fence, landing behind a heap of metal tubes. Almost immediately I had the strange feeling that there was a pair of curious eyes watching me in the dark. To test the water, I picked up a stone and threw it at a cement-mixing machine nearby. At the loud burst of sound, a creature was startled. It was a little cat, which leapt off the top of the machine and scurried through the mud and sand into the building, leaving behind a number of small, narrow paw prints.

I followed the trail of paw prints to the building and found the cat by a wall overgrown with weeds, gazing at me with gem-like eyes. When I approached, it backed further away and disappeared into the building. I parted the weeds by the wall and found the slit of an opening. With a shovel and some hard labour, I was able to widen the opening so that it was large enough for my body to squeeze through. Once I was on my feet again, I began to detect that I was in some sort of fire exit, with a stairway extending heavenward. As I picked my way up, I found those gem-like eyes again, peering down at me from the banister of an upper level. The tiny creature seemed to need a friend, and guided my ascension by always staying one floor above. It was after I had turned a stair corner for the umpteenth time that I finally arrived at a landing without immediate connecting access to an upper floor. There was a metal door on my right. With a slight push it opened to reveal an open space, with the smell of trees and grass and fresh air. It reminded me of what Kaya had once told me: that "some buildings near completion could come with professionally designed mid-level gardens". I wondered if I had just walked into one.

I entered the garden and saw to my left a wooden structure with semi-transparent glass walls. As I got nearer, I found the structure was like a greenhouse with an open front. Aided by the moonlight, some pots of melon vine could be seen strewn across the floor. As I ventured deeper, I found the greenhouse turned into a storage shed with a roof and half-brick, half-glass walls. There were bags of flower seeds, potting soil and empty terracotta pots scattered about the place. In a corner, a bust of a gardening angel lay in a wings-up position. It made you feel as if it would give you comfort and protection. *Not a bad place to spend the night*, I thought.

I walked to the back of the shed and lay down with my back against the wall. When I was on the verge of dozing off, something hairy brushed my arm and woke me up. It was the little cat, which I had not been aware of since I entered the garden. Crouching near my feet, its shining eyes showed a keen interest in the takeaway bag of fish balls and chicken wings on my lap. I gave the fish balls to the cat as a gesture of thanks for bringing me over to the greenhouse which, in my opinion, was quite comfortable as my resting place.

Without a better name, I called the cat a "little cat" because it was bigger than a kitten but smaller than a normal cat. Its body was round and furry like a ball of wool. Its long tail, snow-white in colour with yellow and brown stripes, wagged rhythmically as it enjoyed its meal. Its presence made me feel safe and calm. Without further ado, I closed my eyes and was soon asleep.

I had a bad dream and woke with a start in the middle of the night. Realising that I wasn't in my Khao San apartment but lying on the floor of the greenhouse, I had difficulty in sleeping again. I heard the sound of leaves rustling outside the greenhouse and I thought it was only the wind. But then I knew I was wrong when I saw a shadow emerge from the hedges to enter the greenhouse. In the poor light, the shadow appeared to be slight and slender, with long hair flying around its shoulders as it moved around. I believed it was a female and my question was: Would she be Kaya?

As I kept my nervous watch in the dark, the shadowy figure stumbled and accidentally knocked over a pile of empty pots.

"Shit!" uttered the high-pitched voice of a girl.

An empty pot was sent flying to the corner where I sat. It hit me on my leg, and I couldn't help but let out a little yelp of pain. The girl was startled; she immediately turned around and dashed for the entrance. I sprang to my feet, running after her. Outside the greenhouse she had got herself entangled in the hedges, which gave me the chance to catch up. I drew near to her and grabbed her shoulder. "Kaya? It's me," I muttered.

She paused as if she was trying to understand what she had heard. Suddenly she turned around and stabbed me in the arm with a sharp object. I stumbled back in pain, and she took the opportunity to kick her way out of the hedges and run away. I chased after her, despite my bleeding arm.

When I had first entered the mid-level garden I had gone to the greenhouse to sleep at once, without taking time to familiarise myself with the surroundings. As I now ran after the girl who soon disappeared into the dark, I had only my instincts to depend on for direction. After a series of slips and turns, I found myself standing by the side of a swimming pool filled to the brim with water, its smooth surface mirroring a star-studded sky. Then I heard the hard slam of a door. The noise provided me with a sense of direction. I picked my way along a lane until I reached a metal door which had not been closed completely despite the hard slam. I pushed the door open to enter, without quite appreciating the danger of what lay ahead. With a sense of adventure I was only too keen to find out if the girl hiding was Kaya.

It was not completely dark inside, as there was a candle somewhere up on a wall spreading a weak light about the place. There was a winding staircase before me. I walked down the steps to the beginning of a long, narrow passage. I followed the passage to the end and was faced with the choice of turning left or right. I opted right, simply because there was the flickering light of another candle on the wall and I was attracted to it like a moth to a flame. In my usual careless audacity I was only slightly perplexed by the convenient positioning of candles inside the place. After turning a corner I found I was in a corridor with whitewashed walls and deserted rooms off it. As I pressed on I saw a door suddenly open at the far end of the corridor. I halted behind a pillar to see what would happen. But no one emerged from the room, as if the door had only been thrown open by the wind.

As the silence lingered I decided to move ahead, pulling myself nearer to the room with its door ajar. I waited outside for any sounds. But it was very quiet. I leaned over slightly to look in, and found it was just an empty room, save for a low stool in the centre with a candle on it, burning with a strange white light. On the wall facing the door hung a poster of a beautiful woman dressed in traditional costume, posing in front of a golden tower. As I later learned, the tower was *Shwedagon Pagoda*, a famous landmark in Rangoon, and the woman was *Aung San Suu Kyi*, the icon of democracy revered in Burma and across the world.

I took a tentative step inside the room and saw a pile of rags on the dark floor near the end wall. I probably would have taken my leave if everything had stayed as it was. But the pile suddenly shook. I froze on the spot as it appeared to surge into life, like a cobra responding to the summoning tune of a snake charmer's flute. The pile of old rags, as it turned out, was actually a person kneeling in a folded position. As the person sat upright, I observed in the flickering candlelight that it was a young girl with an unexpectedly pretty face.

"Hi," I said awkwardly, without knowing how to address her when she was obviously not Kaya, much to my disappointment.

"Please help me," uttered the girl. She seemed to be in great pain, with blood trickling from the corner of her mouth.

In a situation like this, compassion springs naturally into action. I immediately rushed to her rescue. But in hindsight, my act of compassion was pretty foolhardy to say the least. As I lunged forward in haste, the ground beneath me suddenly shifted like I was stepping on quicksand. A crack opened up beneath my feet and my body was sucked through it by the pull of gravity. On impulse I seized the edge of the pit and temporarily interrupted my descent. I looked up, and saw the girl peering down at me with large, curious eyes. I had quickly worked out in my mind that it was probably the gangsters from Bangkok who had followed me to the ghost building and set me up with the trap. And I said to the girl, "Take me to your boss. I can explain everything; the Thai girl, the briefcase of money—"

"Stop your pretence now," she shouted down at me. "You're one of those secret agents, aren't you?"

What secret agents? I was perplexed. It then dawned on me that I probably had nothing to do with all this. And I said to her, "I think you've mistaken me for someone else. I'm no secret agent. Pull me up first so that I can make myself clear."

The edge of the pit, which felt like something between wood and straw, trembled violently in my grasp. The harder I tried to hang on to it, the quicker it melted away. Finally it had completely crumbled between my fingers and I went down the hole like Alice. But it was not the sort of hole with bunny rabbits. It was worse than a rat hole, and as I fell, I crashlanded onto the bottom which seemed to be a field of needles. As a result, my body – my back and buttocks in particular – was pierced by what appeared to be many sharp, pointed ends. The pain was so excruciating that I passed out instantly in a dead faint.

It must have been a long time before I slowly regained consciousness. I opened my eyes and there was the girl, sitting several feet from me. In a weak voice, I asked the girl what had happened.

"You've had a long sleep," she said.

"How long?"

"Something of several days," the girl replied.

I found I was lying on top of a pool of bamboo in disarray. I felt enormous pain upon where the bamboo sticks had stuck into my back and buttocks. "You trapped me. Why?" I asked.

"Perhaps I've trapped the wrong man, I'm sorry," she said. "But I'm not sure."

There were some small items laid out in an orderly manner in front of her. I recognised those things as my personal belongings, including my wallet, a black-leather Ferragamo, my AE and VISA cards, my British passport, my driving licence, and some thousand bank notes in Hong Kong, US and Thai currency.

"Be fair. I'm no secret agent," I pleaded. "You have my papers and you can see for yourself."

She picked up my passport and said, flipping the pages, "You don't look anything like the photo of the handsome man in the passport."

I said I had undergone head surgery recently.

"You may have had a facelift to become a spy. Tell me who sent you here," she demanded.

"Nobody sent me. I came here looking for a girl who had once lodged here," I said.

"A girl lived here in the ghost building? You must be kidding," she said in disbelief.

"Yes, a girl like you, alone and hiding…"

"Go on! You have been talking about girls and flowers in your sleep," she said. "You need to do better to convince me. You know I can't let you walk out of this place alive unless you can prove your innocence beyond reasonable doubt."

I knew I had to put my tongue to some hard work if I were to win her trust. And, as I had nothing to hide and no need to lie, I told her a story as comprehensive as I could manage.

"Let's be clear. I'm not a spy. Just an ordinary small merchant who collects antiques. About a month ago, I passed through Macao after a business trip to China and stayed there having some fun in the casino. But as bad luck would have it, I lost everything and owed a large debt to an underground banker. I was placed in the custody of a transporter called Tony who would take me back to Hong Kong for repayment of the debt. Tony was a burly man the size of a bear, who was known affectionately to his friends as 'Tony Bear'. Tony Bear took me to see a Thai girl. He wanted to have sex and some rest before we took the ship to Hong Kong…"

I further recounted to the girl how I'd met Kaya in her massage parlour, how Tony Bear had died of a heart attack as a result of an overdose of erection pills, and how we had eventually escaped to Bangkok with Tony's briefcase of money.

The girl listened with mild scepticism in her expression. To convince her, I told her some other things as well, for instance, how Kaya had been followed by some thuggish men believed to be gangsters from Bangkok, and how we hid the money away in the monastery at Wat Pho. I assured the girl that I had told her the truth, the whole truth, and nothing but the truth.

But the girl only said, "You know what? You've repeated the same story now for a third time, twice in your nightmarish mutterings, without a single discrepancy in the details. I must say I'm impressed. But it is not the same as believing you're innocent."

The efforts of trying to reason with her had proved to be not only futile, but also a total waste of the little energy that still remained in me. Completely exhausted with fatigue and benumbed with an enormous, unspeakable pain, I was too weak to argue with her. I thought I was going to die and I might stop breathing at any moment. I said, in perhaps my last breath, "That's okay if you still think I'm some bad guy, because you don't have to wait very long to see me dead."

She leaned over and gave me a slap in the face. "Keep talking. You haven't finished your story."

"Too late now, I'm sorry," I whispered, feeling my body sink further into the bottom of an abyss.

"Don't be stupid," she said. "This rabbit hole or mousetrap is not intended to be lethal. You've only fallen onto a pile of sharp bamboo sticks. I know it can be very painful, like you have been stabbed in your back and buttocks by a thousand needles. But that kind of injury is not going to kill you."

"Are you sure?" I asked.

"Of course. I have been working as a medical assistant, with experience in helping people with gunshot wounds or landmine injuries," she said, in a voice of pride and confidence. "With proper treatment I think I can help you get back on your feet again."

"You mean you'll help me...and let me live?" I uttered with unconcealed excitement.

"Yes," she said firmly. "I need you to stay alive to prove your innocence."

"Thank you. You're very kind," I said.

"You wait here, and don't fall asleep again," the girl said and left the room.

With a sigh of exhausted relief, I thought my terrible ordeal was coming to an end. But I was wrong. It was only the beginning of something which happened to be even more frightful and monstrous, as it transpired.

Later the girl returned with a pushcart, placed me on it and pushed me outside. I had the feeling that I was being taken back to the mid-level garden but was unsure, as the sun was directly above me. The task of carrying the load of my body from one point to another appeared to be quite a struggle for the girl, who groaned loudly every step of the way as she manoeuvred the cart forward.

Then the cart came to a standstill. My eyes had now become adjusted to the light and I could see that I was indeed back in the mid-level garden where there were trees and grass. The cart had stopped in the space between a swimming pool and something of a clubhouse. The girl entered the clubhouse and came out dragging a plastic hose.

"You stink like a corpse!" she growled. Turning on the hose she shot me square at my body.

Knowing I was in dire need of a clean-up after I had been lying in my own filth for days, I welcomed the shower with closed eyes. But no sooner had the shower begun than it came to an abrupt stop.

"This isn't getting anywhere!" grumbled the girl. She was gone again. I didn't know what had caused her frustration.

When she returned, she carried with her a hunting knife. I thought to my horror that she was about to kill me; but thankfully no, she only used the knife to cut up my clothes into bits and pieces. In no time my body was left in the indignity of stark nakedness, with my male organ unashamedly exposed. She looked slightly embarrassed, with a faint blush across her face. But the blush receded almost as quickly as it had appeared.

She said, "There's no way to give you a full wash with your clothes on. You look as if you're ashamed by your dick hanging like a dead worm. But I can't be bothered. I saw things a thousand times uglier when I was serving as a medical assistant on the border."

Calling my penis ugly was a blatant insult to my body, I thought bitterly. But I knew I must not protest to put myself in danger again, as I should count myself lucky to still be alive.

After a thorough body wash, which at times felt close to drowning, I was on my way again, and carted to the place where I stayed briefly on my first night in the ghost building. It was the greenhouse and shed. As I was dumped on the floor I suddenly remembered my cat and wondered where it was now.

The girl brought me some clean clothes and a glass of milk. She helped me to get dressed and spoon-fed me the milk. She seemed to be a really nice person of exceptional beauty. I thought I was beginning to fancy her.

"You have not eaten anything in the past few days, and you should only do it slowly," she said tenderly. "I know your wounded back needs some immediate attention, but I'd rather wait until tomorrow when you've regained some energy. See you later."

Worn with pain and weak from the hardships I had undergone, I quickly slid into a state of unconsciousness after the girl had left the greenhouse. At midnight I was startled by the presence of a visitor. It was my little cat, who must have caught the scent of what remained in the milk bottle. I poured the milk onto a plate to give it a treat. When it had had enough, it curled up next to me and slept comfortably under my gentle strokes. I was elated by the reunion with my cat, and slept soundly for the rest of the night, little knowing another strenuous day was ahead.

When the girl came in the morning, my cat had already gone. Without much ado, the girl went straight to work on my injured back and buttocks. With me lying on my stomach, she began prodding here and there in the areas of concern with some kind of sharp object. This caused me great pain and made me cry.

"Be quiet," she lightly chided. "I can't work if you keep making those ugly sounds."

After completing the initial examination, she said, 'Now this is what's going to happen. First, I'll work on your back, which to me is like a minefield without landmines. There are thorns all over the place, but again, there are no roses. Pardon me for the expressions. I'm just trying to give you an idea of what we're dealing with here."

"That's fine," I said.

And she continued, "Next I'd attend to your legs which I can see the left one is swollen at the knee. That's all I can say for now. If you don't mind, I'd stop talking and start working."

"Go ahead," I said. "I trust I'm in good hands. I only wish the pain is less punishing."

"Be brave; everything will be all right," she said, and proceeded immediately to work on my back with a hunting knife and something like a pair of pliers.

At first there was only some tingling pain, which had however quickly increased to become sharp and agonizing.

"Ow!' I couldn't help but cried.

"Shh!" she hushed me to keep quiet.

"Ouch! Argh!" The pain was killing me and made me groan, "Oh, fuck!"

She paused, and said reprovingly, "Can you behave more like a man!"

"I'm sorry, but the pain is terrible," I explained, somewhat shamefaced.

She produced a small glass phial and asked me to drink from it if I wanted the pain to stop.

"How does it help?" I asked.

"It's poppy juice; it works like a sedative," she said.

"What if you're trying to kill me with poison?" I queried her.

"Well, you decide," she said. "But what could possibly go wrong when you're no more than a cripple now?"

That was a winning argument, I thought, and obediently gulped down the juice.

She burst into giggling laughter as if she had waited a long time for the moment. "How can you call yourself a man when you would drink whatever is on offer merely to ease the pain?" she ridiculed.

I regretted a little having given my trust too readily to the girl and her juice. But it was too late now, as the drug had quickly propelled me into a state of oblivion.

I woke up a couple of hours later as the effect of the drug had subsided. I was relieved that the juice had not killed me.

She gave me a report of my condition. "Most of your injuries are external. I think I've had removed 99 if not 100 percent of the thorns, spines and prickles which have penetrated in your flesh. Then something about your swollen knee...I'm sorry to inform you that, because of your fall and how you had stupidly landed with your left leg first, you've got something of a torn ligament. It is serious; but the good news is, not sufficiently serious to need surgical intervention. I've already put something of a brace to your affected leg. I reckon the swelling will fade in a few days' time, and six to eight weeks for the torn muscle to fully heal."

I listened with nothing but gratitude, knowing that she had done a great deal to my body while I was sleeping.

The operation, or whatever it was called, was considered a success as I was able to sit up without help in just a couple of days. Another week later, as my body continued to improve, I could manage to move around, by crawling out of the greenhouse like a worm to relieve myself behind the trees.

One day I asked the girl how long it would take me to be able to walk again. It was then that she gave me an update of my condition, which was not funny, because there was still a tiny piece of bamboo stick inside my body. It had penetrated deeply on the side near the appendix, and she had had difficulty in completely removing it during the last operation as I was about to come out of my drug-induced coma. She had therefore decided to wait until the wounds around it were more or less healed.

"Now," she announced, "is the time to get rid of it once and for all."

She explained to me that a second operation was an absolute necessity for my long-term health. I had no objection as I was extremely impressed by the speed of my recovery from the first one. I trusted her fully, not to mention how much I also secretly admired her beauty. She gave me the poppy juice and I accepted it without hesitation. She must have been touched by my courage and remarked, "You're really somebody. There's something special about you for which I don't have a name. Either it is high intelligence or utter…"

I thought she was complimenting me. But I couldn't talk when the drug was taking effect. I could only thank her with a smile before my eyelids dropped like heavy curtains.

As it turned out, the juice I took for the second operation was a lot stronger than the previous time, when it had taken me two days to fully wake up. It was then I discovered that my back was heavily bandaged at the waist.

She congratulated me with news of another successful operation. Optimistically, she explained that I should be able to walk around with the help of a stick in two weeks' time, and try running after a month.

I was very pleased with her report, as I thought it wasn't a bad thing to spend another month with such a pretty girl alone on the mid-level garden.

Ten days later she removed the bandages from my waist. I was befuddled to find that a small area to the right of my back was still covered with adhesive tape. I asked her when that could come off as well. She said for safety reasons she had planted a small metal plate there for support, which would probably have to stay for some time to come.

"Are you sure?" I said with disbelief. "This is absurd."

"Please don't sulk," she said. "The thing you should do is not interfere with it. I promise to do something about it when you can walk again. In the meantime you can always ask for a massage if I can help lessen the discomfort in the area…"

She sounded like she was trying to coax me to understand. I wondered if she would give me a cuddle too should I ask. *But that can wait*, I thought. I told myself not to rush into anything silly, at least not before I had achieved full recovery.

Now my goal was to become physically fit again as soon as possible. Every day I spent hours on end doing workouts, or lifting bricks from one corner to the other inside the greenhouse. One morning, while I was working on my balance, I was delighted to find myself being able to stand erect steadily for a considerable length of time. This was a good sign, suggesting my recovery was around the corner. Anxious to find out if my fitness had returned to a healthy level, I decided to venture outside the greenhouse for a walk in the garden, the first time since my fall into the trap.

After I started, the walk proved to be more difficult than imagined. Depending on the use of a stick, it took me a full fifteen minutes to cover the distance from the greenhouse to the swimming pool.

Although the exercise had failed to prove the return of my energy and vitality quicker than I would have hoped, the effort was not entirely wasted. The moment I reached the low fence outside the swimming pool area, I was lucky to be just in time to catch the sight of the girl climbing out of the pool. She was wearing a one-piece swimsuit in a floral print. Her skin had a healthy, brownish tan, and her legs were long and shapely.

Sitting on the edge of the pool, she had a flower in her hand, and as she gazed at it, to my astonishment she suddenly burst into sobs and tears. I felt as if I had intruded on her privacy without permission, and, as a gentleman, I quickly turned away to save her from embarrassment. As I took a step back in haste, totally forgetting that I was still a pitiable cripple, I slipped and fell clumsily on my face.

The girl must have been alarmed by the noise of my fall. Screaming in horror, she cried, "Just what do you think you're doing? Don't you know your recklessness could get you killed?"

She rushed over and helped me to my feet. She looked extremely displeased with my behaviour. She said, "By my estimation it will be another week before you should start learning to walk again. I don't understand what makes you so desperate!"

"I'm not. I was probably a little over-confident, or even reckless, like you said," I lightly retorted. "But I doubt that would have led to me being killed."

"You never know," she said, still looking cross.

"Can I ask you a question, as a friend?" I said, just to change the atmosphere.

"Not sure if we are friends, but what kind of question?" she asked.

"I saw you crying," I said. "What's your problem?"

She seemed uncomfortable by my spying and answered, "That is a stupid question. If you knew me sufficiently, you wouldn't ask the same question again."

"But you're crying over a lotus flower. Isn't it a bit strange?" I said.

"You're really a curious dude," she said. "You know what? A man could get himself killed simply for knowing too much."

"You don't look so deadly to me," I persisted boldly. "What if I still want to know?"

She laughed. "Well, if you insist," she said. "In the meantime, I happen to have something to tell you too."

"Oh really?" I said, excited by the prospect of a chat.

"Shall we sit down on the bench over there and I'll tell you things you need to know over a drink?" she proposed.

"Perfect," I said.

"Now we'll walk to the bench together. As your back is especially delicate, we're going to do it really slowly," she said gently. "Can I ask you to put an arm around my shoulder?"

I readily complied, knowing it would be rude to say no.

After I was helped to the bench, she said, "I want you to wait here, and promise not to be naughty again. I'll need to change into something dry, and I'll see you later, okay?" She strode away, disappearing inside the building.

As I waited, I had the opportunity to take a full view of the garden under bright daylight for the first time since my intrusion into the ghost building. It was an open space enclosed by a low wall with ventilation holes on much of the perimeter. Divided into sections, the garden was equipped with facilities including a swimming pool, a clubhouse and a golf putting green by the wall on the east side to serve the recreational needs of tenants who were yet to occupy the condominium. It was almost like some holiday resort if not for its state of ruin and decay after the building had been abandoned as a result of the Asian Economic Crisis. The water in the swimming pool was muddy coloured, with rushes and water lilies growing profusely at the far corner. The clubhouse stood with broken windows and a dilapidated roof, and the golf putting green was littered with dead leaves and twigs. Paths of pebbles mixed with dirty sand crisscrossed the garden like a spider's web.

The girl returned all smiles some minutes later. She looked gorgeous in a yellow vest and a light blue sarong tied at the waist. She was carrying a rattan basket in one hand, and something like a cage covered on all sides in the other. The basket was filled with fruit such as apples and bananas, as well as milk and bread.

I was hungry, and helped myself to the food. She peeled a banana for herself and read a newspaper while she ate.

"What's in the news?" I asked casually.

"This is only an old issue of the *Bangkok Post* dated a few days back," she replied. "I've brought it along because there's a story which might interest you."

She passed over the newspaper, and the story concerned, already marked out on the margins with red ink, bore a headline that read:

PALESTINIAN GIRL IN SUICIDE ATTACK IN JERUSALEM RESTAURANT

"This is dull," I said. "Is there a sports page inside?"

"No, you finish reading the story first," she said in a priggish, warning voice. The smile on her face was also gone.

I was a little taken aback by her bluntness, but I wasn't about to argue with her over such trivial matters. I read the story as asked, without realising her brusque manner was a sign of things to come.

"Finished?" she asked, eyeing me with a scowl. "What do you think?"

"Well, I don't know. A Palestinian girl blew herself up at a pizza restaurant in Jerusalem… don't see in what way it's interesting," I said. "Can I turn to the sports page now?"

"No. Let's attend to something else first," she said.

She opened the cage and took out a cat. The creature, which was round and furry like a ball of wool with a yellow and white tail, happened to be my little cat that had first guided me to the mid-level garden and paid me visits whenever it had sniffed a scent of good food in the greenhouse. Looking uneasy and nervous, the cat seemed too tame to escape as if it had been drugged. Even more puzzling, it had been bandaged heavily on the back.

"What's wrong with the cat?" I asked.

"It has hurt its back, like you," she replied. She placed the cat on her lap and began to fix the bandages in place with adhesive tape.

I made no further enquiries and contented myself by watching her. She was unmistakably one of the most beautiful girls I had ever met in the flesh. There was grace in her manner and gravity in her demeanour. She looked brisk and matter-of-fact, pouring herself into her work with love and dedication, to my great admiration.

Finally the girl lifted her hands from the cat and said, "I pray this will serve its purpose."

"Thanks to you, I hope it's all for the best," I said.

She took the cat to the golf putting green some twenty yards away and put it there on the artificial turf. "Okay, dear, you may go," she said.

She returned to sit next to me on the bench. I couldn't wait to compliment her, "You're very kind."

She seemed embarrassed by my praise and said nothing. I thought she was just modest.

On the golf putting green, the cat crouched clumsily near a hole. With the lump of white bandage on its back, it was looking more like a camel than a cat.

"Go, go!" the girl urged from afar.

When the cat was still stationary, the girl picked up a stone from under her feet and aimed it at the cat.

I was wide-eyed, and didn't quite comprehend what she was trying to do.

The stone missed the cat by an inch or two, but was enough to scare it into making a move by crawling to the other end of the turf. The girl followed up with another stone, which hit the cat on the head. The cat gave a grunt of pain and ran for cover.

Near the wall there was a pear-shaped rock as part of the decoration and embellishment in the garden. The cat, apparently unhindered by the burden on its back and with a leopard's agility, made a jump for the top of the rock, just in time to escape another stone coming in its direction.

But it was at this very moment things took a weird turn, almost beyond my wildest imagination.

The cat, while in mid-air, seemed to have been hit by an unidentified flying object from nowhere, like a plane struck by a missile. At the sound of a small explosion, the cat's body fell apart in a whirl of fire and smoke. In the blast, its disembodied head flew over to the other side of the wall, its broken limbs scattered all over the putting green, and its detached long tail, snow white with yellow and brown stripes, plunged perpendicularly into the centre of a hole and stayed there like a standing pole – and, as if with a life of its own, wagging crazily back and forth for several moments before coming to a standstill.

I was completely bewildered and stunned by the violence. The girl looked even more shocked. She buried her face in my lap and cried, "I'm sorry, I'm very sorry."

The cat's blood had reddened the putting green. An odious smell of death and the strong and pungent whiff of the after-blast filled the air in the garden.

I didn't know how to console the girl except stroking her body like I used to stroke my little cat. The girl, calm again later, stopped crying. It was then I noticed that she was still holding a stone in her hand. Now I couldn't be more suspicious and said angrily, "What have you done to the cat? You have killed it, haven't you? With a bomb?"

She was expressionless. She wiped her tears, admitting nothing.

"I can't believe that you could weep like a child when it is you who has murdered the cat," I said. "You're so cruel and heartless."

"That's not true," she retorted. "I also wept for you when you fell down the pit."

"You did?" I said, looking at her tear-stained face.

"I thought you were dead," she said. "Thank God it did not turn out that way. Since you're alive, I have to work things out a little differently."

"What's that supposed to mean?" I said. "By killing the cat with a bomb on its back?"

"It's more than that. It has also demonstrated that when there is a bomb on your back, you must not run or jump. You can only walk slowly with a steady pace; otherwise it can go off and kill," she calmly explained.

"Yeah, now it has gone off and my cat is dead!" I shouted at her, still in indignation. "But what has that got to do with me?"

Without blinking, she declared, in a slow and clear voice, "I planted a similar bomb on your back in the last operation. Only it's ten times more powerful."

The news hit me like a bullet in the chest and I almost fell off the bench. But the girl was quick to grab me by the scruff of the neck and help me to sit straight.

"I know this is hard for you," she said quietly. "But you will soon come to your senses and understand that it is only for your own good."

I lay back on the bench and breathed heavily for several minutes. At last I found my voice again, and asked, "Why are you doing this to me?"

With a sorry sigh she said, "You know, although we have got to know each other much better in the last couple of days, we're still far from being friends. I have many enemies, and you might be one of them unless you can prove your absolute innocence."

"Who are you and what the hell are you doing here by imagining I have anything to do with your world of spies and secret agents?" I said, raising my voice.

She fixed me with a cold, stony stare. I was suddenly aware of my own vulnerability, and I quickly softened my tone and pleaded with her, "Can you just let me leave this place as soon as I can walk again?"

"I'd like to. But it's complicated when you are carrying a bomb on your back," she said. "I reckon it will be a couple of weeks before you can walk properly again. Prior to that, can you do something for me?"

"Anything you say. Just think of me as a friend," I said condescendingly. "Given time, you might even find me quite pleasant and attractive."

"Well, nice to hear that. But listen: I don't need you to be charming or smart, or even interesting. I just need you to cooperate. Can you handle that?" she said.

"How exactly am I to cooperate with you?" I asked. "Are we in a joint venture?"

"We'll come to that," she said, smiling affably. "Now listen…"

"I'm all ears," I said.

"First things first," she said. "There's something you should know about the bomb on your back. Although it's a little uncomfortable because of the bandages and duct tape, you can live your life normally, for example, going to the toilet or taking a bath. In fact this 'little thing' is quite lightweight – it's contained in plastic casing no bigger than a small pocketbook and completely waterproof. You wouldn't even know it was there if I hadn't told you. That being said, as I like to warn you beforehand, you must not ignore it as if it does not exist. What's more, you have to be extremely careful with your every movement, as you should only walk – that is, by the time you can walk again – and not run. And then there's something else I cannot emphasise enough: you must refrain from tampering with the bomb. As a device, it is wired intricately and extremely sensitive. Any attempt to remove it would set it off instantly. Therefore if you make a wrong move you don't walk again, because you're dead. Understand?"

"Understood," I answered feebly.

"Good. Now it's time for our Q&A, and I'm sure you must have loads of questions," she said.

"No. Not loads, just one," I said. "I don't know why you should tie me to a bomb like I was a suicide bomber…"

"Is this your question?"

"No. My question is: How will I ever be free from the bomb and its death threat?" I asked despondently.

"Good question," she said in a formal voice, like a spokeswoman at a press conference. "The answer lies in what I said earlier about cooperation. I've heard your story several times. Honestly, it doesn't add up to prove your absolute innocence. But so far I've given you the benefit of the doubt, because of a certain interesting detail which has kept popping up with unerring consistency…"

"Which is…?"

"Tony Bear's briefcase of money," she said. "You go and find the briefcase, dig it up and show me the money. If you can do that, I don't see why you can't walk out of this place a free man again."

6

A . H . M . A . N .

———

I hated her for killing my little cat.

But hatred aside I experienced a much greater fear when my life was now at her mercy. I probably would fear her less had I known her better. She was something of a mystery – an animal killer, a medical assistant, a bomb-maker, and probably a terrorist too. I never wanted to be near her or speak to her again.

She was quiet after she had spelt out the conditions for my regained freedom, as if she'd become tired of speaking. But before silence had completely sunk in between us, my bowels, irritated by the milk I drank earlier, made a stupid gurgling sound.

"Oh this is important," she suddenly said with a frown. "Shall I remind you not to relieve yourself under the trees again? It is unhygienic, and uncivilised too. For your information, there's a toilet in the clubhouse. Help yourself to it, but don't forget to flush and wash your hands after use."

She had really embarrassed me. As if that was not enough, she added, with a curl of her beautiful lips, "Tell me if you need me to walk you over there."

"No, thanks," I answered bitterly. I swore I'd never ask for her help even if I were to drop dead from fatigue and exhaustion.

I hobbled my way to the clubhouse using my walking stick, under the close watch of her eyes. I somehow managed to reach it without accident, taking the newspapers with me. As I came to discover after I had sat down on the toilet seat – of a certain Italian design – for some serious business, the sports page in the *Bangkok Post* was quite good; the entertainment page with a story on John Travolta was really funny.

At the end of my business I left the toilet to return to the greenhouse. The girl was sitting on the poolside, with her legs dangling above the water and her eyes fixated on the floating leaves and petals. I tottered past her. She pretended not to notice me. Thereby the observance of silence between us for the next couple of weeks began.

I took time to nurse my wounded back. Or, putting it a slightly different way, I was given time to heal, as I could not possibly go to find the briefcase when I could only walk leaning on my crutch. I slept a lot, in the greenhouse or outside on the meadow of tall grasses and wildflowers under the shade of a palm tree. At other times, I would perch behind the wall to appreciate the vista of the city through the ventilation holes, which was beautiful and enchanting like a moving postcard.

Despite the breakdown in communication, we somehow managed to co-exist quite well. Life on the mid-level garden was calm and strangely organised. Normally I would rise after seven in the morning and begin exercising my body on the patch of grass between the greenhouse and the pool. She had also maintained a strict routine of bath and shampoo in the morning, finishing always just before I got up. But there was a rare occasion on which I'd arisen before her routine took place. It was not because I had insomnia, only because I was curious. I hid behind the trees, and through the foliage watched her bathing in the pool. She began by washing her hair, with her head tilted at an angle to the sky, a beam of morning sunlight upon her face. Next she attended to her body, but there was no telling if she was naked, as anything below the neck was obscured under the water. At the end of her shampoo and bath, she climbed out of the pool and her body was revealed to be clad in a one-piece swimsuit. She picked up a stone to aim it in my direction but missed me by inches. I hobbled away and never tried again as I was, after all, only inquisitive, but no voyeur.

There was always food in the right place at the right time: milk, boiled eggs and bread in the morning; barbecued meat, sausages and fish burning like charcoal in the afternoon and evening, plus an adequate supply of fruit on the bench equipped with a conical top for shade.

About twice a day, she would wave me over to check my back, both for the progress of my wounds and also to assess the condition of the cold and deadly device that had sucked deep into my flesh. I held my temper and swallowed my disgust at being someone's hostage. She had asked for my cooperation. I coped reluctantly only because I was under threat and coercion. As a man I had my honour and dignity to defend, and I vowed secretly for vengeance should I find the opportunity. I stayed low, biding my time, and concealed the progress of my recovery from her. I faked shudders of pain when she touched my back, and walked with the help of a stick, which I could have been rid of a week ago.

However she was a much better opponent than I imagined, as she was always one step ahead of my next move. On one overcast day after breakfast, she suddenly decided to exercise her right of speech again.

"I need some help," she said. "Please follow me."

She led the way to the building. I walked dilly-dallying behind her with a pretend limp. Outside the heavy metal door at the entrance, I refused to go further.

"Tell me exactly where we are going?" I insisted.

"To the room where you had been lying for several days on the bamboo sticks," she said. "We have some repairs to do."

"I'm not sure I want to go there again," I said.

"Why?"

"Because you're dangerous."

She bit her lower lip. After a pause she said, "You are the one, aren't you? Otherwise you don't have to be afraid of me."

"I'm the one if you're talking Bond movies," I said, thinking it a clever little jibe.

She burst out laughing. "You live in a very simple world; what envy!" she said. "I am beginning to believe your innocence more each day. But how did you get yourself messed up in all this in the first place?"

"We've been alone in the ghost building for all this time. Aren't you in some way messed up too?" I retorted.

She seemed tongue-tied for a brief moment before she said, with the hint of a sigh, "Perhaps you're right. In a sense we're both trapped here. But in reality I am in much bigger trouble than you. Well, as we're in the same boat, I think we should cooperate and help each other out."

I was still reluctant.

"On the way we'll go past my bedroom. As a friendly gesture I can let you have a glimpse of what it is like inside," she said. "With this further incentive, does it make you feel better coming with me?"

"Better perhaps but not great, unless you ask me to share the bed with you," I said, seizing the opportunity to tease her.

"Please watch your mouth," she said, scolding me mildly. "C'mon, let's go."

I knew, like it or not, that I had to cooperate with her. But secretly I also welcomed the opportunity as a dose of adventure when life in the mid-level garden had been quite boring.

She showed me her bedroom, which was situated in the south wing of the building, a few steps off the main corridor through a side passage. It appeared to be quite spacious, or maybe that was just because it was bare and spartan, with little furniture except a wooden bed by the far wall and a simple table in the centre of the room. I was not surprised to find things like copper-wire coils, tubes filled with a silvery liquid and bottles containing red and yellow powder on the table, knowing her as someone who could manufacture bombs. Near the ceiling there was an east-facing porthole window pouring natural light into the room; perhaps because of the direction of the wind, I thought I could smell the scent of flowers and grass carried along a soft breeze entering through the opening and hear the sound of birds chirping in the garden. There was nothing in particular to suggest it was a girl's bedroom, not until my eyes began to scan around the bed area.

It was at this moment she suddenly cried out, "Oh shit!" and rushed inside to pick up from the floor something white resembling a piece of underwear and shuffle it furtively under the pillow. By now I had also noticed there was a transistor radio, a camping lantern, a standing glass cylinder with water in it (I wasn't sure of its purpose), and some newspapers on the floor near the head of her bed.

After she had securely hidden her underwear under the pillow, she turned to look at me and said, "Well this is it. What do you think?"

"I don't know. To me it's just a room without a view," I said. "Actually you don't have to show me your bedroom in exchange for my cooperation. I'm carrying a bomb on my back and I'll do anything you say."

She said, "As I said, I want to be friendly with you…"

"If you really want to be friendly…" I interrupted her, "… lend me your radio. It's so boring here and if you could let me listen to music and sports news on the radio…"

"No way." She turned me down abruptly. "I've more important use of the radio. I need to monitor the situation of my country every hour of the day…"

"Then forget it," I said with a dejected shrug.

"What about this?" she said, picking up a book among the newspapers on the floor and throwing it over to me.

I caught it neatly in my hands like a goalkeeper catching a ball. The book had a red cover, with a title written in a language I didn't recognise. I threw it back to her, and said, "What's this? Greek or Latin?"

She dropped the book back onto the pile of newspapers on the floor, and said, almost with a hint of relief, "If you don't want to read…"

"I only want the radio." I repeated my demand.

"Okay, okay. I just said I wanted to be friendly with you, and it seems as if I've already owed you a favour. How unfair!" she said, with a little sigh. Then in a split second, her face broke into a big smile as she continued, "What if you help me with some work first, and we'll talk about the radio afterwards? Shall we?"

She didn't expect me to say no. She picked up the lantern on the floor and left the room, closing the door behind her. She said we were going to the north wing of the building. I walked after her between the thick walls, passing deserted rooms and abandoned corridors which were quiet and eerie as hell. Finally we stopped before a room with the door ajar. I looked over her shoulder and saw, to my horror, a stack of bamboo sticks lying in disarray, many still tainted with blood at the sharp ends.

She said, "I'm sorry to have brought you back here. But you have smashed the trap to ruins, and I need to set it up again."

"Why?" I asked, pulling a wry face.

"To catch a thief!" she said. "My deadly enemy will come here sooner or later if you're not the one. Are you or aren't you the one trying to kill me?"

"Am I still a suspect?" I asked.

"Admit it, then we can finish our business here and now," she said, producing a gun.

"Kill me before we find the briefcase of money, and you'll never know the truth," I said, unfazed by her threat, betting that she was only trying to intimidate me.

She put away her gun and said, "Admit it or not, it's useless. You talk too easily, whether awake or in your sleep. You are not qualified."

It hurt my pride to be told straight to my face that I was "unqualified". I vowed to punish her for my indignity someday.

"Come, let's start work," she said.

She briefly explained by drawing on a piece of paper how the bamboo sticks were to be tied: first into crosses, then the crosses to be bound into clusters, and the clusters to be wired together into groups that could withstand the impact of falling. Lastly, the bamboo groups would be placed in rows and layers under the pit like some animal snare.

She left the pit after she had made a dozen crosses as a demonstration for me. She muttered something like "*Hallelujah*" or "*Amitabh*" and left the room, with the excuse of fetching some water.

Half an hour later, I heard her voice in the attic above. She called out something, which sounded like a strange language to me. I shouted back, "I beg your pardon?" but she appeared to have gone again.

I concentrated on constructing the trap, and in the process I was entertained immensely by the exercise, which helped kill my boredom and use up my excess energy. Within barely an hour, I had already finished putting the bamboo sticks into crosses and crosses into clusters, then groups. Then I placed the bamboo bundles together properly for the finishing touch.

"*Aung Min, Hsint Khine-Ye, Than Htay, Kyaw Kyaw.*" Her voice was suddenly heard above the pit, again in a strange language.

Was it some kind of chant? I wondered. However, I didn't give it any more thought as I was busy making sure the bamboo bundles stood firmly in a big group by lacing a strong wire through the clusters.

"Hi!" she shouted at me above my head.

I looked up to find her kneeling at the edge of the hole with a wicked smile on her face.

"Thirsty?" she asked. Without waiting for my reply, she dropped several bottles of water into the pit. The bottles landed in the middle of the bamboo trap, smashing it into disarray.

"Damn it!" I yelled in disgust.

She came to the bottom of the pit through the service stairs. Looking at the shambles, she said, "Don't you see?"

"What?"

"Your trap cannot even withstand falling bottles," she said.

It sounded like ridicule, but she was also right. I stood there feeling like a fool, as someone who was good for nothing.

"If you know it so well, why don't you just do it yourself?" I blurted out at her.

"I did not build it. My team of people built it, and now they are gone," she shrugged, holding up her hands helplessly. "Can you not help me with something so basic, please?"

Looking at the crosses and clusters of bamboo lying in a mess I said, "Exactly; it's basic and primitive. You really believe it can catch your spy?"

"As a matter of fact, I don't," she said. "When I was a child, living in the mountains, I helped my family build all different kinds of animal snare, but we never had much success."

"Then are we not wasting our time here?" I asked, somewhat confused.

"Perhaps a little background will be useful," she said. "But just a little."

I took a bottle from the top of the bamboo sticks and drank from it, while she updated me with "a little background".

"Let me start with a simple theory," she said. "Imagine this: I have in my possession some important information, say, names of revolutionaries and insurgents working to overthrow a rogue government. And there is also someone, a former student activist, who has turned traitor, and he is coming here on a tip to seize the information…"

"I don't see why you can't just leave with your information," I interrupted.

"This is my mission. I have to meet the traitor face to face, identify him, expose his crimes, and put him away," she said, adding hastily, "Well, this is only a theory. I think that is all I can say for now."

"Still, you don't need some age-old trap like this when you have a gun and even bombs…" I said.

"Imagine I have a gun, and you have a gun; then we are even," she said. "Sometimes it pays to use wit instead of pure violence, particularly when it is someone you know and who knows you, too."

"Well, isn't it rather unfortunate to know somebody like you?" I said with a bit of irony.

But she didn't look offended. "Indeed," she said, in a voice close to poignant suffering. "I belong to some of the most unfortunate people in a country that has been ruled by the military establishment through the use of brutality, torture and oppression. Very unfortunate."

She was on the edge of tears, and I hastened to apologise for being inconsiderate. But she didn't cry. She only exploded as if I had touched on a subject of considerable sensitivity. "But we're not weak because we're unfortunate. We will rise in revolt. The revolution is in the air and we'll fight to be free…"

Somewhat regretful, I said, doing my best to placate her, "Let me know if I can be useful to your revolution."

She broke into a quacking laugh. "Thanks, but don't be ridiculous, as you again don't know what you're talking about," she said. "But you're not to blame, as I can't tell you more than… this small theory. Of course we can have another chat, another time."

After a short pause, she continued, glancing at the bamboo trap, "Can I ask that you finish this in the next hour? I think you understand now that it will serve as a last resort in the unlikely circumstances. After all, this age-old trap worked not long ago, didn't it? We only have to adjust the arrangement somewhat and improve its reliability."

Maybe the mockery in her words was unintended, but I had no doubt that she was quite capable of speaking with an unforgiving tongue. I had already grown tired of the inconsequential war of words, and I told myself to keep my careless big mouth shut and focus on the job in hand.

For the purpose of strengthening the trap she told me I could go and take a look in the equipment store for useful things. I went and found some metal rods of various lengths, which seemed perfect for the job. I carried the rods back to the pit, and began arranging them into a triangular base by placing the one with a sharply pointed end in the middle, just like a spire. Once the architecture was in place, I regrouped the bamboo sticks and placed the bundles firmly in place.

When it was all finished, she took a hard look at the trap with the spire pointing upwards at the gaping hole in the ceiling.

"Are you sure?" she asked.

I was rather proud of my pyramid-like construction, and I replied, "Cannot be better."

She shrugged her shoulders and strode away, with unmistakable disdain on her face, much to my bemusement.

I left too, as I found the trap perfect and without need of further improvement. I grabbed a bottle of water, drinking it on my way out of the building to re-enter the mid-level garden. In a moment of absentmindedness, I had left behind my walking crutch-stick in the room, which was rather unfortunate.

The girl was sitting by the side of the swimming pool. As I approached, she waved me over and asked to check my back. I obediently laid my body chest-down on the floor, believing it was only a daily routine.

She pulled my T-shirt up to the neck and asked, as she fingered the flesh around the bomb, "Does it hurt?"

For the first time I was surprised to find her voice extremely tender and sweet. It reminded me of my encounter with a student nurse in a hospital some three years before when I was admitted for a urinary tract infection. The young nurse woke me up in the middle of the night in my ward and asked for my urine for the lab test. She held a kidney dish and told me to pee into it. While waiting, she looked attentively at my prick with her large eyes as if it were her duty to ensure its smooth running. We stood facing each other, heads down, like we were watching goldfish swimming in a pond. At the end of several minutes, when nothing had happened, I decided that she must not have learned in medical school anything about the state of a young man with his trousers down to his knees. "If you don't know," I told her, "let me tell you that you're looking at an involuntary erection induced by the stare of your enormous eyes. It will probably jerk off if you find it so cute and touch it, but I'm afraid the discharge you get won't be what you're after." She got the message and turned her face slightly to the left and asked, in an embarrassed but sweet voice, "Is this better?" Certainly not as good as if she had held me, I thought, but a lot better for the task in hand. Thirty seconds later, I successfully peed into the kidney dish.

The tenderness and sweetness in the voice of the girl, similar to that of the student nurse in my memory, caused me to feel greatly physically excited.

"Does it hurt?" the girl repeated when I was lost in thought and failed to answer the first time.

The pain in my back had subsided days ago, but in order to be consistent with my strategy to fool her, I lied: "There's still this spasm of pain which comes and goes, depending on how and where you touch it."

"How about this?" She suddenly raised her voice, to my astonishment, changing from that of a young embarrassed nurse to an angry matron. Before I had a clue about the reason for the transformation, I was hit on the shoulder by a club of some sort.

I shuddered at the physical pain. "Fuck it! What do you think you're doing?" I shouted at her.

"You'd better stay where you are if you don't want to be blown up like your cat," she said, and beat me again with the club.

"Fuck you!" I shot back, sensing the malice in her tone, and fought with my tongue as my only weapon.

She beat me on the shoulders, arms and legs.

"Are you counting?" she paused temporarily and asked.

I could not believe my ears at her ridiculous question.

"I think the last one was number eight and there are two more to go," she said, reminding herself.

"Please, if you go on beating me, I'd rather jump to my death," I threatened her.

After a moment of consideration, she dropped the club and said, "Okay, I'll spare you the rest for your good behaviour this morning."

"Thank you," I said, gasping in pain. "But why? Where have I fucked up?"

"Do you think you can deceive me about the progress of your recovery?" she said.

"But can't you see I'm in pain?" I stood firm in my disguise.

"Yes, you're in pain because you've just been beaten, not because your old injuries still hurt," she said. "You could move your limbs freely and smoothly when you were building the trap – can you explain that? And you could even catch the book I threw over to you like it was a ball. Did you think yourself a goalkeeper playing in the World Cup? Can you also explain the absence of your walking stick, which you depended upon like it was for dear life when you entered the building with a horrible limp this morning?"

I was mute, angry at myself for being so carelessly dumb.

"So, where's the trust now?" she demanded with a disappointed sigh. After a pause, she softened her tone to say: "But for your good behaviour, I've not only spared the rest of the flogging but also your life."

"My good behaviour?"

"This morning when I brought you to my bedroom, you asked only to borrow the radio, but not the book..." she said.

I didn't know why I should borrow a book which I couldn't read.

"It's a book of poetry," she said, "by a famous poet of my country. Can I give you an example?"

In a clear voice she recited the poem. Although I didn't understand a single word, I liked the accent she uttered; there was something rather pleasant to the ear.

"Does it mean anything?" I asked.

"In plain language, it means: *May a myriad good things with vigour have a chance; may the peacock have its call and dance,*" she explained.

"Never heard it before," I said. "I'm sorry."

"Well, you should count yourself lucky to have never heard about it," she said.

"Why?"

She didn't answer my question, but began chanting, *"Aung Min, Hsint Khine Ye, Than Htay, Kyaw Kyaw…"*

I thought she was making the same strange sounds as she did while I was working on the bamboo trap. "What's that again?" I asked.

She let out a derisive laughter at my ignorance.

"Perhaps it is wrong to describe your behaviour as good, as you're only good because you're stupid and unintelligent," she mocked.

She had insulted me again. Enraged, I retorted, "Perhaps I'm stupid. But it is a strange language I don't understand. And if you let me guess, I'd think you were probably asking me for a fuck!"

"You'd better watch your mouth!" she warned, displeased but still composed. "In fact, I have just spoken a few names in my native language. I called out the same names when you were working down the pit. If you had responded as someone who knows the names or the language, you would probably already be dead on the spot, as the suspected secret agent."

"So, am I cleared of all suspicion now?" I asked.

"I don't think so, because you're worse than some of my deadliest enemies," she said, with a bitterness in her voice I couldn't quite comprehend. "I despise you for the trap you built. Ever imagine what'd happen to someone who falls on a trap with a sharp pointed spire?"

"Killed in an instant, naturally," I replied, in all correctness.

"You are so cruel and pitiless that you don't give a damn about the life of another human being," she said, with obvious contempt in her voice.

I was baffled, and argued in my defence, "But I built the bamboo trap to your order…"

"My instruction was to build it similar to the one you had stupidly destroyed, not something lethal with a sharp and pointed end in the middle," she said.

I thought I had built something to perfection and she'd be pleased. As that did not appear to be the case, I felt frustrated and angry. "Then fuck it. I can go and tear it apart if you like," I said.

"Don't bother. As I said, this kind of basic, primitive trap rarely succeeds in catching the real spies, except some stupid fool like you," she said.

She'd done it again – another personal insult! I was already at the end of my tolerance and growled, "Yes if I'm the stupid fool, then you are just some clever fucking slut!"

"No more F-word, okay?" she warned again.

"Too late now. I'm going to fuck you till you're blind," I said, mad and furious.

"You can't fuck me with a bomb on your back even if I challenge you to!" She was mad too, yelling back at the top of her voice. "Remember, I can always blow you to smithereens at the push of a button."

I became quiet in an instant. The bomb was a real and serious threat, and I thought I'd better shut up before it was too late.

Still looking a little mad she gave me a kick in the buttocks. The kick was quite mild, more from a temper tantrum than a serious intention to hurt. When she raised her foot to kick again, I caught it in the air with both hands.

In a fright she cried, "Release, now! Or you're a dead man."

I loosened my grip immediately. She stumbled a few steps back before she sat down on the floor and broke into sobs.

"Where's the trust now? I've taken the time to observe you and when I begin to think you're above suspicion, you turn against me with your dirty, deceptive tricks. Where's the trust now?" she said through her tears, in a plaintive tone as if she were the victim of my behaviour.

A little guilty perhaps, I suddenly found myself no longer hating her. Instead, I felt sorry for her and sympathised with her troubles, whatever they were.

"Please don't cry," I said. "I confess I've not been very honest with you about the progress of my recovery, my apology. Please forgive me, and let me make it up to you."

"How?"

"What about if I take you to find the briefcase tomorrow?" I said.

She wiped her tears and said, "You'd better. I think now it's kind of farfetched to say you're connected in any way to the spy ring I have been talking about. But as I've said before, I need solid proof of your innocence. And it's time to go and find the briefcase as you've largely recovered."

"That means I'll be free very soon?" I asked.

"Depends if you can find the briefcase," she said. "As a matter of interest, where exactly are we going for the treasure hunt?"

"Wat Pho, the temple of the reclining Buddha in Bangkok," I said.

"And where exactly in Wat Pho, as I understand the temple is very large?" she asked.

I was suddenly tongue-tied, not because I didn't know the answer, but because the answer was complicated. I saw in my head images of stupas and flowers, but failed to pinpoint exactly where they were relative to the location of the briefcase. In my struggle to see things in a clearer light, my head was getting increasingly muddled in the process. I began to perspire heavily under her intense gaze, which was becoming severely intimidating.

"Does your silence mean you don't know?" she said, her tone cold like ice.

I thought I could be in trouble again and felt the need to convince her. "Don't worry," I said. "It's all in my head. But I can't just tell you something about stupas or flowers, which are meaningless to you. What you want to hear is the direction and position, the distance from point to point, etc. Well, you can have it all only if you would be so kind as to let me have a private moment, to concentrate on my thoughts, to ponder about—"

"Fine. I can give you the rest of the day to work it out and we'll go and find the briefcase tomorrow," she said, standing up. "I don't think I need to emphasise that tomorrow will be critical, as it goes without saying, when we go to dig up the briefcase, it'd better be there; otherwise you might as well be digging your own grave."

Then she strode away, disappearing into the building with a hard slam of the metal door.

After she was gone, I sat up, exhaling a huge lungful of air in relief. The tranquility restored to the mid-level garden allowed me to look back at what had happened in the past few hours, not with anger, but with mixed emotions. The girl was still someone of many guises: foe or friend, terrorist or liberator. But how I felt about her had changed dramatically when I could no longer bring it upon myself to loathe her. I had become more forgiving, partly because I was fascinated by her theory of some revolutionary working to overthrow a repressive regime, and partly because I'd found her priggishness and fickleness charismatically complicated and incredibly charming.

Presently, I still had this leftover heart-wrenching feeling in my hands and fingers that had grappled the lower part of her leg, wondering if she was serious when she challenged me to fuck her at the risk of the bomb – to which I had grown accustomed like a tumour on my skin – going off.

Nevertheless, at this very moment, I told myself to stifle the longing for vulgar sensations as I must turn my attention to the more pressing issue of finding the briefcase. To do that, I thought it useful to refresh my memory and go back to the point where Kaya and I first discussed the urgent need to hide the briefcase away.

7

A . H . M . A . N .

━━◦◦◦━━

One evening Kaya returned home after going downtown to pick up some painkillers for my head after surgery.

"I've been followed," she said, catching her breath.

I took a peep through the blind at the window. "Not a soul," I said. "You sure you've been tailed?"

"I first caught the guy's face in a shop window reflection outside Central World," she said with a pale face. "Again, he was two passengers behind me when I bought my ticket at Chidlom Station. Arriving at Nana, I jumped out onto the platform a second before the train door closed. The guy, a short, skinny man who was trapped inside the carriage, glared at me behind the glass door with rage in his bloodshot eyes. I had the feeling that he knew me because of the unquestionable look of recognition on his face."

"Are you telling me that they are close to finding us in Khao San?" I asked uneasily.

"I don't know. I misled the guy by getting off at Nana. I think we're still safe here in Khao San, perhaps for another couple of weeks," she answered uncertainly.

I stole another peep at the front yard. Except for a bundle of electric wires hung between two poles swinging rhythmically like a cot in the breeze, everything seemed eerily still.

"What then, after a couple of weeks?" I asked again. "Will we be moving to another place?"

"Not before you have fully recovered," she said. "After Khao San, we'll leave the big city for good. We'll probably go north, where there are thousands of villages in the mountains on the other side of the border. We'll settle down there. But in order to do that, you must first get fit again."

"You touch me here in the morning and you'll know I'm fit," I said, indicating a certain spot.

"That is only a tiny bit of your body. What about your ear, which still bleeds from time to time?" she said. "We ought to be patient for a little while."

"Does that mean that we'd sit and wait here, doing nothing?" I asked.

"No, on the contrary, we need to deal with the briefcase of money as a matter of urgency," she said. "It's possible that the thugs or the police will find us before we leave. Should that happen, we will lose everything if they get hold of the briefcase."

"So, what do we do now?"

"There's something I learned from my ex-boyfriend, Martchu, who was a bank robber, which is: you can get yourself arrested and you can even spend some years behind bars, but not all is lost if you are smart enough to hide the loot away before your enemies descend upon you."

"It only makes sense if you know where to hide our money," I said.

"Believe it or not, coincidentally I know of a place to put the briefcase," she said. "It's the temple of the reclining Buddha called Wat Pho in Bangkok. There is a stupa garden at the temple where I buried Martchu's mobile phone some years back. What do you think?"

"What a question! Can I possibly think intelligently based on the little I know about you and Martchu?"

"Well, perhaps to put things into perspective, what about if I start telling you what makes me think Wat Pho is a fairly safe place to hide the briefcase?" she suggested.

"I'm listening," I said.

She didn't start straightaway. After a long silence, she said, in a voice brittle with pain, "I know why I have never brought this up; because it was an incident I'd rather forget. Now as I remember, I still find the experience mortifying as to how I was subjected to the humiliation of a body cavity check in the massage centre at Wat Pho."

K.A.Y.A.

IN THE IMMEDIATE AFTERMATH OF Martchu's death, I was expelled from the Chiang Mai massage parlour where I worked as a therapist. At the time I had the difficult problem of raising funds for the ransom of my brother Kiet. Madame Supang, the boss of the massage parlour, was very kind to have found me the money by selling me to a nightclub chain in an Asian city called Macao (as no national entertainment establishments, licensed or otherwise, would employ me because of my connection to the killing of Martchu).

I was expected to go to Macao, with Bangkok as the port of embarkation. Upon my arrival in the capital city, my travel plan was still in limbo. There was a text message left on my mobile saying that "Details of departure will take a few days to finalise", signed off by someone named Oranju. Under the circumstances, I needed to find a place to sleep for the interim. I would have liked to check in at the Peninsula Hotel only if I could afford it. That being unrealistic, I followed the steps of my dead father who always slept in unfinished buildings while working as an excavator operator in Bangkok.

I decided to try my luck at an abandoned construction site opposite the Oriental Hotel on the other side of the Chao Phraya River. I sneaked inside through a gap in the railings surrounding the site and found a corner room on a lower floor which, according to my father, was less cold and windy than the upper floors. Every day I expected to be kicked out, should I be caught trespassing; but during the time I was holed up there, I never came into contact with another human being, and I had a quiet and untroubled stay.

At the end of the week my mobile finally rang. It was Oranju, who said, "A fishing boat will pick you up at Tha Tien Pier at midnight.

Meet me in the evening at eight o'clock at the Wat Pho massage centre. I'll take you to the pier."

"Why the Wat Pho massage centre?" I asked curiously.

"Because I work there." The reply was brusque as if I should not have asked. Then the call was promptly terminated.

I was amused instead of offended by the abruptness, as the call had come as a huge relief. I was thankful for its timeliness, since my mobile phone was already running on standby battery. Furthermore, I also found comfort in the voice of Oranju, which, although kind of coarse and uncouth, belonged unmistakably to a woman. I believed I was in good hands because my contact was female and also a massage therapist. I was, however, a bit naïve, as things turned out.

I checked out from my "five-star hotel" in the evening and took a No. 69 bus to Wat Pho, arriving there five minutes before the appointed time. A large, ugly woman was waiting outside the door. She had a longish face and straight, mid-length hair gathered behind her ears that hung like a pair of handcuffs. Her broad shoulders, large hips and barrel-shaped body were clad in a shabby, loose-fitting uniform, which struck me as suspiciously unfeminine.

"I'm Oranju," she said, when she approached to greet me. "You must be Kaya. You're very pretty, exactly as Madame Supang told me."

"That's very kind," I replied blandly, still feeling disturbed by her masculine qualities. But I was only being sensitive because, before long, my doubt over her gender would be utterly quashed when she shared a shower with me in the massage centre.

"Come in. Let's talk inside. This place is closed for business now," she said, and led the way through an innocuous doorway. We entered a hall behind the reception area. It looked vacant and deserted, with a dozen benches and reclining chairs strewn about the place. A row of lamps near the ceiling spread around a pale, yellow light, casting strange shadows on a long wall where a collection of early monochrome photographs of people in yogi postures was hung.

She asked me to sit down on a chair in the middle of the hall while she kept standing. "Madame Supang said you killed Martchu. We're all very proud of you," she said plainly as if she was informing me of the news of the day.

I was horrified. "I wasn't there when Martchu was shot. I didn't kill him," I hastened to clarify.

She stared at me, stoney-faced. "I'm not your judge. Leave your defence to the court if you don't want to run away," she said. "The arrangement to ship you out is all set. Are you going or not going?"

I nodded, without making a sound, knowing further explanation was useless.

"You are lucky," said Oranju. "It is a fisherman's family. Good people. They agree to take you out to sea at a very reasonable price."

I said my thanks.

"You will be the fisherman's daughter if the boat is stopped and checked by the marine police. So they want to make sure you're clean – very clean," she said, putting heavy emphasis on the word "clean".

"I'm clean," I said, with equal emphasis.

"No weapons, no drugs, and no mobile phones," said Oranju seriously.

I had only a nail clipper and a pair of scissors in my toiletry bag, which in my opinion didn't fit the definition of weapons. And I didn't have a drug habit. Whereas if possessing mobile phones was considered "unclean", I was doubly guilty – other than my own phone (which Madame Supang gave me), I also had Martchu's Nokia with me.

Oranju found my hesitation suspicious, but she had a way to deal with it.

"I'll give you fifteen minutes to go for a walk outside," she said. "You can either call your friends to say farewell or you can have your last joint at your leisure. When you come back, I'll conduct a body check."

"Fair enough," I said, and stood to go.

Oranju pulled open a sliding door at the far end of the hall. "Don't go back to the streets," she said. "Come this way to the central shrine of Wat Pho. Say a prayer to Buddha for your protection before your departure."

At this time of the day, Wat Pho was closed to visitors. When I went into the shrine, the place was empty, with only Buddha and me, as if I had made an appointment for a private consultation with him alone. The gold-plated reclining Buddha was very long; its body of over a hundred feet filled the whole length of the shrine from wall to wall. The eyes of the statue were decorated with mother-of-pearls, and the soles of the feet engraved with auspicious characteristics of the true Buddha. I was told Buddha in the reclining posture was actually dying, but, unlike ordinary men, he had already found a way out with a passage into nirvana. I must count myself fortunate to have found a way out of my present trouble too, but instead of paradise, I was going to a seedy city, which was almost like passage into another hell. Knowing it useless to grieve or complain, I knelt down before Buddha and said a prayer asking for his protection.

I left the shrine after my prayer. As I walked down a path wondering what to do with the mobile phones, I entered through a gate guarded by two giants carved out of rocks. It was in an area with many stupas of different sizes. As I understood stupas are built to contain the ashes of kings and members of the royal family, high monks, as well as rich and powerful men, I suddenly had the idea of burying the phones in the midst of the stupas. I would make a grave and bury Martchu's Nokia as if it were his body so that he could lie in eternal peace in the company of kings and noblemen in spirit, if not in person.

At the far end of the stupa garden, I found a pretty corner overgrown with red flowers. I plucked out the plants and dug into the soil with my hands, making a deep hole. The time had come to lay down Martchu's phone, like a body being laid in a grave. Then I lingered, as parting was always difficult.

I ran my fingers over the carving of our names and the pierced hearts on the back of the phone, reminiscing about the time we slept together. I held the phone close to my chest and, without knowing it, had pushed the power button accidentally. To my surprise, the phone turned on with what little remained in the battery. Some music began to play and seconds later, it was Martchu's voice speaking.

"Hello, this is Martchu. Get lost now if you're not Kaya."

I was overwhelmed by his expression of ardent affection, and I cried, feeling great pain and a sense of palpable loss. But I was sensible enough not to be drowned by my sadness. I shook my head violently to wake up to the stark reality which I must embrace. With a sigh, I kissed his phone goodbye.

I lingered for another second or two, mulling over whether I should first power off the phone. Finally I decided to keep it on as I reckoned there wasn't much battery remaining. After I had placed both phones – his Nokia and my phone – side by side at the bottom of the hole, I recited a little chant which I had learned during the funeral service of my father.

Where does a cloud come from?
Where does it go?
Where was it before it appeared?
And who are you?
All beings arise in time;
Time consumes them all.
Time is the lord who possesses the vajra;
And who's that of day and night?

Knowing I must hurry up after the chant, as Oranju had given me only fifteen minutes and I had already had twenty, I quickly refilled the hole with mud and replaced the plants. In my haste I realised the red flowers were actually roses, whose thorns had inflicted small cuts on my skin and made my hands bleed.

After I had restored the place to its original state, I slipped away with speed. At the gate where a pair of rock giants was standing guard,

I paused and turned around for one last look at the grave amid the stupas. I was a little lost when I could no longer say for sure exactly where our phones were laid in the midst of a wide array of stupas, all similarly pointing skyward with long and short spires.

Suddenly I seemed to hear the sound of music rising in the air. It was nothing soft, but instead intense and urgent. As I listened on, I began to recognise it as the ringing tone of Martchu's phone. It was so absurd, as though someone was trying to call from hell. I froze on the spot, knowing it wasn't possible to take the call when the phone was buried deep down in the earth. A few seconds later, the disturbing buzz died out; probably the phone was at the end of its battery. As peace and silence were restored to the garden, I found I was not as lost as before. The sound of the call had pointed me in the direction of the spot where the phones were buried. I took it as a good sign. My interpretation was that I wasn't to leave the phones behind forever, and I was to return for their retrieval someday at the end of my sojourn in Macao, which I hoped would be brief.

When I went back to the massage centre, I found Oranju was half-lying in a reclining chair with eyes closed, and her skirt hitched above her thighs, exposing her legs thick like elephant trunks. She heard the sound of the sliding door and sat up, looking with wide eyes at my dirty hands covered with blood and mud.

I told her I had slipped and fell in the garden.

"You need a bath," she said.

I welcomed the idea, because I had not had a decent bath for almost a week since my arrival in Bangkok. Oranju took me to a bathroom at the back of the hall, which had a small shower cubicle with a semi-transparent plastic curtain. When I began to unlace my shoes, Oranju said she had to fetch some bath oils and went away.

Once I had stripped myself naked, I turned on the tap and jumped under the sprinkler for the comfort of a good shower. I closed my eyes to enjoy the water streaming through my hair, down my face, my neck, my breasts, to the bottom of my feet where I could feel a small whirlpool was forming at the ankles. Perhaps because of the noise of the running tap, I wasn't aware that Oranju had entered the cubicle to stand behind me. I was startled when her body suddenly touched mine. She was all naked, her breasts dangling like a pair of large papayas. Although I was embarrassed by her presence, I was also relieved to find that she was neither a man nor a transvestite. Just another woman like me.

In a low whisper behind me she said, "I have to frisk you."

"What do you mean?" I said uneasily. "Isn't it obvious that I have nothing on my body?"

"I think you know what a frisk of a naked body involves." She raised her voice as she spoke.

I frowned at her words. In my experience as a therapist, we had regular visits from the police at Madame Supang's massage parlour. Some girls would be checked on the spot with only a strip search. A few others would be taken back to the police station for a body cavity check, where fingers would be poked inside the vagina and anus for drugs or anything not supposed to be stored in those places. It wasn't only embarrassing, it was also extremely humiliating. I had never had previous experience of a body cavity check, not before I entered the massage centre at Wat Pho.

Oranju made me turn to face her with my back against the wall. She grasped my right breast with one hand while squeezing my belly with the other. I refused to make a sound despite the discomfort. When she had found nothing wrong with my belly, she shoved me to turn around to face the wall again.

"You're so pretty; my kind of girl," she said. "I'll let you choose the bath oil of your preference."

She showed me two small bottles of oil, one jasmine, the other rosemary.

"Pick it yourself. I don't really give a damn," I said, with disdain in my voice.

"I think jasmine is good for the purpose," she said, uncapped a bottle and poured the liquid on her palm.

I stuck my face to the wall and closed my eyes to brace for what was to come. She kicked my legs apart and in the next moment I could feel her finger wedge inside my anus, anxiously exploring its depth and breadth, and in the meantime liberally pushing and rubbing the soft walls.

She stayed there for what seemed longer than a century. Finally she withdrew her fingers when she was satisfied that I was "clean". I breathed a huge sigh of relief at the end of a hard struggle against the embarrassing call of nature engendered by the rub inside.

But she was far from finished as it appeared she had something else in mind. She grabbed my crotch and let her fingers swim between the outer and inner labia before honing in on my clitoris, and by exerting a steady and fairly firm pressure on the small bud, made me quiver with a sensation which was both thrilling and revolting.

"Women enjoy my hands as much as men," she said. "I was among the top batch of students to have ever graduated from the massage school."

I thought I had reached the limit of my tolerance.

"It's disgusting," I uttered. I pushed her hands away and ran out of the shower cubicle.

While I was drying my body with a towel in the hall, she emerged from behind and grasped my breasts. I warned her: "I told you I didn't kill Martchu, but that's not to say I'm not capable of doing it." She got the message and took her hands off my breasts.

"Can I put my clothes back on?" I asked.

She looked unsatisfied, and gestured for me to swivel on the spot. I stopped after a full round and asked again, "Okay now?"

She sighed, "You're clean. But what a pity that you should need any clothes!"

I ignored her remarks and started to dress. She got dressed too, by stepping into her one-piece masseur outfit. Then she began fumbling inside my travelling bag when I was still juggling with my bra straps.

"Why don't you have a mobile phone?" she asked.

"I need money. I sold it at Khao San for a few hundred baht," I said. Of course I lied.

She found a hundred-dollar note in my bag and kept it. "This is for the handling fee," she said.

It pained me so much that I was robbed after I had been rubbed so humiliatingly. But if there was any consolation, it was that she had not had the opportunity to confiscate my mobile phones. She probably would never understand the triumphant smile on my face as I gazed out to the stupa garden, foreseeing my return to Wat Pho one day.

A . H . M . A . N .

IT WAS NOW CLEAR WHY Wat Pho seemed a good place to hide our money under the circumstances.

We took a cab to Wat Pho after the clock struck midnight, and entered the monastery through a back door of the massage centre. It was pitch-black inside and dead quiet as we went into the stupa garden via a narrow doorway.

Kaya was right about her memory, as it didn't take her much time to figure out the exact location. Under a crop of flowers, the phones were unearthed. But there wasn't much to say about them when their batteries were long dead and the screen panels had become a colony of earthworms and maggots. I thought she was happy to be reunited with the phones, but she looked sad and mournful.

I began digging a bigger and deeper hole at the same spot to accommodate Tony Bear's briefcase, which was fat and plump, resembling the dead body of my friend. When the hole was ready, Kaya tried to stay poised and collected as she helped lower the briefcase down to the bottom and refill the hole with mud. I replaced the thorny red roses to the area, and my hands suffered minor cuts here and there as a result.

After all was done, we departed, leaving by the gate guarded by a pair of rock giants. I turned to look back and all at once I found I was at a complete loss.

I said to Kaya, "I don't think I'll be able to bring you back to the very spot we have just buried our money."

She replied, "It's only the many shapes and shadows of the stupas everywhere that have caused your confusion. Don't worry. Later I can draw you a map to help you remember."

After we got home, she abided by her promise and put together a map detailing the location of the briefcase in the stupa garden at Wat Pho.

She said, "This is it. Follow the signs and directions and you should never miss it. I hope you won't have a problem finding your way back to the money by yourself, even if we get split up in unexpected circumstances."

Almost like a self-fulfilling prophecy, one night after we had had a big fight over how she, as a young, pretty thing, should work much harder to satisfy the love wishes of her boyfriend, she left our Khao San apartment, without an umbrella and presumably wearing nothing, and disappeared into the heavy, ever falling rain.

8

A.H.M.A.N.

⸻

"Call me Maya," replied the girl, responding to my comment that it wasn't very helpful if I didn't know how to address her properly when we set off together for our expedition.

"I'm Ah Man," I said, extending my arm for a handshake.

She brushed off my friendly gesture.

"When do you think is the best time to go to Khao San to fetch the map?" she asked.

"It'll be sometime after dark, probably after all the people have gone to sleep," I answered vaguely, not at all sure myself.

"Who exactly are the people you're talking about?" she inquired.

"I don't mean anyone in particular, but if you insist…" I babbled, "… it is the King and his royal family, the Prime Minister and his bureaucrats, the Commander-in-Chief and his army, the Police Commissioner and his squads, the Godfather and his lieutenants, the Bangkok gangsters and their buddies…"

"You might as well include Beauty and the Beast; but in my experience, the military never sleeps," she interrupted good-humouredly. "That said, I would suggest we do it around midnight."

"Midnight is perfect," I concurred. "By the way, do you want to hear my plan?"

"We're not overthrowing the government, are we? Why do we need a plan?" she said jeeringly.

"Semantically you should use 'plot' instead of 'plan' as far as overthrowing the government is concerned," I corrected her politely.

"Whatever. I just don't think there is a need for some stupid plan to complicate matters unnecessarily," she said. "I'll let you call the shots as long as we find the money in the end."

I liked what she said. In fact, I never had a detailed plan from start to finish, or of the exact manner and method to make a success of the undertaking, except my own very simple game plan, which was to find the briefcase, split the money and become a free man again. I raised the subject of a "plan" only in an attempt to find out if she had in mind some hidden agenda. But she appeared to be down to earth, purposeful and no-nonsense. I thanked her for her confidence in me and promised that she would not be disappointed.

It was a clear night in September, the air fresh and warm. I was flushed and excited, as I was about to re-enter the outside world for the first time since I'd set foot in the ghost building a month before. After dinner, there was still some time before midnight and we sat by the poolside listening to music from her transistor radio.

A little after the 10. 00pm local news, Maya suddenly asked, "Why don't we go to Khao San now to get the map before we go to Wat Pho?"

I made no objection as it seemed the sensible thing to do, although I was not too pleased that it was not I who had called the shots.

We left the ghost building and took a taxi to Khao San Road. I knew a restaurant at the corner of a side street in Khao San that would stay open for business into the early hours, and we went there for a drink. I ordered a Coke for myself and she asked for a milkshake. I told her I would avoid anything to do with milk here in Khao San if I were her, but she wouldn't listen.

After she had finished her milkshake, she started wondering aloud what we were doing in the restaurant when we should be going to fetch the map straightaway.

I leaned over to whisper in her ear: "We can't work together if you keep questioning the motive behind my every step."

"Fine," she said. "But do you really have to hang your head on my shoulder?"

"No. It is only to avoid eavesdroppers, just to be careful," I said quietly.

She let my head stay, and asked, "Then what?"

"Now, look out the window at the guesthouse across the street with a yellowish neon sign," I said. "At its rear is the apartment where I've lived since I came to Bangkok."

"Yes, got it. What next?"

"If the street outside continues to be this quiet and peaceful, I'll sneak back to my apartment for the map," I said.

She put on a fierce scowl and asked, "Do you mean you're going to the apartment alone?"

"Yes. You wait for me here, as it won't take long," I replied.

"Not a chance," she said sternly. "Once you're out of my sight, there's no guarantee what will happen to the device on your back."

Her warning about the bomb was enough to fill me with despair. "This is not very flexible for our task at hand; it is almost like till death do us part," I said.

"It's romantic of you to describe our relationship as such," she said, with a mocking laugh. "But a bomb is a bomb, and death will be the price to pay if you dare betray me."

I sighed a fatalistic sigh, sensing little chance for my ultimate escape. It was probably from this point onwards that I began to behave a little recklessly and even dangerously.

"Then let's play lovers, if you insist we are to do everything in unison," I said, just to provoke her.

"You mean I'm to take the role of your whore… oh, I'm sorry, I mean your girlfriend? What's her name again?" she asked sarcastically.

"Kaya," I replied. My heart ached with pain for having lost her.

"Call me Kaya," she said, half seriously.

We continued sitting shoulder-to-shoulder in the restaurant for the next couple of minutes, gazing into the dark street outside at people hurrying past the window. When she spotted someone interesting or kind of suspicious, I would explain to her to the best of my knowledge about the inhabitants of Khao San.

"No, the guy only looks like a rat," I assured her. "He is actually one of Bangkok's famous tourist-touting officers said to be government-licensed."

I brought her attention to some other characters in the neighbourhood belonging to the professions that never sleep, for example, the tuk-tuk drivers, children selling flowers, pimps and prostitutes, lady-boys, beggars, yawning policemen, fortune tellers, et cetera. Finally, I said, "Give me your hand."

"Why?"

"Okay, this is what's going to happen," I said. "In a moment we'll leave this restaurant and go to my apartment. We're going to walk down the alley behind the roadworks over there like we are really close. You are Kaya, are you not?"

She mumbled a few words of protestation. I thought she wouldn't cooperate; but to my surprise she stood up, grabbed my hand and led the way out of the restaurant with an expression of steely determination, as if once she had made up her mind to get something done, she'd have no qualms about breaking boundaries.

We walked over to the roadworks, hanging about by the wall at the entrance to the alley, just to make absolutely sure we were not being shadowed. At spotting a guy across the road coming towards us, I drew her near and said, "Let's do what lovers do."

"Like what?" she asked, rather tightly.

"Kiss me."

She looked unsure, but kissed me after a wee moment of hesitation.

The guy walked past without showing any sign of interest in our existence.

I let go of her. She said, breathing heavily after the long kiss, "I'd never have thought..."

She didn't quite finish when I told her to kiss me again upon hearing heavy footsteps on the pavement nearby. This time she obliged more naturally. When a gaggle of people, who appeared to be quite drunk, lingered around the roadworks, it struck me how quickly Maya adapted to her role by engaging my lips in a chain of intense kisses. An elderly drunken sot with a rather boring voice shouted towards us, "Go fuck at home, this is a public place." But Maya wasn't to be scared off. Instead she stuck her tongue in my mouth with defiance, kissing me breathlessly. When it was all quiet around us again, she split from me and said, panting, "Please don't get the wrong idea…"

"That was very good." I praised her for the intimacy.

"It's good, but it's not real," she said coyly. "Do you think we can go now?"

The street was getting darker as more shops closed and became quieter with fewer pedestrians. We could have kissed all night if not for a certain undertaking, I thought, feeling a delicious, intoxicating sense of calmness in the atmosphere that I had erroneously construed as a signal for "All Clear".

We proceeded to the apartment down the cul-de-sac. I unlocked the wrought-iron gate with my key and ushered her into the courtyard. I closed the gate tightly behind me, and led her up the staircase to the upper floor. When we entered the bedroom, Maya was surprised by the strong aroma in the air. I told her it was the fragrant incense Kaya used to burn during her chanting sessions, whose smell seemed to linger on forever in the room when the window was permanently closed. I suspected I had also caught a clinging whiff of the scent of her flesh in the air, or maybe I was just being sentimental.

Without switching on the light, I fumbled under the bed and in no time found the map glued to the bottom. I gave Maya the paper and she sat down on the bed, taking the time to decipher the lines and symbols on the map with the help of her flashlight. Then I started to undress.

"What do you think you're doing?" she asked, with mild shock in her voice.

"I have been wearing these coarse tracksuits you gave me for quite some weeks now," I said. "Can I not change into something better?"

"What about if I wait for you outside?" she said. "Incidentally, I feel like having a pee. Where's the toilet?"

"It's downstairs in the basement," I said.

When she was about to leave the room, we heard some strange, alarming noises outside. I had just put one leg into my trousers, and asked her to check it out at the window.

She took a peek outside and reported that there were shadows of people gathered around the gate. I told her that, in my experience, they might be junkies sharing a joint in the dark. It appeared to be the case, since the men were chatting and laughing amid sounds of matches striking and coughing. After I had changed into my clean trousers and T-shirt, I sat down with her in the darkness, waiting for the men to leave.

Half an hour passed and they were still there. "I can't wait forever," Maya said, "I badly want to have a pee."

It was at this time that the buzz of a mobile phone cracked sharply in the air and all speaking outside came to a halt. Moments later the men began banging the gate with hard objects. I was stunned when someone roared through a loudspeaker, "Ah Man and Kaya, surrender now! This is the end of your running."

Somewhat frustrated, I said, "Why didn't we notice those guys when we entered the apartment?"

"What's the point of your question now? We're trapped, that's it," she calmly said. "I just wonder who those guys are, and if the situation is negotiable?"

Suddenly the loudspeaker boomed again, and the voice that came through sounded more threatening than before.

"Ah Man and Kaya, what are you waiting for? Come out of hiding now. We're going to take you to see our Big Brother."

To me, "Big Brother" sounded sweeter than something like the "Bangkok Police". I said to Maya, "By what they said, it appears that these guys are the Bangkok gangsters, which is not a bad thing. In my experience they are rather nice, reasonable people. Perhaps, as you said, the situation is negotiable."

"How?" she coolly asked.

"Well, the least I can imagine is that you can leave without me," I said. "The people they are after are Ah Man and Kaya, as you've heard. And you're not Kaya, you're Maya. I think they will have no problem in letting you go."

She looked into my eyes and said, "I will not walk away from you just like that. We're together in this, right? But…"

She hesitated in embarrassment, and I wondered if she was about to make a love confession; but instead she said, "I'm dying for a pee. It's urgent. For me, nothing is more important than getting down to the toilet."

I should have been a little disappointed, but I was not; on the contrary, I felt encouraged because what she said had reminded me of something I had long forgotten.

"The toilet, of course!" I yelled in excitement. "Let's go down to the toilet."

"What?" she exclaimed in disbelief.

"Just follow me. I can probably find a way out of here," I said and rose to go, without taking the time to explain that, on the first day Kaya and I moved into the apartment, the caretaker had confided in us, after I gave him a handsome tip, about the existence of a secret passage connecting the apartment to the front block of the guesthouse.

We went downstairs to the toilet in the basement. It was convenient for her because the toilet had no door. She rushed inside and said, as her body hit the toilet seat, "Avert your eyes, or I'll kill you if you steal a look at me," before letting out a huge sigh of relief.

Her warning was unnecessary, as I could see very little with no light in the toilet. I went straight for the part of the wall beneath the sink, pushing and prodding it. Shortly after, my hand came into contact with a wooden board that responded with echoes of a hollow ring when I rapped it with my knuckles. This was the undeniable proof of the existence of the secret passage.

To remove the board, I asked Maya to give me the flashlight. As I waited in the dark, I felt something knock me on the back of my head without warning.

"Are you trying to kill me?" I mumbled unpleasantly.

"It's the flashlight you asked," she giggled.

I took the flashlight, but had a problem clicking it on. Then I realised it was a flashlight that worked with a slider. After several attempts at moving the slider back and forth, the flashlight suddenly blinked to life with a surprisingly bright light. Coincidentally it was also the moment when Maya had just risen to her feet, pulling up her knickers.

"You're despicable. I'll kill you," she said furiously.

"What do you think I've seen?" I said. "Don't be stupid. I'm busy with the board here."

"I'll kill you," she repeated through clenched teeth.

Outside, the noises of shouting and banging at the gate had become more urgent. It looked like the Mafia men would be breaking through any minute.

I said, "Let's get out of here first. You can kill me later if you must."

Then I felt like I had been stabbed and wondered if she had really meant to kill me. But I wasn't hurt except for the hard tingle of something being pointed against my back.

"I found this screwdriver under the toilet seat," she said.

Now I remembered there were other instruments in the tool box and asked her to also get me the hammer.

After I had removed the wooden board with the screwdriver, I began to snip and hammer away at the part of the wall believed to have concealed the passage. As expected, an opening emerged beneath a thin layer of cement, which had enlarged at the impact of the hammer to a bigger hole of about two feet in diameter. I stuck my head inside and found the enclosed space wide enough for my body to squeeze through.

I said to Maya, "I think we've found the way out. Please follow me closely." Then I began to crawl on my hands and knees, with the flashlight showing the way forward. There was a strong smell of urine and faeces inside the passage. I asked if she had forgotten to flush the toilet.

"You shut the fuck up," she grunted behind me.

I knew she was still angry about the flashlight which had exposed her in an embarrassing moment, and I felt I'd better not further antagonise her. So I kept my mouth shut as I pushed forward.

I crawled to the very end and found that the exit was boarded up by a flimsy plank with a crack in the middle, with the diffuse glimmer of a yellowish light. Through the crack I saw some boxes piled up outside the exit, and beyond them a row of urinals fixed to a dirty white wall. Now I knew why there was the foul smell: it was the men's restroom of the guesthouse, which was exactly as described by the apartment caretaker.

It seemed quiet outside, and I broke through the crack to descend onto the toilet floor. I found I wasn't alone. A thin, golden-haired man, apparently drunk, was lying unconscious outside a cubicle, its door stained with puke.

Maya had also emerged from the passage, and as soon as she had managed to stand straight, she repeated, "I'll kill you."

"You mean now? But do you still want to find the briefcase?" I asked.

She looked to have been sickened by the foul smell in the air. "I can wait. Let's get out of here," she said, covering her wrinkled nose with her hand.

We came out of the toilet and found ourselves outside the guesthouse. On the driveway there was a taxi that by chance had just dropped off a passenger. We boarded the taxi and asked the driver to go to Wat Pho. The taxi drove past the Silk Café. I told Maya it was the place where a former occupant of my apartment, presumably a drug dealer, had been gunned down during a police raid after he had made his escape through the secret passage. She looked at me with awe in her eyes and held my hand. Then we sat back and relaxed in a moment of great relief.

About ten minutes later, after the taxi had crossed a bridge, the driver, a ferret-like man, asked us, "Tell me where to drop you off at Wat Pho."

"You mean you don't know?" I asked in surprise.

"Of course I know. I can drop you at the main door on Sanamchai Road. But I don't think you're planning a visit there this late," replied the driver. "The place is closed now."

I remembered that the last time I went there with Kaya, we entered Wat Pho through the massage centre. So I said to the driver, "Actually, we're going to the massage centre."

"It's on Maharat Road, but it's closed too," the driver replied politely. I was mute.

"That's okay," Maya interjected. "We're meeting someone there."

"Oh! I see," said the driver, with a curious glance at us from the rearview mirror.

I knew he found it a little hard to believe us. But who cares? I thought. It's none of his business why we are making a nocturnal visit to a closed monastery.

Nevertheless, things are not always so simple. In the quiet of the compartment, the car phone suddenly rang.

"Who's this?" the driver asked, before he shouted down the mouthpiece, "Why would someone remember the number plate of my car? The police? No way. You mean friends of the police? That's more like it. So what do they want to know?"

We didn't mean to eavesdrop, but we couldn't keep our ears shut either when the driver was blaring at the top of his voice.

"Yes, I was in Khao San, and yes, I have picked up two passengers there – a man and a woman who asked me to take them to Wat Pho. We'll be there in a few minutes." The driver loudly stated the facts.

Now suitably startled by the conversation, Maya and I exchanged a look of genuine puzzlement and sat upright.

"Of course I'll do anything they ask. Trust me, absolutely anything." With flattery the driver kept trying to ingratiate himself to whoever it was on the other end of the phone. "No, you don't have to thank me. It's my pleasure to be at their service. Just tell them I'm also a friend. Cheers."

He ended the call and murmured to himself as if he was getting confused with all the relationships, "A friend of the friends of the police? Then what do they think of me? The police?"

I thought he would tell us something about the call. When he did not, I couldn't wait to check with him. "Is someone asking after us?" I asked.

"Can't confirm. I'm sorry," he said.

"Do you still want to know where to leave us at Wat Pho?" Maya joined in the attempt to make the guy talk.

"That won't be necessary now. I've been ordered to drop you off at Sanamchai Road," he said. Afterwards, he refused to answer any more questions as if his lips were sewn together.

We sat in apprehension, trying to figure out what it all meant.

The taxi made a turn into an area which appeared vast and expansive. There was a great wall on my left, like a long border without end, guarded only by trees and streetlamps standing at regular intervals on the pavement. On my right, there was an extension of neat housing blocks huddled in the stillness of night. It was quiet all around. The driver pulled the car to a halt and said, "Here we are. Wat Pho on Sanamchai Road."

We sat in silence for a moment without knowing what to do. Then I asked, "Will you stop us if we leave now?"

"Why should I?" the driver said. "I was only ordered to deliver you guys to Wat Pho and nothing else. Even if they wanted me to keep you from going, I don't see how it is possible when you're a much bigger man than I."

"Thank you. That's very thoughtful of you," I said.

I threw him some money and told him to keep the change. After we got out the taxi, and stood for a moment figuring out the way to go, we saw some cars, which had just turned into Sanamchai Road, racing at high speed towards Wat Pho. We immediately turned on our heels and ran.

After some twenty yards, Maya seized my arm and dragged me behind a tree. She said, "It's too dangerous for you to continue running like that."

I knew she meant the bomb on my back and asked, "Is there a better option?"

While she was pondering, I glanced back at the taxi and the other cars which had now parked together outside Wat Pho, and saw our driver, only a spindly little fellow, had been dragged out of his car and was being beaten up by a bunch of musclemen.

The taxi driver was heard shouting aloud, "Please don't beat me. I'm a friend!"

"What friend are you talking about?" asked some guys.

"A friend of the police…" answered the driver. Now he was being kicked as well as beaten.

"No! Not a friend of the police, but a friend of the friends of the police," the driver tried to clarify.

The beating stopped and one of the guys said, "You mean just like us? But we are gangsters from Bangkok and who are you?"

The taxi driver shouted out some names which seemed to satisfy the guys at last and they stopped beating him. He stood up and told the guys, "If it is the man and woman you are going after, they've gone down the road this way…" pointing a dramatic finger in our direction.

A bald guy said, "I can't see anything. It's too dark."

"Why don't you take off your sunglasses?" a voice asked.

The bald guy refused to part with his sunglasses, and said, "Sushi, what do you see?"

A short, sparrow-like man stepped forward and reported, after looking long and hard into the darkness, "Somchai, I think I can see some trees."

Everyone in the crowd laughed at Sushi's idiotic answer.

But I didn't find it funny. I shuddered at the names they used to address one another, remembering Somchai as the right-hand man of Big Brother Wichit, and Sushi the birdman by his goose-like voice. They were the same people who had driven me out of Khao San one afternoon when I was having a snooze at a pavement café.

A man with a grim voice said, "Is Sushi trying to suggest something with a local saying that 'Fruits are never far from trees?!'"

"Yes of course!" The bunch of men cheered at the man's wisdom.

"Boon, now I know why Big Brother Wichit has great trust in you," said Somchai flatteringly.

With a dry laugh, Boon called out in an awestruck voice, "Guys, let's go to the trees!"

We knew it was time to run again, however inadvisable running had appeared to be. And we did it with Maya holding my hand to ensure the speed was somewhat faster than walking but a bit slower than running. As soon as we emerged from the trees, the gang had spotted us and howled threateningly from behind, "Stop there. Stop now!"

There was a revolving light at the end of the road. As we drew near we saw it was the light of a garbage collection truck which had parked outside a wide-open gate. I thought we were at the back door of Wat Pho. A sanitation worker wearing a green cap and a large sanitary mask on his face was loading trash into the compactor of the truck. We greeted him with a "Hi!" and "How are you?" Before he had time to respond, we had already flitted past him to enter Wat Pho through the open gate.

It was quiet and dark inside. Somewhat disorientated, we knew only to press forward in search of a hiding place. We went past a field of stupas and flowers. I didn't know if it was the place where the briefcase was buried without first consulting the map. But the briefcase was no longer my concern, at least not now when we were running for our lives.

After a turning we found ourselves in a small garden with a large Bodhi tree. As Kaya had once told me, this very tree was believed to have been propagated from the original tree in India where Buddha sat awaiting enlightenment. I thought we probably had to consider enlightenment in all seriousness should we fall prey to the gangsters.

Inside the garden there was a large building, with an unlocked side door. As we entered, upon seeing a large reclining Buddha statue, we realised we had just entered the main shrine of Wat Pho. Bathing in a flood of lights from the ceiling and walls, the face of the Buddha radiated peace and serenity. All of a sudden I had never felt so calm.

Noises and heavy steps were heard outside in the small garden. Maya looked at me with a strange glow in her eyes. I nodded to her as if I knew what she was thinking. No words were needed. We were a team, a partnership, bound together by the gravity of the situation. Her composure was even more astonishing when a faint smile began to settle on her lips. At the din of frightful footfall rising inside the shrine, I fell on my knees to pray. She picked me up, and said, "Be brave. Let's face it together."

"I've got them!" the leading guy cried in triumph, running straight into me.

He was Somchai, the bald guy wearing Ray-Ban sunglasses. He grabbed me by the shirt and hit me in the stomach.

I didn't yell, trying to be brave. I only moaned at the pain. When Somchai was about to follow up with a kick, a goose voice was heard muttering under his breath behind him, "No, not here; Buddha is sleeping."

It was Sushi, the sparrow-like man.

"Oh, sorry, I thought he was dying, if not already dead," said Somchai. "Anyway, let's get out of here."

I was grabbed by the shoulders and dragged back to the small garden outside, where the grim-faced Boon and his followers were waiting under the Bodhi tree.

I managed to stand with a straight back in spite of the intense pain in my stomach, knowing I must look brave. I greeted Boon with a "Hi", and asked, "Can we please talk?"

"Go ahead," said Boon, in a voice that seemed unvaryingly sober and flat.

"There's no need to manhandle me," I said. "If you're looking for a man who is suspected of killing a debt collector in Macao and running away with a Thai prostitute, you've got him."

A stir was caused among the guys, who seemed to be a little taken aback by my bold confession. They began to look at me as someone with a reputation.

"They are no small crimes," I continued. "And who are you to take an interest in what I've done? Are you the government?"

"We the government?" scoffed the gangsters at the suggestion. "No, the government is sleeping."

"Then I don't see why you should waste your time here," I said. "Why don't you just go and mind your own business, like pimping, extorting or stealing?"

"For your information, our line of business also includes drug trafficking," interjected Sushi the birdman. "Sometimes we murder, too."

"Oh, yeah? What's your story?" I challenged him.

"Ten years ago I killed a man in Tokyo and used a slice of his flesh to prepare a roll of sushi with a topping of *uni*," said Sushi with pride in his goose voice. "That's how I got my nickname—"

"Sushi, you talk too much. You're always talking too much," said Boon, shaking his head. Turning to me, he said, "I like your attitude, my lad. Make no mistake that we are after you because of your crimes. They are not crimes, the same as we are not criminals. What we have here is pure business, and I want to be civilised with you. Please come with me to see my Big Brother."

"No problem. But I'll go to see your Big Brother on one condition," I said.

"What's that?" asked Boon.

"You leave my girlfriend out of our business," I demanded.

"Your girlfriend? You mean the Thai prostitute?" said Boon. "Where's she now?"

Maya was standing a couple of steps behind me in the grip of two musclemen. They made her step forward and stand beside me.

"So, you're the whore?" asked Boon. "What's your name?"

Maya replied, without a moment of hesitation and in a voice which was firm and clear, "My name is Kaya."

Somchai suddenly swore. "Motherfucker! That can't be her real name. She's not even a Thai. She's a Burmese!"

"How can you be so sure?" Boon asked, mild surprise in his tone.

"We've just filled our brothels with a batch of Burmese girls," said Somchai. "Seriously, the Burmese girls are very pretty; this one in particular. Look at her bright eyes, her slender waist and beautiful long legs… she's a knockout!"

While Somchai was admiring Maya, Boon pulled a long face and said in an aggrieved voice, "Why wasn't I informed about the Burmese girls in our brothels? I'd like to have a quiet word with you."

As Boon and Somchai were whispering intently to each other to one side, I took the opportunity to greet Maya. "How do you do, my Burmese girl?" I said, extending a friendly hand.

She took my proffered hand, squeezed it and said, "Nice to meet you. But you need to be braver for a girlfriend like me."

This is very encouraging, I thought.

By now Boon appeared to be satisfied with Somchai's explanation. He said to Somchai in a lecturing voice, "Burmese girls are fine. But don't forget the Chinese and Japanese."

"Most certainly," replied Somchai, bowing his head.

Boon turned back to me, and asked, "But where is your Thai whore now?"

With a sigh, I replied, "She has left me, because she couldn't stand my Burmese girlfriend."

Maya gave me a hard stare of disbelief. I gave her a pat on her shoulder and said, "Don't worry. We're lucky to have met some of the most reasonable people in Bangkok. I trust they'll leave you out of it."

Boon, after a thoughtful moment, asked for the opinion of his men. "What do you think? Are we taking the Burmese girl to see Big Brother or not?"

The guys put their heads together around the bleary-eyed Boon to discuss. It was like a forum conducted with an air of democracy, where everyone was entitled to his opinion and took their turn to speak.

I also had something to say, but only to Maya. "I'll go with them. After I'm gone, you can dig up the briefcase and go back to Burma. You still have the map, don't you?"

"What will they do to you?" asked Maya.

"I don't know. They'd probably take me back to Macao, or they might kill me."

"I won't let them kill you," said Maya, her eyes glinting in the dark. "I own the first right of killing you. Not them."

I hoped she wasn't serious about her right. I thought she only meant she would not abandon me, and I was grateful.

The gang of six seemed to be unable to reach a consensus of what to do with the Burmese girl after lengthy deliberation. Finally, Boon, who must be a man of discretion, said, "I'll give Big Brother a call and let him decide."

He took out his mobile phone, pressed a few buttons, and waited for the connection. But it was a long wait.

"Hell!" Boon grew impatient, shouting down the phone. "Damn it! My phone has no signal. What about yours?"

Sushi checked his. "Not a drop here, but my phone is only a secondhand Blackberry," he said.

The other guys tried their mobile phones, and nobody appeared to be able to set up a call.

Boon, after a suspicious glance around the place, said, "Perhaps they don't allow mobile phones inside Wat Pho. Let's go out onto the streets." He headed off for the entrance, followed by Somchai and Sushi. Maya and I were next in the procession, sandwiched between the musclemen.

Near the main gate, a shrill police siren was heard wailing in the air. Boon stopped under a brick wall for the siren to vanish. When it was all quiet, he was careful to send Sushi to scout the street outside first. Five minutes later, Sushi returned with a stunned expression.

Somchai asked him, "What have you seen?"

"Nothing."

"What do you mean by nothing?"

"No cars, no people, nothing."

"What about our own cars?"

"Gone. The street is completely empty."

"Well it's midnight, and the city is winding down. It all seems normal except for our own cars," observed Somchai.

"I don't know. It's all empty and quiet outside, like a graveyard. I feel bad, terribly bad, almost with the sense of…" paused Sushi, groping for the word.

"We know what you mean," said the thugs standing around us. "It is with the sense of an ending."

Sushi was amazed, and said, "Exactly. How do you know?"

The thugs said, "It's the name of a pop song, don't you remember?"

Sushi shook his head.

One of the thugs broke into a little tune while another thug with a goatee sang, "*The tired old moon is descending, life suspending, country needs mending…*"

Sushi finally recognised the song and joined in with the voice of a soprano, "*Not a perfect ending, just a sad beginning…*"

Somchai shushed them to stop. "Shhh, people are sleeping," he said, rhyming unintentionally.

Boon knew Sushi wouldn't lie about the empty street, but he had his doubts. He felt it necessary to see it with his own eyes, and led the way out of the monastery.

We followed him outside Wat Pho and found things were even more bizarre than what we had just heard. For a main thoroughfare, you always get cars and people, however meagre in number and infrequent, coming and going, in spite of the late hour. But all the while we stood gazing down both ends of the road, not a single soul passed by and traffic seemed to stand still, as if the place had been sealed off from the outside world. The atmosphere was unspeakably sombre and dismal, and the sense of an ending was almost palpable.

Suddenly Boon's mobile phone buzzed, but the call ended before he had time to press the "accept" button; the connection here was probably only a little better than inside Wat Pho.

Everyone was now checking his own phone. Then Boon's buzzed again. He quickly pressed the phone to his ear, and said, "Who's that? I'm sorry, I can't hear you. Can you speak louder? What again? What's on TV? The King? Did you say the King? No, don't go just yet, please don't hang up…"

It appeared the call had been cut off again. Boon said nothing, he only sighed. His men, looking shell-shocked, cried, "What have we heard? What about our King?"

Sushi's response to the patchy news was a histrionic show of slavish passion and sickly dread. As if having some kind of fit, he fell to the pavement and shrieked, "My King! My beloved King!"

"Don't be dumb!" Boon said. "I have only heard that all TV channels are showing nothing but a documentary about our King visiting villages in his youth. I still don't know what it suggests."

"In his youth? What does that mean? I'm lost. I always count myself his most loyal subject; how can I not worry?" cried Sushi. "Oh my King! My beloved King! What will we do without you?"

"Stop it! This is not an opportunity for sacrilege. One wrong word could land you in jail for ten years under the *lèse-majesté* charges for being anti-royal," warned Boon.

Sushi froze on the spot with his mouth agape and eyes fixed at nothing in particular. Somchai gave him a slap in the face, waking him up.

Sushi climbed to his feet and said, "Ten years? That's worse than drug trafficking. Please forget everything I've said."

"We can't. Did you just say something about *The King and I?*" said the thug with a goatee, pulling Sushi's leg.

"No. If I'd said anything about kings, I meant only *Burger King*, okay?" countered Sushi.

Boon's mobile phone rang again.

"Tell me what appears to be the matter?" Boon answered the call, and as he listened, he repeated word for word as if to double check with his own ears. "Troops everywhere. Tanks in position at government headquarters. Abort all operations. Why? A COUP? No, not another coup!"

The call ended just as abruptly as the last one. Boon put down the phone and said, spreading his arms in despair, "How many coups have we had so far?"

"Eighteen in all," answered Sushi swiftly.

"Prior to this, there were seven failed coups and ten successful ones," added another gang man.

"This is unbelievable." Boon sounded surprised. "I never knew you guys took an interest in politics other than beating up people in the streets."

"Well, it's nothing," replied Sushi and his buddy modestly. "Like the Olympics or the World Cup that happen at intervals, our coups are a modern world record that makes the country very proud."

It was at this time all mobile phones vibrated simultaneously. The sound was short and intermittent, different from a call.

"I've got an SMS," announced Sushi.

"Same here," said the other thugs.

Boon checked his phone and said, "I think it's a group message to all of us from our Corporate Communications Department. But it's dark here and the words are too small. Somchai, can you read it out for me?"

Somchai removed his Ray-Bans, which he knew weren't a useful reading aid, before he began: "*State of emergency declared.* What the fuck?"

"Is the last bit part of the message or your own comment?" asked Boon.

"Sorry, it was a slip of the tongue," apologised Somchai.

He began again, "*State of emergency declared. Abort all operations. No more riff-raff on the streets. Fuck!*"

"What's that again?" Boon asked ruefully.

"Pardon me?" said Somchai. "It actually says *Fuck* here."

"Okay, please continue," said Boon with a deep frown.

"*All criminals go underground until the military go back to the barracks*," said Somchai, and concluded the message forcefully, "*Fuck, fuck, fuck, fuck! End of message.*"

"Quite an SMS. What do you think, guys?" asked Boon.

"I like its style. I think our new Head of Corporate Communications has done a good job by sending us an emotional message. It helps to grab our attention," remarked Somchai.

Sushi disagreed. "There's something not quite right."

"Like what?" asked Boon.

"It's the word 'criminals'. The SMS is written and issued by our own people; they can't possibly refer to us as criminals," rationalised Sushi.

The thug with a goatee asked, "If not us… who are the real criminals?"

"Could it be the guy behind the coup?" another thug tried with an intelligent guess.

"If so, he must be the biggest criminal," commented Sushi. "And naturally it is he who should abort all operations and go underground."

Somchai, now totally confused, asked, "Then are we going back to the barracks?"

All eyes turned to Boon for what he had to say, and he said, after careful consideration, "We're not the military, that's for sure. But are we the criminals mentioned in the SMS? Well, it is not important. I only know that we are asked to abort all operations and go underground. Now!"

Just then, the ground beneath our feet trembled violently. Strange sounds, heavy and low, reached our ears like the ripples of a foul sea. Strong lights flared up on the distant horizon; and towards our right, a massive body like a gigantic crab emerged from the darkness.

'What's that? An armoured monster?" yelped Sushi in fear.

"It's a tank, a battle tank!" cried Somchai.

Slowly more tanks came into view, advancing towards us with sounds best compared to volcanic rumblings.

Boon repeated his order to flee. "Go underground! Go now!"

His thugs looked astounded and lost. In a daze they ran in the direction of the approaching tanks. Boon called them back, pointing a finger in the opposite direction. The thugs turned and fled, sprinting like true criminals who had just robbed a bank.

Boon did not follow his men immediately, probably because he still had to deal with me and Maya. He said, "As you've heard, we have to abort all our operations in a state of emergency. We're going underground, and I can understand if you guys decide not to join us."

"You mean we don't have to go with you?" I asked uncertainly, hardly believing our luck.

"That's right. But we'll meet again. I hope to see you soon in Khao San after the dust has settled," he said.

He held out his hand for a handshake, and we warmly shook hands with him and said goodbye.

Before he left, he added, "One last word. Don't stay on the streets, because in our history, all coups are bloody and violent." Then he also took flight, hastening after his companions, and quickly vanished in the smouldering darkness.

On Boon's advice we avoided the streets and took cover inside the monastery. There was a stone hut near the road. We climbed to the top of the hut from a nearby tree and lay on the tiled roof to watch the tanks rattle across. Armoured cars mounted with machine guns trailed after the tanks, followed by vehicles carrying soldiers wearing helmets. Sirens like air-raid warnings were heard near and far. Deployment of troops to place the city under siege seemed urgent and intensive. It was as if the military, in a rush to drag the country to embrace self-destruction, were hell-bent on the path of crushing a functioning democracy.

Maya said, with tears brimming in her eyes, "I feel really sorry for the Thai people. Their hearts must be bleeding this morning to see how their country has been taken over by a military establishment through the brutal use of force and oppression."

Her words reminded me of my friend, the attendant at Erawan Shrine and also a self-serious poet, who had written a poem called *Breakfast at Café Democ*, describing how blessed he always felt about the democracy in his country. I told Maya about my friend who must be devastated by the coup.

Maya said, "There's very little you can do, even when such stark abuse of freedom and democracy is occurring right before your eyes. I really hope I would have the courage to stop the tanks from proceeding, just like the tank man."

"The tank man?" I said, mild shock in my voice. I'd read the story of the tank man who had tried to stop the procession of tanks like a mantis trying to stop a chariot. But it was something that happened in the last century, and I didn't know if it was the same tank man Maya had in mind.

"I don't think you're old enough for that," I said to Maya.

"Don't be stupid. For crimes against humanity like the Holocaust or Hiroshima or the My Lai Massacre, you don't have to be a direct witness to believe. Last year when I was working at a clinic in a refugee camp on the Thai-Burmese border I was shown a documentary about the tank man," she said.

That explained it, I thought.

"It was a solitary man in a white shirt and dark trousers standing in front of a column of tanks and barring their way," she reflected. "I was enormously impressed by his courage. I will not forgive myself if I let this brutality go unchecked before my eyes."

"You mean you're going to stop this coup single-handedly?" I said, not sure if I understood her.

"You know there is the saying: a man does what he must in uncompromising circumstances in spite of personal consequences," she asserted.

"But that's easier said than done," I countered. "What can you possibly do even if you fancy trying to defy the troops outside?"

"Just watch," she said.

To my astonishment, she picked up some broken pieces of brick from the roof and threw them at the passing troops like she was throwing grenades.

As the shreds hit the army vehicles and caused a commotion, she muttered hurriedly, "Let's duck!" and pulled me down the roof.

We huddled against the wall, listening to the noises outside. The movement of vehicles appeared to have come to a halt after they were attacked. Hollow sounds of boots tramping on the pavement were heard on the other side of the wall. Amid shouts of soldiers in alarm, a rather harsh voice cried out, "Attention!"

All footfall ceased, and all voices became heavily muffled.

In the hushed silence, I dreaded that it was only a matter of time before the soldiers broke into Wat Pho. Then somewhere up in the air came a distinct swishing sound, splitting the quiet of the night. A moment later a metallic scraping and clinking was heard, like a flying object that had crashed on a soldier's helmet or his shield.

"Was it a bullet?" a soldier groaned.

"No, it's a nut," another soldier said.

"So it's only nuts!" other voices chimed in with obvious relief.

A soldier must have shaken a tree on the roadside, and nuts fallen down like a small rain shower. Some soldiers burst out laughing while others cried "Tough nuts!" as they were hit. Believing it was only a false alarm instead of a real attack, the soldiers returned to their vehicles and carried on with their quest to seize control of the country.

Not long ago I had felt that dread possessed my body and mind when I thought the soldiers were about to break into the monastery. After the troops were gone, my fear had transformed into a pleasant rush of adrenaline coursing through my blood. Elated by the daring adventure, I congratulated Maya for her heroism.

"Don't be vain. It's pure madness," she said with a dismissive smile. "You should have stopped me from being so reckless."

"But you're my hero!" I said. "You risked your life for what you believe. That's very respectable. I'm so proud to be your partner."

"Don't mention it again," she said. "You should instead think of the coup-maker as our best partner. Now this place is effectively lawless, and therefore there is no stopping what people have conspired to do – whether it's ripping the country apart or digging up secret treasure under the stupas in Wat Pho. Wouldn't it be wonderful?"

"Then what are we waiting for?" I cried excitedly. "Let's go!"

With the help of the map, we traced down to a corner in the stupa garden and found Tony Bear's briefcase in a small grave underneath a bed of red roses. I watched apprehensively as Maya opened the briefcase, and was greatly relieved to hear her exclaim with incredulity,

"Unbelievable; all this money!"

"Didn't I tell you?" I said, almost with a sense of justice. "Now it's clear that I've never been the man you've always wanted to catch. As such, I wonder if you would be so kind as to split the money with me before I go."

"No, you're not going anywhere," she said very resolutely.

"What do you mean?" I said, surprise in my voice. "We have a deal, don't we?"

"But where can you go when there's a coup underway?" she said. "I might as well kill you now and bury you under the flowers rather than let you run into the coup with a bomb strapped to your back. They'd think of you as a protester working against the military. Just like the Palestinian girl."

"What Palestinian girl?"

"It was in the newspaper I gave you to read the other day, of a Palestinian girl who blew herself up at a pizza restaurant in Jerusalem. You mean you didn't read it?" she said.

"Well, perhaps I should read it again. But then, what's your point? That the bomb kills, right?" I said uncomfortably. "Seriously, when do you think you can remove the bomb and set me free?"

"Settle down," she said. "You know I can't do it now. I'll need the necessary tools for the safe removal of the bomb. It can only happen if we walk out of this coup unscratched and return home in one piece."

By home I knew she meant the mid-level garden of the ghost building. But to me it wasn't a home, just a place of torture and ordeal. And as it looked like my life would continue to be at her mercy, my ordeal wasn't going to be over any time soon, I thought miserably.

"Shall we go?" She gave me a slap on the back and said, "Cheer up, dude. It's going to be all right."

I sighed, not knowing if I could trust her one more time.

9

A.H.M.A.N.

By some miracle we survived the coup and returned to the ghost building unscathed, after hours following a dim path along Chao Phraya River under the cover of darkness.

But as we later found out, to our good fortune, we had a lot to thank the coup-maker for. This last coup, number eighteen according to the gangsters from Bangkok, was widely hailed as a bloodless "good" coup. Since it began in the early morning, there were no opposing troop movements, and no reports of armed clashes or even stand-offs in the city. Not a bullet was fired and no one was killed. For a *modus operandi* which was planned, deliberate, strategic and methodical, the coup-maker had provided a textbook example of how all future coups should be executed, and offered an intelligent alternative to the world's failing democracies for the peaceful transition of power.

The public appeared to welcome coups which are peaceful and non-violent. An opinion survey carried out by a university in Bangkok found that eighty-four percent of those polled supported the coup. The remaining sixteen percent were not entirely against it; they were only a little ashamed of themselves for being ambivalent. Another survey carried out by a student society asked only one question: "*What will history say about our democratic conscience if we let our future stay in the hands of coup-makers?*" While a small number answered, "*Fuck the democratic conscience*" or "*Fuck the coup-maker*", the majority of respondents offered "*No comment*".

On our return to the ghost building, we stayed alert for all uncertainties, little knowing we were lucky to be taking a stroll through a fairly "good" coup. I was filled with all kinds of troubled thoughts. Other than minding the bomb on my back and my walking speed, my heart was with my friend who must be devastated by the coup. My friend, although only a shrine attendant, could speak with a noble air on subjects of freedom and democracy. Should he know I was a firsthand witness to the coup, he would most certainly ask me for my observations. I felt I must be prepared by knowing everything surrounding the coup and keeping track of its development. Maya's transistor radio should come in handy. For what we had gone through together tonight, I thought she should have found me as someone likeable, if not loveable, and she would have no problem lending me the radio if I asked. Even better if she should treat my back first thing after we returned to the mid-level garden as she had promised. We could listen to the news together in her bedroom while she worked on my back to remove the bomb with care and tenderness. How nice! Such wonderful thoughts were spirit-lifting, which had the effect of making an awfully cheerless journey home less insufferable.

But then, I had probably misjudged her again. Something rather trivial happened as soon as we were back at the ghost building, against which I sensed the first error in my judgment. I had been carrying Tony Bear's heavy briefcase all the way from Wat Pho and, without knowing how, it changed hands the moment we stepped into the mid-level garden. This would not have perturbed me if it weren't for the extremely cold and aloof expression she wore as she went through the heavy iron door that led to her room on the south wing of the building, without a word or a backward glance.

I shouted from behind and begged her to stay awhile. She paused at the doorstep, made an about turn and asked me what the matter was.

I didn't want to accuse her of being forgetful after she had got what she wanted. I only asked if I could borrow her radio.

"Why?" she grunted in her throat.

I was taken aback by the lack of warmth in her voice. I told her I wanted to keep track of the developments of the coup.

"What for?" she said icily.

"I have a Thai friend who is quite proud of the democratic system in his country," I explained. "He must be deeply concerned by how this coup will change the lives of the Thai people. He would probably discuss all the big issues with me, like how freedom and human rights will be eroded as a result of the coup, when we meet next time."

"Well, for the little you know, it'd do more good to seal up your big mouth with Band-Aids," she said harshly. "Radio news won't be much help to you because the situation is complicated."

I swallowed the insult and said, "Please tell me what is so complicated."

"Freedom and human rights? What a joke!" she snorted. "Let me tell you what your friend's government has done about freedom and human rights as far as the Burmese people are concerned."

"Please," I said fawningly. "I'm all ears."

"The Prime Minister of your friend's government, as soon as he was elected, initiated a 'forward engagement' policy in collusion with the Burmese generals by investing in the building of dams inside Burma," she said. "To facilitate the construction, the Burmese military had set up some heavily militarised areas along the Salween River by violently evicting villagers and destroying their homes; as many as 300,000 civilians have been forcibly displaced, many fleeing to Thailand. To please the Burmese junta, your friend's Prime Minister ordered crackdowns on Burmese dissidents living in Thailand, banning Burmese pro-democracy groups from holding public demonstrations, arresting and repatriating refugees with no guarantee for their safety."

This was all new to me, and I frowned uncomprehendingly. "You speak as if my friend's government is bad, and the coup is good. I probably should clarify with him the next time we meet," I said.

"You'd better do that," she said bitterly. "I hate this coup, or any military coups attempting to take over the country with banditry, but it doesn't mean I have sympathy with the downfall of your friend's government."

"You're excellent," I praised her. "Thanks for the clarification. If you don't mind, can we change the subject?"

She was as smart as a fox. She said, "It's been a long day and I'm very tired. Let me have some sleep first. We can continue with whatever you want to discuss tomorrow. OK?"

"No, please listen to me," I said hurriedly.

She yawned. "Be quick with what you have to say. Oh I'm so tired."

In a most ingratiating voice I said, "Can you do me a small favour by taking the bomb off my back now?"

"No." Her reply was quick and clear-cut. "You have to wait until tomorrow. Goodnight now."

She picked up the briefcase from the floor and turned to go, closing the iron door behind her with a slam.

I was so furious and yelled after her, "Are you being forgetful or is there a problem with your fucking head?"

The door was swung open again. She took a half-step forward and said, "Okay, let me tell you why it's better to wait until tomorrow. Because I can't do it without first having some rest, as the job requires concentration and precision."

I knew it was just a lie. She simply wanted me to carry the bomb forever so that she could manipulate me any way she liked. Worse still, I suspected that she might have already decided to get rid of me as she had now got the briefcase and all the money.

She must have noticed my face convulse with anger and felt the need to placate me. In a gentle voice accompanied with a smile, she said, "Can you please let me have some sleep first? What if I give you the radio now and leave the bomb till tomorrow?"

I was speechless when I saw nothing but deception behind her pretty smile.

"Must you behave like a spoiled brat?" she cooed. "If you want the radio, just come and get it, OK?"

"I think you're impossible… impossibly unreasonable…" I stammered, trembling with a mix of anger and fear.

"Well, goodnight now," she said and quickly disappeared into the dark passage behind the heavy iron door.

Not knowing what more I could do after I had begged, argued and cursed, all to no avail, I returned to the greenhouse to rest. But I couldn't sleep and I began to ponder my chance of walking out of the ghost building alive and free.

By my analysis I was no longer of any value to her after she had secured Tony Bear's briefcase and all its money. She could, as she had promised, give me my freedom back. But she wouldn't, because of the things I knew about her: a Burmese girl hiding and waiting in a ghost building in Bangkok on a secret mission. As she had once said, "Someone could get himself killed for knowing too much." It must be in her best interest to see me dead instead of alive. Not long ago, within only a matter of hours, she had repeatedly said that she'd kill me at the next opportunity. It seemed she didn't just banter about it, but had all along meant to do it in all seriousness.

I felt sick all over when I imagined that she was going to kill me the way she killed my cat. The feeling of powerlessness to turn the situation around further compounded my sickness, which had caused havoc in my system. My stomach, among all my organs, was complaining the loudest. Although my life was at stake, it appeared that I had to attend to an urgent call of nature first, as if it mattered at all in the face of death.

I hurried to the toilet at the clubhouse, and relieved my bowels sitting on a throne of some Italian design. Spread on the toilet floor was an old issue of the *Bangkok Post*. There was a picture of John Travolta on the entertainment page. I thought that if Maya entered the clubhouse now with a gun I probably would die like Travolta in the movie *Pulp Fiction*. It's as if there's something about shitting that makes you vulnerable. But John, after his fake death, would rise, wipe his ass, and collect millions of dollars for acting, whereas someone of my nonentity would never stand up again, forever saving his butt from wiping.

On the floor was also the front-page story that Maya had asked me to read when she was about to kill the cat the other day. I had only had a quick scan at the time, knowing roughly it was about a Palestinian girl who blew herself up in Jerusalem, without paying too much attention to the details. In my present plight I found my situation was curiously similar to that of the Palestinian girl who was killed by the bomb, and I decided to pick up the paper for a reread.

> "*A Palestinian teenage girl, identified as fourteen-year-old Haifa, blew herself up at a pizza restaurant in the centre of Jerusalem, killing fifteen people – mostly young families and tourists – and wounding more than ninety...*"

I paused, and began again. Then I paused after the line "*wounding more than ninety*", when these words for some reason struck me as not only awful but also terribly illuminating.

The key message of the article that "the bomb can kill" continued to stand out loud and clear, which was what Maya had intended to use for the purpose of intimidation when she asked me to read the story. But as I reread it, at a time when I was filled with rage and fear of my own impending death, I had suddenly become conscious of the fact that the bomb was not only capable of killing the one who commits suicide but at the same time taking down all others in the vicinity of the blast as well.

This was to me a complete eye-opener. To the common reader a bomb that kills the bomber and the people around is quite obvious as a fact. But I had the feeling that I was about to discover something of a lifeline in my hopeless situation.

To clear my mind, I took a bath in the cool water of the swimming pool. As I sat down on the bottom of the pool, holding my breath underwater, suddenly I had something of a eureka moment as I seemed to have found the meaning behind the fact that "the bomb can kill one and many". It was, in very simple terms, that if Maya wanted to kill me she would only do it when we were some distance apart; otherwise she would have killed herself too by setting off the bomb on my back if she were close by.

This could be the key to my survival, I thought excitedly. As long as I could be near her, so near that I could hold her in my grip, then I'd probably be safe.

I climbed out of the pool and, lounging by the poolside, tried to imagine how I could possibly cut down the distance between us. After some uncomplicated ruminations I came to the conclusion that there was no better way than to wait outside her room for the opportunity. As soon as she appeared she'd be quickly subdued and forced to succumb to my demand to remove the bomb. Then I'd be free.

There was, however, one technical flaw in my simple thinking, which was that she could, in the unfortunate circumstances, set off the bomb in haste and desperation, then I'd be doomed. Nonetheless, should that occur, my consolation would be that as I died, I wouldn't be alone as she would die with me in our mutual annihilation.

This was one bloody plan of life and death. But in the final analysis I was sure as hell that it was the only way if there was any ultimate escape.

I slowly climbed to my feet, and to psyche myself up for my audacious plan, I pictured her in my mind as some extremely dangerous enemy with a pretty and wicked smile, her eyes dancing with malice, her body writhing and twisting like that of a poisonous snake.

"Bitch!" I swore aloud. "Have I told you I'm gonna fuck you till you're blind?"

I jumped up and down on the edge of the pool like a madman in a fit of bitter laughter. Knowing I had reached the point of no return in my life, I didn't even bother to put my pants back on but let my cock whoop and hop like an angry rooster as I set out in search of whatever chance for my survival.

The corridor leading to Maya's room was dark and cold. Dark because I had left the flashlight in the clubhouse toilet; but I didn't really need it, because I felt safe in the dark. The cold was simply due to my own nervousness. I had no difficulty in finding her room situated in the south wing of the building, a few steps off from the main corridor through a side passage. Her room was shut tightly, leaving no crevices or space at the bottom of the door, and I was unable to observe if it was dark or light inside. I gave the door a slight push and was not surprised to find it locked. I wondered if I should sit down and wait, but worried that it could be a long wait, so long that I might have dozed off outside her room.

As I stood indecisively, pondering my best move, her voice suddenly rose on the other side of the wall. "I guess you still want the radio," she called out.

I was amazed at how she had discovered my presence. But there was no time to think and I promptly answered, "Yes, I do."

"Come in," she said, with a yawn in her voice.

At the sound of a click, the door stood back an inch. Through the gap, I looked past the long table in the middle of the room to the bed under the far wall. In the yellowish light from a camping lamp, I could see her lying on the bed, her body clad in a green vest and white shorts, her face to the wall.

Without turning to me, she muttered, "The radio is on the table. Get it and get out immediately. I'm very tired."

I entered the room quietly and tiptoed past the table to stand at the side of her bed. Meanwhile, the door behind me closed automatically with the soft sound of the kiss of metal. She must have heard my approaching steps, and spun around with the quickness of an animal disturbed. Staring at my naked body with astounded eyes, she bawled in horror, "What do you think you're doing?"

I knew time was simply too deadly precious to give a reply when she could go for the kill any second. The key to my safety was to be really close to her. And I took the leap, as if I were to plunge down a precipice, with my body landing on top of her.

She screamed. She seized my shoulders, trying to push me away. "Get off me now, or I'll blow you up!" she warned.

Her old trick still worked on me and I froze on the spot, but only for a split second. Remembering I was only a suicide bomber who would be dying anyway, I said with a sneer, "Go ahead. I'm going to die with you. We'll make a perfect couple, heaven or hell!"

She ceased to struggle instantly. I thought she must be regretting now having momentarily let her guard drop. To my admiration, she was being careful not to show any frustration on her face. She could have begged me to let her go in exchange for the removal of the bomb, but she was either too proud or too dignified to consider those options. Instead, her eyes shifted haphazardly around the room, obviously in search of what might come in handy for her rescue.

I knew she wasn't someone who would submit easily unless she had first learned her lesson the hard way. And just to humiliate her, I took away her flimsy green vest in a swift snap, exposing her bare breasts. This seemed a cruel thing to do, after all. But I had been waiting long enough for the opportunity to punish her and I must be cruel, really cruel. And once it had all started I had also begun to find a beastly pleasure in my cruelty. In a renewed struggle, she hit me full in the stomach. I swallowed the pain, which only hardened my determination to punish her.

I spat in her face. "Bitch, let's have a good ride before we're dead!" I said, ripping her short pants into pieces, and barged into her.

"Stop it!" she cried. "Please don't hurt me."

I paused at some threshold, whatever that might be.

"Can we make a deal?" she asked.

"Another deal?" I said with incredulity in my voice. "You seem to be the last person to honour any deals."

"I'm sorry if that's what you think," she said. "But what is it you want? Is it about money?"

I was appalled. She still pretended my concern was something other than the fucking bomb on my back. This was absurd. It exasperated me so much that I resumed my attack on her with double intensity.

"No, stop there, please!" she prayed, swaying her body in small defensive struggles. But it was too late now, as I was seized with a raw desire to do some horrible, sordid things.

But quite inexplicably, at this very juncture, whatever was occurring between us came to an abrupt stop. She had all of a sudden withdrawn even the slightest resistance to my earthly muscles, rendering my aggression not only unnecessary but also a bit ridiculous. I had also halted in the middle of my invasion. I didn't advance further because it was never my intention to molest her as such, even though I had always wanted to punish her in my revenge, but it was also because I saw her pretty face in a fleeting moment take on an alarming expression of fear and anxiety.

She placed a finger on her lips. I was baffled by the sign for silence and my body stiffened into rigid attention.

A strong gust of wind entered the room through the porthole window near the ceiling. Blue liquid bubbles inside a large glass cylinder standing by the wall next to the bed raced up and down, making small wheezing sounds like a boiling volcano. In a worried voice, she whispered, "Turn off the light, quick; someone is in the building."

I hesitated, not sure if it was one of her tricks.

She fixed me fully in the eyes and said, "We have a situation here. I need your cooperation."

While we were locked in a deadly embrace, I welcomed the idea of some cooperation. I switched off the camping lantern at the side of the bed as she asked. The boiling sound of the bubbles had also settled down to complete silence.

Keeping her voice low, she said, "Trust me, we have a critical situation. When someone opens the main door to enter the building, I can always feel it by the wind coming through the porthole window.

The thermometer near my bed will also alert me with its rioting bubbles when there's a sudden change in temperature."

That explained it. Now I understood why she knew I was outside her room even before I had knocked on the door. "Is it somebody you expect?" I asked.

"Yes, very probably," she said. "It may be the definitive proof that you're not the spy and traitor who I've been waiting for to appear, although I'd already dismissed you as a suspect after you came clean with the briefcase and money. Still, I blame myself for having prematurely considered you no longer a threat… but say no more for now."

She spoke into my ear in a voice scarcely above a whisper. I was enormously excited by the great intimacy and my body reacted exaggeratedly with an upsurge of blood and unrest. As a result the bed creaked beneath our combined weight. To my amazement, she moved her hand purposely down my groin, and gave the piece of unsettled flesh a pinch. "I need you to calm down," she muttered.

"I'm deeply sorry," I said, "but you know I can't help it."

But somehow my body cooled off without needing another pinch when footfall was heard outside. It was the sound of leather shoes scratching the unpolished surface of the ground, moving from one end of the main corridor to another. We could tell it was a man when he coughed as he walked. Sometimes he raised his voice to shout something. We didn't hear clearly what he was saying as the voice still seemed far away. As he came closer, we could hear sounds as if he was tapping the wall with a metal object. Three taps, then a shout of something. At its closest to our room, which was only steps apart from the main corridor at the end of a little passage, the man as usual tapped the wall three times and followed with a shout. This time we heard clearly what he said.

"I have come to speak on behalf of Maya."

At hearing her name, Maya started with a jolt.

"She has asked me to convey the following message," continued the man in a hoarse voice. "Rangoon is burning! I repeat: Rangoon is burning!"

Maya quivered in my arms, sobbing quietly, with tears streaming down her face. The bed beneath our bodies creaked. I had to hold her really tight to keep her still.

The man, who must have decided he was only speaking to thin air, moved on. He kept knocking on the wall, repeating the name of Maya, and reciting the message as he walked down the corridor and started off toward the north wing.

The instant the man's voice and his footsteps had completely vanished in the distance, Maya could no longer restrain her emotions and wept openly. She snuggled in my arms like a child, her chest heaving agitatedly beneath mine.

"Who is that guy? What has he done?" I asked.

"His name is Hsint Khine Ye, who is believed to be behind the murder of my boyfriend in a prison in Burma," she said. "The sad thing is that there's no clear proof. So his friends and I set something up here for the purpose of tracking down the true culprit. It has been a long wait, over a month now, and I thought of giving up the whole scheme after we went digging up the briefcase. But he has turned up, eventually, speaking my name and reciting the message 'Rangoon is burning'. This is the solid proof of his crime, and himself as the out-and-out traitor and murderer."

"I'm glad for you. Your time here has finally paid off," I said. "I believe no crime should go unpunished. I think it's time to claim justice."

She shook her head ambivalently.

I was curious and asked her, "What's stopping you?"

She made a grunt in her throat and said, "For many weeks I've been waiting for this very moment. I've worked out every detail, ready for every eventuality. There could be an arm wrestle or a gun fight; I'm more than prepared."

After a short pause she raised her voice slightly with irritation: "But how anyone, by any stretch of the imagination, could have anticipated that I'd have been rendered utterly useless at the crucial moment. What nonsense is it that you ask what's stopping me? What am I supposed to do with you climbing on me and a bomb ticking above us? You fool!"

"I'm sorry," I said. "I never meant to intrude in your privacy in the first place. You'd like me to shove off? Just tell me if it's safe to dismount and—"

But I didn't finish my sentence, which was cut short by a sudden piercing scream out of nowhere.

She gripped my shoulders in fear, and I could almost feel her nails in my skin when heart-wrenching scream after scream was heard coming through the porthole window. They were extremely awful screams, like those of a man whose soul had been trapped in hellfire, or of a bull dying violently under a butcher's knife.

Then the horrendous screams came to a halt, as abruptly as they had first burst out of the silence.

"I didn't know there is a slaughterhouse in the area," I said, wondering if they were the most horrible sounds I had ever listened to.

Maya looked stunned, her face a whiter shade of an extraordinary pallor. She said, "Oh my God! This is crazy! This is absolute madness!"

"What is the matter?" I asked.

In a voice splintered with pain, she said, "Hsint Khine Ye is dead. Your trap has killed him!"

Quite astounded, I exclaimed, "Oh, shoot me now! What have I done?"

I felt a chill down my spine and a cold sweat all over my body as I could almost picture the ghastly face of a man who had died by falling on the sharp spire of the trap. Struck with guilt and fear, I experienced dizziness and excessive shortness of breath. I thought I was going to die.

"That's okay. It's not your fault," she said, holding me tenderly in a loving embrace. "You're freezing. Let me warm you up."

She kissed me and touched me and told me to hold her tight. Slowly I began to feel blood running through my veins again. She rubbed her body against mine, as if she could pass warmth to me by vigorous friction.

"It's no fault of yours," she repeated. "On the other hand, please know I'm immensely thankful for everything you have done for my cause."

She had greatly boosted me, both mentally and physically. When I was feeling less guilty, I was already inside her without knowing exactly when we started fucking. She was totally compliant, with eyes closed and a half-smile of satisfaction on her face. I found myself in such a curious predicament because things were pretty good for a while as if it would continue forever. As I got better and better, working myself into a nice rhythm which was quickening by the second, she suddenly opened her eyes and said, "We've gotta stop. The bomb will kill us."

I would probably have risked myself a few more thrusts, but reluctantly pulled my body to a halt.

"Don't ask me to separate from you," I implored her.

"Of course not. We're at the point of becoming almost inextricable, now or forever," she said smiling at me. "Now hold me by the waist and carry me over to the long table for the tools."

And we, without disconnecting from each other, made it to the table in the middle of the room. I placed her on the tabletop and stood hovering over her. She found a small screwdriver to work on my back. I felt almost nothing except some minor discomfort, like tingling of the skin. Then she changed the screwdriver for a pair of scissors and said, "Please lean closer. I want you to hang your head over my shoulder so that I can see the wires."

I did as I was told. She let out a string of giggles, "You've infiltrated me through and through. Don't make me laugh because I must concentrate."

I knew this was going to be crucial and tried my best to stay really cool. After seconds of probing and prodding, she said, "I think I've got the one wire which, sorry to inform you, could make or break both of us. Do you really want me to proceed?"

I wondered if I had a choice and didn't know what to say.

She muttered, with a degree of earnestness, "Don't worry. Think you're going to die and everything will be all right."

She scared the shit out of me. As I waited I suddenly remembered how she had always wanted me dead. In the suspense, my heart seemed to stop beating. Images of my cat blown out of the mid-level garden in the explosion passed before my eyes with perfect clarity; I wondered if I were already dead without even knowing it. Then in the silence came the sharp, clear sound of the snapping of wire. One sharp click, followed by another. She held my head, looked me in the face and kissed me.

"I think we're safe now," she said, with relief in her voice.

But I wasn't so sure, as there was still something uncomfortable stuck to my back.

"It's only the bomb case, and the tapes and bandages," she said. "Don't worry. They can't harm you anymore."

I had learned my lesson of not entirely believing her, and asked her to remove everything.

"Are you sure? It's going to cause some pain," she warned.

I insisted, though nervously.

In a quick snap, she tore away the adhesive tapes and bandages on my back. I experienced a severe burning pain and jumped back like a bolt, effectively detaching myself from her.

She sat up slightly, one hand holding onto the edge of the table for support and another grabbing the case of the bomb, which was black and thick like a paperback.

She said seductively, "Come here. Let me give you a massage to lessen the pain."

But I wasn't to be seduced. I was feeling angry and even violent instead of sexually aroused. Although the threat of the bomb had been lifted, the fear and shame which had enslaved me for weeks and months lingered. I took a step forward and gave her a hard slap in the face. She fell back, lying motionless on the table.

I thought she might have passed out. I leaned close and found there was blood at the corner of her mouth, but she was conscious.

She raised her body slightly and said quietly, "You may leave now if you want."

I quickly became sensible again after I'd vented my indignation.

"Where can I go now when there's a coup outside?" I said.

"Do you want my advice?" she asked.

"Please."

"Forget about the coup, and attend to whatever is unfinished here," she averred.

Her message was clear: "Make love, not coup."

I took the cue, and she took the plunge from me as she sprawled on the tabletop with a groan.

Before her lips were sealed with my kisses, she said, "Of course you're gonna stay."

Without the bomb on my back I felt things were even better in our reciprocal and perfectly harmonious embrace. I could not describe how beautiful it was when we reached the crescendo at the moment of consummation, with our bodies climaxing almost concurrently. Afterwards we lay blithely exhausted in each other's arms, never having felt so good after we had left our enmity behind.

We fell asleep, but our sleep was interrupted when our room was invaded by a strong stench. It was the stench of death, and we remembered that Hsint Khine Ye was dead.

The time was four thirty in the morning. Gathering a large blanket around our bare bodies, we ambled our way towards the room fitted with the deadly trap in the depths of the pit in the north wing.

Down in the pit we were met by the horrendous sight of a dead man whose body was hung like an animal carcass hoisted on a meat hook in an abattoir waiting to be broken down into serviceable cuts. It was an ordinary man of about fifty, with a dark, overcooked brown complexion. His eyes stared blandly at the ceiling, with dilated pupils and enlarged eyeballs bursting at the rims of the sockets. His angular body frame was clad in a black silk suit, and his large feet were encased in a pair of glossy leather shoes. The spire had pierced him through the chest at the point between the breastbone and stomach, where blood – imagined to have been spouting like a small fountain about an hour ago – had stained the whitewashed wall with impressionistic marks and was still dripping from the torn tissues. A gun was held pointing at his head, probably in the middle of committing suicide when the wound had become too painful to bear. But it seemed that he had run out of time before pulling the trigger; and he died, saving the trouble of killing himself.

Maya had not uttered a sound since entering the pit. She appeared to be brooding over how things had turned out this way. Her mouth was slightly twisted, her eyes smouldered with rage, and her face was a mixture of despair, bitterness and pain. She shook her head time and again, sometimes in disbelief, other times with grief.

"I pray for the evildoers to receive their recompense. But I never wished your retribution to be as terrible and savage as this," she murmured.

Her hard expression slowly softened to one of sympathy and compassion. She knelt down and started to chant with closed eyes. I had to follow suit because of the blanket we shared.

There was a soulful quality to her chanting, characterised by mercy and profound kindness. I was touched beyond myself, and my heart was seized by a pang of sadness. It was then that I noticed Hsint Khine Ye, despite being dead, respond positively to the chanting. He let loose his grip of the gun, which slid soundlessly from the surface of the bamboo sticks to the floor. I have heard Buddhists are experts in death and specialists in obsequies. I thought Maya's chanting might have helped Hsint Khine Ye move on without further clinging to his mortal coil. The dead man, who must have finally recognised himself as dead as a nail, gave up fighting to stay in the realm of human reality. His eyeballs rolled back in his sockets, and his eyelids descended like the fall of a curtain. Then he departed, almost with an air of peace and serenity.

"I guess he's finally and absolutely gone," I said.

Maya stopped chanting. She opened her eyes and fixed them on the body of Hsint Khine Ye with a quizzical stare. She said, "My boyfriend died a death no less horrible not long ago. His skull, smashed out of shape, had to be stitched together like a baseball for the funeral. I think the score is even now."

"I don't know if I should congratulate you," I said carefully.

"No. You are the one to be congratulated," she said with a smile. "Hsint Khine Ye is a traitor of the highest order. You have killed him and saved my people from further damage."

I was shocked. "I-I didn't kill him," I stammered. "It was only the trap I built on your orders. I think you should take the full credit. If you like, you can think of me as having made a contribution, and a small one, all things considered."

"You're too modest," Maya said, leaning against my body under the blanket.

I sighed and didn't know what to say. I shuddered at the thought of having yet another murder attributed to my name. This was so unfair. I was only a forced labourer conscripted to build the trap under threat of death. Perhaps my only problem was that I actually enjoyed the process of building it, and perfected the original design with a slight modification. But I'd never meant to cause harm to anybody, not to mention actually killing them. The cruel reality was, however, that Hsint Khine Ye had been killed, and Tony Bear was still dead. Already a fugitive hiding in Bangkok, I probably would be fleeing again very soon for my complicity in the death of Hsint Khine Ye.

"What's troubling you?" said Maya. Before I could say anything, she stood up and dragged me out of the pit.

Outside we found that dawn had broken over the Bangkok sky. Birds were chirping noisily in the trees in the mid-level garden. We sat down by the side of the swimming pool, our legs dangling above the water as we observed the light reflections on the water surface in silence.

"Fancy a swim?" asked Maya.

I was unsure. As a matter of fact, during my whole stay here in the mid-level garden, I had only washed my body in the pool, but never tried swimming. I thought that in a proper swimming pool the water should look a pristine blue and crystal clear, with the smell of chlorine or ozone. Here the pool was basically filled up by Bangkok's abundant rainfall. The colour was a light green and the smell, something like moist earth, could not be described as pleasant. I told her I had doubts about the water quality.

She said, "You're wrong to think of the water here as dirty. Perhaps you as a city dweller would not be able to appreciate the simple pleasure of swimming in the countryside, in a lake, a pond, or a river. You know, me and my twin sister used to swim in the river that runs past our village in Shan, completely without clothes."

I was wide-eyed.

"The water in this pool reminds me of my old days in Burma and the pleasure of swimming, happy and carefree," she said. "You know, I swam naked every morning here in the mid-level garden… until you came. This is perhaps one of the reasons that I always wanted to kill you."

All smiles, she opened the blanket and slipped down into the pool. After a few crawls and kicks she reached the centre and waved at me to join her. Eager to share the simple pleasure of swimming without clothes, I dove in and swam after her. Then we reached the shallow end of the pool. She stood up on her toes and cried out excitedly, "Look, isn't it lovely?"

I came to stand beside her. As my feet landed on the muddy bottom, I realised that the swimming pool, having over time accumulated layers of sand and silt at the shallow end, had evolved to become something of a pond, with the growth of aquatic plants.

She was gazing at a group of water lilies in front of her, and the object of her enchantment was a lotus that had blossomed into a large flower. Its colour was an innocent white, and it was so beautiful, so pure and immaculate. There was also an alien quality about it, something spooky and otherworldly. I felt almost a reverential awe, finding it hard to imagine a thing of such beauty and purity could have sprung from a place of dirt and mud.

Cupping the flower softly between her hands, she said, "Ko Ko, is that you? Is this your soul, appearing before me on the morning after justice is served?" Her voice was a low whisper and kind of weird.

When I wondered what it was about, she said to me, "Ah Man, this is Ko Ko. Please say hello."

I felt it polite to oblige without knowing what the name Ko Ko was about. "Hello, Ko Ko," I greeted the white lotus flower. Then I asked Maya to remind me who Ko Ko was.

She gave me a hard stare. "I've told you: Ko Ko was my boyfriend who died in a prison in Burma," she said. "I went to his funeral last month with a lotus flower of exactly this size and colour."

"Oh, what a coincidence!" I exclaimed.

"This is no coincidence," she said. "I can feel the spirit of Ko Ko, who has come to say goodbye. I think he can finally rest in peace now. Goodbye, my love."

She prayed and chanted, "*Om Mani Padme Hum.*"

She asked me to chant after her, and I chanted after her. She paused after six rounds to ask me, "Do you know the meaning of the mantra?"

I answered no.

"It means '*Praise to the jewel in the lotus*'," she said.

We resumed chanting and stopped after 108 rounds. She wanted to swim again, and I welcomed it. I was already a little in love with the sport for its quality of freedom and pleasure. Afterwards we took a rest by just keeping our bodies afloat on the water, and looking up at the Bangkok sky tinged with the many splendours of the morning sun.

She asked me what I was thinking.

I said nothing in particular. "And you?" I inquired back politely.

She said the visitation from Ko Ko's spirit had brought back to her a flood of memories of her Burmese days. "I am thinking it is something I can share with you, if you're interested."

I replied, "Of course," as I didn't want to be rude. I thought she was trying to find consolation in the supernatural after having lost someone dear to her, and I was reluctant to dismiss that as purely superstitious. I told her I'd be honoured if she confided in me about her personal experiences. She was overwhelmed by my response, as if she had seen generosity and kindness in me for the first time, and she cried happily. I was glad that I could please her simply by lending a listening ear.

We climbed out of the pool to lounge by the poolside. Still sobbing, she started telling me her story. I guessed it would be one of those stories about the adventures of a rebellious girl running away with her lover, some dissident, against the wishes of her family. I thought I could have nodded off before long.

But I was wrong.

I was hooked shortly after she had begun, by what appeared to be a mesmerising account of revolt, treachery, slaughter and ruin. I was left horrified and stunned by a story of crimes against humanity, and of a humanity contaminated by the most hideous crimes on earth. I thought it must be the most unforgettable story I had ever heard in my whole life.

PART TWO

THE RANGOON BOMBING

I do not hold to non-violence for moral reasons, but for practical and political reasons, because I think it's best for the country. And even Ghandiji, who is supposed to be the father of non-violence, said that between cowardice and violence, he'd choose violence every time.

Aung San Suu Kyi

10

M.A.Y.A.

A hba, Ahmay, Meena... shall I tell you how much I miss them as my most beloved family members when I look back at the past of my youthful days?

Just to be clear, Ahba and Ahmay are not actual names, only a form of address. At home I call my father Ahba and my mother Ahmay. Meena is the name of my twin sister, who is younger than me by a couple of minutes. She is by nature an artist, whereas I could probably be best described as some sort of brave-hearted nerd. Sometimes I cannot help but wonder: if I were like my dear little sister, with a certain artistic leaning towards music, would my life carry less of the trials and tribulations that I've known? But there is no easy answer because you don't choose your own birth or your family. And you don't choose your country either, which is a shame. I guess many of my countrymen would have wished to be born elsewhere if they had the choice. It is a wretched time and place to be alive. With the country brought to its knees by military brutalisation, one has to battle for one's survival. In the age of persecution it is simply not good enough merely being stoic and defiant. More often than not, it would be foolish to stand tall when you should instead flee far and fast if staying alive is what matters at the end of the day.

I first experienced fleeing when I was in my early teens, living with my family in one of the 2,000 villages on the Shan plateau, which is a combination of hill ranges straddling central eastern Burma and northwestern Thailand. My father was a teacher in a monastery school and my mother worked at home, tending a tiny plot of vegetables in addition to her domestic chores. A small creek ran past our village, where Meena and I went swimming after school. The place was serene and peaceful, and life was happy. Then very suddenly the rural idyll turned into a nightmare. One day, the soldiers came. The village was torched and we fled, never to return. My mother lost her life by stepping on a landmine at the riverside. At only twelve years old, this happened to be my most dreadful, traumatic and incredibly tough experience. The effect on my adolescence couldn't be more profound and lasting.

After the horrendous death of my mother, Ahba was determined to teach us something more practical than reading and writing or doing mathematics. He taught us to build bombs and how to apply them effectively in the warfare against the junta.

But before anything there was a psychological issue which had to be dealt with first. For quite some time I had struggled to explain my father's behaviour since he had become a widower. I quietly condemned him for issues of infidelity, and suspected him of running a clandestine parallel life alongside being a schoolteacher.

He must have guessed my misgivings and felt it useful to come clean before the lessons. He acknowledged that he had been working as an explosives specialist for a faction in the resistance under the leadership of a man called Dr Rice to carry out subversive operations against the junta.

Hearing this revelation, I thought I was quite mature at my age to have absorbed the news. I soon got over the surprise and felt rather proud of him as an explosives expert affiliated with the democratic movement.

Meena was more curious than shocked by Ahba's secret identity. Always a bit of an oddball, with a penchant for asking uncomfortable questions, she inquired, "Has anyone called you a terrorist?"

Ahba looked positively discomfited. He squeezed a bitter smile and said, "My dear girls, I received formal training from the Tatmadaw on the manufacturing of landmines, grenades and bombs for two years. No one called me a terrorist then. Why would anyone call me a terrorist now when I have only changed sides to serve the resistance?"

The mention of Tatmadaw made me cringe. We as children had learned in school that Tatmadaw (the official name for Burmese armed forces) is patriotic and an undisputed aspiration for a better country. It is very powerful, but it does not terrify people when its goals are to achieve national unity and strive for better health and education in the country. It is only terrifying when we hear stories of people speaking from their experiences of forced labour, child soldiers, torture and the use of rape as a weapon of war. I found it hard to believe Ahba was formerly linked to the Tatmadaw but was glad that he had made the switch.

"I'm not a terrorist," he stressed, "for the fact that I never make bombs with the malicious intent of harming others. I only make bombs for the purpose of dazzling with sight and sound, like fireworks; to cause awareness and raise the spirits of the people who are oppressed; to act as a sounding board on behalf of the people who are lost and silenced; to give them hope when it seems to have all but vanished. Bombs to me are like thunder in the sky and precursors to the long-awaited rain which will someday make the wasteland of our country fertile again."

Suddenly he said, visibly vexed, "Meena, I'm answering your question, but I don't think you're paying attention!"

All tearful in the space of a second, Meena said, crying, "I'm busy composing a song in my head. I'm sorry. What if you let me work on something else, like playing my little piano?"

My twin sister could be shy and diffident, but she was also not afraid to tell people how she truly felt. Ahba knew it better not to insist, and released her to focus on her favourite pastime. As someone who had displayed a natural affinity for music since she was small, Meena later went on to become the student of an old maestro and learn how to play the Burmese harp and perform classic songs in the Mahagita tradition.

I probably could be excused too had I demonstrated similar disinterest. But I was both nervous and excited when I was about to be indoctrinated into the world of explosives, as if I were kind of expecting it as a matter of course. I wanted to learn everything about it and had a strong desire to excel in the field. This was only understandable if one happened to know that I had actually witnessed my mother being killed before my eyes, whereas Meena was fortunately spared the experience. I needed no persuasion to stay, and my enrolment into the revolutionary movement was almost automatic and voluntary.

Ahba might have liked to sign up Meena too if it were practical. As we know, we are fighting a prolonged war of attrition which could continue for generations. In time, not only would our children join the struggle for freedom and democracy but also our children's children, if the war should protract indefinitely. But Meena's exclusion might have been just as well. I guessed Ahba was glad to have avoided putting both his daughters in the grave danger of fighting a rogue regime for the liberation of the country. It was perhaps wrong of me to say he was "glad" as if he had a bigger love for my little sister. It wasn't so. I never doubted my father's love; on the contrary, I felt his love for me might be deeper and more complicated with an earnest desire to wish me well.

Hence my years of living dangerously as an explosives practitioner began.

For my learning, Ahba had designed a comprehensive programme mixing theories, easy-to-follow recipes and hands-on experiments. I still remember his opening remark at the first lesson: "Like Man, not all explosives are created equal. In general, explosives can be classified according to their power. At the top of the ladder you would have RDX, PETN and nitro, and a few of their close cousins. In the middle, TNT is a typical example. And then a lower group includes black powder, mercury fulminate and lead azide. While Man's behaviour can vary from the very violent and destructive to rarely speaking above a whisper, the same can be said about the performance of explosives:

some can explode so fiercely that they destroy everything within range, while others are merely useful for recreational purposes, like firecrackers."

Starting as a novice in the first year, I laboriously built up a pool of knowledge of the materials, tools, methods and testing procedures. It was extremely hard work which caused me to suffer many sleepless nights trying to memorise a litany of explosive substances by rote. At other times I broke down hopelessly at failing to pass tests designed by Ahba for the purpose of gauging my progress. Stretched to the absolute limit of intensity, I temporarily lost confidence, feeling frustrated and filled with self-doubt. But I was never discouraged to the point of giving up my studies. I thought I had found solace as well as a sense of purpose in the subject matter of my training, and decided nothing could break my resolve to succeed in the end.

Twelve months later I became an advanced beginner. One day I was taken to the depths of a forest to conduct the first of a series of field tests under Ahba's supervision. I perched behind a large rock, peering out into the distance as the bomb was set off. At the sound of a loud blast, a large fireball rose in the air, expanding in all directions. An accompanying shockwave which felt like a supernatural force bearing down on creation hit the trees, uprooting some and flattening others around the epicentre. I was thrilled as never before by the spectacular sights and sounds, feeling heroic and valorous.

At the end of my two-year apprenticeship, having tested hundreds of bombs built from a wide range of formulations and their variations, I had not only gained an appreciation for many of the finer points of explosive technology but also become proficient in employing explosives for special targets and situations. My extensive knowledge of the variety of fuels and detonators and a deep understanding of the intricacies of the devices proved an important asset in my chosen career.

A week after I turned fifteen, I was given the assignment to bomb a township post office in the capital city. I visited the site beforehand to determine the kind of device to be used, before a prototype was made and tested in the woods. On the night of the assignment, which was rather cool and moonless, I went with Ahba to install the bomb on a dark, deserted street outside the township post office. At midnight sharp, the bomb was detonated using a time-delay trigger mechanism. The blast brought down the front door of the post office and demolished part of an adjacent wall. I was really pleased with the result; from the extent of damage to the zero casualties, everything had been planned meticulously from the start and nothing was left to chance.

As we stood on a dark corner across the street, watching the dancing flames of the fire outside the post office, Ahba held my shoulder and said, "Maya, you've done it! Congratulations! Do you realise you could probably be the youngest explosives specialist ever produced in this country?"

At the sound of police sirens in the distance, we decided to take off. At the end of the road we turned to look back at the fire, which was getting smaller. Gazing at the red embers, Ahba said, "This is the day of your graduation, as I think I've taught you everything I know."

"Does it mean I can now make myself useful in advancing the cause of the democratic movement?" I asked excitedly.

"That has always been the idea. But there's no rush, as you're still very young. I'll get you some small jobs as a start and see how it goes. Someday I would like you to meet Dr Rice and discuss how your talent can help with the campaign," he said. "For the time being, I want you to go and experience the world at large, which you'll find more confusing and ambiguous than you already know. You're going to learn what is meant by being independent after you've matured to become more intelligent with sharper eyes and better judgment."

I saw the arrival of fire engines and police cars outside the post office and asked Ahba if we should start running.

"No, it's still early," he replied calmly and walked on at a leisurely pace. After we had turned down a path with trees on both sides, he paused to pick a flower from a low-hanging branch. He gave me the white flower, which turned out to be just a piece of folded paper. I opened the paper and saw three large words written in red ink: *Time to run.*

Ahba was already running ahead, and I couldn't help laughing as I turned on my heels to run after him. I had always prided myself in my ability to run very fast due to my long legs, slender body and light weight. I was soon running parallel to him and told him I was impressed.

"I didn't even know you'd planted the flower on the way. What's the trick?" I asked.

He slowed down to sit on a picnic bench and I sat beside him. He looked grave and serious. He said, "Do you know it is my biggest worry that once you're out there in the field, you've only yourself to depend on for your safety and protection?"

"Ahba, I'll be okay," I said. "Can't you see I'm an extremely good runner?"

"Don't be silly," he said. "It takes a lot more than being a good runner to stay out of harm's way."

"Then tell me: what is the trick?" I asked again.

With great solemnity, he said, "Now listen to this carefully: I don't care what you've done, whether you've just bombed the post office or set the parliament house on fire, I don't want you to make the mistake of getting caught in the act. And the trick is about planning your escape routes and covering your tracks with utmost care, which is more important than dabbling in your explosives with tact and sophistication."

He paused for a moment to let this sink in before he continued, "Remember, there is no reason to assume that you're more resistant to danger or even immune from calamity because you're doing something good for the people. I therefore cannot stress enough the importance of caution. You must always watch your every move, skip no minor details and don't overlook what seems to be the most obvious. One misstep is too many, which might have left the door open to catastrophe."

"I'll always be careful," I said briskly, wishing he'd stop worrying.

But he wouldn't stop. In a burst of emotions, he spoke rapidly, as if it were a matter of great urgency: "At the same time, you must always have faith in your own survival even in the most difficult situation. Although you risk your life to perpetuate the cause of the democratic movement it doesn't necessarily make you a sacrificial victim or a martyr. No, you deserve to get away with it every time without fail. You'll always come back to me safe and sound, because you will promise me that you'll treat your safety as a matter of uttermost importance…"

"I promise," I said earnestly.

He wanted to carry on, but his voice, which had become strained, failed him. After a bit of a struggle, he heaved a deep sigh, cleared his throat and muttered, "I am sorry."

Bemused, I didn't know if he was apologising for being a little emotional or if he really meant he was sorry as an expression of contrition. I was, however, too young for this kind of analysis. I just left it at that, believing only time would tell.

And time did, as time always does, with startling revelations and accidental discoveries. In time I not only found out there was always a religious side to my father, whose love, though true and profound, was also ridden with guilt. In the process I had also come to have a glimpse of my own complexity which, if I had to find words to explain it, was a combination of pride, defiance and recklessness, as well as a willingness to put my life on the line for values I believe in. My realisations didn't come about easily, but only after I had roamed about the outside world, learned my lessons the hard way and paid a heavy personal price.

At the beginning of my career, I knew it was unlikely I would get into the thick of the action anytime soon due to my inexperience. However, I never expected it could be such a poor and lacklustre start. During the first three months, I ran some secret errands, inspecting locations on the list of potential targets or collecting information about the activities at key structures considered for future strikes. I compiled my observations into reports which Ahba would pass on to a higher level via a man called U Kloh or Uncle Kloh (where U is the Burmese honourific for senior males) living in Dala, a township located on the southern bank of the Rangoon River. At other times, I dismantled old devices sitting idly in the backyard and invented new, ingenious ways of reconstructing them. I was greatly bored by the idleness, but knew Ahba was not to blame as I noticed even he wasn't getting a lot to do.

One day I went to Ahba for an explanation when I could no longer conceal my impatience.

"This is political," said Ahba. "The Prime Minister of the junta government, who is also the country's military intelligence chief, has recently announced a seven-step 'Roadmap to Democracy' for political reform with the promise of a new constitution and the first elections since 1990. The Opposition is tempted and open to negotiations. As such, the more bellicose members in the Opposition are being asked for restraint in order not to 'rock the boat' when secret talks are being held behind the scenes. Dr Rice, whose party has pledged nothing less than 'wiping the military dictatorship from the land', has reluctantly agreed to a period of hiatus. It is very quiet, I know; but if we are lying low now, it won't be long."

And Ahba was right. Not long after, the government's tall claims of national reconciliation proved just another sham and the Opposition pulled out of the reconvened national convention. So we were returning to some active business.

I was getting a batch of jobs that I had successfully pulled off by applying my skills and knowledge. But to my disappointment, because of the small scale of the jobs and at locations outside Rangoon, they had failed to cause much of a stir in society.

In the spring of the New Year, I turned sixteen, and so did Meena. Exactly one month after our birthday, I saw Ahba and Meena off at Rangoon Central Railway Station. Meena was going to Bagan for her music studies and would stay there with her maestro for a year. Ahba was sent by Dr Rice to Mandalay on a special assignment. This was the first family separation since my mother's death, and we all dressed up nicely for the occasion on the day of departure.

Meena, wearing a bright dress of yellow and red, had attracted quite some attention from other passengers at the railway station. Physically, she was slender and tall, with long black hair, clear eyes, and a ripe body with fully developed breasts. She was a hot teen, looking older than sixteen by a year or two, just like me. Actually, many boys and girls about our age tended to look very grown-up once past fifteen or sixteen, and people said it was a sign of hard times when children were expected to mature faster to take on adult responsibilities early in life.

I thought my outfit, a white shirt and a light blue skirt, was quite plain in comparison, as I wanted to maintain a low profile. But Meena told me that I was beautiful. She was always honest and her remark did not come as a surprise as we were twins. We had a lot in common, including our good looks, although we could not be more apart in other things like temperament and personality. She was more inquisitive about changing bodies, and talked about menstruation blood and bodily fluids quite openly. She made comparisons of our breasts while we were having a bath together, praising mine for their shape and size, much to my embarrassment. She fell in love with a boy who played guitar in a band when she was only fourteen and broke up three months later. She said the boy preferred girls who looked calm and composed, and wondered if she should arrange for me to meet the boy. I told her to forget about it because things like falling in love did not interest me. In my mind I had made a serious commitment to the revolutionary movement, which was almost like a vow of chastity. I thought I would remain unwed for the rest of my life. How naïve I was then.

When it was time to board, Meena was on the verge of tears. Ahba told her not to make a scene. She protested, "I'm not Maya. She's cool and contained, with graceful manners, whereas I'm always hyper and crude and impulsive!" Then she cried openly.

"That's not true," I consoled her. "You are a gentle and lovely girl, and my prettiest little sister!"

At the whistle of the train about to depart, we hugged and said our final goodbyes.

Home alone, I spent my time toying with the devices and waiting for the early return of my father. Then I received the bad news that Ahba was behind the explosion at Mandalay Marketplace. The operation, which had gone awfully awry, had killed four people and injured fifteen; and because of a possible intelligence leak, Ahba and his team members from Rangoon had gone into hiding. I couldn't help feeling depressed at the prospect of a prolonged period of doing nothing in the absence of my father. But Uncle Kloh (Ahba's friend and not a biological uncle) who brought me the news, said something that cheered me.

"Now you're the only one in Rangoon who knows how to work with explosives. I'll talk to Dr Rice to see if we can enlist your assistance on the coming *Tatmadaw Dei*."

Tatmadaw Dei, or Armed Forces Day, is held in March every year to mark the anniversary of Burmese resistance to Japan's occupation of the country during World War II. A military parade by the junta government would usually be part of the celebrations. The briefing I later received from Dr Rice via Uncle Kloh was that "at a time when all hopes for national reconciliation and political progress have been dashed, we need to send to the junta a loud and clear message that political setbacks will only serve to strengthen people's resolve in the struggle for the restoration of democracy to the country. Look forward to seeing something spectacular on *Tatmadaw Dei* from you."

In the past I had only worked on small projects that had gone almost unnoticed and I was thrilled to be given the opportunity to handle work of such importance. I thanked Uncle Kloh for Dr Rice's confidence in me and promised that he would not be disappointed.

As I worked on the project, after some careful analysis, I came to understand that the challenge was not so much about the construction of a high-powered device but to identify a suitable location for the bombing. And that challenge had been further compounded by the authorities which, prior to *Tatmadaw Dei*, had beefed up security in the capital city to defuse any threat that would disrupt the celebrations. Riot police and soldiers could be seen combing the streets with bomb-detection and landmine-clearance devices.

Eventually, after much location scouting, I found a spot near a landmark colonial architecture perfect for the operation. I put together a plan, describing in detail the time and location and the sort of devices required. I got the approval within the next twenty-four hours, and also received the materials needed for the construction of the bombs from Uncle Kloh.

On the early morning of the *Tatmadaw Dei*, two unoccupied sampans riding the waves of the ingoing tide drifted noiselessly to the jetty in front of the Strand Hotel, mixing inconspicuously in the group of floating planks moored there. At 5.00am, the bombs attached to the sampans exploded. Half of the jetty was destroyed, with its iron bridgehead collapsing in the water. The façade of the hotel was lit up at the moment of explosion and some windows on the lower floors facing the jetty were shattered by waves of the blast.

I was observing from a sampan anchored at a distance from the jetty. The city of Rangoon was still in deep sleep when the bombs went off. With black smoke rising at the jetty and police sirens wailing in the air, I laid low in the sampan to take a short nap and savor the moment of success.

At 6.00am the city of Rangoon sprang to life as a new day began. The waterway was buoyed with ferryboats shuttling between the Pansodan Jetty and Dala Township. I rowed to the nearest bank, climbed ashore and went to a teahouse for my breakfast.

Later in the evening I boarded a ferry at Pansodan Terminal for Dala, carrying the spare bomb not used in the operation with the purpose of returning it to Uncle Kloh. I would have dinner with him and debrief him on the operation.

Dala, a small but charming rural town grown out of a collection of villages and numerous ponds, is home to about 100,000 inhabitants. Uncle Kloh's house was on a street in the southern part of the town. I had visited him with Ahba before, and also a few times recently by myself to work on the *Tatmadaw Dei* operation. The narrow streets, the clock tower, and the tiny tin bell under the roof of his house had already become familiar to me.

After I walked past the clock tower, a gentle drizzle fell from the darkening sky, which became more intense as I turned into the street where Uncle Kloh lived. Without knowing why, I suddenly had the feeling of something untoward in the atmosphere.

Outside Uncle Kloh's house, as I reached for the tin bell that was tied to a rope under the roof, I noticed to my astonishment that the yellow ribbon, usually dangling at the tip of the bell, wasn't there. I was perplexed to find the windows unlit and, as I listened, it was dead silent inside. I looked at the floor and found the yellow ribbon lying flat in a crop of muddy footprints. Considerably alarmed, I immediately took my leave. At that moment, some men emerged from the darkness in the street corner. I turned to run, and the men ran after me with hounding cry and yelp as if they were chasing a hare.

I sensed great trouble and was a little desperate. But I wasn't lost, knowing clearly that after about half a mile, I would reach the town's border where there was a stretch of woods, a beach, and beyond that, a river that would take me back to Rangoon. I was, however, unsure if I would make it that far when the noises of men chasing me were getting louder and louder.

I saw a church ahead with an open door. I decided it was a place for people on the run and seeking refuge. I entered the church, walked down the aisle and found myself inside a dimly lit hall. It was almost empty except for a grey-haired old man with a crooked back sitting at the front pew. I told the old man I was in trouble and asked if I could sit down with him. He nodded, with an avuncular smile on his wrinkled face. At hearing boots thumping past the church outside, he held my hand and prayed. Then there was a moment of silence which did not last very long. The boots returned. But instead of the earlier heavy rumbling, it was the crisp sound of the boots of perhaps a single man. Now the footfall was inside the hall. They went on rising and falling in the aisle until a man appeared before the altar with his back towards us. The man, wearing a tight military outfit of dark blue and a pair of black boots stained with mud, stood looking at the crucifix on the side of the altar for a couple of seconds before turning to us and said "Hi."

My general impression of the military was people usually looking coarse and rugged, always staring about in a most alarming manner and wearing expressions from the very unpleasant to extremely disagreeable without any cause or reason whatever. But the opposite was true in this instance, and I could never forget my huge surprise as my eyes came into contact with a strong, clear-cut and handsome face. He looked mature but young, probably in his late twenties. He was a tall figure with an imposing presence. He took a card from his chest pocket, brandished it before our eyes for a fleeting moment and said, "I am Bo Tin Aung, Military Intelligence Service."

I guessed Bo was a military rank in the Tatmadaw but wasn't sure if it was the equivalent of a sergeant or a captain.

"Can I ask you if you have come across anyone who could be described as kind of suspicious passing through the church?" asked the military guy.

Without knowing how to address him, I only shook my head and muttered, "No one." To my relief, the old man supported my claim by saying, "There's absolutely no one, officer!"

"So who are you? I mean, are you related, if you don't mind?" asked the officer again, sizing me up with his clever eyes.

"Grandpa and granddaughter, officer!" returned the old man in a firm voice.

Bo Tin Aung, whose eyes had never left my face, said, "I should have guessed it. Very well then, I've no more questions. Before I go, please accept my apology for the intrusion."

He offered to shake hands with the old man, who ignored him by praying in concentration. When Bo Tin Aung asked for my hand, I felt it would be rude to refuse him. I put my hand out and he caught it, giving it a strong yet gentle squeeze. The handshake lasted much longer than I thought it should, and the sensation of his fingers touching mine almost made me swoon. He must have seen the blush on my face and loosened his grip. The old man broke his prayer and said, with a slightly befuddled expression, as if he did not quite understand all the fuss, "I'm sorry. Is my granddaughter delaying you?"

"No, not at all," said Bo Tin Aung. "But you reminded me: I'll be meeting my soldiers in a minute and I'd better go. Goodbye now." He straightened his body, raised his hand to his temple for a two-fingered salute to the old man and added, as an afterthought, "By the way, you've a very beautiful granddaughter."

He flashed me a wink before he stomped down the aisle and out of the hall. I felt both embarrassed and flattered.

The old man waited until it was safe to talk. "The guy makes me sick. What a pest!" he whined.

I felt differently about the officer and I said, "I think he has been quite friendly."

"Because he said you're pretty?!" asked the old man incredulously.

"No. But if he was honest, what's the problem with that?" I retorted.

"Nothing, except you're in big trouble," returned the old man grimly.

"What do you mean by that?"

"You don't know these people. When they say you're pretty, you're dead."

"Are you serious?" I asked in disbelief.

"If I were you, I'd be running for my life now… if it is not too late," said the old man in a grievous tone as if he had seen the end of the world.

It was unmistakably a danger warning. I was by now well over my swoon or whatever stupid sensations I had from the physical contact with the handsome officer. I stood up to go, but sat down again when I heard the sound of boots tramping on gravel and men shouting outside in the courtyard.

Someone called out in a raised voice, "Hey, guys, are you all here?"

I recognised the voice of Bo Tin Aung who went on to say, "As I can see, you've got nothing from your chase. How disappointing!"

A soldier said, his tone shy and deferential, "Boss, it's not always easy to catch someone in the environment of Dala, with the narrow streets, the ponds and all that. Besides, it's dark, and it's raining. If you go as far as the woods and the beach, you might as well swim back to Rangoon by the river."

Some soldiers laughed. Bo Tin Aung laughed with them good-naturedly. He said, "I know, I know. But that's okay. You guys have already made me proud with the arrest of the guy named Kloh…"

I almost dropped to the floor at hearing that they had got Uncle Kloh. My heart ached like it was stabbed.

Outside, Bo Tin Aung continued in his commanding voice, "It's been a long day. You have been working hard since morning. You deserve a good rest. So I think I'll call it a day and end our operation this very minute. Now, guys, you're all happily dismissed."

The soldiers burst into an explosion of jubilation. They thanked Bo Tin Aung, calling him a good man and telling him how much they loved him. They were shouting all sorts of nonsense as they left the church.

"Oh, I'm so hungry!"

"Yes, let's go back to Rangoon to eat."

"Eat, eat, eat. Doesn't anybody fuck anymore?"

When it was all quiet again, I thought I should go. The old man asked me to wait as he would go and find out if it was safe for me to leave. At the entrance, he pushed open the door slightly and poked his head out, but quickly withdrew with a gasp. He returned to the front pew and said, with an expression of awe, "I don't understand what this guy is doing. He's all alone in the courtyard, drinking like a fish!"

"Who are you talking about?" I asked.

At that moment there was a sound at the door. The old man took a quick glance at the entrance and said, "There you go. It's Bo Tin Aung."

As Bo Tin Aung entered the hall and walked down the aisle, I could see that his face was reddened and somewhat bloated, perhaps because he had been drinking; otherwise he looked normal to me. But when he came close and opened his mouth to speak, I began to detect strong alcohol on his breath.

"Grandpa, are you checking on me?" asked Bo Tin Aung.

The old man, after an awkward silence, said, "No. I didn't know you were still here... working outside in the courtyard when your soldiers are all gone."

"Yes, I've sent all my soldiers home. And you should be glad that they're gone. They are like a pack of wolves. They'd go feral if they saw your granddaughter and they'd tear her into bits and pieces," said Bo Tin Aung, chuckling as if it were only a joke.

But if it was a joke, it was not funny, I thought apprehensively.

"Grandpa, if you don't mind me asking, why are you still here?" demanded Bo Tin Aung. "By the way, have you other grandsons and granddaughters?"

"A grandson and a granddaughter, six and eight respectively, officer," returned the old man.

"Very well. Now, Grandpa, if you don't mind, can I give you a piece of friendly advice?" said Bo Tin Aung.

"What's that?"

"You are right that I'm still working while my soldiers have gone home. As a matter of fact, when I'm working, I don't like to be disturbed," said Bo Tin Aung. "I'd therefore ask you to get out of here now and leave us alone."

I was confused by what the officer meant by "us". The old man had also chosen not to understand and said, "Does it mean that I can go with my granddaughter now?"

"No, you go, she stays," said Bo Tin Aung, removing any ambiguity. When the old man still hesitated, the officer bellowed, "Move your fucking ass now, you old fool!"

The old man, looking frightened and sad, stood up to leave. But he was a brave man and he made one last attempt to save me despite the hopelessness of the situation. As he went to the entrance, he paused there and turned to say to Bo Tin Aung, "What do you want, officer? I beg you. Please don't do bad things to her."

"What makes you think I'd do bad things to her? Are you demented or what?" growled Bo Tin Aung. "Do you know me? I'm the good Tatmadaw, one of the best! I'll only protect her and permit nothing bad to happen to her, okay? But I'm sorry I cannot give you the same guarantee. And please be warned: if you don't go now, you will not be able to see your real grandson and granddaughter for a very long time."

I knew the old man had to go if he didn't want to get himself into trouble. But I didn't want to see him go and I turned my face away from the entrance to the altar and the wall at the back where there was a statue of Jesus nailed to the cross. Then I heard the sound of the door opening and closing and my heart sank, knowing the old man was gone.

Bo Tin Aung sat down next to me. He said, "I know you're afraid, but that is not necessary. I'm a good Tatmadaw. I only want to ask you some questions. You satisfy me... with your answers, and I'll let you go."

"Promise?" I said, sitting up to look him in the face. "Promise you won't do bad things to me?"

"Upon my word, okay?" he said. "Now, tell me what you were doing outside the house of U Kloh."

I had anticipated the question coming, and I had the story ready. I said, "U Kloh is my uncle. He is a kind and harmless man, a Buddhist, who would not step on an ant if he could avoid it. He is also weak in health, suffering from tuberculosis. I think you've got the wrong man. He's innocent."

"It's up to me to decide if he is innocent or not," he said coldly. "Please continue, perhaps with something about yourself."

"I lost my parents in the civil war, and Uncle Kloh, as my only remaining relative, has taken care of me like my own father…" I told my story confidently because there was a lot of truth in it. Uncle Kloh, a lecturer at Rangoon University, was sacked for having taken part in the 1988 demonstration. He had contracted tuberculosis during his incarceration in Central Prison Insein. After being released on conditional amnesty, he found a job as a nightshift doorman in a company making industrial products. I knew I could not be too honest with Bo Tin Aung by telling him everything about my parents, but again I had not lied about the fact that I had lost my mother in the war between government troops and the insurgents. When I thought of my mother, I broke into tears.

Bo Tin Aung showed a surprising sensitivity to my emotional outburst. He patted my shoulder and let me cry. I felt thankful, but only briefly. I was completely turned off when he, not long after I began telling my story, scratched the area around his crotch as if to ease a perpetual itch from time to time. It was disgusting for a man of his good looks to behave with such vulgarity in public.

He asked me to resume my story.

"Uncle Kloh lives alone in Dala. Because he is weak and poor, I visit him regularly with food and medicine…" Then I stopped again when he moved from vulgar to gross by fumbling with the buttons of his trousers.

"Can I be frank with you?" I boldly said. "You know what you are doing is rather indecent."

He grabbed his crotch and said, "You mean this?"

"I believe you're a different Tatmadaw who is good and handsome and civilised. Please don't ruin my good impression of you."

"Then marry me," he said, totally out of the blue.

"That's not funny," I said angrily. "If you don't mind, please stop doing a thing like that."

"I'm sorry, but here's something you don't know," he said, looking at his crotch. "I have been drinking and want a leak. I can't just walk away when you're telling me something personal, as I don't want to be impolite or arrogant. But you know it's always hard to try to hold a pee. If I've embarrassed you, I apologise."

I said nothing. I felt better when he apologised and stopped fumbling in his trousers.

"What's that?" he suddenly asked, looking to his right. "Is it a confessional box?"

On the right-hand side of the hall there was a wooden box by the wall and a model of a manger with a cradle and little Jesus near it. Bo Tin Aung rose to his feet and said, "I don't mean to be rude, but you know I cannot leave you here and go to the toilet outside. I think I'll use the box in the circumstances. Please excuse me."

He teetered away as if he had real trouble with his bladder. Then I had an idea. I shouted after him, "Can I make a request, officer?"

He rushed inside the confessional box and shouted back. "What is it?"

"While you're doing… what you have to do, can I light a candle for my dead parents at the altar?"

"Go ahead! Ohh! Ahh!" he groaned loudly as he relieved himself.

Judging from the gushing sound coming from the box, I guessed it was going to be a long piss. I took the opportunity to walk up to the altar. At the end wall where the crucifix hung, I found the main switch, which I had spotted earlier when I was sitting in the front pew. I pulled the switch down and the hall was blacked out in an instant.

In the dark, I could hear Bo Tin Aung curse loudly, "Shit! Power outage again when I'm having a leak!" Then he must have remembered that I was lighting a candle at the altar and called across the hall, "Can you bring a candle to the mobile toilet?"

I answered back in a clear and most reassuring voice, "Yes, of course, officer!"

While the guy continued with his long piss, I tiptoed down the aisle and went straight for the entrance. As I opened the door to slip out, I heard the guy scream from the box, "Where is my candle?!" Without wasting a second, I slammed the door shut behind me and started to run.

The rain outside, which had been going on since the evening, seemed to have grown heavier with an easterly wind. I felt nothing but grateful for the bad weather, believing it would discourage whoever it was on my trail and help my escape.

I ran and ran, and after about a quarter of an hour, reached the stretch of woods on the border of the town. I waited among the trees. After some time, as all I had listened to was the sound of rain pattering on the thick canopy of leaves, I decided it was safe to push forward. I stayed low, so low that at times I had to crawl on my belly through the narrow spaces between the trees. Though it was dark I never lost my direction. An hour later I began to hear the pleasant sounds of waves and knew I had made it to the river.

At night, Dala beach was all but deserted in the wind and rain. The Rangoon River was obscured by thick darkness. As I scanned the long, desolate expanse of sand from left to right, I found no sampans except some loose wooden logs pitting against each other in the nearby water. As such there was nothing to do except wait, in the hope that the wind and rain would in time abate and a fishing boat would appear that would carry me away.

I found a relatively dry spot in the woods where I sat down with my back against the trunk of a tree to wait. I felt a little hungry and took an apple from my backpack to eat. Then I closed my eyes, just to relax, as the bad weather wasn't going to disappear anytime soon.

I didn't know if I had nodded off or not. In the boredom of waiting I might have felt drowsy or even slightly sleepy, but I knew I had always maintained a high level of alertness to changes in my surroundings.

Yet, when I opened my eyes after some time, I was surprised to see that the weather had turned from bad to clement, almost without a noticeable transition. I thought I had probably had a momentary lapse in concentration, or even a nap. I didn't exactly know.

I stood up, feeling chilly. I thought I might have caught a cold after sitting idly in the woods for the past hour. I sneezed explosively and the muscles in my right leg suddenly ached and cramped. At this moment I wasn't sure if I had seen a flickering light on the river. I stepped out of the woods in order to see clearly whether it was a fishing boat that I had been waiting for. The sand under my feet was soft like mud after the rain, and I laboriously dragged myself farther and farther out of the woods for a better view, despite my cramp.

But there was no fishing boat. Instead, the light concerned was only the reflection of the Shwedagon Pagoda, perched on a hilltop and beautifully illuminated at night, throbbing and shimmering in the water of the Rangoon River. Given my sorry plight, I felt the need to say a little prayer to the Buddhas residing in Shwedagon. When I had just begun crossing my fingers to pray, I suddenly heard a sound in the air, which was loud like a howl in a vacuum. Aghast, I turned in the direction of the sound and saw the shadow of a man racing towards me like a cannonball. I took fright, trying to retreat into the woods. But it was too late; within seconds, I was knocked to the ground as the man collided into me. I struggled to stand up, flinging my arms about and kicking with my legs.

"Now will you stop fighting me?!" the man said, and I immediately recognised the voice of Bo Tin Aung. I refused to yield, but he eventually succeeded in overpowering me and restrained me from further struggle by handcuffing my hands behind my back.

He helped me to sit on my haunches. Kneeling beside me he said, "Isn't it romantic that we should meet again here on the beach, enjoying an excellent view of the Shwedagon Pagoda?"

I never imagined things could go from bad to worse with such rapidity and I began to cry.

"What is this?" he asked. "You should be glad that I've found you first. Didn't I tell you some soldiers are just like beasts that'd eat you up alive?"

I stopped crying and I asked him, "What about you? Are you going to rape me?"

"No, I don't do rape, even though some people say we're licensed. But there's no truth in the accusation," he said solemnly. "I only do marriage. I wanted to marry you from the very first moment I set eyes on you in the church, and I want to marry you now!"

"It is still rape if you're going to do it by force," I said.

"Don't worry. I despise violence, as I am, after all, a peace-loving man," he said. "I'd only marry you after you'd settled down quietly and peacefully."

What he said seemed to carry a glimmer of hope. I felt I needed a strategy, and said, "I don't know how serious you are about marrying me..."

"Very, very serious," he interrupted with a quick answer.

"If so, what about this: if we were to get married, I think we should do it properly, by having a small ceremony in Shwedagon Pagoda with the blessing of a high monk; as you know, I am only sixteen," I said, thinking this would perhaps buy me some time if he agreed.

"Only sixteen? Just like a babe!" he said with undisguised excitement in his voice. "A ceremony at Shwedagon Pagoda with the blessing of the monks? What a great idea! It's so beautiful, almost like a wedding vow."

"Does it mean a yes?"

"I can't say yes just yet," he said. "I would like to have a drink first."

He took out a wine flask made of tin or stainless steel from the inner chest pocket of his uniform and drew a large gulp from it. He passed me the flask and said, "Drink with me and I promise you that we'll have our wedding in Shwedagon Pagoda."

I declined, as I didn't want to drink with him in spite of his promise.

"Just a sip, okay?" he said. "You only have to open your mouth."

I knew I'd better cooperate just to be friendly. I opened my mouth for a sip. The liquor was very strong with a pungent smell. I coughed and spat out what was in my mouth. He waited until I was feeling better and asked me to open my mouth again. When I refused, he forced my mouth open with one hand and poured the wine into my mouth with the other. The wine went all the way down my throat. I spluttered and choked, thinking I was about to drown.

"I can help myself if you uncuff me," I mumbled, feeling my tongue stiffen under the effect of the alcohol.

As if he hadn't heard, he went on dispensing the wine down my throat the inhumane way. I choked and coughed violently. As he did it again and again, the stuff turned my mind into a horrible muddle.

"Please! More… no more…" I cried incoherently.

"Oh, I'm sorry. Did you say you want me to uncuff you?" He uncuffed me and said, "You may go now if you like."

I clambered to my feet and, in spite of feeling an unbearable heaviness of body and mind, I managed to stagger a dozen steps without falling down.

He had all along been following me and whispering in my ear as if to encourage, "Very well done. Just keep going, one step at a time and you will soon be able to swim in the river."

I tried, but my feet were so heavy, as if they were rooted in deep mud, and my vision of things around me had turned into a horrible blur. Then he went for the kill with a tap on my shoulder and a shove in my back. This proved to be my undoing as I collapsed face down on the sand, losing my consciousness. As a consequence I was violated and defiled while I was perfectly ignorant of what went on in my knocked-out state.

How long I was unconscious I did not know. I woke up lying on the soft sand of the beach, my clothes in disarray. I pulled up my jeans and found my inner thighs stained with blood. I also felt an incisive pain in my belly. I knew I had become a new victim of rape. This was simply too much for me to bear. I felt devastated and completely hopeless, as though it was the end of the world. I began to contemplate killing myself.

I remembered there was a spare bomb in my backpack, which I had been carrying for the purpose of returning it to Uncle Kloh. It seemed quite handy now that I was thinking about committing suicide. Although it was still night and dark in the woods, it did not take me too much time to recover the backpack under a tree. I took out the bomb and connected the key wires. Next I set the trigger to detonate with a five-minute delay. Then I changed my mind and reset it to ten minutes as if I were the God of Death who could lengthen or shorten one's life on a whim.

On second thoughts I reset the device to five minutes, thinking why would I need another five minutes of a life damaged and wasted? Then I lay on my back, waiting with closed eyes and listening quietly to the sounds of the universe that were going to vanish forever with my demise.

I heard the rustling of leaves in the wind and the waves lapping on the shore; I also heard the beating of my heart, and the flow of air as I breathed in and out. But in the midst of all this, I also heard, to my bewilderment, the snoring of a man.

I rose to my feet and went around in search of the ugly sound. And to my astonishment I found the body of Bo Tin Aung sprawled under a tree nearby. Asleep and snoring, he was strangely clad in full uniform, as if whatever he had committed earlier was just routine in his daily duty. In my outrage and humiliation I picked up the backpack and threw it at his body. He didn't move a bit, he only snored. I kicked him in the buttocks. He awakened, and sat up, staring blandly at me for a long moment before he said, "Good morning. How are you doing?"

I was so angry that I couldn't utter a word.

He looked out to the river with a yawn, and announced he needed to wash his face. I noticed that he was sitting on the backpack without knowing it contained a bomb which was ticking toward the point of oblivion. I knelt down before him, barring his way. In my mind, I wanted him dead as much as I wanted to kill myself.

He stayed where he was. "What's it you want?" he asked.

"You did something horrible to me. Why?" I said.

"Oh you mean… well it's hard to say exactly," he said. "I think it is because I love you."

"That's bullshit," I said. "I'm a girl, only sixteen, and now I have woken up without my virginity. My life is now totally ruined by you. I don't think I can live anymore."

"Calm down," he said. "There's nothing that cannot be fixed."

"How?"

"I think we discussed earlier about getting married at Shwedagon Pagoda with the blessing of a high monk. Let's do it," he said. "You might have imagined there was a rape. But there was no rape – only premarital sex – should we become husband and wife."

It was a clever argument, I thought. But I wasn't to be fooled. Rape is a horrible crime, and no one should be able to get away with impunity. I said, "I'm sorry. But I'm going to die anyway. If you truly love me, then you're invited to join me in death."

"Always a pleasure," he said casually, with a charming smile. "But shall I remind you, if you die now, you won't see your father ever again."

"My father?"

"U Kloh, your uncle, who has brought you up like your own father," he said. "He should now be languishing in a cell in Central Prison Insein. Here is the simple fact: you die, he dies too. But if you marry me, I can promise you that he'll not be tortured as long as I am around. And I can arrange for you to visit him too; how about that? Do you want to see your father again?"

I cried as if he had struck me where I was most vulnerable. The mention of Uncle Kloh had reminded me of Ahba and Meena, whom I thought I also wouldn't be seeing again if I died now. That would be tragic and I cried fiercely, feeling a deep and unexpected sadness.

"Now stop crying like a baby. You're with me, and everything is going to be fine," he said, holding me and stroking my hair.

It felt cosy and warm in his embrace. I was surprised that I didn't put up any resistance. I wondered if there was some kind of secret force at work which was changing me. If I was stubborn and impractical a moment ago, I was now malleable and open to persuasion. Suddenly dying was no longer an option. And I must live because I wanted to save the life of Uncle Kloh, and I badly needed to see my father, Ahba, and my little sister, Meena, again.

As I was becoming more realistic and accepting, I began to find the man who was holding me in his arms not so detestable but quite likeable instead, not to mention he was also very good looking.

He fixed my face with a stare and asked, "Will you hold your breath a moment for me?"

I thought he was going to kiss me and I was not going to turn him down. But he didn't. He only waited in silence for a couple of seconds before he said, "It is strange but I keep hearing this buzz, like the ticking of a clock."

Oh shit! He had reminded me. I felt that I had to be honest with him in the circumstances. And I told him that he was sitting on a bomb.

He couldn't quite comprehend what I said and he asked, "What kind of bomb?"

"The explosive kind, of course!" I answered.

His face went pale and he mumbled nervously, "You mean there's a bomb here! What do we do now? Are we going to die for real?"

Realising the bomb was about to explode any second now, I dragged him up and said, "Yes, if we don't get out of here at once!"

With great urgency we sprinted away towards the river, and threw our bodies in the water the moment the bomb exploded with a thunderous bang. Sand and loose twigs were blown in all directions by the strong blast, like a multitude of missiles, and we stayed underwater waiting for the blitz to subside. Later, as we rose to the surface, we saw some trees in the woods were still burning like a bonfire.

He said, his voice filled with awe as well as gratitude, "You've saved my life!"

I said nothing, daunted by the thought of having to explain about the bomb. I fell back in the water and let my body drift along with the waves. He swam after me, yelling from behind, "You're my saviour. I'll go wherever you go!"

When the fire in the woods had turned to dying smoke, we swam back and made for the shore. He was the first to reach the shallow water near the beach. As soon as he could stand upright and walk on the sand, he picked me up and cradled me in his strong arms. My heart beat violently when I felt we were like characters in a fairytale of mermaid and prince supporting each other after a shipwreck in a stormy sea.

Advancing up the beach, he paused a while when the water was still waist-deep, and said, "If I haven't made it clear, let me say this: I have meant to marry you ever since I first set eyes on you. Therefore, may I formally ask you: Will you marry me?"

He completely caught me by surprise. Perhaps there was a fine distinction between a good and a bad Tatmadaw, I thought. He could have arrested me for possessing a bomb, or he could kill me after he had raped me and dump my body in the river. But instead he was asking me to marry him, which seemed too good to be true in my untenable position.

"Say something, please," he urged, his face flushing. "Will you marry me?"

"Yes, I will," I muttered, deciding that 'marrying my rapist' was the best option available if I didn't want to become a girl to disappear unaccountably.

11

M . A . Y . A .

———

Rape notwithstanding, Bo Tin Aung was actually a terribly good Tatmadaw, as I came to discover.

Once back in Rangoon, he could have arrested me and thrown me into a ring of wolves in some dark dungeon. But he didn't. Instead he took me home, which was an apartment on the top floor of a multistorey building situated in a quiet residential area on the fringes of the city.

As a result of my battered experience, I fell sick for a whole week, and he took good care of me. Then I recovered, and he asked me to stay because we were getting married. I had to stay, as it was impossible to leave his apartment. He locked the door from the outside when he went to work; the windows in the living room with the view of a newly constructed road some distance away were covered with an iron grating. Another window in the kitchen was very small, almost like a hole on a jail door; even if I could manage to squeeze my petite body through, I probably would fall to my death from the height.

Claiming to be my husband-to-be, he did exercise his right to use my body for carnal purposes, but always with the decency of first asking my permission. When I refused, he'd sulk and get drunk. Every time he was drunk, he'd complain loudly about the outside noise of vehicles screeching to a stop before the traffic lights at the newly constructed road. Then he'd go ahead with what he had in mind without asking my permission a second time. As always, he'd apologise for his beastly behaviour afterwards and beg for my forgiveness.

A month into our cohabitation, he stopped raising the subject of marrying me with a ceremony at Shwedagon Pagoda, as if he had a better idea. This happened after he had asked me about the bomb that went off at Dala beach. I could see the question coming and I had the story ready.

I first told him something about my uncle, U Kloh, who worked for a company which provided high-quality explosives to large and small-to-medium-sized businesses in the mining, quarrying and construction sectors. Each day, industrial explosives were packaged according to orders received, and special blasting devices included on request. These products were nicknamed "firecrackers". Uncle Kloh, to supplement his meagre wage as a nightshift doorman, would also help with the delivery of the packaged explosives to companies in the Rangoon Division during daytime for some extra income. His firm would sometimes give him delivery orders to companies somewhat remote, and because of the long distance, Uncle Kloh would usually ask me to go on his behalf. And what had happened was: on *Tatmadaw Dei*, I delivered about a dozen packaged explosives to a construction company in Hmawbi Township in the northwest of the city. But it was a bad day, and the transaction went kind of sour. One of the goods was found to be defective and had to be returned. Because the order was left incomplete, it meant that not only had I not earned my fee, which was usually paid by the client (sometimes with a tip), I also had to return to the company in Hmawbi later with the replacement. So I really wasn't in the mood when I went to see Uncle Kloh on that fated evening with the defective "firecracker". When I was chased by what appeared to be "a pack of wolves", I only acted on my instinct and ran for my life. Then I was tracked down on the beach and without knowing why, the defective "firecracker" went berserk and exploded accidentally; but fortunately nobody was hurt in the incident.

I thought my story was nearly flawless because it was true to a large extent. Uncle Kloh did work for a company specialising in commercial explosive products as a doorman and a temporary deliveryman. What

I didn't say was that he also had the key to the store of explosives, and provided my father with materials for the manufacture of devices for anti-junta activities.

Bo Tin Aung was not totally convinced. As if he had spotted the weakest link in my story, he asked, "How did you know the firecracker was defective? You don't just take it back when someone tells you it is defective!"

"I did a test with it!" I blurted out in a hurry to defend my story. "I only agreed to take it back when it was proved to be defective." Then I realised I needed better imagination to prevent my story from falling apart, and I said, "Uncle Kloh has taught me tests to determine if the explosive goods are functional. It is very useful, as I can tell if something is actually wrong with the product or if the customer is only being difficult."

Bo Tin Aung was not persuaded, and he followed up with a more deadly question, "Has your uncle also taught you how to make bombs?"

Pretending not to notice his face tight as a fist, I replied casually, as if I had absolutely nothing to hide, "Firecrackers, yes; bombs, no. I've learnt how to make firecrackers that can blast off with a really loud noise to scare away stray dogs."

It appeared that he was finally satisfied with my answer as his dark, frigid demeanour began to thaw by returning to his good looks and charm. At twenty-nine (the age he claimed) he was boyishly handsome and could pass for a college student when he was wearing jeans and a white T-shirt instead of his dark uniform. But I couldn't quite explain the subtle change in his expression, as the more I talked, the more I felt he was developing some special interest in me. My guess was that he had probably conceived a genuine fondness for me, that of a man towards a woman.

Then, out of the blue, he said, "You know how much people would pay for anyone who can successfully bomb the City Hall in Rangoon? Ten million kyat! It is very attractive, isn't it?"

I played dumb, without reacting to what he said. I told him I was tired, and wanted to go to sleep. He followed me to the bedroom, and asked perfunctorily for permission to sleep with me. I refused, but he went ahead as if he had not heard me.

After two months locked up in his apartment, I was beyond bored with my life of captivity. I began putting up more resistance when he asked for permission to fuck me.

"What's the matter with you?" he said angrily. "Are we not husband and wife?"

"No, not until we have had our wedding ceremony at Shwedagon Pagoda," I insisted.

"That means you don't know the law," he said, explaining, "In our country, there are three ways of becoming husband and wife. First, a man and a woman are brought into marriage by their parents, then live and eat together; second, a man and a woman are brought together by a go-between and then live and eat together; and third, a man and a woman come together by mutual consent, then live and eat together. A ceremony is not a prerequisite, and marriage in Buddhism is purely a contract founded with the consent of the parties, evidenced by openly living together."

"That is bullshit. In our country we don't even have a constitution. We also don't have proper functioning law, except perhaps the law of the jungle," I retorted. "You call this a marriage? I call it a crime, an abduction!"

He did not want to argue with me. He thought he was big and muscular, and could easily tame me into submission. He beat me up; I had bruises all over my body. I fought back, and he received claw marks and bites on his face and arms in return. Slowly he began to get tired of the fights and wanted peace. One day he said, "You know I love you. Can't we just live like an ordinary couple without killing each other every time we go to bed?"

"That could only happen if you honour our relationship with a proper wedding ceremony." I stood my ground, and gave him a kick in the loins when he was looking in the other direction. This time I had really incapacitated him, and it took him a week to recover his manliness.

At last he seemed to have learnt his lesson and proposed a solution to the situation after exactly a hundred days of me being confined to his apartment. "Let's get married at Shwedagon Pagoda if the idea appeals to you."

By this time I had also undergone imperceptible changes in my emotional life as a result of the physical closeness and intimacy while in captivity. Every morning I felt sorry to see him leave for work, and waited with impatient expectancy for his return in the evening. He was a rough man with a temper, never an ideal companion in my imagination. But I might have been desperate in my predicament and allowed myself to be charmed. I craved more and more of his company as well as the physical love that I was beginning to enjoy.

"So, it's really happening?" I sounded incredulous. "When?"

"I've talked to the monks at Shwedagon Pagoda," he said. "They'll choose a date for the ceremony. But they want to first interview us because you're only sixteen."

I had always thought that he would bury me instead of marrying me after he had grilled me about the bomb. But I was wrong. I began to think his love was real.

"Please marry me," he said, kneeling down before me with a glittering gold ring in his hand.

"Oh! It's very beautiful!" I yelped, with tears brimming in my eyes. "This must be very expensive."

"Yes, it has cost me a fortune," he said. "I have been saving up my salary to buy it. That's why I could not have gone ahead with the ceremony earlier."

It didn't sound like he was lying. I became so emotional I wept. He placed the ring on my index finger and held me. I sat crying in his arms, hardly believing my dream had come true. The past three months, with all the domestic fights and spousal rape, as well as the emotional and human affection inherent in our stormy relationship, must have changed me significantly. They had also fully prepared me psychologically for the role of a good wife worthy of a terribly good Tatmadaw officer.

He said, "There's nothing I value more than making a permanent commitment to you. We're going to build a happy family together, and we'll have many children…"

"Many children?" I cried out. "You think me some sort of pig?"

"That's not it. I might have exaggerated. If not many children, give me a son, and I'll be very happy," he said, his eyes tearful as if he really wanted to have a son. "We'll need a bigger house for it. I therefore want to get rich and get rich really quick. You must help me to achieve that."

I thought he had said something standard and conventional, similar to what any man would say when they propose. And I replied, also with something I believed to be typical of an acceptance speech, "Of course. As your wife, I'll do anything to contribute to your wealth and success."

He responded with a big smile and kissed me. Then we went to bed, and for the first time, he fucked me with well-granted permission. Also for the first time, I came to appreciate what conjugal felicity was about.

Afterwards, when we were spent and lying exhausted in bed, he suddenly said, "Tomorrow is going to be important."

"Why? Because we're having this interview with the monks?" I asked.

"That too, of course," he said. "But you'll also be meeting my best friend Shit-Lone later in the afternoon."

"Shit-Lone? What sort of name is that?"

"His full name is Aung-Myint-Tin-Oo-Pan-Thi-Ta-Lone," he said. "Obviously for a name it is very long, and for purposes of convenience, he is more commonly known as 'Shit-Lone' which means 'eight words'."

"Why should I be meeting him?"

"Shit-Lone is the vice-chairman on the board of the township's 'Restoration of Peace and Stability' committee. Recently we have had a serious problem in the military intelligence bureau, and he's working with me for a solution. I think it is useful to get you involved, thinking you could be bored living here," he said. "You'd be interested to hear that Shit-Lone has the idea of making us filthy rich in the process."

I was perplexed by what he said when we were still sweating between the sheets. But I felt exhausted after the physical exertions, and I said, with a yawn, "Can we not talk about this Shit... now? I need some sleep so that I look my best when we go to see the monks at Shwedagon tomorrow."

He showed himself to be very considerate. "Very well," he said, and kissed me goodnight.

We arose early in the morning and went to Shwedagon Pagoda for our meeting with the monks. I was beyond excited when I saw the Pagoda from afar, perched upon a green knoll at the top of Singuttara Hill, with its spire soaring skyward and its main stupa looking like a gigantic mass of gold in the shape of an inverted bowl.

Our taxi stopped at the southern entrance. We alighted and began to climb up the covered stairway lined with shops selling Buddha images, incense, antiques, flowers and other offerings. Before entering the Pagoda, we left our shoes behind at a flower shop. The shopkeeper, a tiny old man with betel-stained teeth, after a fearful glance at Bo Tin Aung, handed me a bundle of the flowers of the season. I accepted the bundle and asked him the price.

But Bo Tin Aung interrupted dismissively, "No bother. It's a gift."

The old man agreed meekly, "It's a gift, of course. No pay, officer."

I did not feel very comfortable about it, but Bo Tin Aung marched ahead without concerning himself by at least acknowledging the old man's kind gesture with either a nod or a charitable smile, as if the gift was part of his military rights and privileges.

We showed up at the Visitors' Registration Office on the west side of the Pagoda and informed the staff we had arranged to meet a venerable monk for the counsel of our marriage. We were asked to put down our personal particulars, like name and date of birth, on a piece of paper. A young monk told us to wait, explaining that all the senior monks on duty were engaged at the moment. Bo Tin Aung looked impatient and the young monk suggested we take a walk outside and he could come and fetch us later when a senior monk had become available.

The time was about ten in the morning. The sun was on an ascending path and the air was cool. It was very comfortable to walk on the ground with our bare feet when the marble floor had not yet been heated up by the sunlight, which would become fierce approaching noon. In a clockwise direction, we strolled around the main stupa on a route of planetary posts. Each planetary post has a Buddha image. Pilgrims go through the ritual of offering flowers and prayer flags and pouring water on the image.

Bo Tin Aung, wearing a black longyi and a long-sleeved white shirt, was extremely handsome. He had bought me an outfit of a white-silver sarong and a matching green shirt. I thought the dress must fit me well when people kept turning their heads to look at me. Strolling in light steps, my small hand in the grip of his large hand, I felt so sweet, thinking we must be among some of the happiest couples visiting the Shwedagon Pagoda.

As we were walking towards the Hall of Great Prosperity, we saw two novice monks waiting in our path. The one on the left, a boy of about thirteen with a smart face and eager black eyes, greeted us.

"Good morning," he said. "My name is Balu. May I have the pleasure of informing you that my master is now waiting to see you?"

"At last," Bo Tin Aung grumbled.

"My master would like to meet the lady first," continued the boy-monk. "And the gentleman to follow in turn, if necessary."

Displeased, Bo Tin Aung groaned, "How long will it take? One hour, two hours? What am I going to do with all this time?"

"Perhaps my colleague can show you around inside the Hall of Great Prosperity if you like," Balu suggested politely.

"Is it all right if I go alone?" I asked Bo Tin Aung.

"I don't see why not," he said with a shrug of his shoulders. "In fact, the monks don't need to see me at all, as they know me well. You just go ahead; it's no big deal. I think you'll probably get a lecture on how to serve your husband properly and satisfy… all his needs without fail under the doctrine of Buddhism. Well, I hope you'll have a good time. I'll see you later."

He turned away, starting for the Hall of Great Prosperity. Balu's colleague, also a novice monk of about the same age, hurried after the officer with a low-bowing head as if he was fearful of him.

At Balu's request, I followed him to the south side of the pagoda. After we had walked past the University Boycotters' Memorial, we arrived at a corner where there was a large banyan tree. Under the shade of the tree stood an old monk in his late fifties, whom I believed to be Balu's master. I walked up to the monk and bowed in obeisance. The monk, wearing a robe of coarse material in a dark tan colour, had a calm face and serious eyes. He looked at me and said, "Maya! Is it really you, my little Maya?"

It sounded quite odd to me, and I wondered if it was some monks' way of talking with a big heart of love and compassion. I replied, "Yes, I'm Maya. How do you do, my Venerable Master?"

He ignored my greeting and went straight on to say, to my huge surprise, "Maya, what you are doing is totally inappropriate. Do you know why?"

I was confused. "Master, what is your question again?" I asked.

"You are marrying a *Tatmadaw Bo*. Why?" he said, in an unmistakable tone of disapproval.

I felt the old monk seemed to have a bias against the Tatmadaw, and I replied, boldly, "Because I love him, and because he is a terribly good Tatmadaw."

The old monk shot back almost at once, "But what will your father say?"

"My father?" I said. "I filled out a form at the Visitors' Registration Office when I came in this morning, on which I've declared both of my parents dead."

The monk took out a paper from inside his robe, which I recognised as the form I had mentioned. He said, "I no longer advise on marital matters these days. But I saw your form and I have decided to take it up myself. Now, will you tell me if you have lied about the date of your birth?"

"No," I said. "I was born on the day of the *Pyatho* Full Moon, exactly as I have put down on the paper."

"Then you must have lied about your parents," the monk said. "Shall I tell you that one of your parents is not dead? Your poor mother is dead, I'm sorry; but your father is still alive and going strong. Shall I also tell you that, my little Maya, he is now hiding in Mandalay?"

I could not have been more stunned by what he said. After a long awkward silence, I was finally able to utter, "Who are you, my Venerable Master?"

The old monk said, "I am U Vicitta. I have known your father since I was the abbot of a little monastery in Shan and he was a Tatmadaw officer some years ago."

I looked around, afraid what we said would be overheard by the passing visitors. But we were in a quiet corner of the pagoda, and there was only me, the old monk and Balu, who was standing some distance from us and looking in the other direction. I asked U Vicitta if it was safe to talk in the presence of his novice monk, and he replied, "Don't worry. Balu is my best disciple."

I asked, "May I know, if you don't mind, as you are an acquaintance of my father, if you had a problem with my mother marrying a Tatmadaw?"

"No."

"Then I don't understand, if my mother could marry a Tatmadaw, why can't I?" I pursued.

"Did I say you can't?" said U Vicitta. "Maya, my only fear is that you, at only sixteen, are way too young to make a decision which you'll regret later."

Unfazed, I said, "Bo Tin Aung is a good man. Of course he's not perfect. Same as everyone, he has his faults and weaknesses. But I'm confident he'll make a good husband."

"Oh, you're still a child, a silly little girl," said U Vicitta. "You are the same as your mother who was also quite stubborn."

"And you knew my mother well?" I asked curiously.

"Yes. Do you know your face is a striking reminder of how beautiful your mother was? She wasn't only pretty but also graceful and elegant, every inch the descendant of a true princess of the Shan Sao Hpas royal family."

"And stubborn too?"

"Yes, yes," U Vicitta answered with a smile. "She was very stubborn, particularly about the choice of husband. But I did not have a problem with the man she chose. In fact, I married them in my monastery."

"Then give me your approval. The man I'm going to marry is also a good Tatmadaw like my father," I said.

U Vicitta sighed. "Maya, it makes me sad that you know almost nothing about your father. If you think your Tatmadaw officer and your father belong to the same crop of men, you are very wrong."

"How can you say that I know nothing about my father...?" I stammered in protest. I thought I had my suspicions about Ahba's secret life in the past but he had already come clean about it.

U Vicitta said no more. He began to walk away, out of the shade of the banyan tree and down a lane off the main circuitous route. I walked after him, the novice monk Balu keeping one step behind me. After we had come to the level ground again, U Vicitta led the way into a modern three-storey building surrounded by iron fences. Balu told me it was the Museum Library and Archive. No visitors were permitted at the time when the museum was under renovation.

After the old monk had turned the corner he paused before a low wall and a pavilion behind it. Balu whispered to me that it was the Museum of the Buddha. U Vicitta unlocked the door of the museum with a large key. Before we entered, he said to Balu, "Can you keep an eye on the gentleman, please? I'm tired of getting complaints about him drinking in the prayer halls behind the Buddha statues."

Balu took the instruction with a reverential bow to his master. He also bowed to me before he took his leave.

U Vicitta took me to the shrine room in the museum. The place was dimly lit probably because the museum was under renovation. After we had sat down before a platform with the statues of five sitting Buddhas, U Vicitta pushed a button on the wall and the little light that had remained also went out in an instant.

I was a little scared, and I asked, "My Venerable Master, what is this about? I can't see anything."

"Because you're blind," said the voice of U Vicitta.

"No. I'm not blind. It's dark," I said.

"Maybe it's dark. But if you look at the world with only your eyes and not also with wisdom, you are the same as blind," said U Vicitta.

"My Venerable Master, what are you trying to tell me?"

"Because of the little you know…" U Vicitta paused, and resumed after a while, "… I'm going to tell you the story of a man who was made to traverse miles and miles of a pitch-black forest which was also heavily strewn with landmines. In the end he made his escape unscathed."

"But how does it help… in my case?" I asked.

"I believe the story will lead to a deeper understanding of your situation," replied U Vicitta. "At the end of the story, if you're stupid you'll become a little cleverer. If dumb, smarter. I hope you'll also gain some wisdom about the human condition. If not, you can at least tell the difference between a good and a very bad Tatmadaw."

12

Z.E.Y.A.

—❧—

His name was Zeya.

His father died when he was only three years old. When he was five, his elder and only brother died. When he was six, his elder and only sister also died. His mother married again, but soon afterwards, his stepfather died too. His mother died six months after the death of his stepfather. The causes of death of his parents and siblings, some natural and some accidental, through sickness, suicide and sometimes murder, were no more banal than the seasons in a world of vicissitudes; only with the small consequence of setting the scene for the little Zeya to become a *samanera* (novice monk) at the age of thirteen. In the monastery, he was taught Buddhist scriptures by the abbot, the Venerable Sayadaw U Okka. At the age of seventeen, Zeya attended a sermon on *Abhidhamma*, whose ideas and doctrines had greatly steeled his mind to become a monk for life. In the year he turned twenty, he was made a *bhikkhu* (ordained male monk), fully and formally. In that same year of his ordination, when he was still adapting to his newly acquired status of refuge and learning to renounce body and mind, life's vagaries took another twist, which had him thrown right back into the everyday world of the torments of the damned.

The abbot of the monastery, the Venerable Sayadaw U Okka, with over fifty years of monkhood in the observance of *Dhamma and Vinaya* (Buddhist understanding and discipline), was well versed in the Pali Canonical text. He was a known authority on *Abhidhamma Pitaka* (the psycho-ethical analysis of things in the ultimate sense in contrast to conceptual forms). He set up a monastery school in his township to provide free education to the poor, and a village hospital to care for the sick. It was on his fifty-ninth birthday, at noon, when he was practising *vipassana* meditation under a Bodhi tree in the monastery, that he was carried off by soldiers to serve as a porter for the army at the frontline.

Zeya, who had gone out to collect alms when the soldiers came, had returned to find the abbot was not in the monastery. He saw a soldier dozing under the Bodhi tree where the abbot used to sit for meditation. The soldier, startled by the sound of Zeya's footsteps, pointed his rifle at him.

"Don't move or you're dead," warned the soldier.

Although Zeya didn't know much about firearms, he could see that the soldier, who must have been awoken in a panic, held his rifle in reverse, pointing at him with the butt end instead of its muzzle. Zeya kindly alerted the soldier to his mistake. The soldier was embarrassed and his face, which was slovenly with a skin disease, turned the colour of a dead pig. But he was also relaxed by Zeya's kind gesture and lowered his rifle.

"Where is the abbot?" Zeya asked the soldier.

"Not sure what abbot you're talking about. There was a man sleeping under the tree when we came. A lazy man, we thought, and we made him a porter," said the soldier matter-of-factly.

"Are you serious?" Zeya cried in horror. "That man is the abbot of this monastery! He is an extremely learned man! Besides, he is an old man who has just turned fifty-nine today."

"Good to hear that. We don't take people over sixty for porterage. And don't tell me your abbot belongs to those who are blind, cross-eyed, lame or deformed, because those aren't excuses for exemption," the soldier informed him dutifully.

Zeya asked the soldier if it was possible to use him as a porter in exchange for the freedom of the abbot.

"I don't know," said the soldier uncertainly. "I can take you to see my commander and you may ask him for the exchange."

"Where's your commander now?"

"He's resting with his troops at the village community hall," answered the soldier. "I'll go with you. I think you may also find the porters there."

The community hall was located at the other end of the village. Zeya rushed out of the monastery, thinking he must hurry or he wouldn't see his abbot again. When he hurried down to the village, he found the place unusually quiet and desolate. Some houses were empty, with open doors; others were locked, with soldiers guarding the front, and the weeping of women and children could be heard inside. A chicken had been beheaded and trampled in the middle of the road. The sky was dark and it was raining, and the atmosphere was as miserable as it was sad.

After turning to the left of a large palm tree round the corner, they reached the village's community hall which was a wooden structure with a thatched roof and timber walls on three sides. Several soldiers were seen idling at the entrance, where there were also some villagers chained together by a rope, squatting on the floor and left soaking in the rain.

The slovenly-faced soldier told Zeya that the villagers bound with the rope were the newly conscripted porters. Zeya took a close look at the villagers and recognised most of them: there was U Tu, the village headman; two farmers named U Zaw and U Khai; a primary schoolteacher called U Dun; and U Min, an MP elected in the last election but who was never invited to the National Convention. To Zeya's disappointment, his abbot wasn't among them.

"Are there others?" Zeya asked the soldiers at the entrance. "For mercy, I'm looking for my abbot, who has been conscripted to work as a porter. Tell me where I can find him."

"Go to see our commander over there," replied a soldier. He indicated the farmhouse next to the village community hall, which was now serving as a temporary battalion office. A military flag had been hoisted on the roof and guards were standing sentry at the front.

Zeya was brought to the farmhouse and passed to a mid-level officer who asked Zeya to wait outside while he first had a word with the commander. It was a long wait, something like an hour. The mid-level officer reappeared, and said to Zeya, "My commander is very kind to have agreed to hear your grievance. Please come with me."

Inside the temporary battalion office, Zeya was caught by the strong smell of a certain medicinal ointment; he wondered if a part of the farmhouse was also being used as a first aid station. Then he saw a man – a big man, with a large skull round like a coconut and a neck thick like that of a bull. His eyes were tired and bloodshot, as if he had been roused in the middle of his afternoon catnap. The mid-level officer introduced the big man as General Naing Lwin, commander of the battalion.

Zeya lingered at a distance from the man because he couldn't at once secure an accurate idea of everything that was to be seen. General Naing Lwin was very unlike the conventional image of military commanders sitting on a high seat, overlooking spread-out maps with coloured pins. Instead he was half-lying on a long rattan chair, and his right leg was wrapped in bandages. Probably because he was having a nap, the trousers of his dark green uniform were unstrapped, his shirt unbuttoned, and his golden revolver and cartridge belt were left dumped on a side table. Zeya also found it strangely unsoldier-like that the commander's face was heavily plastered with makeup. Although it is quite common for the locals to wear a thanaka paste on their face for the purpose of sunblock, it was completely mind-boggling why a commander, while at war, should have taken the trouble of having his face masked with the substance like a woman having a facial treatment.

General Naing Lwin noticed Zeya's hesitation and waved him to come forward. "My lad, tell me, what is your problem?"

Zeya found the commander with the highly decorated face only queer, but not unkind. Weighed down by anxiety over the safety of his abbot, Zeya rushed over when beckoned, and blurted out almost incoherently, "Your soldiers have taken my abbot to serve as a porter… I'm here to get him out… but he's nowhere to be seen. What have you done with my abbot?"

General Naing Lwin immediately took offence at Zeya's impertinence, and gave him a hard slap in the face. But it didn't deter Zeya, who protested loudly, "Are you a Buddhist? Do you know my abbot is a Venerable Sayadaw, not only in this area, but the whole country?"

General Naing Lwin was a little taken aback by Zeya's juvenile behaviour. He thought, given a different commander, who didn't have a soft heart like him, the young monk could have already been summarily executed for his insane boldness. But he decided to give the monk a chance, because of his weakness for the beauty of youth. The young monk's cheek, reddening like the blush of a girl after a slap in the face, had greatly excited him.

He said to Zeya, "I was once a Buddhist, but not anymore. I cannot be a Buddhist at the same time as being a soldier. War is now my only religion, and I have only time to practise killing my enemies and meditating over their death. With regard to your abbot, you should know that the country is at war. In wartime, it is the patriotic duty of every citizen to join the army. I'm afraid I can't see why a mere abbot should be exempted."

"But do you know that what you have done is highly immoral and anti-religious, by sending a fifty-nine-year-old man, also a widely respected abbot, to the killing fields?" said Zeya with an angry voice, as he could hardly contain his agitation. "It is a crime against the Sangha! And you'll be burnt in hell for eternities to come as your punishment."

General Naing Lwin couldn't avoid feeling somewhat shaken when he was told that he could be burnt in hell for making an abbot a porter, and for eternities – which seemed a very long time. He knew these things could be superstitious but who knows when modern science, however advanced, has yet to disprove the existence of other worlds in the hereafter? His first instinct was that it was better to believe it now rather than suffer the consequences later, and he decided to be a little more accommodating with Zeya.

He said, "Young lad, I never meant to be discourteous to your abbot. But when my soldiers brought him in, we were simply incapable of telling a high monk from an ordinary farmer. Perhaps your abbot was too proud to ask for a favour from the soldiers by identifying himself. Now tell me, how can I be of help?"

"I don't know. I'm afraid he might have already died in the battle," said Zeya dismally.

"That's impossible. Porters don't fight; they are only required to carry loads of food and supplies," explained General Naing Lwin. "What's more, we're not advancing, but retreating. The monsoon season has come. If we don't leave now we'll be wrestling with the rain and mud rather than our enemies. We and the insurgents have agreed to a ceasefire and my troops are going back to Rangoon."

"But where is the abbot now?" asked Zeya anxiously.

"If your abbot isn't outside with the captured villagers, I believe he would have gone with the main battalion, which departed three hours ago," said General Naing Lwin. "They should be arriving in Rangoon in ten days' time. Why don't you go with us to Rangoon and find the abbot there?"

"But are you leaving this place anytime soon?" inquired Zeya.

"No. I as the commander am staying behind with a regiment of soldiers to oversee the retreat," said General Naing Lwin. "Besides, I have twisted my leg and can't walk properly. I need to rest and will not leave until tomorrow."

"Tomorrow will be too late. I think I'd better go and find the abbot now," Zeya said, and turned to go at once.

The mid-level officer blocked the way out and said, chastising Zeya, "You little monk, don't be such a prick. Show some good manners. If you want to go, you should first ask my commander for his permission."

Zeya apologised. He also asked for permission to leave, with a deep bow.

But General Naing Lwin wouldn't let him go. He said, "We don't have enough porters and I'm making you one. So you're gonna stay with us."

Zeya was horrified. He said, "I'm a monk! You can't make me a porter against my will!"

General Naing Lwin picked up a bayonet from the floor. "Don't move if you don't want to get hurt," he said, and in a few flicks cut Zeya's monastic robe to shreds.

Standing naked and in only his loincloth, Zeya said with a trembling voice, "What do you think you're doing?"

"I've disrobed you and you're not a monk anymore," said General Naing Lwin. "When you're not a monk, you can be conscripted to work as a porter. Is that clear? Now get the hell out of here."

Zeya was dragged out of the temporary battalion office. He was given a blue uniform to wear, and made to squat with the villagers in the soaking rain outside the community hall.

With heavenly mercy, the rain stopped an hour later. Then evening came and the soldiers moved around for a new shift. Taking the opportunity, the village headman, U Tu, began to brainstorm with the porters around him about the possibility of escape. He said, "We could all be dead tomorrow if we don't run away."

The farmer, U Khai, concurred. "I know there's a river. My sister's family lives in the village downstream—"

The primary schoolteacher interrupted, "We all know there is a river, but not everyone can swim."

U Zaw, the other farmer, said resignedly, "I can't swim. I'm not escaping."

Zeya also said, "I'm not escaping either. I'm going with the troops to Rangoon to find the abbot."

The headman said, shaking his head and gazing sadly at Zeya, "I really doubt if the abbot at his age could make it to Rangoon at all."

Just then a bunch of soldiers emerged from the temporary battalion office. The porters stopped talking at once and watched in alarm the commotion that had begun. It was a kind of procession, with General Naing Lwin being carried on a stretcher, escorted by armed soldiers in front and at the back and also on the flank. The procession passed the community hall. General Naing Lwin asked to pause a while. He scanned the group of squatting porters, found Zeya among them, and told him to join the procession.

Zeya, who was squatting behind the headman, stood up and asked, "What do you want?"

"You're going to help me with my bath," returned General Naing Lwin, "and attend to my wounded leg as well."

Once the procession had reached the riverside, General Naing Lwin told the soldiers to leave him alone with Zeya. The soldiers went away but weren't completely gone, as they could be seen guarding at a distance near the river.

General Naing Lwin asked Zeya to help him strip. He was a stout man with a large torso, and his chest was hairy like an ape. He asked Zeya to strip too, and to come down to the river to help with the washing. Zeya was embarrassed. He only removed his porter uniform but kept his loincloth on. His boyish shyness greatly excited the commander.

General Naing Lwin first took time to clean his whitish face. Zeya asked why the mask. The general replied, "I have had this skin disease, some kind of rash, since childhood. It occurs once a month, like a woman's menstrual cycle. There's no cure except the thanaka paste."

Zeya remembered the soldier at the monastery whose face was slovenly due to a skin disease and wondered what he was about to witness once the commander had taken off his mask. But to his surprise, the commander's face looked positively fine after the paste was removed.

"I can tell that you're amazed by the soft, delicate skin of my face," said General Naing Lwin, expressing a certain pride. "The thanaka paste is magic. It not only cleanses and tightens the pores, it is also anti-ageing."

Zeya didn't know what to say in response. He found the commander old and ugly, despite having smooth skin on his diseased face.

After the bath, General Naing Lwin asked Zeya to give him a massage. Sprawling naked on the flat surface of a large rock, Zeya noticed that the commander's body was dotted with numerous black moles and the skin coarse and leathery. As he worked at it reluctantly and after a dozen strokes, the commander's pygmy-like penis doubled hideously in size. Nauseated by the ugly sight, Zeya gave the commander's wounded leg a hard squeeze, effectively checking the erection.

Zeya studied the leg wound and found it had swollen with infection. He told the general that he knew how to treat his wound with a herb that could be found on the riverbank. General Naing Lwin agreed to give it a try. The herb, a nameless palm-shaped leaf with the smell of mint, is a common plant that grows profusely along the river. After Zeya had collected a bunch of the herb, he used a pebble to grind the leaves into a mucilage, and carefully pasted it on the wound.

While he was preoccupied with treating the commander's bad leg, he suddenly felt a hand reach for his behind, stealthily slipping under his loincloth. Zeya tried to move away, but it was too late when he was grabbed firmly by the groin.

Zeya's mind ran wildly in a tumultuous vortex. Humiliated, he found the teaching of tolerance, non-resistance and self-sacrifice couldn't easily be reconciled with the repulsion he felt so strongly. He quickly finished applying the herbal medicine and broke away. It was a tug-of-war. In the end, the commander, whose strength had been seriously affected by his wounded leg, unwillingly gave up his most prized possession. With deep remorse in his voice, he sighed, "What's the point of having the most marvellous youth if you let your beautiful dildo sink into disuse?"

On returning to the village, General Naing Lwin gave up the stretcher and asked Zeya to carry him on his back. He clung to Zeya's shoulders meekly and obediently, like a bride in a village wedding procession. The air was hot before the next downpour. Zeya, encumbered by the weight of the big man, was perspiring heavily. Large beads of sweat appeared on Zeya's nape, like morning dew before the eyes of the general. As young flesh was always a temptation too great to resist, the commander, who just couldn't believe his luck, pulled out a long tongue and started collecting the bodily fluid that tasted like nectar from heaven.

Disgusted by what was happening behind his back, Zeya began to think of throwing the commander off the bridge by feigning a misstep. He could almost imagine the commander's body hitting a rock in the river, his skull cracked open like a coconut. For the first time, Zeya realised when he wasn't a monk he could be frighteningly violent and vengeful, the same as any ordinary man when stretched to the limit of tolerance.

But he wasn't there yet; not even remotely close. He kept his balance and walked on steadily. Helped by his religious belief and years of practice, he was able to keep his turbulent mind in check. He carried on walking, oblivious to how General Naing Lwin kept feasting greedily on his virginal flesh.

Early the next morning, General Naing Lwin's regiment of soldiers departed the village for the journey back to Rangoon. All porters were made to walk ahead of the main troops. U Tu, the village headman, was assigned to detect landmines with a stick. The other porters were made to carry heavy supplies of food and ammunition like human pack mules.

After the troops had covered about ten miles, the village headman stepped on a landmine and was killed instantly. When the soldiers lay low on the ground at hearing the explosion, the elected MP, U Min, and the schoolteacher, U Dun, took the opportunity to escape and vanished into the forest.

So it had now become the turn of the farmer, U Zaw, to go up front with a prodding stick. He was old and slow, and also overcautious for fear of stepping on an undetected landmine. The troops were now moving at crawling speed. General Naing Lwin lost his patience and ordered the execution of the farmer if he could not move faster. Upon overhearing the commander's order to kill, Zeya volunteered to become the front man.

Affected by his troubled leg, General Naing Lwin had slept badly the night before. Low on appetite, he now felt the young monk was expendable like the rest of the porters. He made no objection to Zeya's offer to replace the farmer by walking ahead of the troops.

People thought Zeya was very foolish indeed, albeit respectably brave, to have volunteered to become a minesweeper. Zeya had his reasons. As a monk, he could not possibly stand idly to see the farmer, U Zaw, getting killed simply for being too old and too slow. The First Precept of Buddhism states: "*I undertake to cultivate compassion and find ways to protect the lives of people, animals and plants. I am determined not to kill, not to let others kill, and not to condone any act of killing in the world.*"

Secondly, in his calculation, it would only be a matter of time before it eventually became his turn to take up the human minesweeping after all other porters had disappeared one way or another. As he boldly stepped forward, he thought he would have the protection of his religion. Owing to his attainment in grace and intimacy with Buddha as a monk ordained, he told himself that he had nothing to be afraid of.

Other people took a dim view of Zeya's chance of living. The use of human minesweepers in the war between the junta and the rebels had proven, time and again, an effective measure to ensure the safety of the soldiers. The jungle had become a treacherous minefield after decades of fierce internecine warfare. The consensus was that Zeya would need a miracle if he were to survive the journey back to Rangoon.

It was a relatively quiet first day after the village headman was killed. On the second day of the retreat, several landmines, which had been washed up to the surface by the torrential rain, were spotted in good time and safely defused.

There was nothing extraordinary to report on the third day. Then something happened on the fourth day. While the troops were about to enter a field of tall grass, a swarm of bees had caught Zeya's attention. The bees had strangely avoided a cluster of plants decorated with brilliant red flowers. Zeya, who had spent time doing meditation with his master in the wild from a young age, knew what harmony was like when men co-exist peacefully with nature. And the strange behaviour of the bees was evidence of nature having been molested and upset. Zeya informed General Naing Lwin of his suspicion. Soldiers were sent to investigate, and detected under the flowers a dozen connecting landmines. General Naing Lwin was hugely impressed. He felt the young monk was extremely lucky to still be alive.

Now the troops were about to withdraw completely from the conflict zone; only a day remained before they were back in Rangoon. It was then that Zeya's luck dwindled considerably. He might have become too tired to stay alert after a long and strenuous journey. As the first one to attempt crossing a ditch that separated the jungle and the village beyond, he was tripped by a coil of wire and took a horrible tumble. It was a heart-stopping moment when everyone behind expected the worst to happen.

But there was nothing: no sound of explosion, no flying disembodied arms and legs. When Zeya was helped to his feet, the soldiers found that he had stepped on a trap-wire landmine. It was a Vietnamese-made M14 anti-personnel landmine, which had, however, failed to detonate because its key component had become dysfunctional after years of being buried underground.

General Naing Lwin and the soldiers congratulated Zeya for another great escape. They were all happy for him – as they were, after all, human beings, not beasts. When they weren't killing each other, they could always have a good laugh over an anti-personnel landmine that had expired.

Ten days after Zeya had been forcibly conscripted to serve as a porter, the regiment of soldiers under the command of General Naing Lwin returned to the army headquarters in Rangoon without losing a single man, with the exception of the village headman; but the headman didn't count because he was only a civilian, and therefore wouldn't be considered for either casualty compensation or military commendation.

After a night's rest in a shed behind the army barracks, Zeya left in the early morning in the hope of finding the old abbot in Rangoon. He was stopped at the gate. Brought before General Naing Lwin he was charged for AWOL or "absence without leave". Scratching a mole on his chin with his golden gun, the commander said, "As a deserter, death by firing squad will be the punishment."

Zeya was appalled, and pleaded for leniency. General Naing Lwin said, "I quite like you, lad. I can drop the charge only if you enlist in the army."

Zeya said, "But what about the abbot? I need to find him before anything."

"As far as I know, the abbot is fine," said the commander. "The main battalion already arrived in Rangoon three days ago by taking a shortcut through the jungle. I'm glad to inform you, of the twenty porters recruited at the village, only five have died and seven were injured; but your abbot isn't one of them. As I have also learned, the abbot didn't stay more than two days with the battalion; he has escaped, with the help of his fellow porters."

Relieved to know that the abbot was alive, Zeya demanded to be released immediately to be reunited with the abbot, who was his master for life, and he'd follow him wherever he was. But General Naing Lwin was quick to remind him, "You have now only the choice between enlisting in the army and facing the firing squad. My advice to you is that you are done with being a monk, and your affair with the abbot is over for the time being." Then he added, in a most trusting voice, "C'mon, stop being such a pussy. I need you; the Tatmadaw need you.

If you become one of us, I'll write you an excellent recommendation for your distinguished service during the retreat."

When Zeya still hesitated, General Naing Lwin called in two soldiers to put Zeya away, pending a date for execution. Realising that he was left without much choice, Zeya agreed to join the Tatmadaw. As he was inescapably drawn back deeper into the secular world, he wondered if he still had the protection of his religion from the worst consequences that might ensue.

Once enlisted, Zeya was sent to the Army Training Centre at Thingan Gyun for a programme that lasted four and a half months. Together with a batch of 250 recruits, Zeya was taught how to stand in front of the officers, how to salute, how to answer and how to not question. As far as the business of killing was concerned, he was taught skills to set and defuse landmines, strip and repair weapons, and work with mortar shells. He had also learned shooting at obstacles at ranges of 100, 200 and 300 feet with accuracy. After graduation, he was formally assigned to Light Infantry Battalion 117. But a day before Zeya was to report to his battalion, there was a change of plan. Zeya's supervisor at the training centre, while signing off Zeya's service record prior to deployment, had read something interesting in the letter of recommendation from General Naing Lwin.

It said, among other things, "… the lad has mystified me by having an uncanny ability to detect landmines. In my experience of using him as a drafted minesweeper, he has proven to be incisively brilliant, able to spot dangerous signs well ahead of others with more experience. His superb gallantry and total disregard for his own safety had put my soldiers to shame. A valuable military asset to Tatmadaw if put to further training in ammunition and landmines."

The supervisor, acting on General Naing Lwin's recommendation, sent Zeya to a production plant at Prome in central Burma, and had him groomed for the Ordnance Corps. The plant, owned by Defense Products Industries, manufactured ammunition for rifles, grenades, bombs and landmines designated MM1 and MM2, modelled after the Chinese Type 59 stake-mounted fragmentation mine and Type 58 blast mine. During his attachment to the plant, Zeya worked his way up from apprentice to semi-skilled worker, and graduated as an all-round ordnance technician after two years. Placed in a specialised military engineering unit responsible for landmine laying and clearing, he was given the rank of *Du Tat Kyat*, equivalent to lance corporal, which was the lowest rank among non-commissioned officers. But that could still command the respect of foot soldiers and privates.

In the first year of active duty, Zeya was stationed with the battalion LIB-352 on the western front in Arakan State along the Bangladesh border. It was a relatively quiet time. The Rohingya, though always a problem, had not yet developed into a humanitarian crisis as in later years. With little ethnic armed resistance, the military regime didn't have to resort to ruthless counterinsurgency tactics to assert control as was the case along the Thai-Burmese border.

Zeya, a landmines officer, didn't have to fight like foot soldiers with rifle and bayonet. What he did was merely lay landmines around the border posts for defence purposes, and clear landmines for the protection of men and animals. This meant that he was able to maintain peace of mind as well as a clear conscience. Living the unexceptional life of a nobody, he subsisted like all other passive and nameless little men in the crowd; invisible like a drop in the ocean. For a while, his terrible nobody-ness served him well, by keeping him out of the path of collision with the worst of human depravity. But nothing lasts.

In August of that year, he was redeployed to the eastern front. Baffled by the suddenness of his posting, Zeya had learned through the grapevine that a massive attack against the insurgents in Shan State had been planned after the rainy season. A landmines team was sent to prepare for the stage of invasion, which was expected to carve out a path through the landmine-contaminated forest. The progress was disappointingly slow. Before a mile had barely been cleared of the hidden landmines, two landmines officers were killed. The work was suspended temporarily, and Zeya was appointed the replacement officer to lead the mine-clearing team.

Zeya was flown over to the Southern Shan State. He was met by Major Htun at the military camp who told Zeya that they had not only lost all their mining engineers, they had also lost precious time. The main battalion would be arriving in two weeks' time for the dry season offensive. The first part of the campaign was to reach the villages on the other side of the forest, and push out the people suspected of harbouring the insurgents in the hill areas. A road relatively clear of landmines was the key to success.

The commander of the arriving battalion, a highly decorated general, was renowned for his "zero tolerance policy". Major Htun warned Zeya that he could expect the worst form of punishment should Zeya fail to complete his assignment in good time.

Zeya carefully studied the landmine records left behind by the dead officers and carried out field inspections with his assistants. He was impressed by the work of his predecessors, but sorry for them to have sacrificed their lives for the construction of the warpath. Although he was able to deduce a rough pattern of the distribution of landmines, he wasn't confident as to how he could extend it for an extra mile without the cost of casualties.

In fact, he was rather ambivalent about the job at hand. He knew porters would be used as human shields during the attack and a path relatively clear of landmines would mean a great deal to them. On the other hand, he was deeply disturbed by the impending fate of the villages on the other side of the forest, where many families were presently cooking their meals, farming their fields, tending to their poultry, rearing their children, and unsuspectingly leading a basic pastoral life which was about to come to an end once an unimpeded thoroughfare was opened up.

Faced with the dilemma, Zeya asked his team to work only on clearance within the distance of the first mile but no further, until he had a better plan. It was still no good. Within days of the work restarting, one of the de-miners stepped on a landmine and was seriously injured. The clearance work was again brought to a halt.

Zeya's reaction to the incident was mixed and complicated. He thought he should naturally feel a little desperate, as only a week was left before the arrival of the main troops. Instead he felt a certain relief by the disruption, as if he had unconsciously wished it to happen. By his reckoning, Zeya thought his life had reached another crossroads, and it was time to pause and do some serious thinking.

It was midnight at the end of a very hot day. The pouring rain had stopped several days before – a sign of the immediate resumption of war. As an ordnance officer and because of the dangerous nature of his work, Zeya lived away from the main barracks, occupying one of the three connecting thatched huts used for the storage of ammunition, landmines and mine-clearing equipment on the edge of the forest. He was content to be far away from the boisterous soldiers, as he could have some quiet time to himself. Although there was a stable some twenty yards away where a horse and several mules were kept for military transportation, an occasional nicker or bray at night didn't bother him.

Zeya was sitting cross-legged in his room, meditating by a wall pinned with maps of areas of the forest concentrated with landmines. Although a soldier by profession for some three years, Zeya had never abandoned meditation, as the spiritual practice always gave him calm and peace of mind when he was agitated and confused. For the present crisis, he once again resorted to meditation, to plunge into a world of mindfulness, and grope for clarity with questions like, "Who am I if not a mere nobody in a fallen world?" and "Where am I going from here?"

In meditation, his mind was connected back to the time when he studied under the Venerable Sayadaw U Okka, who said, "People live their lives reacting to their surroundings because they have been conditioned to do so. These feelings and thoughts are perceptions conditioned into one's mind through pain, through having been born as a human being."

Zeya was struck by the timelessness of the abbot's teaching, as well as its relevance to the problem of humanity. How he missed the old abbot, Zeya thought with sadness. At this moment he was startled by the neigh of a horse. Zeya ignored the sound, as if it were only a reflection of the unrest in his mind. Taking a deep breath, he tried to regroup his drifting thoughts and return to the meditation. Then there was a sharp cry outside in the forest that almost made him jump. It was the high-pitched voice of a girl who yelled, "Stop it! Please stop it!"

Zeya had the strong urge to go outside to find out what had caused the tumult. But the noise ceased just then, and he remained seated, without changing his posture. By remembering the abbot's counsel that said, "Much of the lesson in life is learning to understand what we don't like in ourselves and in the world around us; to be patient and kindly, and not make a scene over the imperfections in the sensory experience", he was pleased with himself for maintaining his calm.

Again he tried to resume meditating, but again he was distracted by the terrible cries outside.

"Will you just leave us alone?!" the girl with the same high-pitched voice said vehemently. She was joined by another girl who begged between sobs, "Please don't hurt me. I'm a virgin. I'm getting married tomorrow!"

When the cries became painfully urgent, Zeya gave up his meditation and decided to intervene. Armed with a torch that cast a fairly long and wide beam in the dark, Zeya went outside in search of the source of the distressing noises. Passing the stable, he saw the horse of a peculiar dapple grey poke its head through the fence, looking restive, as if it wanted to go for a trot with Zeya. But the horse wasn't needed when Zeya quickly discerned that the commotion was near the stable on a meadow half-concealed by the trees.

There were three soldiers. Two of them were in the process of jointly stripping a girl whose view was largely blotted by a low tree. A third was trying single-handedly to subdue a girl clad in white, who resisted courageously by yelling and kicking to ward off the assault.

As Zeya came near, he recognised the soldiers as Ko, Aw and Chaung, belonging to the unit under Master Sergeant Tun. They were ordinary rank-and-file soldiers assigned to night patrol duties; and Zeya, as a lance corporal, had every right and authority to intervene in their beastly behaviour.

"Now, what's this?" Zeya shouted over to the three guys. "This is ridiculous, and it must stop immediately!"

Ko, mounting the girl behind the tree, froze like a statue. His accomplice, Chaung, who was working near the mouth of the girl, said contemptuously, "Don't worry. He's only a *Du Tat Kyat*," and urged Ko to keep going.

Zeya knew his authority as a lance corporal over the rank-and-files was exceedingly limited. In normal circumstances he would complain to the soldiers' commanding officer about their inappropriate behaviour. But this was urgent and Zeya felt he must act now to save the girls, even if he risked enraging their boss.

"Attention!" he roared at the trio.

The soldiers, knowing disrespecting the structure of power in the military could have grave consequences, reluctantly stood up from their positions. Chaung and Aw, bare-chested, were looking around furtively for their uniforms, whereas Ko had to quickly pull up his trousers which were down at his knees.

"I think you are supposed to be on night patrol duties?" asked Zeya.

"Yes indeed," replied Ko. "We have just arrested two suspects."

And the two suspects, once freed from their confines, rushed into each other in a fearful embrace. The girl in white, about fifteen or sixteen, her hair tied in a ponytail, consoled the other girl who looked to be more mature, judging by the state of her nakedness.

"What are their crimes?" asked Zeya.

"We made a search of the village and found these offenders, unrelated as family members, spending the night together without reporting to the authorities," Chaung duly reported. "The names and numbers on Form 10 don't tally with that of the names of the offenders. They are therefore arrested for breaking the law of Unreported Guests."

The law of Unreported Guests requires a visiting guest who intends to stay overnight with the host to register with the local authority before nine o'clock in the evening. It is designed to give the government the right to carry out guest checks at households suspected of sheltering dissidents or insurgents. Offenders would be brought before a magistrate and given a fine of fifty kyat, or imprisonment from two weeks to six months if found to be unrelated to insurgency. It is, however, highly unlikely that the court would sentence the offenders to be raped by the soldiers.

Zeya wanted to help the girls, and he asked them, "What if I let you go for a fine of fifty kyat?"

"It's not fair, officer!" said the girl with a ponytail. "My name is Ingjin, and my friend is Nilar; she is getting married tomorrow. My friend has invited me to spend the night with her before her wedding. We don't think we need another Form 10 because we are adjacent neighbours."

Zeya told the soldiers with a harsh stare, "I don't think you have a strong case here."

"But there's something you don't know!" Ko yelped exaggeratedly. "Can you see they're not Burmans, but Shans? If we marry them, the government will pay us an extra 3,000 kyat on our salary."

"Forget it. We are not going to marry you!" Ingjin replied at once, looking angrily at the soldiers with girlish pride which Zeya found adorable.

Nilar had now put her clothes back on with Ingjin's help. She had also stopped weeping as she said to Zeya, "Whatever the soldiers have done to us, we're not going to make a complaint. I'm getting married tomorrow. I just want to go home now."

"It's useless to make a complaint against us," the soldiers laughed with a sneer. "We're only performing our duty for homeland security."

Zeya decided to end the matter quickly and let the girls go. He said, "Hey, guys, I don't think what's happening here has anything to do with the government's policy regarding mixed marriages. What about this? In a minute, I'll go back to my hut over there as if I have seen nothing and heard nothing. I promise you that I'll not say a word about your disorderly behaviour to your commanding officer—"

"Best for everybody," said Chaung with a clear note of cool sarcasm, as he had been quite ill at ease with the low-ranked officer all along.

Zeya ignored him and continued, "And the girls should be allowed to go home to sleep."

The soldiers were appalled by Zeya's decision. But there was nothing they could do other than look on with disgust at being deprived of their prey.

Ingjin and Nilar thanked Zeya and left quickly. Zeya watched with deep anxiety as they went down the road. Just before they were about to disappear around the bend, Ingjin paused and turned to bow as a gesture of thanks to Zeya. Zeya waved back politely. Engrossed by Ingjin's warmth and cheerfulness, he forgot to lower his arm long after the girls had vanished in the darkness.

Then Zeya went back to his hut. In his haste he had forgotten to order the soldiers to dismiss. When he entered the hut, he saw in the corner of his eye that the soldiers still remained standing to attention. Zeya wasn't about to rectify his mistake as he closed the door behind him, secretly believing it was better for the safety of the girls.

Zeya tried to return to meditation but failed to concentrate after the disruption, so he went to sleep. He saw the girls in his dreams, and perhaps due to a lingering anxiety he seemed to hear the girls' terrible cries for help. Believing it was only a dream, he thought what he saw or heard was unreal, only illusions that would ultimately disappear. As the old abbot had kept reminding his disciple: "A wise man doesn't act or react to worldly imperfections and injustice as if they are real, so he escapes suffering." Zeya decided not to be troubled by the sad cries. And he resumed his sleep. The cries had also stopped, as if he had willed them away with the teaching of Buddha.

But in a sensory world, sometimes it is difficult to tell a dream from reality. After a brief sleep, Zeya was awakened to find his dream had turned out to be a real nightmare. There was heavy pounding at the door of his hut. When he climbed to his feet, the pounding had stopped. He opened the door but saw no one outside, except fast-moving shadows down the lane. He thought he had caught a glimpse of white clothes as well as hair gathered in a ponytail. Then he realised it was Ingjin, and she was in grave danger.

Zeya experienced fear and fits of outrage never known before. He rushed into the stable, climbed onto the dapple-grey steed and rode into the woods. The horse, which had been rather restive, was excited by the opportunity to stretch its legs. To its delight, this time it wasn't being driven to war, but committed to something of a much higher and nobler purpose: the rescue of Ingjin.

Zeya found Ingjin near the hillside with soldier Chaung. Her clothes had been torn at the shoulder. She was screaming as she tried to run away, but was grabbed at the heel by Chaung. Zeya drove up and hit Chaung with the whip. Chaung, trying to protect himself from the lashing, let go of Ingjin. In one swift scoop, Zeya lifted Ingjin onto the horse and held her in front of him.

"I thought you'd gone home. What happened?" Zeya asked.

Ingjin replied, panting between breaths, "The soldiers followed us to the village. We saw them in the distance and ran. I lost Nilar as I escaped. I don't know where she is now."

Zeya asked Chaung, "You got any idea?" When Chaung wasn't forthcoming with an answer, Zeya hit Chaung in the face with the whip, leaving a clear mark in the shape of a crow's claw across his nose bridge.

Chaung cried out in pain and said, "Okay, stop hitting me, and I'll talk! I think the other girl has gone straight to the camp of Master Sergeant Tun. I guess she should be safe there."

The mention of Master Sergeant Tun, who was Zeya's senior by a few levels, was enough to discourage Zeya from taking further punitive actions on Chaung. As it appeared that the other girl was out of danger, it remained for him to deliver Ingjin to safety. Before he left he said to Chaung, "I want to see the three of you in half an hour at the stable. I'd like to hear what you guys have to say about your despicable behaviour. If I'm not satisfied with your explanation, I'll ask your commanding officer, Master Sergeant Tun, to take disciplinary action against your misconduct."

Then Zeya rode away, taking Ingjin back to her village at the foot of the hill. As the horse trotted down the country road, Ingjin described to Zeya what had happened earlier.

They had been at the end of the road when they were ambushed by the same three soldiers. They escaped into the forest, but not long after, Nilar turned back because she was afraid of the landmines. Ingjin didn't have the same fear, as the forest had been her playground since she was a child. Moreover, she would rather be killed by a landmine than raped by the soldiers. But Nilar didn't want to risk losing a limb before her wedding and headed back. Ingjin had no choice but to follow her friend. As they emerged from the forest, they saw Zeya's hut, with a dim light, and decided to knock on his door for help. But before they got close, the three soldiers appeared from behind. In a panic they fled in separate directions and lost each other. Finally, Ingjin had struggled to reach the hut and was able to alert Zeya just in time.

Fearing the soldiers would come back to arrest her in the middle of the night, Ingjin didn't want to go home.

"What about your parents? They must be worried about you right now!" said Zeya.

"I have no parents. They died when I was a child. I live with my grandmother, who is eighty-nine years old, deaf and half-blind. She doesn't even know I sleep the night at Nilar's place," said Ingjin. "Will you please be so kind as to take me to the monastery on the hilltop?"

"Will the monastery give you shelter?" asked Zeya.

"The abbot has known me since I was a child," replied Ingjin.

As they went uphill, they were quiet for the rest of the journey. They were probably a little embarrassed by the physical closeness within the limited space of the saddle and the need to hold onto each other when the horse trotted its way up the slippery road.

It was a horrid, hot night. The abbot of the monastery couldn't conceal his astonishment as he saw a horse enter carrying a girl and a man in a soldier's uniform. He recognised the girl as Ingjin. The abbot knew Ingjin and her grandmother well. He listened to Ingjin's awful experience and felt sorry for her. But he was suspicious of the officer. An abortive rape? It is almost unheard of in the history of the army. He wondered what this young officer actually wanted in return for what appeared to be a meritorious deed.

But the officer was very quiet, almost shy, without making any specific demand for gratuity. He seemed to be in a hurry to go. The abbot then invited him to stay for a cup of tea.

"That's very kind," replied Zeya, with reverence in his voice. "I'm still on duty. It would be improper of me to stay any longer." He made a deep bow to the abbot, with the graceful manner of a veteran practitioner of Buddhism, to the abbot's amazement. Then he remounted the horse and set off.

"Wait!" Ingjin said, looking up at Zeya with her crystalline eyes. "I can't thank you enough for what you have done for me. I'm sorry that you have to leave now. Must you go?"

"I don't know," Zeya mumbled. Ingjin had made him so nervous that he didn't know what he was trying to say.

"Must you really go?" asked Ingjin again.

Zeya began to feel a twinge of pain in his chest as the parting was prolonged. He wanted to end it and said, almost abruptly, "Yes. I really have to leave now. Goodbye, and goodnight."

Ingjin ran her fingers through the grey strands of the horse's mane, hugged it around the neck, and said, "Thank you, horse." The horse held its head high, its ears forward, and emitted a soft, long neigh before galloping off.

On the way back to the camp, Zeya struggled to process what was happening to him. He was in a strange mood, dreamlike and fantastic. He continued to feel vividly the warmth of Ingjin's body in the saddle space, which he had found difficult to dismiss as unreal and illusory.

He entered the camp, completely forgetting his order to the soldiers to assemble at the stable for his return. But they remembered, and they were there already, lurking in the darkness as Zeya drove the horse into the stable.

Almost without a sound, Chaung leapt from the roof of the stable, hauling Zeya down to the ground from the horse's back. Aw and Ko joined in, overpowering Zeya after a fierce fight. They tied Zeya's hands behind his back with a rope, and dragged him by the hair to make him stand on his feet. Zeya was aghast by the trio's behaviour, wondering what they were trying to do. Before he had hardly opened his mouth to ask the question, Chaung came forward and beat him in the face with a whip.

"You know it's a serious crime insulting an officer," Zeya warned them.

"No crime is more serious than rape and murder," said Ko with an evil smile. "Officer, you are under arrest."

"What are you talking about?" asked Zeya, astonished.

Ko and Aw didn't explain, whereas Chaung kept lashing at Zeya's face and body with the whip like a madman. Chaung didn't stop until he'd had enough of his revenge, and also, someone was just entering the stable. It was Master Sergeant Tun, the commanding officer of the soldiers. He looked at Zeya with eyes so cold, as if he were looking at a dead man. In a wretched voice he said, "They said you should be shot by firing squad. I couldn't agree more after what I have seen with my own eyes."

Zeya was taken back to his hut. As the soldiers raised their torches to aim a strong beam into the interior of the hut, Zeya saw a naked body lying spreadeagled on the floor, its head towards the back wall and feet to the door. By the colour of the clothes beside the body Zeya thought the woman was Nilar, the girl who was getting married the next day. Bruises were seen at the veins of her neck, her mouth agape, her tongue sticking out – all signs pointing to a violent death of suffocation by strangulation. With her legs spread wide apart and her vagina a mess, and blood stains all over her thighs like red paint, Zeya believed the poor girl to have been gang-raped before she was brutally murdered.

"Is rape not enough? Why must she be killed as well?" lamented Master Sergeant Tun. "Now, will you guys tell me what you have witnessed?"

Then Zeya heard a corroborated story that alleged him to have raped the girl and murdered her afterwards. Master Sergeant Tun raised genuine concerns about the soldiers' account which was not without holes. To Zeya's disbelief, the soldiers were quick to correct their "oversights", making the case watertight and indefensible. Zeya, knowing he had been framed, felt it useless to defend himself. As he listened on, he felt sorry to have failed to heed the counsel of his master. On the other hand he was also consoled by his own failure. Because, should he have succeeded in the strict observance to the principle of "not making a scene over the imperfections in the sensory experience", Ingjin would have been dead by now.

After further deliberation, the soldiers decided that Zeya was guilty and recommended sentence by death and execution without delay. However, Master Sergeant Tun, although Zeya's senior, didn't have the authority to order capital punishment. He said, "The main battalion will be arriving in a week's time. Let's wait for the commander to decide on the final fate of this evil man."

Zeya was taken away to be locked up in the prison ward to await his court martial hearing. On his way past the stable, he saw the grey horse gaze out at him behind the fence with large, round eyes of incomprehension. It made a soft, low nicker, as though it was worried. With heartfelt sincerity, Zeya whispered to the kind beast: "Tell Ingjin I miss her if you happen to see her again. Goodbye now, my friend."

13

Z . E . Y . A .

———◦∿◦———

On one fine day of brilliant weather, the main troops, comprising Light Infantry Battalion 213 and 224, Infantry Battalion 33 and 36, Signal Battalion 212 and Artillery Battalion 19, drawn primarily from Burma Proper and under the command of General Naing Lwin, arrived in Southern Shan for the dry season offensive.

The prison guard informed Zeya of the troops' arrival and told him his days were numbered. Zeya asked the guard, "Do you really believe I have actually committed the horrible crimes of rape and murder?"

"In the army, rape is regrettable and murder inevitable, not exactly horrible crimes, as both can be justified in the name of protecting the country," replied the guard shrewdly. "But if Master Sergeant Tun wants you dead, there's no escape regardless of the nature of your crime."

Two days later, Zeya was brought before a special military tribunal for the court martial proceedings. Inside the commander's office there was an assembly of people, including Major Htun, the ghost-faced Master Sergeant Tun, and the witnesses represented by Privates Chaung, Ko and Aw, and a slew of soldiers.

Zeya, in handcuffs and a waist chain, stood up from the bench as he heard a soldier call out, "All rise!"

The presiding judge entered, who was, coincidentally, also the commander who had arrived two days before with the main troops.

Zeya immediately recognised him and shouted out his greeting, "Good morning, General Naing Lwin. Do you remember me?"

Master Sergeant Tun at once squeaked, "You stupid idiot! As the accused, you don't speak unless you're asked!"

General Naing Lwin sat down and said, "So you were the monk Zeya I made a soldier three years ago in Rangoon?" and added, half-jokingly, "I know all our soldiers take rape very seriously. And you have made them proud to have murdered, too!"

Zeya pleaded, "I have been framed, commander! I'm innocent."

"I'd like to think so. As I now remember, I was quite fond of you when you led my troops out of the landmine-infested jungle like Moses led his people out of Egypt. Don't worry, for this one time, the court will presume you innocent until, one way or another, proven guilty beyond reasonable doubt," said General Naing Lwin; he didn't sound like he was joking again. "Soldiers, will you uncuff and unchain the accused?"

Master Sergeant Tun squeaked again, begging the commander to reconsider. He said, "I think it is a little too charitable for someone who's extremely cruel and dangerous."

"What are the reasons for restraint?" retorted General Naing Lwin, drawing a long golden gun from his hip holster. He plonked the gun on the table and said, "Is there danger of violence or escape? Of course not!"

Master Sergeant Tun cowered and said no more. After all the buzz and fuss, the court martial began properly.

Major Htun represented the prosecution. Privates Chaung, Ko and Aw each took the witness stand and parroted a perfectly corroborated and well-rehearsed testimony. Master Sergeant Tun was the last witness to speak; his delivery was eloquent, convincing and damningly noxious, doing everything he possibly could to hammer the last nail in the coffin.

Major Htun made the closing statement on behalf of the prosecution by saying, "This court has established the accused guilty of rape and murder, and recommended him to be sentenced to a supreme penalty. Now, may I request the presiding judge, the honorable General Naing Lwin, for the concluding remarks?"

General Naing Lwin was just scratching a dark mole on his chin with his golden gun. He was not pleased to be interrupted when he was enjoying a continuous flow of sensation, half-pleasurable and half-painful, which had sunk deep in the roots of the few hairs growing out of the mole. He launched an attack on Major Htun, to the surprise of the audience. With a darkened face, he said, "I'm very disappointed with you, Major Htun. The accused man here, whose guilt is absolutely unpardonable in the Tatmadaw, should have been executed straightaway a week ago. What's your excuse?"

"I'm afraid I don't have the authority to order the execution," answered Major Htun carefully.

"If so, the guilty man should at least be allowed to continue digging up the landmines." The commander kept up his reprimand. "Now we have neither swiftly served the cause of justice for the dead woman, nor made the progress necessary for an early advance on the villages. Again, what's your defence?"

"There's no defence for my gross oversight; please pardon me," said Major Htun timidly. "But I've been a soldier all my life, who's better at war than interpreting this country's law of rape and murder, which is beyond my comprehension. And as a veteran soldier, my advice for the loss of time is to double the number of porters to work as human minesweepers to protect the advanced army."

"It's certainly a solution, but simply too obvious," said the commander. "When it's too obvious, it would appear to be strategically unsound, even if we have access to an unlimited resource of expendable human material."

Major Htun knew it best to stay quiet.

General Naing Lwin continued, "Anyway, we can discuss more about our country's greatest invention of human shields later. Now let's refocus our attention on the case. Can I ask the defendant to speak about anything he has in mind before the sentence?"

Zeya repeated that he was innocent. He was, however, unable to really explain why the dead body of a young woman, found raped and murdered, was inside his hut. He could have argued his case by providing the court with an alibi, proving that he was in some other place at the time the alleged offence was committed. But he could not possibly cite the evidence for reasons of Ingjin's safety. It was therefore far from sufficient just to say, "I didn't do it." And he could sense the coming doom even before he had finished talking.

General Naing Lwin, knowing the defendant was now entirely at his mercy, went on to announce the sentence. "We have here a master sergeant and three soldiers who have testified against you, with accounts generally considered credible and reliable. I therefore have to inform you that you're guilty of one count of rape and one count of murder. I hereby sentence you to death by firing squad."

This was the second time Zeya had been sentenced to death by firing squad, and by the same man who appeared to hold an inordinate fondness for him. The court was adjourned after Master Sergeant Tun reminded the audience in a most satisfied voice that the execution would be conducted within the next twenty-four hours.

Before Zeya was led away, the commander, who had a soft heart, almost wept. He said, "I'd like to have a private moment with the defendant. In the name of compassion, he who shows remorse can be considered for a full or partial pardon."

After all others had left the room, General Naing Lwin said, "Tell me, are you guilty or not? Last chance."

Zeya said, "I'm innocent. I swear."

General Naing Lwin sighed. "I believe you. I never trusted those soldiers from the beginning. They're professional liars, a disgrace to the Tatmadaw," he said. "But they have all sworn under oath to speak the whole truth and nothing but the truth. This is a court martial, not a place to talk trash. I therefore can only use my authority, on the basis of the trash I have heard, to sentence you to death for the crimes you are alleged to have committed."

Zeya said, "If you'd listen to me, the truth is: the same soldiers kidnapped two girls from a village while on night patrol duty and

I stepped in when they were just about to force them into having sex—"

"But what does it matter now?" interrupted General Naing Lwin loudly. "You'll be dead in the next twenty-four hours! No one can save you now except me. You have only one question to answer for yourself before it is too late: Do you want to live?"

"Of course I want to live. I don't want to die," Zeya blurted out without thinking. It was apparent that he would do anything possible to avoid death, like all people and living things.

"Then consider me a friend and a confidant, as I have something important to share with you," said General Naing Lwin.

"Tell me, if there's anything more important than life and death," said Zeya.

"We're going to have a heart-to-heart and man-to-man talk," said the commander. "You can decide if it is more important than life and death."

"Heart-to-heart and man-to-man…" murmured Zeya after the commander, incapable of seeing what was coming.

"Yes indeed, man-to-man, in the sense of a man, a pen, a man and a pen," explained the commander. "Don't forget that we're not ordinary men. We, I mean, you and I, who have a lot in common, belong to a very different breed of men."

Completely stupefied, Zeya said humbly, "You're an important man and I'm just an ordinary soldier. I don't see what we have in common."

"Don't you see our backgrounds are wonderfully similar?" the commander pointed out for the benefit of Zeya. "You were a monk and then a soldier, whereas I've been a soldier all my life. In our professions, woman is no-no; forbidden, inadvisable and off limits. But what the heck! What do we need women for if we can be as good as them in every other way?"

"I'm sorry," said Zeya. "I still don't see what else we have in common."

"Adversity! We're in a war, and we are both vying for survival," cried the commander with emotion. "Adversity makes strange bedfellows, and you're welcome to creep inside my hole when there's no other shelter hereabout." He finished with a most flirtatious grin.

Zeya was not sure if the commander was gay or a freak, or both. What he knew was that the commander was trying in a roundabout way to figure out if he was a freak too. Zeya knew himself not to be a freak. But he did not want to deny it categorically as yet, when the idea of being a freak seemed to have its appeal in the present situation. He wondered a little, in the crooked times in which he lived, if it was the freakiest rather than the fittest that would eventually prevail. So he played dumb by staring blandly at the commander with an open mouth and said nothing.

General Naing Lwin gave up being circumspect, as after all he was not a very patient man. He went ahead with an upfront question. "Are you a virgin?"

"Yes, I am," answered Zeya blushing with embarrassment.

"I knew it!" cried the commander excitedly. "I always fucking know it!"

"I don't know what it has to do with saving my life," said Zeya despondently.

To his surprise, General Naing Lwin responded by saying, "I don't know either," before wheezing a hoot of masochistic laughter. Then he went on, panting and laughing, "What I know is: if you want to be saved, you must cooperate with me in every possible way. Then you might not have to die."

That is not the same as I can live, thought Zeya grimly.

"Of course this is not the same as you can live," the commander said, as if he could read Zeya's mind. "But even if you die, you should be glad that you have died for truth and knowledge. In this world, many people have lived their lifetime in utter ignorance and died not knowing a single thing about themselves. That's pathetic and pitiable. I don't want the same fate to happen to you. I'd help you understand yourself by knowing your true nature, which is the highest thing worth dying for."

"But I don't want to die!" Zeya groaned with desperation in his voice.

"I know, I know," the commander softly cooed. "We'll try to work something out." Then without being specific about what that something would be, he ended his private session abruptly and called in the soldiers to put Zeya away.

Zeya now realised that he, in all probability, was going to die. His last night on earth, as it appeared, had presented him with the best opportunity to practise meditation on mindfulness of death. But he gave up meditating after fifteen minutes, realising that when one is actually dying it is a bit late to begin doing something serious about death. He went to sleep, wondering, in that sleep of death, what dreams may come. He had a dream. He saw that he was dead; his body decomposed and turned to dust; his soul, after having traversed *Bardo* - the intermediate state between death and the next life - re-entered the world of *samsara*, by returning to the same old country and the same small village where a sixteen-year-old girl named Ingjin had once lived. He woke up and seemed strangely consoled by the premonition in his dream.

A new day arrived. At noon, the guard brought him lunch and a report on the latest situation. "I've heard no news of your pardon, full or conditional. Nor have I heard the exact time of your execution. You're just like the rest of us: death is certain, the hour is uncertain. Therefore, be sure to eat something, because your life still needs your active participation. Ha-ha-ha!" he quipped.

Then evening came, with frightful punctuality. Zeya heard voices outside his cell, which he recognised as of those of General Naing Lwin and Major Htun.

"Shall we set the time of execution at midnight, your excellency?" asked Major Htun.

"Very well," answered General Naing Lwin. "Give the condemned man some good food for his last supper. Three years ago he treated my twisted leg with a miraculous herb grown along the river. I had a speedy and full recovery thanks to him. I'd like to see to it myself that he has something to enjoy towards the very end."

For probably his last meal on earth, Zeya was provided with a whole chicken and a bottle of wine. Paradoxically, Zeya found life much easier when the illusion of hope was completely taken out of the equation. He devoured the entire chicken and finished the wine to the last drop. He was never a drinker, but found a little drunkenness was useful, like a balm to the terror of dying, a means of facing up to the firing squad without countenancing the horrible sensation of bullets tearing into his body.

The final death rite, at about an hour before midnight, was simple but suitably formal and official, attended by General Naing Lwin in full uniform tied smartly by a pigskin belt at the waist and a hip holster on his right where his golden gun was kept. Major Htun, attired sombrely for the occasion, as if attending a funeral, was accompanied by three soldiers from the firing squad. It was a warm night, with a cloudless sky and a large bright moon providing good illumination for the stage of execution. Zeya, shackled at the knees and hands cuffed in front, was taken to the edge of the forest where a pit, meant to be his grave, had been dug.

General Naing Lwin walked with Zeya in front of the pack, whereas Major Htun was ten steps behind, with the firing squad tagging along. Deliberately keeping his voice low, General Naing Lwin said to Zeya, "You should know that nothing is too late, even at this stage. Whatever you ask, I can give you."

"Like what?" asked Zeya.

"One or several stays of execution until, one way or another, you're ready to die," replied General Naing Lwin. "Or an absolute pardon if you really want to live."

What the commander said was so tempting it completely upset Zeya's composure. "Of course I want to live," uttered Zeya with despair. "But what do I have to do to be worthy of a stay of execution or a full pardon?"

General Naing Lwin said, "Although I am a soldier, I'm an exceedingly sentimental man with a soft heart. I wept unstoppably after our conversation yesterday. You have made me feel that a brotherly love, which I have desired secretly and fervently all my life but always in vain with disappointment, is finally within reach. I was overwhelmed, and am tremendously grateful to you. You should be pleased to know that, with brotherly love, everything is possible. As a general, I can give you the absolute pardon, in return for your total and unconditional love as a brother."

Zeya got the message, which was as sick as it was clear. General Naing Lwin had hinted at a *fucking* way out. But if it was a way, it was a hellish one, thought Zeya. He wanted to tell the commander to get lost and get on with the execution. But he was also awfully split between an animalistic craving to live and a soul desiring to remain unsoiled. In his inner struggle, his willpower began to wane. He felt nauseous and uncomfortable. His belly churned, his breath came in short gasps, and his face twisted horribly when he could almost see his life flicker like the flame of a candle in the wind; now it was bright and now it was dark.

General Naing Lwin lifted Zeya's face to the resplendent moonlight and sampled it like a most prized possession. "Love me tender, love me now, and you're there," he said softly. "To be or not to be, is not the question. We are brothers. Readiness of the flesh is all."

General Naing Lwin unlocked the shackles at the knees of the condemned man but kept the handcuffs on. He said to Major Htun and the members of the firing squad, "The prisoner has requested to make a last-minute confession. Will all of you step back fifty yards to keep your guard?"

He waited until the footsteps of the soldiers were out of earshot before he took Zeya by the arm into the forest. They arrived at the site at the start of the first mile where landmines had been largely cleared. Zeya was pushed down to lie on his back, facing the cloudless night sky, for the aggression to begin. The commander's course of action was crude, obvious, gross and sickeningly bland. Crouching on his knees beside Zeya, he quickly removed Zeya's trousers, and began sucking like a baby sucks his mother's nipples for milk.

With fear and shame, Zeya thought: *Why can't I just die when life has become such a dreadful and deplorable existence?* As a former monk, he had helped many people to go through the torments of death by telling them there is nothing to be afraid of, when "death takes place around us every moment as the continual dissolution of the psycho-physical life form conventionally called living things, including human beings". But when death had come to be his own, he had great trouble accepting it with complete equanimity.

There was a stir in the woods which made General Naing Lwin spit out what was in his mouth and pause to look around. It was only the breeze, the rustle of leaves, and there was nothing to be alarmed by, the commander thought. He quickly returned to his plaything, grabbing and pawing it with guilty pleasure.

Suddenly, without warning, the commander was hands-off, leaving his plaything standing stiff and erect in the night air, touched only by the wind that whisked across the forest. Zeya stole a look at the commander, and found that the big man was in the process of stripping off. Separate pieces of his military uniform fell in piles onto the ground, his military medals and decorations dropping like diamonds from the sky. Zeya knew what was to come, and closed his eyes to brace himself for the next stage of the brutality.

As Zeya waited for the coming onslaught, there was for a while only absolute silence – not a rustle, not a whisper. Then he heard the commander speak again, in a theatrical, velvety voice, "I'm ready. Please take me."

Zeya opened his eyes and was astonished to find the commander had got down on all fours: his body naked, his legs kneeling and wide apart, his head resting in the cradle of his hands, and his rump rising at an angle as if asking for a good, hard spanking. Glancing askew at Zeya with passion and affection, General Naing Lwin, assuming the role of the weaker sex, implored with the voice of a woman begging her man, "It feels like my cunt is on fire. Please take me now."

Zeya clambered to his feet, but did not quite know what to do with a bum sprayed with moles and thick hairs overgrown at the cleft like an unmown lawn. General Naing Lwin took a look at the watch that he still kept on his wrist after he had offloaded all his clothes, and said with urgency, "We must get it done before midnight or you don't get a full pardon."

Zeya continued to dawdle until he had thought of doing something useful in his situation. He held out his hands and asked to be uncuffed.

But General Naing Lwin, even though his "cunt" was on fire, was not stupid. He said, "I don't need your hands. I need only your prick. Stick it inside now."

"What a cunt!" grumbled Zeya under his breath. He gave the "cunt" another look of disgust, and said, "I'm afraid it's too dry."

Amazingly, General Naing Lwin did not seem to be offended by the remark. Instead, he found it a fair observation and said, a little apologetically, "Sorry. I've brought with me the lubricant. It's in the chest pocket of my uniform."

Zeya did not have to reach far for the uniform lying just at the feet of the commander, and quickly found a polythene bag containing a light yellow oil. At the same time Zeya had also found something which made his heart jump. It was a belt and a hip holster with a golden gun. The gun, as well as the packs of military medals and decorations glinting under the moonlight, looked ridiculously out of place as their master now lay prostrate, putting his asshole up for foreign invasion.

"Found it? It's the extra-virgin olive oil from Sicily. I never leave home without it," whispered General Naing Lwin. "Anoint me, now."

Zeya bit a small hole in the polythene bag to let the oil drip down onto the commander's mound. As the oil crawled its way inside, the commander groaned, "Oh. It's time. Fuck me now."

Zeya, with the polythene bag clasped between his teeth to keep the lubricant running, slowly moved his hands to open the holster and fish out the golden gun. When General Naing Lwin's moans got louder and his appeal for Zeya's mercy to enter more urgent, Zeya pointed the nozzle of the gun at the commander's asshole and pushed it hard inside.

General Naing Lwin's response was a combination of great pleasure and pain. He shrieked like crazy, not that he did not enjoy it, but he had a complaint. "You're naughty. It's cold. Where's your hot rod, my lord?"

Zeya froze temporarily clutching the gun, as he was surprised he had come this far. Although he had not the slightest idea how to proceed further, he knew he had to continue improvising as best he could to deal with a situation of his own making, one that began from the moment he tried to save the girls, to the present point of screwing his own commander in the asshole.

After some pondering, he decided to be completely honest with General Naing Lwin. He said, "Dear sir, your excellency, please note that I'm not the kind of man you think. Unlike you, I'm normal. I think I'm attracted to the opposite sex rather than the same sex; as only lately, I've found myself falling in love with a girl who gathers her hair in a ponytail."

The trees nearby were suddenly astir. If there was a wind, neither Zeya nor General Naing Lwin noticed it.

The commander tried to move his buttocks, but Zeya stopped him by pushing the gun another inch inside and told him to stay still. In great pain, the commander acknowledged this was the end of his game. As a strategist and a member of the country's highest military board, he knew it was time to call for another ceasefire as one of the many ceasefires the junta government have agreed with the ethnic rebels through the years. He said, "You've my full and absolute pardon. Withdraw the gun, and you're a free man."

"You mean I can go?" asked Zeya, amazed by how rapid the situation had turned around.

"It's up to you. In fact, you can stay. I can promote you to Sergeant, as we still need experts like you to clear the landmines," replied General Naing Lwin.

"I wonder if you'll ever forgive me," said Zeya.

"Well, if you don't trust me, what about this?" said General Naing Lwin. "Leave the battalion and make this your opportunity to escape. Go now, and I'll not stop you. If you are lucky, you could reach the village on the other side of the forest before daybreak."

Zeya peered into the landmine-infested forest, which had already killed two soldiers and wounded a third during the preparatory stage of the dry season offensive. Although uncertain of his chance of survival, he somehow felt the forest was his only route to freedom.

General Naing Lwin said, "You know you would be a dead man now if I were less sentimental. The forest is now your only chance… ouch!" To his embarrassment, he produced a loud discharge of gas from his back end with the sound of low thunder. Then he resumed, with urgency in his voice, "It feels very uncomfortable in my anus, which is demanding a quick and dirty solution. I'll give you one more minute. At the end of the minute, I'll get up regardless of whether you want to kill me or not. Take my advice. Leave for the forest now. I promise I will stay very quiet when you go. But please hurry up."

Zeya thanked the general for his advice and prepared to go. He loosened his clutch on the gun, which miraculously remained stuck with great obstinacy in place without slipping to one side, probably because its stem was long and the penetration firm and deep. He found the key in a pocket of the general's uniform and used it to unlock the handcuffs. Then he began to put his trousers back on.

General Naing Lwin, noticing Zeya's legs were somewhere in the legs of his trousers, knew it was his opportunity to fight back. He sprang up and made a lunge at Zeya. Zeya was startled and took a step back. He was tripped by the legs of his trousers, and slipped and fell.

General Naing Lwin, the man with the golden gun stuck loyally in his arse, rushed forward to attack. But he slipped too, having stepped on the polythene bag of olive oil. He took a big pratfall, which was not funny. As his haunches landed on a hard rock in the grass, the butt of his gun crashed under the enormous pressure of his massive body weight. Without knowing how, the trigger was pulled. A shot was fired, or misfired, to be precise. A bullet was sent travelling in an upward trajectory inside the commander's body, and by mercy it did not go all the way to the top of his head when its ascension was intercepted by a rib near his heart, whereupon it stayed and blasted off.

When Major Htun and the soldiers of the firing squad heard the loud sound of a gun, they all knelt down and prayed, believing that Zeya had been executed, without knowing it was the ghost of their commander that was now hovering above their crew-cut heads.

Zeya, who was still lying clumsily on the ground with his legs twisted in his trousers, watched with awe at General Naing Lwin sitting on the rock, majestically, as if it were his throne. His mouth was wide open as if he wanted to chastise Zeya for his naughtiness. But no words came out; instead, a gush of blood spurted forward, spraying the grass all around with a fine, obscene scarlet red. A moment ago the commander had promised to stay very quiet when Zeya took his leave. Now, as his giant, coconut-like head bent down to the point of kissing his own genitals, Zeya found there was no reason not to trust his commander this time. He quickly put his clothes on and, on a hunch, took the commander's watch for his own use. Then, upon hearing the approaching steps of the soldiers, he made a dive into the dark and deadly forest.

When Zeya embarked on his great escape, the first mile was not such a challenge, as the landmines had mostly been cleared. He also had a fairly good memory of the landmines' concentration for the next mile or two. He moved on carefully but confidently, and after about an hour, he reckoned that he should be at a distance of several miles from the garrison camp and fairly safe for the time being.

He sat down for a rest and took stock of his situation. He knew he had now become a fugitive. Soldiers would be sent to hunt him down very soon, probably at the first streak of dawn, as to the military regime, General Naing Lwin was too important to have died like that and the culprit must be apprehended at all costs. Zeya knew that he must try to reach the other side of the forest before daybreak. But the surrounding darkness was a nightmare, and he had no idea how he could proceed without stepping on a hidden landmine. Then exhaustion got the better of him and he dozed off.

He had only had a brief snooze, when he woke up to a sharp pain in his leg. He felt something like a stone had hit him. He sat up to look around. Slowly he began to realise that he was not alone. It was not something he saw, but the sounds he heard. There were the whistles of wind, the rustle of leaves, the short and continuous beats of nocturnal insect wings, and the intermittent burps of frogs in deep waters underground.

Suddenly, a few yards away to his left he saw a ball of fire emerge out of nowhere in midair, floating like a dream. He shook his head and rubbed his eyes, believing it only an illusion. As the fireball continued to flicker before his puzzled eyes, he thought it was perhaps the fireflies. But if he were right, it must be a collection of a thousand fireflies to produce such a concentrated mass of fire. Otherwise, he must have a problem with his eyes, which might have lost their sense of proportion after having gazed into the impregnable darkness of the forest too hard and for too long.

Zeya, mesmerised, followed the fireball, which kept floating at a distance ahead. A notion of the supernatural took shape in his head as he began to think of genii, sylphs, gnomes and, more particularly, nats. In Burma, nats, as a group of thirty-seven ghost spirits symbolising prominence of life and violence of death, are worshipped in conjunction with Buddhism. Zeya believed the thousands of fireflies were messengers of a nat that had come to his rescue. Feeling thankful at a time of great danger, he followed the fireball as though it was his guiding angel. By placing his faith totally in the power of the nat, he moved on mindlessly and effortlessly as if he were walking in the clouds.

And blind faith has its advantages, of living painlessly when one doesn't have to wrestle with a conscious mind that keeps feeding you with rubbish thoughts in nanoseconds. But a conscious mind that is shut down also has its problems, of bending time and distortion of the sense of space. Trailing after the fireball, Zeya experienced only a brief interval of time. But in reality, a couple of hours had elapsed ever since.

He wasn't aware of a trick of the mind or of time, not until the fire in front of him suddenly went out in a snap without warning. In the abrupt darkness, his mind jerked awake. He checked his watch and was astounded to find that what he assumed was only the briefest time was in effect the great stretch of a long night. In his reckoning, he thought he must have traversed quite a distance in the forest, and felt very lucky not to have stepped on a landmine so far.

When he was pondering the way to go, he saw the fireball spring back into life a few yards ahead. But he was not as trusting in the nat of fireflies as before, having become conscious again of the danger of the treacherous minefield in his surroundings. He didn't go after the fireball even though it began to drift away.

As if confused by the behaviour of its follower, the fireball paused in the air. Then it went a small distance ahead, and stopped again when Zeya was still not following. When neither the fireball nor Zeya was moving, a kind of impasse ensued. But it didn't take long to break the impasse when dawn suddenly came. Faint streaks of glimmering light penetrated the dense leaves, causing subtle changes to the spectrum in the atmosphere. Zeya thought he saw the shadow of a figure. He gave his eyes a brisk rub and checked again. Now, as the crack of dawn widened and the light in the forest increased, Zeya was able to see clearly that the figure beneath the fireball was that of a girl dressed in white, her hair tied in a ponytail. He shouted out to the figure, "Is that you, Ingjin?"

Ingjin lowered the torch of fire to her face and said, "Hi."

"Why are you here?"

"I knew you were going to be executed by midnight, so I came."

"This forest is a minefield. It is very dangerous," said Zeya.

"Don't worry. This has been my playground since I was a child," she said. "I'm sorry I can't take you to the other side of the forest. But I can take you to the monastery and I'm sure the abbot will give you a place to hide."

"But how can you be so sure walking in the dark?" asked Zeya.

"I rely on my instinct, which has never failed me in the past," replied Ingjin.

Zeya was horrified that Ingjin had been paving the way by exposing herself to the danger of the hidden landmines. He rushed over to her side and said seriously, "I forbid you to become a human shield for me. Let us walk out of this forest together. If we are to get killed, let us die together."

Under the flickering fire of the torch, Ingjin's cheeks flushed crimson. Her eyes swelled with tears in an instant.

She said, "You've saved my life before, now it's my turn to save yours. We'll walk out of this place together but please always stay behind me."

Zeya would only agree for Ingjin to take a half-step in front of him, as he had to depend on her for direction. Then they set off with Ingjin leading the way. She was confident, but sometimes overconfident, so that Zeya had to pull her back from stepping on objects that looked dodgy. After they had covered a mile, Zeya began to lead, as his expertise and experience as a landmines officer had proved to be as important as Ingjin's familiarity with the forest landscape. Forging ahead, they held each other's hand tightly and never let go. It was not just because they understood they had each other to depend on for survival, they also felt a deep desire waiting to be fulfilled.

They came to a small pond. While they took a short rest, Ingjin told Zeya how she had come to find out about his execution.

She said after Zeya had brought her to the monastery where she stayed the night, she returned home the next day and was told Nilar was dead. The official version was that Nilar had been raped and murdered by a low-ranking officer on the edge of the forest. She went with the village headman on one of his trips delivering food supplies to the army base, and found out the prisoner accused of rape and murder was actually the officer who had saved her. She had her suspicions, believing Zeya was innocent. On the night Zeya was destined to die, Ingjin hid herself in the forest, tracking the progress of the execution. She saw how Zeya was marched in front of a procession of soldiers, and how his commander molested him in the forest. Zeya was mortified to know that Ingjin, who was so worried that she could not turn her eyes away from what was happening, had witnessed everything a young girl was not supposed to see.

"What would you have done if they had executed me?" asked Zeya.

"I would say a little prayer for you," replied Ingjin. "Then I'd bury you. You're a good man. I hope you deserve a next life better than this."

Zeya was greatly touched. He had suddenly become so bold that he said, "I don't care about my next life. I only want to know, while you've saved this present life of mine, would you promise to spend the rest of it with me?"

Ingjin didn't know what to say. Blushing profusely, she turned her face slightly to escape Zeya's intense eyes. She was happy, but her happiness also made her weak. She froze on the spot, as if she had suddenly lost her bearings in the forest which had been her playground since childhood. She had never before thought a landmine could hurt her, but now she was not so sure, as if the forest was jealous of her happiness and not friendly anymore.

Zeya waited anxiously for her reply, with eyes filled with love. Suddenly she was not afraid anymore as she could now depend on Zeya to protect her. And she said, "I promise."

After they had emerged safely from the landmine-strewn forest they went to the monastery, where the abbot agreed to give them refuge. A month later, when Ingjin turned seventeen, they married under the supervision of the abbot in a simple Buddhist ceremony attended by Ingjin's grandmother.

Then the dry season began, and the troops were making final preparations for war. Soldiers ransacked the villages, drafting porters and grabbing livestock and food supplies. Zeya and Ingjin, who were hiding in the basement of the monastery's storehouse, lived in constant fear of arrest.

But the dry season offensive had in the end not taken place. There were commands and countermands with regard to whether an attack should be launched because of the death of General Naing Lwin, which had seriously impacted the morale of the soldiers. Finally, the Senior Head of the military government, after consultation with his most trusted fortuneteller, called off the operation by announcing a unilateral truce. The troops withdrew, and the villagers that had been living under the menace of an impending war for months were finally able to heave a huge sigh of relief. They were allowed to return to their pastoral habits and duties, if only temporarily.

Ingjin's grandmother had been unselfishly praying to her god every day. This time her prayer was heard and duly answered. The threat of war, which everybody said was looming near, was lifted, and she and her granddaughter could live in peace again. Now at eighty-nine and counting, she remembered she had come from a royal family of the Shan Sao Hpas and was the daughter of a Shan princess. During the years of a protracted civil war fighting the old Burmese monarchs and the junta government, she had lost all her sons and close relatives except her granddaughter from her youngest son who had also gone missing. Now Ingjin had grown up, and thank God she had found a husband as soon as she had come of age. Her last wish was to stay alive long enough to see with her own eyes the arrival of her great-grandchildren. But what a pity that this last wish was not to be granted. She passed away ten months after she had relocated with the newlyweds to a village in the deep jungle of Southern Shan. Three weeks after her death, Ingjin gave birth to a pair of beautiful, fair-skinned, identical twin girls.

14

M.A.Y.A.

———

The Venerable Master U Vicitta, looking tired, wanted a break. He asked me to meditate on the story, which I believed had only been half-told. He too closed his eyes to meditate, and dozed off seconds later in a sort of trance.

I confess I didn't quite get the moral of the story. But I wasn't blind. This was a time when people often changed names to avoid repression and persecution. Although Zeya and Ingjin were unfamiliar names to me, I could confidently say that Zeya was my father and Ingjin my mother, whom Meena and I affectionately called Ahba and Ahmay.

The story of Zeya had made it easier for me to understand why Ahba was such a taciturn man, quiet and thoughtful, who would opt for a walk instead of a talk at times of crisis or uncertainty.

Ahmay was just the opposite. She was bright and cheerful, loving and caring. I didn't remember having seen her sporting a ponytail; perhaps I was too young for that. The Ingjin I knew was already a beautiful young woman in her prime, always draped in a watery-blue longyi, with her hair knotted into a bun pinned with a seasonal flower like the yellow padauk or white jasmine.

Perhaps because of Zeya's inglorious past, it was no wonder that we lived our life nomadically.

Moving from place to place, Ahba would take up anything on offer to make a living. He had been hired for a few thousand kyat a day to work in the paddy fields during the harvest seasons; or labouring under a scorching sun at rock quarry sites.

There was this one time he took up business selling red rice, and went bankrupt the first day. He didn't realise that one needs to be shrewd, and even cunning, to do business for a profit; whereas honesty and sympathy are dismissed as worthless. He couldn't bring himself to bargain with housewives juggling a meagre income to cover the basic needs of the family. He felt disgusted that he had to squeeze really poor folks for money. In the end, when he was selling his rice at a loss, he gave all the rice away to the poor and quit doing business forever.

In those days, we also lived dangerously.

There was many a shocking moment at midnight when Meena and I would be startled in our sleep and told to pack and run. The reason for fleeing was either the outbreak of another civil war or a new wave of forced relocation programmes. Now I also knew, at various times we were on the run, that it was because of Ahba's connection to the murder of a junta commander.

It also explained why we had never joined the exodus going to the relocation camps set up by the military government. When the soldiers came, we took to hiding in the forest and returned a few days later. In circumstances when the village had been destroyed, we moved on to settle elsewhere.

But in spite of the difficult times, my childhood was not as sad and miserable as it sounds.

When I was about nine or ten, Ahba found a teaching post in a village monastery school, and things settled down to a more natural pace. These were some of my halcyon days. In the early morning, Ahba went with us to the school where he taught and we studied, while Ahmay worked at home growing vegetables on a small strip of land behind our thatched cottage. Nam was the name of the river that ran past our village. A tributary of the Salween, it makes a loop across a little plain towards the south, turning gradually north again before it falls in torrents over a cliff. At the end of the loop there was a small lake, where Meena and I used to bathe and swim. Dinnertime was among the best of my memories. A happy family is a family without someone absent or missing. We were all present at the table, the food was sufficient and the meals were delicious. Ahmay was an excellent cook. She had learned cooking from her grandmother who died days before Meena and I were born. She said her cooking was not simply Burmese style, it was also blended with Shan flavours; when it was fried rice, it was Shan fried rice; when it was mohinga – a rice noodle and fish soup eaten for breakfast – it was Shan mohinga. It was when I learned cooking from Ahmay that I knew I was endowed with a sense of proportions and a natural ability to mix ingredients, which I put to good use when I later dabbled in explosives.

Entering a third year living in the tranquil village in Shan, we had probably outstayed our welcome after the kindness shown to us by the time and place. On one rather sad and gloomy day we left, never to return. This was after the family was dealt a tragic blow.

It happened one afternoon when I was lying in bed with a hot forehead. Ahba came home before school finished. He said soldiers had come. The village headman and four others suspected of insurgent activities had been arrested. The villagers were being gathered to assemble in the school courtyard for relocation to a camp a hundred miles away.

"This is not a drill," Ahmay, who was always graceful and calm in all situations, lightly joked as she packed things into a suitcase. Ten minutes later we quietly slipped away through the backdoor when the sound of soldiers doing a house-to-house search came near.

On our way we made a stop at the riverside, as a last chance to store up enough water for use in the next few days before we went uphill to the forest. The river ran in a rushing torrent, and Ahmay had to steady herself by holding onto a lower branch of a tree on the riverbank as she stepped down to fill the bottles while we waited with the suitcases. After she had returned with the bottles of water and as we were about to set off again, she suddenly asked us to wait a moment.

She stepped back into the river, paddling across to some trees blazing with white and yellow flowers. Standing on tiptoe, she hesitated a little about what colour flower to choose before she decided on a yellow one. As she pinned the flower to the coiled hair at the back of her head, she flashed us a beautiful smile, looking somewhat embarrassed for the delay. Then she hurried back to join us when Meena cried, "Ahmay, give me water. I'm thirsty."

We went into the forest, intending to stay there for a couple of days to a week. But the situation had become critical, as we were quickly running out of water in just three days because of my persistent fever. At times my forehead burned like hot charcoal and Ahmay had to cool it constantly with a wet towel. On the morning of the fourth day, Ahba couldn't wait any longer. He decided to venture back to our village and find out if the soldiers had gone to see whether we could all go home as soon as possible.

Due to the distance to the village and back, we thought Ahba would only return in the evening. But to our surprise, he reappeared a little after noon. He said we could probably go home now. This should have been good news, yet as he went on describing what he had seen and heard on the road, his tone of voice was pensive, almost sad.

He said he had met a man who was residing in the same village as ours. His name was Yaw, a former dissident. He was dying of AIDS, which he had contracted while serving time in prison for crimes of endangering state-security activities. After his release, he lived in isolation in our village because of his troubles with either AIDS or with the junta government, or both.

He was on the verge of dying when the soldiers came four days ago. His appalling sight had frightened off the soldiers, who left immediately without opening fire at the man for disobeying the relocation order. A bullet was saved. A life – or what remained of it – was spared. But to his dismay, he was still alive three days later. Realising he probably would have to be around for longer still, he decided to pay a visit to his mother living in the village on the other side of the mountain.

Stepping out of his house, he found the village was totally abandoned. The houses were vacant, and the street was empty, with no sight of soldiers. Except for a stray dog, there was not a soul in the entire place. As he teetered away, he was perplexed as to why the soldiers had left without setting fire to the village.

When he met Ahba on the way, he informed him that the soldiers had gone. Ahba thanked him for the news, and was glad to know that he could finally go home. But Yaw couldn't understand why the soldiers had not burnt down the village.

Ahba, speaking from his knowledge of the military, explained that the soldiers would sometimes destroy villages to punish people for insurgent activities, but at other times keep the villages intact for future resettlement by different people.

Yaw sighed, "It sounds like even brutality has a pattern."

Ahba agreed, thinking it important to be aware of the pattern if one was to survive against the odds. With a confidence he was later to regret, he concluded that he could now safely return to the village with his family. So he said goodbye to Yaw. But noticing Yaw was not seeing all that he was supposed to see in his wasting condition – his eyeballs bulging at the rims and the irises enlarged with a dark yellowish colour like the eyes of an ailing dog – Ahba wondered if the poor man would ever make it to his destination. He said a little prayer for him as he watched Yaw hobble away under a blistering sun.

Ahmay was overjoyed to know we could finally leave the forest to return home where there was fresh water from a river nearby and medicine was at hand. Acting on the urgency of my condition, we set off in great haste.

But the journey back turned out to be an extremely excruciating experience.

I was too sick to walk on my own, so Ahba had to carry me on his back. As we led in front, Ahmay tried to catch up, struggling with the burden of the suitcases. Meena never saw the need to hurry. Lagging behind, she went in and out of the trees, singing and picking flowers. Lying in semi-consciousness on Ahba's back, I could sometimes hear Meena's voice complaining loudly, "Ahmay, I'm thirsty!" But we had completely run out of water, and I guessed everyone was at varying degrees of dehydration.

We took a rest later under the shade of a large rock surrounded by huge trees. Ahba, who looked tired and exhausted, quickly began snoring as soon as his body hit the grass. Ahmay, sitting next to the suitcases, was panting softly. Meena took a nap, but not for long, and woke up whimpering, "Ahmay, I'm going to die of thirst."

"Oh dear, I'm sorry," crooned Ahmay. "Let me see what I can do about it."

She stood up to straighten her dress. As she smoothed her hair and arranged it in a lovely knot behind her head, she looked slightly uneasy for not having a fresh flower to adorn it. Ahba was still snoring. She picked up a bottle and said, "I'm going to find something to drink. Tell Ahba I'll be right back."

When she returned a little over half an hour later, she hadn't found any water. But she had instead brought back a handful of wild berries. As she sat down to prepare the berries by removing the kernels inside, she explained that her grandmother had told her the berries were not only an excellent thirst quencher, they were also a heal-all for almost every ailment, especially effective for bodies with a temperature. She insisted that I swallow at least a dozen of them, even though I found the green berries bitter and sour. Meena stopped after taking several, and complained again of thirst, as the berries could only help wet the tongue somewhat but were in no way a substitute for water.

When we resumed our journey, Ahmay suggested leaving the suitcases behind, hiding them in the bushes to be retrieved later. She planned to go ahead, searching for water by travelling light. She gave Meena her word that her thirst would be over very soon, as she thought she might find watermelons or strawberries in the area. Meena was cheered up by the mouthwatering promise.

Ahmay felt my forehead with her hand and said excitedly, "I think the berries are working. Your temperature is going down."

I couldn't tell, and I only managed to respond with a weak smile. She said, "Don't worry. Water will be with you girls right away."

She spun around to go and hurried down a rutted lane with bouncing steps. This was the Ahmay I always fondly remembered: loving and caring in her bright looks; kind, courteous and long-suffering.

We hit the road after Ahmay had gone ahead. I slept on and off in semi-consciousness on Ahba's back, occasionally awaking to his footsteps tramping heavily on sand and dry mud, or sometimes startled by the noisy chirping of small grey-headed parrots perching above in the trees. After a glimpse of the long dusty road without end, I would quickly drop back to sleep.

The next time I woke up, it was near evening. A black eagle was circling in the twilight sky where dark red-purple clouds gathered.

I asked Ahba, "Will we be home anytime soon?"

"Yes. We're getting near," he replied. "In fact, the road drops from here on its way to our village."

I asked again, "Does it mean the river is also not far away?"

"Indeed," he said. "We'll see the Nam in no time."

I was feeling much better now, thanks to the wild berries probably. My temperature had subsided, and I was experiencing a cool forehead for the first time in days. I told Ahba to put me down and let me walk on my own. As I was lowered to the ground, I stumbled a bit at first, but quickly found the strength to walk steadily.

Meena shouted from behind, "Ahba, wait for me!"

Ahba, still on his knees, waited with open arms as Meena raced into his embrace. He lifted Meena and asked, "You tired, my dear?"

"Yes. I want a nap," purred Meena, resting her head on Ahba's shoulder and shutting her eyes immediately.

Ahba, as dutiful and deferential as any father to his daughter, carefully cradled Meena in his arms as he resumed the way.

After another half a mile, we came to the point where we could see in the distance our village of thatched huts set in a clearing in the forest. I thought I'd also see men returning from the paddy fields after a day's toil and the smoke of stove fires rising to the sky as housewives prepared their evening meals. But it was all quiet in the village; not even the barking of a dog was heard. Then, I realised, the village was now forbidden ground and all the villagers had been forced away to the relocation camp.

I crossed a meadow and paused at the edge of the hill. The River Nam came quite suddenly into view. From my perspective I had an extensive panoramic vista of the river that left the high plateau to rush down an elongated bend before pouring over a steep cliff to join the main stream. Looking down the steep slope, the river at its closest skirted past the foot of the hill where I stood. Trees with a sprinkle of red flowers lined the riverbank; the water looked placid and calm as dusk fell.

It was at this moment I had spotted Ahmay mid-hill. She was on a narrow path that went meandering down to the river. Standing on a rock, she was waving vigorously to catch my attention.

Ahba was resting in the meadow after he had carefully placed Meena, who was sound asleep, on the grass. I shouted excitedly to Ahba, "Ahmay has found water!" Ahba came over to the edge of the hill. He yelled over to Ahmay, "You need me to go with you to the river?"

"No, I'm already halfway. You stay with the girls and take a rest," Ahmay shouted back. "I won't be long."

Ahba called back, "Be careful!" We were not sure if she had heard it clearly or not at all, as she continued straight to make her way downhill.

We followed her closely with our eyes when she was getting in and out of the narrow leafy forest path that seemed like a maze in the dense trees and grasses. But she was someone born and bred on the Shan plateau; if she wanted to find the way to the river there would be no obstacle too big that she couldn't overcome.

She seemed to spend a long time in the bushes and I was beginning to worry. But then she suddenly reappeared out of nowhere, standing on the bank and waving at us merrily.

Then she went ahead to get water by stepping into the river. She ventured out as far as waist level, where she stooped to wash her face and the bare parts of her body. She then filled the bottle with water, drank from it, and refilled it afterwards. Knowing we were all very thirsty, she quickly returned to the bank for the way back.

We were relieved, for a splintered second, that all was well.

But then, to our surprise, something had caught her attention. Pausing before a clump of trees that lined the riverbank, she seemed as if transfixed by the flowers in full bloom. I knew she had sorely wanted to adorn her hair with something becoming since morning, and she must have found the flowers of an unequalled daintiness irresistible. When the flowers above her were out of reach in spite of her standing on tiptoe with a lengthening arm, she changed her mind to aim for the flowers from some lower branches hanging over the river's surface. She twisted round so she could lean her body on the trunk of the tree, and this was where she suddenly slipped. She had, however, quickly seized a stem and regained her balance.

"Haven't I told you to be careful?" Ahba grumbled quietly as we watched anxiously as Ahmay, after having picked a flower, began to retrace her steps.

Just then, something exploded under her feet. Amid flying sand and a cloud of odious black smoke, she was hurled inhumanly high up into the air, and left hanging there for what seemed to be an ungodly time before her body fell crashing into the river with a mute splash. Tiny shreds of leaves and thousands of red flowers flew around like a heavy shower of confetti. The water appeared placid and calm, but was actually rough and wild as it carried the body away like something placed on a high-speed conveyor belt. Swirling in the waves, she was only visible by her light-blue dress, which had grown murky and dark as the body was jostled en route. Arriving at the end of the river where a steep cliff stood at the ready, she flew over it like a bird as if she could defy gravity. When she looked as if she would float further away, her body suddenly turned and plunged precipitously downwards before landing in the deep river below and vanished completely underwater.

I must have been screaming senselessly throughout. It was one long, drawn-out scream that had begun from the moment of the explosion and sustained its piercing, sad sound long after the body of Ahmay had become invisible.

Ahba, overwhelmed by the evil that had befallen Ahmay, took a misstep and fell down the slope of the meadow. Just when I thought I was to lose both parents within minutes of each other, his fall was obstructed by the trees and he was able to climb his way back.

I must have still been screaming when he sat beside me and took me into his arms. He said, a little incoherently, "Ahmay is gone. But she can swim, can't she?"

I buried my face into his chest and cried. I cried and cried for a long time until someone suddenly touched my back. I sat up and saw it was Meena, who must have been awoken by my morbid screams and cries. Rubbing her eyes, Meena asked, "Where's Ahmay? I'm hungry." Then we all sat together in silence, staring into the void and striving to make sense of what had happened.

In our world, you don't have a reason to explain every tragedy when tragedies just inexplicably occur around you. There was, however, a clear reason behind the murder of Ahmay, which we later learned.

It is called the strategy of area denial. To enforce relocation of a local population, the military would bury landmines in the cleared villages at places like wells and riversides where villagers do their washing and cleaning. Landmines were also planted in fields with crops to be harvested, sheds keeping the harvested crops, and even kitchens with the remains of the last meal still on the table, thus barring the return of the banished villagers.

Ahba might rightly have been aware that even brutality had a pattern. But the thing he had failed to see was: when the military was determined to win the war over their most hated enemy (which, coincidentally, happened to be their own people), they would from time to time change the pattern of their brutal behaviour. And the junta, being capable of the most horrible crimes on earth, always won.

Ahba was devastated by the tragedy. He spent ten days searching in the river, but Ahmay's body was never recovered.

In the days after we moved to a village downstream, he sank into bitterness and depression. Deeply affected by Ahmay's death, he did not work anymore. On a normal day, if he was not at home, you could probably find him loitering along the river. He would gaze blankly at the waterfall in the distance, with tears streaming down his face. When we went to fetch him for dinner in the evening, he would tell us to leave him alone. What he needed was some private time, as well as a drink.

One day when Meena and I brought him food at the river, we saw a woman offer him a bowl of rice. He accepted it after the woman had successfully talked some sense into him. We were relieved to see that he was eating again.

One evening, when it was raining, I went to the riverside with an umbrella. From afar I saw a woman (I'm not sure if it was the same woman who brought him rice) just walking away from him. She looked somewhat dishevelled as there was a wind blowing her way. But she also looked kind of pretty. She greeted me with a faint smile but I turned my eyes away uneasily, without knowing why.

Then Ahba stopped going to the river. At home he would lock himself in his room, drinking, chanting and meditating. When he slept, he cursed loudly in his dreams. Skipping most meals, he overdosed on wine, religion and, as I later discovered, sex. His state of mind deteriorated, and his behaviour worsened to the point of insanity.

One midnight when I went to the back garden for a wee, I walked past his room and heard the giggles of a woman inside, begging for mercy between heavy gasps. I was stunned. I quickly moved away from the window and hid behind a hedgerow in the garden, totally forgetting my urge to pee. Crouching there, I asked myself exactly what it was that he had done wrong which had induced such a burning revulsion inside me.

As I waited, the door of his room suddenly sprang open. Two women, faceless in the darkness and telling only by their curvaceous figures, came out and slipped away through the rear gate. They sniggered, giggled and laughed out loud when they were out of the gate, as if they were the conquerors rather than the conquered. I wondered if Ahba would come out to see them off, but no; as soon as the temptresses were gone, he was heard chanting in his room again.

Utterly dazzled by the preposterousness of suspecting adultery that had transpired to be an orgy of sorts, I didn't know what to think. I was too young and inexperienced to say if his behaviour was infidelity in the wake of the death of Ahmay, or only mindless sexual dalliances. He was, after all, my father. I could have hated him based on whatever moral judgment of the day, but ultimately I had only pity for everything he was made to endure. I therefore stopped analysing this or that and accepted that Ahba was sick and needed help in an unbearably sad time.

THE VENERABLE MASTER U VICITTA jerked awake in his meditation. He lit a candle and asked, "Where are we?"

"Zeya and Ingjin gave birth to a pair of twin girls…" I replied.

"That's right…"

To confirm my belief that Zeya and Ingjin were my parents, I asked him, "Did you know Ingjin was dead?"

He nodded with a sigh. "Ingjin was a girl in a million; a true Shan princess. I always miss her and her ponytail."

"And Zeya was mad?" I said, further proving my theory.

U Vicitta answered affirmatively. "Yes, he went mad at the death of Ingjin. But Zeya, who had been an ordained *bhikkhu*, had a way of dealing with a mind that had gone crazy."

"How?" I asked.

"Madness is only an escape from great pain," answered U Vicitta. "One day he woke up to his situation and thought he'd had enough of it. He went to the hilltop monastery in Shan to find me, but I had already moved to the city. Later he tracked me down in Rangoon. When he saw me, he asked for my help to become a monk again."

"If Zeya had become a monk, what about Ahba?" I thought with a mixture of doubts and suspicion.

With a mysterious smile, U Vicitta went on to describe what Zeya had encountered as he made his attempt to return to the monastic order.

At Zeya's request to rejoin monkhood, U Vicitta arranged for him to stay in the monastery's meditation centre in preparation for ordination to be readmitted to the Sangha community. He was required to meditate nonstop for a month. But it was only after three days that he interrupted his programme, emerged from the meditation cubicle and requested a private session with U Vicitta.

"I've found it very difficult to almost impossible to sit still in my meditation," Zeya told U Vicitta. "Weird images of fiery colours keep popping up before my eyes all the time. In the back of my mind there are all kinds of violent and vengeful thoughts battling for my serious attention…"

"They're illusions, but they don't exist without reason," remarked U Vicitta. "What do you reckon is the reason?"

Zeya paused for a long time before he answered, "It is my anger. I've become really angry this time."

In a tone of abject pain, Zeya said he had never experienced anger of this magnitude before. When he was a child, the loss of his parents and siblings only made him sad but not angry. He was confused and upset when he was conscripted and made a human minesweeper. His commander molested him and he felt ashamed and downright disgraceful. When he was later framed and sent to death by firing squad, he felt just sorrow and grim resignation. As a wanted criminal, he and his family were constantly on the run from village to village across the Shan plateau, which had only made him feel desperate and woeful with a heavy heart.

But the death of Ingjin was entirely different. He was hit by some really powerful stuff emotionally. He was mad at the military, and the idea that the brutal government was to blame had been lingering in his mind ever since. On the verge of being consumed by his undying anger, he decided to seek refuge with Sangha, so that he could forgive and forget under the grace of Buddha. But after meditating for three days to pacify his mind, he only found his anger to have grown more pronounced. He didn't understand how he, as a former monk, could have become so unforgiving.

U Vicitta was able to empathise with Zeya. He said, "If your anger is about the military government, you're not alone. We monks are all very angry, too."

Zeya was shocked. "Monks by profession don't easily get angry. Is it really that bad with the military regime?"

"To say the junta government is bad is an understatement," answered U Vicitta. "The problem is that they never trust the monks who always crave to live according to the rules of Buddha's *Vinaya* in the spirit of democratic tradition. To control them, the government created the Sangha Organisation Law by placing all nine Sangha sects in the country under a State Sangha Organisation. All monks, as members of the organisation, are required to strictly abide by the rules and regulations stipulated by the military regime."

To enforce the draconian rules and regulations, U Vicitta continued, military intelligence personnel and members of USDA (Union Solidarity and Development Association) were assigned to the monasteries to keep an eye on the behaviour and conduct of the monks. As a result, many monks and novices had been disrobed and imprisoned for non-compliance.

"Besides, our anger is also mixed with enormous sadness," sighed U Vicitta. "There are monks whom I've known personally, for example, the Venerable Dhamma Wara, the Venerable Vithoadda, the Venerable Meenana, the Venerable Zawtika, the Venerable Arsara from the Thayettaw Monastery in Rangoon, the Venerable Bhaddanta

Yewata, the Venerable Zana Theyna, the Venerable Neminda and the Venerable Neymira, all have perished in prisons or labour camps. And many are still locked up in state prisons."

Zeya was saddened by the mention of the dead and imprisoned monks. He was reminded of his master, the Venerable Sayadaw U Okka, whom he always wanted to rejoin should he have found out his whereabouts. With a helpless tone, he asked, "What can the monks do about their anger?"

"Not much indeed," answered U Vicitta. "We wish we could free the country from the military dictatorship. But monks are bound by the doctrines of Dhamma of Tipitaka, which prohibit all forms of violence and extremism. Rebellion is absolutely out of the question. I must confess that I envy you who have no such constraints."

"Why should you envy an angry layman like me?" asked Zeya. "Is there anything I can do which you can't as far as expelling all those bastards in government and liberating the country?"

"The country is in a shambles; people are poverty-stricken. A man with your expertise and without the constraint of the robe is in an excellent position to put things right," said U Vicitta. "Use your anger positively. Ask not what is wrong with those bad guys in the military government; ask what you can do to right the wrong and make those guys disappear. I have a secret to share with you if you are interested."

"What kind of secret?" asked Zeya.

"Yesterday, there was a conference held here in the basement of the monastery, attended by people driven by a passion to find a solution to the problems of the country," said U Vicitta.

Zeya looked curious and intensely interested. He said, "I don't think I'm returning to the monkhood anytime soon with this level of anger. Please tell me more about how an angry layman like me can help exert pressure for the necessary social change."

So U Vicitta confided in Zeya that the *Sangha Samaggi* (Young Monks Union) had just held an underground conference in the monastery the day before, attended by representatives of monks from monasteries all over the country. The agenda was about what the Sangha community could possibly do to save the country from further destruction by the regime. A number of democratic organisations ranging from the moderate to the radical were also invited. All sides argued passionately for what they believed in and what they thought would work. In a way, all participants agreed unanimously that the junta government was shit and must go. But opinion was split seriously on issues like non-violent struggle advocated by the leading Democratic Party, or the use of armed resistance to overthrow the government. At the end of the conference people left without being able to agree on a concrete action plan, which was not unusual for this kind of political debate when there was not enough emphasis on the great urgency of the situation.

"This is disappointing," said Zeya. "Where's the leadership in the country?"

"The Lady is our highest leader," said U Vicitta reverentially. "But after the Lady has been incarcerated under house arrest, her movement of non-violent struggle as the only approach and strategy to achieve democracy has deteriorated to a manner of non-struggle. It is the great fear of some people that if we wait too long until the day the Lady is free, the country will be beyond rescue."

"Let's do something now or never – is that what you're trying to say?" said Zeya earnestly. "I'll do it. Just tell me what."

With a wry smile, U Vicitta said, "I can't tell you what to do as I'm only a monk. But there are people who can." He told Zeya that while most participants had left at the end of the conference, some others who had businesses to deal with in the city had stayed behind for another night in the monastery. He suggested Zeya have a chat with them to explore the possibilities.

Later in the evening, Zeya went to the Dhamma Hall to attend a sermon. After the sermon, U Vicitta brought Zeya's attention to a guy who had just slipped out of the back door for a smoke. He was a short, sallow-looking man in his late forties; he had sharp, hawk-like eyes and a scar on his left cheek.

U Vicitta said, "That's the man you probably should meet. He is very interested in your expertise. You'll find him in the garden behind the Scripture Hall waiting to talk to you."

"Who exactly is the man I'm going to meet?" asked Zeya.

"Simply put, the man is a radical," said U Vicitta. "Of all the people I know who have their own vision of a new Burma, this man is the most determined about doing something revolutionary to change the current situation. To be clear, his is not the popular 'resistance' of the Lady's camp. The party he belongs to is among some of the most bellicose factions, and he himself is a radical who scoffs at the idea of open dialogue and reconciliation with the junta government, and sneers at those who insist on non-violence strategies. He once shared with me the crazy idea of blowing up the notorious Central Prison Insein to free all the political prisoners there. I didn't know how to respond except to give him my blessing."

"Well, he definitely can use me if there's anything to blow up," remarked Zeya. "By the way, how shall I address him?"

"That's a good question," U Vicitta said. "He has several names. Some call him U Nyo Thein, others call him Dr Nyo Thein as he, in addition to being a party leader, is also a medical practitioner working at a refugee camp on the Thai-Burmese border. He also has an interesting nickname that people gave him after an insurrectionary speech he made to an assembly of young monks. I was there in the audience, and every word he said on that day still rings clearly in my ears as if he were speaking to me now.

"The title of his speech is '*A farewell to Alms – Burma's Road to Democracy*'.

"In the speech, U Nyo Thein praises the Sangha community as a moral authority, the most respectable and influential in civil society. At a time of moral decay as we have experienced, like now, he considers that the Sangha community should take up a more industrious role by joining forces with the democratic parties to put an end to the vicious rule of the regime.

"Then changing to a tone of regret, he says: 'The monks seem reluctant, because they have found it objectionable to express themselves politically in the form of demonstrations or direct resistance to the repressive government.' And he points out, unequivocally, that that's not how moral authority is won; that's how it is lost.

"To illustrate, he tells the audience the story of Arjuna, the warrior prince, on the battlefield of Kurukshetra in *Bhagavad Gita*, the song of God and the eternal message of spiritual wisdom.

"Facing duty as a warrior to fight the righteous war between Pandavas and Kauravas, Arjuna, as the battle draws close, is overcome with self-doubt about the righteousness of the war against his own kith and kin. He is distraught at the thought of having to fight with his friends and family such as his dear teacher, Drona and grandsire Bhishma.

"Arjuna asks Lord Krishna, 'I do not see how any good can come from killing my own kinsmen in this battle. Why should I wish to kill them, even though they might otherwise kill me? Nor do I know which is better – conquering them or being conquered by them?'

"Lord Krishna tells Arjuna, 'Happy are the fighters to whom such fighting opportunities come unsought, opening for them the doors of the heavenly planets. You should know that there is no better engagement for you than fighting on religious principles; and so there is no need for hesitation.

"'If, however, you will not fight this righteous fight, failing your duty and losing your honour, then you will incur sin. The world will forever recount the story of your disgrace, and your enemies will deride your strength and speak many unspeakable words about you. What can be more painful than that?'

"U Nyo Thein uses the story to emphasise that non-violence, or the practice of non-resistance, which is equivalent to some perfect ideals of pacifism, has no place in a broken world. If it is of a righteous cause for the common good, fight for it; otherwise, it will incur sin as the result of neglecting one's religious duty.

"Some young monks in the audience argue that they are fighting all the time spiritually.

"U Nyo Thein tells them that they are wrong about fighting. And he asks them these questions:

"'What is the meaning of fighting if it is in the form of praying in obeisance for the mercy of Buddha and waiting in line with begging bowls for alms from the poor?

"'Where do people get their rice for alms-giving purposes when they are themselves starving and poverty-stricken?

"'As a Buddhist country, does it mean that Burma has to continue to tolerate the oppression of a totalitarian government for eternities to come?

"'If so, where is the moral fulcrum as represented by the Sangha community located on any given day?'

"Some young monks burst out crying. They want U Nyo Thein to tell them the answer.

"And U Nyo Thein says, 'Words are useless. Action is all we need. The answer is: Rise up for rice and democracy. There's no rice without democracy, except those who think they can continue to depend on the patronage of the military. It's not about *metta* (world peace); it's about struggle. And it has to begin from the point where you say *no* to alms from a repressive government and have faith in that democracy is our common rice, and without democracy, there will never be enough rice to feed the nation. So, my brothers, rise up now, for rice and democracy!'

"The young monks are thunderstruck. They applaud U Nyo Thein and give him a standing ovation, shouting, 'Rise up for rice! Rise up for democracy!'

"Since then, U Nyo Thein has a new nickname. He is well known amongst those who respect him and endorse his views as *Dr Rice*."

1 5

M . A . Y . A .

———✦———

"**R**ise up for rice… Rise up for democracy!"

I mumbled the words quietly, imagining myself in an excitable audience overwhelmed by an awe-inspiring speech.

"I would like to meet Dr Rice one day…" I mused.

"I don't see why you'd have anything to do with him," interrupted U Vicitta. "In fact, I regret a little having introduced your father to him."

"Why is that? He appears to be a man of action and great determination," I said. "Doesn't he offer the right kind of leadership this country seems to lack in the absence of Daw Suu?"

"Don't be disrespectful," said U Vicitta.

I was confused. "Have I said something wrong?" I asked.

U Vicitta sighed. "No, but the issue is complicated. As you're still young, you don't really need to know how grown men run the business of the country, whether it is through violence or non-violent struggle."

I disagreed, but I didn't say anything.

"Now may I ask you," continued U Vicitta, "after I've told you the story of Zeya, can you now tell the difference between good and very bad Tatmadaw?"

"Thanks for the story. Maybe Zeya is a good Tatmadaw, but he's not perfect," I said. "The same goes for Bo Tin Aung. Maybe he's far from perfect either but I'm not going to change my mind about marrying him."

"Don't be silly," said U Vicitta, raising his voice. "You're not marrying the Bo."

"Why not?" I shrieked. "Is it because Bo Tin Aung is a Tatmadaw officer like my father, or is it because you monks are angry and hostile to the Tatmadaw in general?"

I thought U Vicitta would chastise me for my impudence. He didn't. He only shook his head and lamented, "You're just a child who should still be picking up shells at the seaside, flying a kite, or riding a bike! What has happened to you that you're yelling at me for telling you not to marry a Tatmadaw?"

"I'm sorry." I quickly apologised most humbly for my rudeness. "But I'm sixteen and a half, going on seventeen. I'm more grown-up than you think."

"Grown-up in what sense?" U Vicitta snapped. "This is one unmistakable example of the country's social ills – a society dominated by the military that allows the younger generation to grow up in fear and insecurity, never acquiring a set of rational expectations about the future. Children are practically pressured to mature fast in order to take on adult responsibilities early on in life; and almost inevitably, they wither fast and die young in their fight for survival. What will history say about the inherent moral responsibilities in the human society within which we live today?"

I wasn't sure what he was talking about. I coughed as if choked. I was only pretending, as I was afraid that he would launch into another long lecture.

He looked at me, his eyes brimming with pity. He said, "Maya, I have the responsibility to protect you. Can I ask: Are you safe... with the officer?"

I felt "safe" was not a suitable word to describe my relationship with Bo Tin Aung, and I simply replied, "He is a good man, probably a good Tatmadaw, if you like."

"I'm surprised that you describe Bo Tin Aung as a good Tatmadaw, because my impression of him is quite the opposite," said U Vicitta.

"How much do you know him?" I asked uncomfortably. "And how do you rate him as a Tatmadaw?"

In a most unambiguous voice, U Vicitta said, "He is a freak of a human being, and a monster of a military officer."

His emphasis on the words 'freak' and 'monster' made me squirm.

And he went on: "We monks here working in the Pagoda are all familiar with Bo Tin Aung, who is assigned to conduct checks at Shwedagon for the Military Intelligence on a regular basis. But Maya, must I tell you everything about him as a freak?"

"By all means if it pleases you," I shrugged, "although there's no guarantee I could be dissuaded from marrying him."

U Vicitta sighed a deep sigh. He said, "You look as if you're living under the spell of a kind of deceit; either he has deceived you or you are deceiving yourself. Now listen carefully to what I'm going to tell you and decide for yourself."

Before he began, he took the time to light another candle. I narrowed my eyes uneasily at the monk's gaze, which became increasingly severe in a room that had become a little too bright. Then he cleared his throat and started, with obvious resentment in his tone, by declaring that Bo Tin Aung was to him something of an anomaly – an average and egotistical man, and a soldier with an indecent amount of boorishness rolled into one.

He was twice married, both times impulsively at the age of twenty and twenty-five respectively, and both marriages ended in tragedy. His first wife died in labour giving birth to a stillborn baby. His second wife became a drug addict after several miscarriages and died a few years ago, reportedly of substance abuse. Now approaching his mid-thirties, the fact that he was still childless made him feel incomplete. The monastery would never have known these things about his private life had he not volunteered to confide his secrets to our monks in the hope of receiving some sort of healing benediction for the need of a wife and numerous progeny, said U Vicitta.

Formerly a member of the *Swan Ah Shin* (Masters of Force), a pro-government community group acting as the informed eyes and ears for the military regime to counter and contain protesters, he later joined the Military Intelligence Bureau, where a distant uncle of his held a senior position. He moved to work in Rangoon when his uncle was made a commander of the Rangoon Division. Despite his uncle's influence, Bo Tin Aung had never advanced beyond the rank of Bo Gyi (Captain) because of his low education.

But that was not to say he was unimportant just because he was not clever or scrupulous enough. On the contrary, he was a man to be feared, because he was entrusted with the responsibility of taking care of his uncle's many interests. Officially he represented the commander on a number of township committees involving matters from university education to religious affairs, and unofficially assisted his uncle running the city's largest corruption ring.

Higher education had almost ceased to exist since 1996. To repress dissent, campuses were repeatedly closed to prevent students from gathering in protest; lectures were conducted via distance learning and examinations were handled through correspondence. In Rangoon, Bo Tin Aung had contributed significantly to the development of higher education by making correctional behaviour an integral part of the curriculum. A special physical education programme was introduced in which students (and their recalcitrant leaders in particular) were required to serve time in state prisons and labour camps.

He also played an important role in religious affairs, with Shwedagon Pagoda on top of his list of monasteries under surveillance. When there were new directives issued by the State Sangha Committee, he'd arrive in full military uniform and pronounce with solemn officiousness the new rules to an assembly of monks. As part of his agenda, he'd take the opportunity to pick on monks suspected of disobeying the laws laid down by the government, with threats to defrock them.

On occasions of routine visits and checks at the pagoda, he'd do it less formally by appearing in civilian clothes. Mixing among the worshippers, he would hide himself inside the prayer halls behind the Buddha statue and spend time eavesdropping on what the monks or nuns and other visitors said in their prayers and chants, looking for signs of suspicious anti-government behaviour.

"A pest and a weasel," grunted U Vicitta disdainfully. "His behaviour in the prayer hall can only be described as filthy and disgusting. Usually after he had left the hall, the cleaner would find cigarette butts, wine bottles, remains of betel nuts, tin foil, and dirty stains all over the space where the officer had nestled. It is not hard to imagine that he was drinking and smoking and chewing betel nuts when he eavesdropped on the pilgrims.

"We have recently banned smoking inside Shwedagon Pagoda. In the near future we'll also restrict betel nut chewing. That, of course, is not enough to stop the military intelligence officer from doing whatever he wants inside the prayer halls. But smoking and chewing betel nuts aside, he is also suspected of drawing offensive graffiti on the back of the statues. It is an act of sacrilege against Buddha. It is a sin!"

I frowned at the word "sin" as I struggled to understand Bo Tin Aung's motive. I did not know why he would have done something so childish. When I pictured in my mind a raffish and handsome officer, who, without obvious purpose, busied himself by drawing graffiti on the back of a Buddha statue in a dark corner of the prayer hall, I couldn't help allow a half-smile to form on my lips when I felt the guy was so mad and so cool.

"Maya, this is not funny," said U Vicitta with a reproving look. "A man with the habit of alcohol and substance abuse is dangerous."

I bit my lip and asked, "Has he committed anything worse than the… laughable sin you have just described?"

"You think him laughable?! No, he is abominable!" uttered U Vicitta in a voice of dire exasperation. "So you want examples of something far worse? Seriously, what do you think of the arrest and imprisonment of students and monks over the years? What about his use of brutal force by working with the vigilantes in the suppression of civilian dissent? And what about the city's rampant corruption since his uncle's arrival? I just can't stress enough that this man is extremely dangerous and detestable. I don't know why he would have agreed to marry you. I suspect he's only using you for some unspeakable purposes. Maya, you must leave him now before it is too late."

"But I love him!" I contended. "What am I supposed to do?"

"Do something, whatever it is, for the sake of sanity," cried U Vicitta. "Imagine, with just one careless slip of the tongue, you could have easily landed your father in the gallows for a third time."

I thought this was the least of my concerns. To assuage him, I said, "I told Bo Tin Aung my parents are dead."

"Maya, you're not stupid," said U Vicitta, with a tone of relief. "But why have you got yourself mixed up with a Tatmadaw officer in the first place?! Do you know you're only a child?"

"That's not true. I'm a big girl now," I said, genuinely meaning it.

"I'm not sure about that. In my eyes, you're only a defenceless child who is yet to mature mentally and emotionally," he said. "You don't really know what you're doing, do you?"

His question had made me excessively uncomfortable. The air in the hall was stuffy and suffocating. I yearned to end the discussion quickly and leave the place at once. And I said, "My Venerable Master, I'm not as simple and innocent as you think. You know Ahba is behind the explosion of the Mandalay Marketplace…"

"I, of course, know," he cut in abruptly, shaking his head. "I wish I had never heard about it. Everything, from plan to execution, is nothing but a pure mess. I condemn all activities causing bloodshed to civilians. But I don't blame your father, who only contributes his skills and expertise. I don't blame people who are a little radical either, except that they should understand radicalism is not the same as terrorism."

He might have noticed I was waiting with gaping mouth in mid-sentence, and he asked me, "What is it you want to tell me about the Mandalay Marketplace explosion? You should be working doubly hard at your studies when your father is out of town. What have you been doing these days?"

"I have something for your ears only, OK?" I said in confidence. "In fact, I was busy. I worked with Uncle Kloh to blow up the Strand Road Jetty on *Tatmadaw Dei*. My uncle has been arrested and locked up in Insein ever since. I'm still figuring out how to save him."

"This is absurd!" he growled in frustration; his face contracted horribly in gloomy despair.

I was a little shocked by his reaction, not knowing what to say.

Suddenly he swept his large, scrawny hand sporadically across his wrinkled face, as if to swat an annoying fly that had ventured near him. But there was no fly. I was perplexed by the sad, painful expression on his face and asked him, "Have I said anything wrong?"

"No, I'm only a bit tired. Perhaps you can go now," he said with a resigned voice.

I stood up to go. But he asked me to wait. "Maya, don't think I'm disappointed with you," he said. "On the contrary, you have made me proud. At only sixteen, you are already following in the footsteps of all those young men and women who have poured their souls into the revolution since 1988. Come here, my child, to receive an old monk's blessing."

His words gave me goose bumps and made me speechless with embarrassment.

At his prompting, I lay prostrate before him. He placed a hand on the top of my head and started chanting a weird chant. When he stopped, I asked, "Can I go now?"

With a nod, he said, "Forgive me for being a little long-winded. But please listen: your *Tatmadaw Bo* is never serious about marrying you. I suspect he is only using you for some despicable purpose. Leave him at the first opportunity."

"Yes, I will try," I answered cursorily, and rose to leave.

As I was moving towards the door, he still had not finished. "Come to me anytime if you need help. Remember, you're the daughter of Ingjin. I love you like you're my own child."

As he had again evoked the name of Ahmay, who was the font of grace and wisdom and always demanded that her daughters display the most exemplary manners, I feared she'd be disappointed if I just popped away without a big formal farewell to the monk, even if I was desperate to be gone. Hence I paused at the threshold, bowed graciously to the monk, and spoke in the most reverential voice, "Thank you, Venerable Master. Goodbye."

Then I pushed open the door and dashed off.

Outside, I found the pea-eyed novice monk Balu waiting under the shade of a tree. He said, "I'll take you to the officer. Will you please follow me?"

He took me to a prayer hall on the south side of the pagoda. I waited at the entrance while he went inside to find Bo Tin Aung. Moments later, Bo Tin Aung emerged as the crowd split in two to make way. He was pleased to see me, greeting me with an exaggerated grin. He said, "You don't look too happy. Why?"

I didn't know where to start. Despite the things I had heard about him, things that were dangerous and alarming too, I was glad to see him again. He was such a handsome man, with beautiful hair, fine teeth and a charming tone of voice. I must still be deeply and unreflectingly in love with him.

I said, "The monk who interviewed me doesn't seem to be very keen to marry us anytime soon. Shall I not feel upset about it?"

"Silly girl!" he said. "It's only a small delay. I don't really mind. The monks at Shwedagon Pagoda are busy. You know, there is this fat monk in charge of matrimonial affairs, whose name I forget, who is now having fun outside Rangoon at some anonymous, stupid place."

Balu looked eager to help with the missing information. He said, "It is the Venerable U Wayama. He is now in Bagan, helping a class of young monks to prepare for the *Payiyatt Sangha* examination."

"Shut up!" Bo Tin Aung knuckled Balu on his shaved head. "Don't try to be clever when I'm talking. If you are really that smart, inform me of the monks who are anti-government."

Balu said, "I don't know," rubbing the sore spot on his head.

"You don't? Or you won't?" said Bo Tin Aung with a fierce scowl on his face. "What if I pay you for the information?"

He took a handful of money from his pocket and tossed it in Balu's face.

"No, I don't want your money!" cried Balu.

As the money fell on the floor, the coins hitting the marble tiles with a shower of metallic sounds and the paper notes flying all around like butterflies in the wind, Bo Tin Aung said, glancing contemptuously at Balu, "Pick it up. It's yours now!" Then he strolled away, dragging me with him.

We turned to look back when we reached the exit and saw that Balu was salvaging the money that had scattered all over the floor. Bo Tin Aung sneered, "All people love money. Monks are no different."

It was at this moment Balu stood up, waving at us with fistfuls of money. "Officer, your money!" he shouted in our direction.

Bo Tin Aung shouted back, "You think you're virtuous or what, you greedy bastard?! If you don't want the money, give it to anyone who can come forward with the information."

"No, wait!" said Balu. "You take it back, or I'll give it to charity on your behalf!"

"Does it make any difference?" said Bo Tin Aung sarcastically.

Balu staggered across the marble pavement to the other side of the hall where there was a donation stand, and tossed, with a gust of childish laughter, all the money into the box. He spun around, hoisting his bare hands at us merrily. "Thank you, officer!" he whooped from a distance, and fell on his knees for a most humble kowtow, his forehead barely scratching the floor.

What a lovely, clever child, I thought.

Bo Tin Aung, however, disagreed. "This despicable little fucking shit makes me sick," he snorted. "Let's get out of here."

We left through the southern stairway after we had reclaimed our shoes. At noontime, Shwedagon Paya Road was bustling with traffic and pilgrims. Bo Tin Aung flagged down a taxi and told the driver to take us to Zawgyi's Café.

Zawgyi's Café was situated on the corner of the Bogyoke Aung San Market. We took a table on the front patio of the café facing the road. Bo Tin Aung ordered red curry chicken, fried watercress and Dagon beer. We watched the throng of people flowing like a tide on the busy Bogyoke Aung San Road while we ate our food.

By the time coffee was served, Bo Tin Aung checked his watch and grumbled, "The guy is late again." He dropped his head resignedly on the table and took a nap.

He was snoring when a short man wearing a long-sleeved white shirt and a dark green longyi strode into the restaurant. The guy seemed to know where he was going and walked straight to our table. He took the chair opposite me, and after a moment studying my face, said, "I'm sorry. I know all his girlfriends, but I don't seem to recognise you."

Bo Tin Aung must have been only half-asleep. He sat bolt upright and warned, "Be careful, old fool. She's my fiancée."

"Oh, I'm terribly sorry. You must be Maya," the guy said, offering his hand for a handshake. "I'm Shit-Lone, nice to meet you."

I gave him my hand, but he quickly withdrew his when Bo Tin Aung picked up a fork to stab him.

"You're late by a full hour," said Bo Tin Aung. "Have you been drinking?"

"What a question? Never deny I've been drinking non-stop for the past thirty-five years since I was born," he said, with pride in his voice.

He didn't seem to be lying, as evidenced by his appearance of a certain physical infirmity: a dark-yellow face with an unnatural puffiness, eyes small and bloodshot, and hair – coarse like straw – thinning around the crown.

"But I don't do drugs, except *yaba* occasionally," he continued. "Do you still remember the year when we celebrated our thirtieth birthdays together with a cocktail of ketamine and amphetamines...?"

Before he had even finished, Bo Tin Aung gave him a kung fu kick under the table. The chair on which Shit-Lone sat toppled over. He fell back, his body thrown to the floor. It was so funny that I just couldn't resist bursting into laughter.

Shit-Lone crawled his way back like a crab and said angrily, "What's the problem with you? Oh I know. I said something about the birthday. I'm sorry. I forgot that you're only twenty-nine. As we're the same age, I'm also twenty-nine. Okay now?"

Bo Tin Aung said, "No more nonsense. Let's have some serious discussion."

Shit-Lone fixed his chair, sat down and said, "Where do you want me to begin?"

"Say something, just to let me know you're sober," said Bo Tin Aung.

"Shall I give you a recap... of the situation?" suggested Shit-Lone.

"By all means," answered Bo Tin Aung.

Shit-Lone picked up an empty beer bottle from the floor, playing with it absentmindedly, as if searching for his thoughts before he said, "The situation is very simple. Essentially it is about burying you and your commander when both of you are dead."

Bo Tin Aung was infuriated, pouncing upon Shit-Lone at once. He tried another kung fu kick at Shit-Lone under the table. Shit-Lone must have anticipated what was coming and jumped aside in the nick of time. His chair flew away like a rocket before it hit a tree.

He returned to the table, and apologised. "Now you know I'm sober," he said, laughing.

What a jerk! I thought.

"Don't make fun of me again, or I'll kick the shit out of you, motherfucker," warned Bo Tin Aung.

"Hey, man, what have I said? It's the truth, isn't it?" argued Shit-

Lone. "Imagine what'd happen if your commander was transferred to Mandalay. He's finished, and you too…"

My heart skipped a beat at hearing the mention of Mandalay where Ahba was presently hiding.

Bo Tin Aung flashed a glance at my disturbed face.

I knew I couldn't pretend to be uninterested, and asked him, "Will you be going with your commander to Mandalay?"

"No. We are working out a plan to stay," answered Bo Tin Aung.

Shit-Lone pulled another chair over to sit down. "I haven't finished my recap yet. Now listen to the man as sober as a tombstone," he said.

"Go ahead," Bo Tin Aung said. "It's also useful to keep Maya in the loop. We must all work together if we were to succeed at anything."

I didn't know why it was useful to me but said nothing.

"This is a tale of two cities: Rangoon and Mandalay," Shit-Lone began earnestly. "They have much in common, for both have been attacked by bombs recently – the Mandalay Marketplace explosion and the Rangoon explosion on *Tatmadaw Dei*. Both cases have remained unsolved. The generals are very unhappy about the progress of the investigation. It is rumoured that they are considering a swap of commanders between the two cities."

After a pause, Shit-Lone suddenly said, "My mouth is very dry. I can't go on without a drink."

"No," said Bo Tin Aung sternly. "Finish your story first."

"That's not fine, but that's okay," said Shit-Lone with a shrug. "Where were we? Right, the swap. No one understands the logic behind the swap except that it is purely political. The Mandalay explosion that killed only a few people and injured several others is no big deal. Everyone knows it is the usual suspects, such as the NCGUB, ABSDF and NLD-LA, who have all gone into hiding. As far as the Rangoon explosion is concerned, the case is largely solved with the arrest of a guy named Kloh. We all suspect that the generals are actually warming up for another round of political reshuffle, but are using the explosion cases as a smoke screen."

"That's too bad," I said.

"Indeed," Shit-Lone hastily concurred, without knowing I was only mortified at the thought of Uncle Kloh.

"The swap would spell the end for my handsome friend's uncle-commander," continued Shit-Lone. "You know, over the years, the commander has earmarked a big trunk in his annual operation budget to cater for the city's unrest. Fortunately or unfortunately, except for some small incidents, there has been no major unrest in the past five years, and the commander has been investing the unused funds like a tycoon. Today his assets include a restaurant in Sanchaung Township, a condo and a flat worth millions of dollars, a sedan, a wife and two mistresses."

"Yeah, my uncle lives like a king," remarked Bo Tin Aung. "I have always asked him to practise moderation, but he won't listen."

"Who's talking now?" cried Shit-Lone. "You as the king's man have made good money too, you hypocrite! I envy you, being the owner of some high-class residential property in Rangoon."

"Don't mention it," said Bo Tin Aung bitterly. "It's a bad bargain. Only a three-room apartment on the edge of the city; nothing compared to my uncle's palace. I'm particularly pissed off by the traffic lights at the junction of the newly constructed road outside. I just can't stand the noise of the braking cars; they always irritate me."

"Well, you can always find enough money for a second property," said Shit-Lone, "so long as your uncle can glue his ass to his throne in Rangoon."

"That's why we need some fucking-hell incidents to occur in Rangoon, which would change the mind of the generals," said Bo Tin Aung. "By the way, have you found the guy we want?"

"Yes, but let me ask you a question first," Shit-Lone said. "Has your commander agreed to throw a few bombs?"

My heart skipped a beat, as I couldn't quite believe what I heard.

"His Excellency the commander is entirely OK with the idea," replied Bo Ting Aung solemnly and respectfully as if the commander were listening on the side. "Ten million kyat for three powerful bombs."

"Terrific," uttered Shit-Lone excitedly. "Now I should finally have the money to marry my girlfriend who's four months pregnant! We must celebrate with a drink. Waiter!"

There was no waiter around. Shit-Lone would let nothing dampen his good mood and went away to fetch the drinks himself.

As Shit-Lone walked away, Bo Tin Aung said with a sigh, "The guy is hopeless," and added, with even greater emphasis, "I need you to help me with the bombs."

I didn't want to talk about the bombs, which I had decided were none of my business. "Please don't count on me because I know nothing about bombs," I said.

"What a pity!" he said, looking disappointed. "But what do you call the thing that almost killed us on Dala beach?"

"The thing on Dala beach?!" I exclaimed. "Haven't I explained it enough?! It was called a firecracker, not a bomb."

"To me, a firecracker and a bomb are the same thing."

"No, they are not!" I rejoined vehemently. "To be exact, firecrackers are, as I told you, industrial products used for mining and construction. I can't have any without my uncle U Kloh, who was a doorman at an industrial company before you put him in prison."

He met my explanation with a long and sceptical gaze as if I was trying to fool him with a lie. Then after a flirtatious blink of the eye, he smiled a sly smile and said, "If you want to be exact, let me be exact with you, too. Your uncle is not in prison; he is only in the prison hospital. Thanks to me, he lives there like a VIP. Neither is he tortured nor starved. What's more, he's getting the best care in the hospital for his tuberculosis."

"That's very kind, thank you," I said, relieved to have learnt something about the situation of Uncle Kloh since his arrest.

"You know why I do that? It's because of you," he said, in a most sincere and serious voice. "Now don't you think you should repay me, by helping me out of my contemptible situation?"

Under his intense gaze, I felt I should at least appear to be supportive. "Well, if you really need me… to help, I can ask around."

"Good girl," he said. "Your uncle will thank you for that. Just imagine what a new commander taking over the intelligence branch in Rangoon would do to him."

"What would he do?"

"Under the pressure of the generals, he'd very likely close the case of the Strand Road explosion immediately," he said. "That means your uncle would be shot in no time."

I was petrified. "But my uncle is innocent!" I insisted, and cried.

"I know, I know, but who cares? The reality is: ninety-nine out of a hundred prisoners in the Central Prison Insein are innocent. Your uncle is unfortunately one of them," Bo Tin Aung said. "As a matter of fact, if practical, the junta would not hesitate to have them all shot, notwithstanding their innocence. The generals, you know, are all bastards."

His dislike of the generals made me wonder if he was, after all, a good Tatmadaw, even by a long shot.

I said, "People overhearing what you just said might think you are anti-government."

He stole a furtive look around and said, "I don't mind being a little anti-government when there's money to be made. I don't mind being democratic too; if democracy means cash on the table, I would certainly be the first to grab it. Like now; we've a real opportunity that we can save your uncle, and draw some hard cash in the process. You won't regret it if you help me."

Democracy and money? He seemed to be somewhat mixed up about the two things. But I kept an open mind. I thought, if he wasn't already a good Tatmadaw, he had the potential to become one. The possibility of helping him and making him a convert appealed to me, as I was still thinking of marrying him. Now I was not as against the idea of becoming involved in the bombs as before.

And I asked, "Exactly how would you like me to help… with the bombs?"

"Shit-Lone is contacting a guy who claims to know a few formulas for mixing explosives," he said. "But as I told you, I can't trust him completely…"

He stopped short when Shit-Lone showed up at the table with a large bottle of beer. He filled the glasses and proposed a toast, "To wealth and success."

I politely took a sip. Bo Tin Aung took a large gulp, and Shit-Lone emptied his glass in the blink of an eye. When he proceeded to refill his glass, Bo Tin Aung blocked him and said, "Bring me up-to-date with the bomb maker first."

Shit-Lone stood still and pondered a minute; then he sat down and opened his mouth, but only to belch noisily.

Bo Tin Aung scowled, looking like he was about to explode.

Shit-Lone then said quickly, without further delay, "I think we've got the right guy. But he is not cheap. Five hundred thousand kyat for three bombs."

"Money is not a problem if he's good," remarked Bo Tin Aung. "Tell me if he is good."

"I don't know…" answered Shit-Lone uncertainly.

"You don't know?!" exclaimed Bo Tin Aung, annoyed.

"Hey, man, let me finish, will you?" cried Shit-Lone. "What I mean is: I don't know yet. Later today the guy will give me a small demonstration," adding, after a glance at his watch, "I'll be meeting him at four thirty at Danyingon Station. Let's take the Circular Train. You're all invited."

Bo Tin Aung was thoughtful for a moment. He said, "People like him don't usually live very long. I'm not sure if I'm too keen on meeting a dying guy."

"That's easy; just think of going to his funeral," Shit-Lone said cruelly. "Bring him some flowers, real or plastic, if it pleases your conscience."

He got up from his chair, as though on the point of starting off at once.

Bo Tin Aung told him to wait outside. "I'll have a word with Maya first," he said.

Shit-Lone strutted away, taking the beer bottle with him.

Bo Tin Aung, who waited until Shit-Lone was out of earshot, said, "Here's how you can help."

"How?"

He said, whispering in strict confidence, "I want you to go to the bomb test with him. I want you to be my eyes and ears, and advise me if we can count on the guy for three very good bombs."

I didn't think I understood him. "Your eyes and ears? What about Shit-Lone?" I asked.

Shit-Lone, pausing by the reception, shouted towards us between taking swigs from his bottle, "Hurry up, we're going to miss the train!"

Bo Tin Aung ignored him and continued in his whispering tone, "What about him? He is my best friend, dependable and trustworthy, so long as he is sober. But to my dismay, he's constantly on the booze. I need you to give me an independent assessment."

"An independent assessment? You mean you're not going?" I asked nervously. It was almost unthinkable that he would for once relax his control over me since he had locked me up in his apartment.

"Correct," he said with a nod. "I'd like to go with you but just can't. I'm meeting my uncle at the bureau to report on how we proceed with the plan."

Shit-Lone was again urging loudly from afar.

"But you don't have a problem with me running around... out there... alone?" I stammered, still unsure of the possibility of liberation from confinement.

He might have sensed the unease in my tone, and replied, "Why should I? You're my fiancée and I have full trust in you. You should know that you are absolutely free to do what is required of you to get things done. Have I made myself perfectly clear to you?"

"Yes, very clear," I answered diffidently.

He put some money on the table, which he said was for my personal expenses. Then he kissed me goodbye, and went to join Shit-Lone in the reception. He spoke to Shit-Lone for a long time. I couldn't guess what he was saying, as I could only see his back. Shit-Lone, facing me, rolled his eyes in quick succession like he was having some kind of epileptic fit as he was being talked to. He made no rejoinder; he only drank his beer indifferently. Then Bo Tin Aung raised his hand, giving a two-finger salute and left abruptly, without another glance towards me on the patio.

I took a deep breath, wondering if I had been set free at long last. For a while I still couldn't quite believe my luck. And I was right because it was moments later that Bo Tin Aung emerged from nowhere almost like a ghost, standing on the other side of the wire fence that separated the patio from the street. He waved cheerfully for my attention. I waved back, with an equally cheerful expression. He blew me a kiss all smiling and shouted over something which I couldn't hear for the hubbub of the street noise. It could have been something like: "I trust you," or, "I love you." I was not sure. I mouthed something similar in reply without actually saying it out loud. He was satisfied and turned to go, entering the crowded Bogyoke Aung San Road like he was stepping down a busy stream. Soon thereafter, he was engulfed by the multitude of people and lost without a trace.

Perhaps overwhelmed by my unexpected freedom, I suddenly found the atmosphere warmly convivial. The hubbub from the street was not as head-splitting as before; instead I could almost enjoy the animated conversations and eruptions of laughter which occasionally passed over to my side of the fence. I closed my eyes, savouring the moment of joy akin to a bird that has taken a small step out of a cage that has had its door swung wide open. The air around me smelt fresh and sweet. My body felt so light that I could almost take flight. *How nice it is to be free again!* I thought.

Just then, a hand touched me and a voice thundered into my ear, "Get up!" It was Shit-Lone, who said, "Shall we go? We'll catch the 4.10pm Circular Train."

16

M.A.Y.A.

———◦◦◦———

I was curious to meet the man who was pronounced as "not having long to live" by Bo Tin Aung as if he had been diagnosed with a terminal illness.

What kind of person is this guy? I thought, almost like a counterpart in a similar line of business to me. The most puzzling question might be why he would agree to work for Shit-Lone, the vice-chairman on the board of the Township's "Restoration of Peace and Stability" committee, to cast a couple of bombs around Rangoon?

We arrived at Central Station perfectly on time, but the Circular Train was late to start again.

Passengers were used to the small inconvenience and waited patiently inside the cramped train carriage. I didn't mind the waiting either. Sitting on a bench, I gazed out the open window at the bustling platform with people hopping on and off carriages, as if the delay had given them pause for thought for a last-minute change of direction in their journeys. In a moment of hard-earned freedom, I watched with interest the everyday life which felt like a rolling movie in which no one in particular was in a leading role; or conversely everyone was a main character of sorts by virtue of their self-importance, all carrying an expression of hope and desire with a peculiar mix of loss and discontent. I reflected that I was looking upon the river of life, flowing nonstop, with so many men, hundreds and thousands of them, converging one moment, dispersing the next, adrift all over the place and lost without a trace moment to moment.

As I sat brooding, my thoughts were interrupted, much to my resentment, by Shit-Lone. Sitting beside me on the same bench, he had dozed off, head drooping on my shoulder. There was an unpleasant smell about him that made me want to raise an elbow at him. Fortunately the train started, and Shit-Lone was awakened. He asked, somewhat disorientated, "Have we arrived?"

I told him the train had only just left Central Station.

He murmured something unintelligible before he quickly nodded off again. This time his head swung the other way round to his left, resting on a fat boy who was also fast asleep.

A few stops forward, my carriage became almost deserted when most passengers had got off. Among those who remained were Shit-Lone and the fat boy, sustaining each other in their sleep like a couple, an old man sitting in a far corner with a basket of vegetables, and me. At the next stop, the fat boy was also gone. He stood up abruptly, jumping off the train at the very last minute. Shit-Lone now had nothing to lean on; his body tipped to one side, his face smacked on the hardness of the metal bench. With an "Ouch!" of pain he woke with a start, and asked again if we had arrived. I repeated no. With a shamefaced grin and a yawn, he said, "Talk to me, just to keep me from falling asleep again."

I took the opportunity to ask him about the man we were to meet upon arrival. I was not sure if he minded talking about it; but to my surprise, his response was ready and prompt. "I am lucky to have found this guy, who is like the last of a dying breed," he remarked.

"The last of a dying breed?" I said, "You make it sound as if people like him are becoming extinct! How particular is his kind?"

He said, "Well, by 'a dying breed', I mean those people who think they passionately espouse the cause of democracy, justice and liberty, and they are opposed to the regime government…"

Slightly baffled, I said, "I'm not sure if these people are hard to find."

"No, in fact they're everywhere, all over the country. But many espouse democracy only because it is fashionable, by succumbing to its Hollywood appeal of western values," he said. "I'm sorry, these people don't really count."

I disliked the lofty contempt in his voice, and I retorted, "If the people who espouse democracy don't count, then who does?"

"In my opinion, those who not only talk the talk but also walk the walk," he replied. "They are fierce and uncompromising men who practise what they preach and engage in perils as they come with an indifferent air to seek the enemy, to run to meet the bullets, to offer to shed their blood… you think these men are easy to come by?"

"I don't know. I believe they exist," I answered carefully.

"They exist, for sure, but they are quickly becoming an endangered species when more and more people have embraced non-violence as the chosen strategy to achieve democracy," he said with a sigh.

Perplexed, I asked, "But isn't it a good thing for you as someone on the board of the 'Restoration of Peace and Stability' committee when the number of non-violent people is on the rise?"

"That's very charming of you, I mean, of your innocence," said Shit-Lone with a smirk. "There's something you don't know, which is, in order to restore peace and stability, one must see to it that peace and stability are disturbed and disrupted in the first place. I therefore don't need people who only want to play safe, as they embrace non-violence not because it works, but because it gives them a sense of achieving the impossible without the actual risk. These people make me sick!"

And he went on, "The crisis we're having at the moment is not because events like the Mandalay Marketplace explosion or the Strand Road explosion on *Tatmadaw Dei* are commonplace, but instead their occurrence is rare – a suggestion of a society becoming passive and inert. This would be disastrous for the ruling class as it makes our generals look redundant, posing a grave threat to the military government's ambition to rule the country for eternity."

I was silent. His logic was so queer and iniquitous, almost criminal; yet he seemed to have got at least one thing right, which was: if the military were to rule the country for eternity, one might as well forget about peace and stability, not to mention democracy.

Then he began to lament, "I miss those fierce and uncompromising men, and how their daredevil deeds, time and again, dazzled the military government whom they consider, wrongly and most unfairly, extremely brutal and repressive. This is the end of a heroic era. In the absence of those men, there are no heroes *per se* to speak of. How unexciting for the land that has only villains!"

"Well, you've now found the guy you need, haven't you?" I said. "But in what sense is he the last of a dying breed?"

He sighed again, shaking his head. At length he answered, "Last week I met the man in his home. The guy seemed to be still in possession of a certain revolutionary spark within him; the moment I raised the idea of bombing Rangoon, he was all pumped up in an instant and cried, 'Let's do it!'"

"He's a hero, isn't he, by your definition?" I said.

"A hero or not, you decide," he said. "But there's something he said which might qualify him as one..." He paused, as if trying to remember the exact words, before he resumed, "The guy, despite his age and horrible infirmity, declared: 'I can't go on fighting the junta. I must go on fighting the junta. I will go on fighting the junta.'"

I was intrigued. I found the man's words, of deep defiance mixed with intense helplessness, almost inconceivable.

But then the train was drawing to a stop at a busy station, and I said no more. A gaggle of commuters got on. There were office workers, betel-nut sellers, monks, tourists, a farmer's wife and some crying children. The carriage quickly became fully packed. It was very loud and noisy, as if it is easy for people cramped in close quarters to strike up a conversation when travelling. Or they were just like members of a large family, and the talking and quibbling between them never stopped. The noisy, lively atmosphere reminded me of my own family, where Meena and I always bickered over really trivial matters, for example, whether one can sleep with eyes open, or in the hare-tortoise race, whether the animals would have agreed to run the stupid race in the first place as they don't even speak the same language. We were a happy family though when Ahba and Meena were around and Ahmay was still alive. *But where's everybody now?* I sadly thought. *Are all families alike in that they will in time disintegrate for various reasons?* As the Circular Train drew in and out of stations, the "large family" in my carriage fell apart; members arriving at his or her "destined" station went separate ways to go about their business in the world. A few stops down and after Aung San Station, the carriage was deserted and became quiet again. But there was no time to pick up the conversation where we left off, as we had also arrived at Danyingon.

We alighted from the train, descending immediately into a sea of people with baskets of fruit and vegetables. Danyingon was a village where most of the agricultural farming was done for the Rangoon region. The station was busy like a virtual marketplace where every available space between the tracks and the platform had been taken up by vendors selling a huge variety of fresh produce and consumer goods. After we fought our way through the crowd to enter the large covered market beside the station, a young man, in his late twenties, sidled up to Shit-Lone, putting his arm around him like an old pal. Shit-Lone, caught by surprise, brushed off the young man's arm, and said angrily, "Hi, man, I don't know you. What the fuck is the problem with you?"

The young man, who had a little thin face and a little thin body, said, "Don't tell me you've already forgotten me. We've a date for the bomb test."

Shit-Lone, glancing around surreptitiously, said in a hushed voice, "Let me warn you: we must pretend not to know each other in a public place. And please say nothing about the test."

"Okay, I don't know you," drawled the young man with a shrug, and added, upon noticing my presence, "I didn't know you were bringing along your girlfriend, either."

Shit-Lone said, "I wish she was my girlfriend, but no. She's my friend's fiancée."

The young man greeted me: "Hi, I'm Moe Chit."

I admitted the young man scared me a little because of his fiercely pale face and hideously wild red eyes, and I only responded with a polite smile. Shit-Lone at once snapped, "Moe Chit, will you just take us to the site now? We're busy and have no time to waste."

"Okay, okay." Moe Chit quickly set off after another shrug of his thin shoulders. He paused some ten yards ahead when he noticed we were not following him immediately. Shit-Lone waved him to move on, like waving at a dog. Moe Chit got the message that we wanted to keep a distance from him, and turned to walk ahead dropping his head with perceived sluggishness.

I found it hard to believe that the young man, who looked like a little rascal to me, had anything to do with bombs. I said, "Don't tell me this guy is what you call the 'last of a dying breed' who'd get you the bombs?"

"Well, I'm not at all sure if the guy is dying. If that happens, it's only because he is a drug addict and nothing else," replied Shit-Lone. "But you're right. It's not him but his father on whom I'd have to depend for the bombs."

And he explained, "When Bo Tin Aung asked me to help his commander by spreading panic and fear in Rangoon with a few bombs, thereby making the generals trust the commander again to end the strife, I made a visit to the place with the largest collection of fierce and uncompromising men."

Somewhat bemused, I asked, "Is there such a place in the country? Almost like a select club?"

"The Central Prison Insein," answered Shit-Lone, in a deadpan voice.

Of course, I thought.

"But to my disappointment, many of the guys who have been admitted to this exclusive club are serving terms ranging from twenty-five to seventy years. They could perhaps play a role in some future revolutions, but are of no use to our immediate mission," he said.

"That's too bad," I said.

And he carried on, "So I used my authority as the vice-chairman of the 'Restoration of Peace and Stability' committee to gain access to the records of former inmates, and put together a list of people who have the appropriate qualifications and experience. Then I spent some time tracking them down. Things at first didn't go well, as I came to find that some of the guys are dead while others have gone missing. Finally I got a lucky break; after a series of twists and turns, I finally located this guy in a small village here in Danyingon."

Now as we walked, we had left the marketplace and the boisterous crowd behind; human noises were reduced to a minimum; except for the sound of barking dogs and the chirrup of birds in the trees, it became quieter the farther north we went on a mud path with paddy on both sides. Shit-Lone felt he no longer had to keep to his cautionary tone, and switched back to his normal voice as he went on to describe his meeting with the guy.

"I sat down with him in the front porch for a chat. I called him 'Siha', which is his nickname meaning 'lion'. I knew it from his prison record. He was surprised but very pleased, because it was a name of great respect for the high opinion accorded to him by his comrades. I told him I wanted some bombs. He didn't ask me why, assuming, correctly, that they were intended to target the regime. He only whined, 'A people's revolt at last!' He said he had been waiting for me to come to him for the bombs since his release from prison five years ago. He didn't understand why it had taken such a long time for a people's revolt to occur, for the ultimate removal of the junta that has grown, in his words, 'like a tumour in a man's brain'.

"I followed his use of the tumour metaphor, just to please him. I said the tumour has already swelled to a monstrous size; it has grown so big that it has taken control of the man's whole being and all his actions. Like a cancer of permanence and pain, the tumour is going to stay, because if it were removed, the man himself would probably die too.

"'Then why now?' Siha asked. I said not everyone has agreed that the tumour cannot be removed; some people even think it is better to do it now than to wait until the tortured flesh rots and festers. Siha, touched by what I said, became so emotional that he began to cry, tears all over his face. Suddenly he asked me, 'How's your brother Htin Oo? Is he still fighting in the jungle?' I was confused because I have no brothers or sisters. Then I realised he must have recognised me as somebody else. I lied to him on the spot; I said my brother was dead, killed by the junta soldiers, just to please him. He cried more, wiping away the tears with his hand.

"It was then that I saw what I didn't see when I first sat down with him on the porch. It was his hands; his left hand was completely gone, whereas his right hand had only the remains of two fingers permanently bent like a crow's claws. I remembered in his prison record that he was arrested ten years ago outside Rangoon City Hall when a bomb exploded in his hands; he was released some years later because of his deteriorating health. I further observed one of his eyes was blind, the other yellowish and misty."

"What a pity! It looked as if he was totally wasted," I said.

"Forget about pitying him, because he is more unyielding than his shabby, wasted body seems. When I asked him if he could still fight the junta in his condition, it was then that he cried, in a firm, damning voice, 'I can't go on fighting the junta. I must go on fighting the junta. I will go on fighting the junta.'"

I was almost moved to tears, as I was now able to appreciate the man's strong defiance mixed with a heartbreaking helplessness. And I asked Shit-Lone, "And you as a member of the junta, what did you say in reply?"

"I said thank you very much. Then I was silent, thinking my plan was in tatters when the man I had found was virtually a useless cripple," said Shit-Lone. "I thought I'd better leave. As I stood up, someone emerged into the porch from the back of the house. He was the son of the old man. He offered to walk me to the railway station.

Halfway we turned back, after he had said something that made me change my mind."

Suddenly he raised his voice to a loud shout, "Moe Chit, what the fuck are you doing there? Haven't I told you to go ahead?"

Moe Chit was squatting under a tree at the side of the road. He slowly rose to his feet as we came near. He said, a hand pointing into the distance, "We're almost there. My father has put together something very powerful. I hope you'll be impressed."

"We'll see," said Shit-Lone nonchalantly. "You know you'll get no money from me if I'm not happy with the test."

We resumed our way quietly. A couple of minutes later, we turned up a narrow path and arrived at the site behind a dense tangle of trees. It was a surprisingly neglected spot, a kind of rubbish-dumping ground where there was a dilapidated house with a ramshackle front. An old man was sitting by the wall for a little shade from the afternoon sun. He might have heard our approaching steps, and stood up. He was a stout man of medium height, with silver hair and a statue face covered with heavy wrinkles; there was a certain sense of strength and fortitude about him in his fearsome countenance. We were still at the outer edge of the grounds, and the old man, after gazing around for a second or two, seemed not to have noticed our presence. He sat down again, with a tired sigh.

I thought this must be the man nicknamed Siha (the lion) – the 'last of a dying breed' who had vowed to go on fighting the junta in spite of he himself being blind and lame; a hero too, or to be precise, a fallen hero in a bygone era when there were still heroes on the land, not just villains, according to Shit-Lone.

Then of course, he was also the father of Moe Chit, who called out, "Dad, they are here. Are you ready?"

Moe Chit slithered off to join his father for the preparation of the test, while we waited sitting on a broken tree branch that lay on the ground. Shit-Lone, glancing after Moe Chit and his old man disappearing behind a brick wall, said, "There's no truth in the saying 'Like father, like son', as all you see is a lion, albeit old and weak, and a rat!"

I said, "Earlier you told me Moe Chit suddenly showed up and made you change your mind. Yet you're calling him, instead of a lion's cub, a rat? How is a rat useful to you?"

"Well, a rat sometimes makes excellent cannon fodder material," he said, but quickly added, with a dry laugh, "It is, of course, unfair to think of him as merely a rat, because he is also an assistant to his father in getting bombs made."

I frowned, feeling ill at ease by knowing the little rascal was a kind of second-generation bomb-maker like me. Shit-Lone must have misunderstood the dismayed expression on my face, and said, "Have I jumped too far? What if I tell you what Moe Chit said that made me change my mind?"

I said, "Please," just to conceal the cause of my displeasure.

"All right," he went on. "On our way to the railway station, Moe Chit said, 'I heard you want some bombs. You've come to the right place.'

"I said, 'I don't think so. Your father can't work anymore.'

"'That's not true,' said Moe Chit. He took me to a shed in the backyard of his house. He trained a torch into the shed. In its light I was shocked to see a wide assortment of bombs of different shapes and sizes on the floor.

"Moe Chit said, 'This is my father's only pastime since my mother died two years ago. You want bombs? They are all yours as long as you have the money.'

"I quickly moved away, not because I was not interested, but because of the sickening smell which had filled the shed. I told Moe Chit, 'Money is not a problem. But I also need someone to plant the bomb and set it off. Who's going to do that now?'

"Moe Chit answered, 'That will be me. I can carry the bombs around town, plant them anywhere you like, and set them off at the precise time of your choice. As long as you pay me handsomely for the job, you won't be disappointed.'

"His repeated emphasis on money alarmed me. The ghostlike paleness of the guy's face and his really bad breath as he spoke caused me to be suspicious. I thought I knew his kind of men. I said, 'It seems you are in urgent need of money. What for?'

"He shrugged, without an answer.

"'Drugs,' I suggested.

"With an embarrassed smile, he said, 'Yeah, something like that.'

"'What kind of drugs?' I pursued.

"'Ice,' he replied.

"'Ice is expensive,' I said.

"He nodded his head, biting his lip.

"Now his profile was becoming clear to me, and I asked him, 'Are you working? What is your job?' He again said nothing. I said, 'Don't be ashamed. I can't give you money unless you're honest with me.'

"A little irritated, he said, 'Why should I be ashamed? You are only a criminal plotting against the junta government! You're no better than me.'

"I said, 'Yeah. We're all criminals. That's why you should have no problem sharing your story with me.'

"I thought I had convinced him. 'Yeah, I use drugs, I sell drugs,' he confessed. He told me he was only out of prison at the beginning of the year, after having served a two-year sentence for drug trafficking. He was unemployed at that moment, and he needed startup cash to revive his drug-selling business.

"I thought to myself, 'my efforts after all have not been in vain. Now I have found two men: one makes bombs, the other plants them and sets them off. This is perfect.' So we discussed the money and everything. He asked for half a million for three bombs. I said okay, but for that kind of money, I needed a test, or a rehearsal."

At this moment the father and son re-emerged from the house and came over to meet us at the edge of the grounds. Shit-Lone rushed forward, greeting the old man: "Siha, you pave the way for a new Burma. You're a great man."

The old man replied, "No, I'm not, you are. My brother, the Burmese people are hopeless without you."

Shit-Lone gave no answer, but smiled with unabashed pleasure and pride.

Moe Chit was impatient to get started. He said, "Hopeless my ass. Will you all just sit down for the show to begin?"

Still smiling, Shit-Lone brought the old man before me and introduced us. We helped the old man settle down onto the tree branch as Moe Chit went back to the house to attend to the preparation of the bomb.

The old man said, "My son told me you are a pretty girl. I wish my eyes could see better these days."

I replied that I was just an ordinary Burmese girl.

He said, "What is an ordinary Burmese girl doing here? Are you not afraid?"

"Maybe, but I'm curious," I replied.

"Well, it can be a little scary. But have no fear, as I'm here with you," he said gently, and lightly touched my hand with the remains of a hand that had only two claw-like fingers.

Moe Chit ran in and out of the house, busy like a bee. I didn't quite get what the fuss was about. Finally, he rushed back, shouting, "One minute," his hands over his ears as though to protect them from the impending sound of explosion. There must still have been plenty of time remaining when he reached a tree stump near us. Crouching on it, he said panting, "Thirty seconds."

Shit-Lone looked both excited and nervous, and followed the good example of Moe Chit by putting his hands over his ears. Moe Chit took a glance at his watch and began counting down, "Five, four, three, two, one... NOW!"

In an unnerving moment, Shit-Lone inadvertently uttered a low cry, despite nothing actually happening. As time slipped by the sound of silence became so loud that it was almost embarrassing. After a full minute, Shit-Lone dropped his hands and swore furiously, "What the heck is going on? Is the people's revolt now or never?"

After a considerable pause, the old man said, "It's now, of course.

But if we're experiencing a delay, it has probably got something to do with the trigger mechanism."

Shit-Lone said, in a tone feigning moral indignation, "Siha, you know it is the junta we're waging this war of justice against. A single delay would suffice to irrevocably render all revolutionary attempts in vain. See where we are now?!"

Moe Chit stood up from the tree stump, and said with a guilty expression, "Seems like I've messed up a wire or two. Give me a second, and I can fix it right away."

"No, wait," the old man said. "I don't think it is a good time for a last-minute repair."

Moe Chit ignored the old man's advice, charging ahead with quick, short, swaying steps. When he was about ten yards from the house, suddenly, a loud explosion erupted which made the ground shake. Moe Chit, as if hit in the chest by an unknown force, stumbled and dropped into a rubbish heap. The house swayed in trepidation, its dilapidated front leaning precariously to one side as a portion of the wall on the right had collapsed. Bricks and cinders flew in all directions in a dusty mist, some landing yards away on the body of Moe Chit who was lying motionless as if dead.

The old man gazed for a long time at the rubbish heap where Moe Chit lay, and asked, "Is he all right?" His tone was, however, not particularly worried.

I was inclined to trust the old man's judgment. I didn't think Moe Chit was seriously hurt either, as the bomb that exploded with a loud bang was, after all, only a tester, and a small one by any standard.

But Shit-Lone seemed more concerned than us perhaps out of vested interest in the scheme of things. He called out to Moe Chit, in a voice of great sympathy, "Hey man, don't you dare pull a stunt like that! This is only a rehearsal. If you die now, who's going to die later?"

Although his words were gibberish, they seemed to work on Moe Chit whose body began to shake a little. Shit-Lone, encouraged, raised his voice even higher, "Stand up now, and I'll make you a very rich man!"

Moe Chit's response to this latest appeal was almost instantaneous. He clambered to his feet, wobbling horribly as he struggled to maintain his balance. He looked heavy-eyed and frail, but appeared to be fine, without any injuries. Eventually he was able to function properly like a normal man as his senses returned. Glancing at the collapsed wall, he cried, "We have done it, haven't we?"

Shit-Lone was, however, not pleased by the 'resurrection' of Moe Chit. He said, "Why the hell did you have to rise up at all? There's a dead man in the script I wrote. Where's he now?"

Moe Chit, confused by Shit-Lone's words of reproach, murmured uneasily, "All right, all right," and slowly sank back into the rubbish heap.

Shit-Lone let out a guffaw of laughter, and said, "Don't be a fool, I'm only joking. Come here; let me congratulate you, Moe Chit, upon the wonderful success of your endeavour."

Moe Chit stood up, rushing over for a rapturous hug with Shit-Lone, who said, in a voice of great compassion, "My brother, you don't die for real unless it is necessary, okay?"

Shit-Lone also shook hands with the old man, assuring him the revolution would erupt without further delay and the days of the junta were numbered. As he talked, he gave me a sideways wink. It was the sort of wink one would give to a friend and confidante, keeping him from bursting out laughing at all the nonsense he spoke. I felt uncomfortable by his falsity, but I played my part as required by the circumstances and returned the wink.

He grinned back at me, before walking away with Moe Chit for a private chat. They talked, huddled under a leafy tree. Moe Chit rolled a cigarette, lit it and passed it to Shit-Lone. Shit-Lone took a long draw from it, and shut his eyes as if he were in some pain, before exhaling with a sigh of pleasure. Then the rolled-up cigarette was passed back and forth, between sighs of pleasure and moans of pain. Knowing the guys as men with an established predilection for drugs, it was not hard to imagine that they were presently happily sharing a cannabis joint.

As I watched them chat and smoke, the old man sitting next to me suddenly said, "Did you say you're just an ordinary girl? But that's a lie."

He startled me. "I beg your pardon?"

"I might not be able to see or hear very well at my age, but my feeling is as sensitive as if I were young," he said, "and you don't fool me."

"What have I done to fool you?" I murmured in protest.

"When the bomb blasted off, did you scream or shriek? No. Did you shake or shiver? Not that I was aware of. There was not even a telltale shudder through your hand to my crippled hand," he said. "Your composure is astounding. Who are you actually, my girl?"

This guy was a real *pro*, I thought. Out of admiration and respect, I decided to be a little more honest with him. But I first asked him, "Can you keep a secret?"

"Why?"

"Because if you don't, I'll be in trouble," I said.

He nodded with an avuncular smile. "Don't worry. Keeping secrets is what this business is about, isn't it?"

When I pondered how much I could safely reveal to him, I saw Shit-Lone and Moe Chit appeared to have nearly finished sharing the joint. Shit-Lone took out a wad of cash, handing it over to Moe Chit who pocketed it, and it looked as if they were wrapping up whatever they were discussing. I knew I didn't have time to go into detail with the old man, which was, however, also not something I intended to do anyway. I therefore simply said, "Siha, trust me, I'm just an ordinary girl, but I'm also someone who's on your side."

"My side?" he said.

"I mean on the side of the democratic movement and the Burmese resistance under the junta rule…"

"That's too vague," he said. "Can you be more specific about people of the resistance like me?"

"You are someone who not only dares to dream about bringing an end to oppression and tyranny but also works tirelessly and fearlessly towards the goal," I said.

"I'm flattered," he said. "But there's more to this side of the resistance."

"What's that?"

"This is a side that doesn't flinch or waver. We never speak the language of reconciliation, only overthrow. We start by being violent because if we don't we'll never get justice. The world likes to glamourise non-violence, not because it works miracles, but because the world has chosen to turn a blind eye to the destruction of the lives of ordinary people who die, not with a bang but a whimper," he said. "And this is my side, rough and tough and turbulent. Can you still honestly say this is the side you belong to?"

"Please don't doubt me," I said.

"Very well, but here is the thing: I belong to some of the most maligned people in the entire resistance movement, in spite of how we work literally side-by-side with death for the collapse of the regime," he said. "My girl, it takes a lot of guts to be on this side. Nobody will blame you if you choose otherwise."

In a firm and unequivocal voice, I said, "I've witnessed the cold brutality of the repressive regime and I've seen how our people are being driven to flee in desperation. I don't need to choose again… for justice."

And I quickly added, as I noticed Shit-Lone and Moe Chit were heading back toward us at the end of their chat, "Now you know a secret of mine that not even my friend knows. They're coming back, and we'd better stop talking now. If you still have any doubts, you only have to hear these words: we have a common goal, which is to galvanise our people to come out into open rebellion to overthrow the regime; for that matter, there's nothing better than to wreak havoc with a spree of bombs in Rangoon."

The old man lifted his leonine head, looked at me a moment in silence, and replied, "Well, my girl, whatever may occur, let's stand our ground and do what we believe to be our duty."

17

M.A.Y.A.

———※———

For a short time I was free from my confinement, allowing myself to be dragged into the conspiracy of terrorising Rangoon with a spree of bombs, with the enthusiasm for an explosive specialist who doesn't quite know what he's getting into. Under the circumstances, in the absence of a marriage, I thought that by providing my support, I'd make myself useful in a way that might lead to the end of my captivity. But in fact I was only being led straight into an ambush, as it later emerged.

I considered my continuing freedom would depend on the conspiracy thriving, and when Bo Tin Aung, after having heard from Shit-Lone a most dramatic account of the bomb test at Danyingon, turned to me for my opinion, I replied most positively. I praised the expertise of the old man, at the same time casting doubt on his infirmity and the unreliability of his son, and strongly advised the need for close supervision if we were to work with them.

Bo Tin Aung complimented my observation. He said, "Now you know why I sent you to the test. From now on, you'll be the main liaison with the father and son to ensure the bombs function without fail."

"Are you sure?" I exclaimed, looking uncertain but secretly pleased.

"Of course. Your role in the operation is no less important than ours," he said. "This afternoon my commander gave me three million kyat for the first payment. I propose splitting the money equally between the three of us."

Shit-Lone looked stunned, as if he had just been robbed. "Then what's my role for my one million?" he asked sarcastically.

"You can drive, can't you?" asked Bo Tin Aung. "I want you to find a car, a stolen car preferably. You'll give it a repaint and a false registration so that nothing is traceable afterwards. We'll navigate the streets of Rangoon for suitable bombing targets."

Bo Tin Aung gave Shit-Lone extra money for the vehicle. "At the end of everything you could either get rid of the vehicle or make it yours," he said, as if that would console Shit-Lone for having to split the money three ways.

The gesture did indeed cheer Shit-Lone, who said, "Thank you very much. My girlfriend has always wanted to own a car. Immediately after the business here, I'll visit her in Bagan and show her what a nice gift I've got for her."

Two days later, in the evening, Shit-Lone drove over to pick us up for a ride. The car he had acquisitioned was a four-wheel-drive Mazda. I had never seen an uglier car – its fat body was hearse-like and its colour, a demoralising dark blue, looked funereal in the descending gloom. When he turned the ignition key to start the car, the engine only buzzed and hummed, reluctant to wake up. It was after a few more attempts that the car finally puttered into action, grunting like a pig.

After we had had dinner in Chinatown, our clandestine tour began. Shit-Lone drove confidently down Mahabandoola Road as if he knew where he was going. He pulled up outside Rangoon City Hall, and asked, "Shall we put our first bomb here?"

Bo Tin Aung, sitting in the front passenger seat, gazed out quietly at the massive light blue building adorned with nagas and peacocks on the portico. I thought I would not be surprised if the City Hall, which was home to many protests and demonstrations as well as several bombings in recent years, was selected. But Bo Tin Aung, after a moment's pondering, decided to wait until he had seen other potential targets.

Shit-Lone drove on, leaving behind the sombre Ministers' Building to enter the busy Bogyoke Aung San Road. The night was cool. It was quite a pleasant ride sitting all by myself in the back of the car, enjoying unobstructed views from both sides. The car moved onto Strand Road, which runs parallel with the Rangoon River. As it passed the Strand Hotel, I couldn't help but steal a quick glance at the jetty on my right whose bridgehead I had destroyed with a bomb some time ago.

"You OK?" asked Bo Tin Aung suddenly, his eyes staring at me from the rear mirror.

"I'm fine," I replied. Not knowing what was playing on his mind, I tested him: "Found anything suitable?"

"You mean the Strand?" he said. "I don't think so. The police have more men walking the beat in the area since someone bombed the jetty. Anything along the road, for example, the Strand Hotel, the Pansodan Jetty, or the Nan Thida Terminal, is a no-no."

Shit-Lone smartly drove the car off Strand Road into a side alley. We thought he knew where he was going, but soon became aware that he was all but lost in a maze of dark, sleepy streets. After crossing and re-crossing a certain path that had in time become almost well-trodden, Shit-Lone eventually rediscovered his bearings and found the way back to the full blaze of the city of light and sound. Entering the bustling Bo Aung Kyaw Street, he breathed a huge sigh of relief, and announced he needed a toilet break. He stopped the car outside the splendid St Mary's Cathedral, and Bo Tin Aung went with him.

As I sat waiting inside the car, I heard singing voices emanate from behind the thick cathedral walls. The accompanying music was beautiful, and familiar too, as I came to recognise the piece as 'Amazing Grace', which Meena sometimes sang while playing the guitar. In a moment of homesickness I fell to imagining her as one of the choirgirls inside the cathedral, standing at the altar before a large congregation and singing to the organ with hands above her bosom. I must have missed my little sister terribly.

The guys returned. As Shit-Lone slowly pulled the car off the pavement, he asked Bo Tin Aung, "What do you think of this place?"

"No, not the church," answered Bo Ting Aung genially.

As our tour resumed, our Mazda continued to wander about like someone who is out of his mind. It went on and off Bogyoke Aung San Road, weaving between streets using numbers for names: 40th Street, 39th Street, 38th Street, 37th Street, etc. I was getting bored when nothing seemed to stand out as a potential target. Then we were on 27th Street, with Rangoon General Hospital appearing on my left. Suddenly I felt a vague and indescribable discomfort in my belly. Alarmed, I feared my monthly period, overdue for weeks, had finally come. I asked Shit-Lone to drop me off at the main entrance of the hospital. As I thrust open the door to get out of the car, Bo Tin Aung grabbed my arm and asked, "Where're you going?"

"The toilet, of course," I replied.

With a wrinkled nose and a frown, he said, "Don't make me wait. This place stinks."

I knew he meant the strong smell of antiseptic in the air. I promised I'd be quick and he let me go.

The antiseptic smell got stronger as I entered the redbrick and yellow-painted building. But it didn't bother me. On the contrary, I quite liked the sharp, pungent smell without knowing why. Perhaps with a background of dabbling in explosives, my nose had learned to be receptive to chemicals. I went to the Ladies', checked between my legs and in my underpants and found no sign of menstrual blood. Fortunately the discomfort had come and gone, and I quickly took a pee and returned to the car. Bo Tin Aung told Shit-Lone to get out of the area immediately. "I'm dying for some fresh air. Let's go to the park," he said.

There was a public park in downtown Rangoon, the Mahabandoola Park, which was not far from the hospital. Shit-Lone might not have clearly thought out the route, and by heading west, he had steered the car straight into the midst of a traffic jam outside Mingalar Cinema on Anawrahta Road. The next picture show was due in a few minutes. A large poster of the film, *Sa Tai* (Style), gleamed brightly under a line of spotlights on the façade of the cinema building. Late-arriving moviegoers hopped like naughty rabbits between the traffic lanes as car horns blew frantically in the air.

"Where have you brought me? A park or a zoo?" grumbled Bo Tin Aung.

Shit-Lone chose not to react. He forged ahead, pressing the horn so hard that pedestrians blocking his car were made to jump and flee. Eventually he succeeded in leaving the hubbub behind by turning into a side street at the back of the cinema. In sharp contrast to the noisiness outside the cinema, the place was surprisingly quiet and dark. But to everyone's distress it was a dead-end street.

Going no further, Shit-Lone had to reverse back out. Bo Tin Aung cleared his throat audibly as if he was about to grumble again. Shit-Lone quickly apologised. To my surprise Bo Tin Aung held his temper; he only said, "Thanks for the ride. I'll remember this backstreet. But now, can we go to the park without further delay?"

The car returned to the main road. Shit-Lone had learned his lesson and was clever to have avoided the crowd. A couple of minutes later, the car entered Mahabandoola Garden Road and the park was within sight. The Independence Monument came into view. It was a strong, upright stone pillar rising from the centre of the park to such a height it looked as though it could touch the clouds in the night sky. Shit-Lone put the car in a low gear, cruising around the park at an unchanging moderate pace, passing the line of tall trees and the fountains. After a few turns we were on the Merchant Road. Bo Tin Aung, as if he had seen something of interest, asked Shit-Lone to stop the car.

Shit-Lone parked the car neatly on the pavement under a government propaganda sign mounted on some scaffolding. Directly across the road stood an imposing colonial-era structure with a roofed entrance. Some men in uniform could be seen looming inside in the dim light behind the glass-panelled door. I thought it was a bank, but if it was a bank, it should have closed for the day by now. Then I heard Bo Tin Aung mutter under his breath, "I think I've found it."

Shit-Lone nervously jerked his head and said, in a voice of huge surprise, "Are you sure? This is the US Embassy!"

"Why not?" retorted Bo Tin Aung. "Think how the Americans have hurt us with their sanctions."

"That's true," said Shit-Lone, adding agreeably, "It's time to teach the bastards a lesson."

I thought it was over-ambitious to bomb the US Embassy. I said, "I'm not so sure. We'd need a truckload of gunpowder to bring down an enormous building like this. Not a bomb."

Bo Tin Aung said, "It's not my intention to destroy the entire building. I need only an event that would generate enough noise that the Rangoon folks can read about it in the next day's newspapers. Do you think you can get the old man to make the bomb and his stupid son to set it up?"

I wasn't at all sure when I was reminded of Moe Chit, the son who sometimes behaved like a lunatic. And I said, "I'll try."

"Very well. I know what you're capable of, and I trust you," he whispered, in a warm, affable voice.

That said, it concluded our clandestine city tour as a prelude to bombing Rangoon, which was scheduled for two days later, after dark.

THE FIRST BOMB, AS IT HAPPENED

IT WAS A HOT AND HUMID Monday night in late May. We set off at the appointed hour for our destination. The sky was unusually forlorn and grey for Rangoon; a pale moon gleamed cautiously through the dusty windshield of the ancient Mazda. The guys were talking all sorts of nonsense on the way, arguing, swearing and apologising. If they were noisy, they were not alone because the night was far from tranquil. Strange winds slammed unhinged doors, dogs barked, nocturnal bugs buzzed, women cried; a man cleared his throat at some stony steps; above all the clang and clamour, a distant temple bell also tolled.

Five minutes after we had parked our car on Mahabandoola Garden Road, Moe Chit showed up. He was wearing dark clothes for the occasion. He got into the car, carrying a bulky plastic bag.

Bo Tin Aung, who was sitting in the front, decided to join us in the back. Mo Chit held out his hand and said, "I don't think we have met. My name is Moe Chit. How do you do?"

Bo Tin Aung ignored the gesture. "Will you just move over?" he scoffed and scrambled into the back.

"You're sitting on my leg!" squeaked Moe Chit, shifting his body to make room.

Shit-Lone said, "Moe Chit, if you need a formal introduction, this is my partner, and Maya is his fiancée."

"Shut up," snorted Bo Tin Aung. "I need no introduction. Will you go to Merchant Road straightaway?"

Shit-Lone drove the car off without another word.

Moe Chit, squeezed between me and Bo Tin Aung, was looking uncomfortable and unhappy about the inhospitality. He must have thought he would be treated more kindly. He said, "I think we need a formal introduction. Shall I repeat that my name is Moe Chit? And shall I ask you to tell me yours again?"

Bo Tin Aung wanted to reveal nothing. "There's no need as long as you know I'm the one calling the shots," he said.

"I can't deal with anyone incognito," insisted Moe Chit.

Bo Tin Aung was furious. He gave Moe Chit a slap in the face and roared, "You're not dealing with anything here. You only have to take orders from me."

Moe Chit rubbed his face, groaning in pain. "Who are you?" he wailed. "A beast?! I can't relate to you as someone in the resistance. I wouldn't be surprised if you're with the military."

Bo Tin Aung was astonished by how easy it was to have his cover blown. He didn't like that and hurried to explain. "You're wrong. Junta is my enemy, and that's why I'm coordinating tonight's operation," he said, adding, as his face turned from harsh to less unkind, "I might have been a little too rough. Sorry."

Moe Chit said nothing, still rubbing his face.

"I'm a good guy," Bo Tin Aung softened his voice to say. "You don't trust me? Ask Maya."

Moe Chit turned to consult me. I gave him a reassuring nod, and said, "He's all right."

"Okay," mumbled Moe Chit, "I think I can trust Maya. She seems to be the only sane person here."

Bo Tin Aung said to Moe Chit, "Sorry again. Have I hurt you?"

"No, no, I'm fine," replied Moe Chit. "If you don't want to tell me your name, how about I call you Big Brother from now on?"

"As you please," Bo Tin Aung said, grinning at Moe Chit. "Now tell me, what is in your bag? Looks like you're carrying a football or a watermelon?"

"Good guess," said Moe Chit, opening the bag to reveal a watermelon.

Bo Tin Aung was startled. "What the fuck! But where's the bomb?"

Moe Chit chuckled derisively. "The watermelon is for disguise. You cut it open and you'll find the bomb."

"Is it safe to carry the bomb around like that?" asked Bo Tin Aung.

"Safe? Who are you, my Big Brother? Are you a guy or a gal?" Moe Chit said with disdain in his voice. "Face your fears, dude, you're going to die! Hahaha!"

Bo Tin Aung put on a grim face, waiting for an answer.

With a grimace, the facetious Moe Chit said, "Yes it's safe. Is that what you want to hear?"

"Explain it," demanded Bo Tin Aung.

"I'm afraid it's somewhat technical," said Moe Chit. "All I can say is you don't need a formal education to become a terrorist if you shop with my dad, who doesn't make bombs, but toys – toys with a dial and a switch that any brainless dumbass age three and above can handle without a problem."

Bo Tin Aung was impressed. In awe he said, "Are you saying anyone can carry it around and toss it anytime, anywhere he likes?"

Now the car had arrived at our destination, and parked where it had parked two days before, beneath the government propaganda sign mounted on metal scaffolding. In the deepening night, the street was dark and quiet without a single pedestrian. The embassy compound across the road stood very still, human activities inside observed to be down to a minimum, with only some watchmen looming dimly behind the glass-panelled door under foggy ceiling lights in the hallway.

"To answer your question promptly, yes, it is anyone but you, my Big Brother, unless you can prove yourself not to be some brainless dumbass," said Moe Chit, passing the watermelon to Bo Tin Aung. "Now will you take the challenge?"

Bo Tin Aung hesitated for a moment, and said, "No thank you. Perhaps another time."

"Hey man, don't be a spoilsport," cried Moe Chit, raising his voice but just trying to be funny. "Are you telling me that you're worse than a three-year-old dumbass?"

"Me afraid? You must be kidding," retorted Bo Tin Aung. "The watermelon is too small for the challenge."

Moe Chit countered, just to provoke him, "Okay. There are two more bombs in the loop, and I'll make sure they are bigger and more powerful. So are you going to handle them personally, just to prove you are not a coward?"

Bo Tin Aung was cornered, and after a second's delay, said with an ominously darkening face, "Fine. I'll handle the last bomb, supposedly the biggest."

"You sure?"

"Fuck you. I said it, and I mean it, okay?" rattled Bo Tin Aung.

"Don't eat your promise, or you're worse than some fucking chicken shit," said Moe Chit with a wicked smile, attempting to be more facetious still.

Given a different time, Bo Tin Aung would have thrown Moe Chit out of the car for calling him chicken shit. But it was not happening tonight. He just said, with a vicious curl of the lips, "Now shall we move on with what we've planned?"

"Always my pleasure, Big Brother," quipped Moe Chit.

"Good," said Bo Tin Aung, his voice grave and serious in sharp contrast to Moe Chit's playful tone. "This is what you're going to do. Imagine yourself an errand boy who goes to the embassy to deliver a night snack. Now you take the bomb which you called some toy, go inside the embassy and kill all the guards there."

At once Moe Chit protested sharply. "Hey man, this is crazy. It is the equivalent of urging me to commit hari-kari. What is this all about? You want the bomb, you have the bomb. Now you want some corpses too?!"

"Are you afraid?" said Bo Tin Aung with a cold sneer. "Who are you if you don't have the chutzpah to do it? Some three-year-old dumbass?"

"Of course not," answered Moe Chit vehemently. "I can bring down the wall of the embassy with the bomb, or I can even destroy its roofed entrance. But I'm not going to drop the fucking bomb inside the embassy like a suicide bomber."

Bo Tin Aung, after fixing Moe Chit with a long, taunting stare, burst out laughing.

"Why your crazy laugh? This isn't funny," said Moe Chit uncomfortably.

Still laughing, Bo Tin Aung said, "No, this is funny. Because I have only been testing you."

"What do you mean by that?" asked Moe Chit. "Do you want to bomb the US Embassy or not?"

"No," returned Bo Tin Aung in a deadpan voice.

Shit-Lone gasped over this unexpected answer, and bawled at once, "I thought we were going to punish the bastards for the sanctions. Otherwise what the fuck are we doing here?"

Bo Tin Aung shot back, "And what the fuck do you know? Must I remind you that the US is a friend?"

"A friend? You mean a friend of the junta government?" exclaimed Shit-Lone. "This is absolutely ridiculous. When have the US become so morally corrupt?"

"No, not the junta, but a friend of the 'Lady!'" said Bo Tin Aung. "Don't forget who we actually are!"

"But excuse me, who are we actually?" asked Shit-Lone stiffly.

"We're the resistance, okay?! And we're the Lady's staunchest supporters, okay?!" stressed Bo Tin Aung. "Therefore we can't bomb the embassy because the US is a friend."

Shit-Lone nodded as if he'd finally got the point. He said to Moe Chit, "Now we're not bombing the US Embassy. Are you happy now?"

Moe Chit shrugged. "I don't know. It depends what other crazy things you guys will dream up as a friend of the Lady and the US."

"Well, I'm going to make it really easy for you this time," said Bo Tin Aung. "I don't need a corpse now, provided you owe me one in future."

"Not sure about that," returned Moe Chit, "but I'm listening."

"I want you to take this thing down with the bomb," said Bo Tin Aung, gesturing at a certain object outside the car window.

We followed the direction of his pointing finger and saw he meant the government propaganda sign mounted on scaffolding that stood next to our car on the pavement. It was a large banner with slogans painted in white on a red canvass.

Moe Chit stared hard at the banner, and said, "Hey man, what has gotten into your mind? Don't you see it says *People's Desire* in the slogan? If we take it down, what will the Lady say? Does it make us an enemy of the people?"

Bo Tin Aung smirked. "Don't be a fool. Read the words carefully, and decide for yourself."

Obliged, Moe Chit began to read, aloud:

"*People's Desire:*

Oppose those relying on external elements,

Acting as stooges, holding negative views,

Oppose those trying to jeopardise

The stability of the state and national progress…"

He paused, scratching his head. "This doesn't make sense."

"Go on," urged Bo Tin Aung. "Read every line and read every word and you'll understand what I mean."

Moe Chit continued:

"*Oppose foreign nations interfering*

In the internal affairs of the state…"

He interrupted himself again, and said, "I'm sorry. I can't see the last line from here."

Shit-Lone had a better view from the driver's seat, and readily helped:

"*Crush all internal and external destructive*

Elements as the common enemy."

"Now what do you think of the *People's Desire*?" asked Bo Tin Aung.

"If I could speak on behalf of the people, I'd desire no such thing," replied Moe Chit honestly.

"That's exactly the point," said Bo Tin Aung. "No people would want to oppose this and crush that almost as if it were a national pastime."

"So this has nothing to do with the people's desire, when it's actually the junta's desire," remarked Moe Chit.

"Exactly," said Bo Ting Aung. "So let's burn it down and show what people truly desire."

"Absolutely, Big Brother, absolutely," cried Moe Chit overeagerly.

Hence, after all the quibbling and squabbling as well as all that had been said and argued about, the moment of action had finally come. Moe Chit got out of the car, carrying the watermelon. We wished him luck and said "goodnight", knowing that we would part from this point and go our separate ways after the strike.

We drove off the target site to park the car at the corner of 34th Street. Under the shelter of darkness we kept our watch on the government propaganda sign from a comfortable distance. At midnight sharp, the bomb blasted off with a loud bang. The scaffolding lit up brightly in the explosion. A fire ensued, spreading quickly to the banner which was made of some combustible material. In time, as the banner was swallowed up by the raging fire, the state-invented *People's Desire* melted away, the slogans liquefied line after line, and a masterpiece of the most mendacious rhetoric was completely obliterated.

Suddenly we saw a shadow at the back of the burning scaffolding, and recognised it to be Moe Chit as he moved into the firelight. We thought he should have left after the explosion and couldn't quite comprehend what he was still doing there. He jumped over the debris, like a stuntman leaping through a hoop of fire, and landed on the pavement where our car had been parked. Then he went on to baffle us by throwing his limbs about in a sort of dance as if he had made the burning scaffolding his stage, and we, watching from afar, his audience.

The loud explosion had triggered off the alarm at the US Embassy, which rang like a ghostly wail; there was also the howl of police sirens in the distance.

"Okay, you've done it," muttered Bo Tin Aung, gazing out at Moe Chit, who carried on gyrating like crazy against the backdrop of fire. "Now go before they come to get you."

Moe Chit lingered on. He turned around and waved at us as if he could see us peering gloomily at him from the car. If that was not enough, he further amazed us by making a pistol with his hand and banged away some imaginary bullets, obviously targeting our vehicle. Now some men came out of the embassy, and shouted across. Moe Chit took flight. The men didn't chase after him, they only watched. Moe Chit darted away, jumped over a fence and scampered off behind a patch of dark trees.

Bo Tin Aung, completely baffled by Moe Chit's stunt, said, "What did he think he was doing by banging at us?"

Shit-Lone thought a moment, and said reflectively, "Let me guess, if I may. This guy is high all the time. You've humiliated him and he fought back. He seems to be saying to you: I'm brave, you aren't. Can you fucking do it like me?"

"That son of a bitch!" growled Bo Tin Aung through clenched teeth. "Can I do it? Can I fucking do it with a toy called a bomb? Does he think he can beat me at my own game? I only hope he lives long enough to see!"

He continued railing at Moe Chit for another minute about nothing specific except that a man who had taken his recalcitrance too far by committing the crime of ridiculing a military man must be condemned.

"How convenient!" laughed Shit-Lone as he put the car in gear and drove out of the area along a backstreet as the police siren got louder and clearer in the night air.

THE NEXT MORNING I FOUND I had been locked up in Bo Tin Aung's apartment again when he went to work. Without newspapers to read, nor radio to listen to, I had absolutely no idea of the Rangoon people's reaction to the bombing on Merchant Road. When he returned home in the evening, he was tight-lipped about the situation. I was keen to get on with more actions, but careful not to show my true emotions. As the week went by, the suspense became intolerable.

Then one Saturday afternoon, he took me to watch the movie *Sa Tai* (Style) at Mingalar Cinema. When we arrived, Shit-Lone was already there, sitting idly in an empty corner away from the crowd in the upper circle. I sensed I was going to hear something more interesting than the movie itself.

Shit-Lone was excited by our arrival. He jumped to his feet and whispered under his breath to Bo Tin Aung, "Have you got our fee?"

Bo Tin Aung gave him a paper bag. "This is the second payment."

"Thank you," said Shit-Lone after a quick peep inside the bag. "Now tell me what your commander wants."

"Let me first give you guys an update," answered Bo Tin Aung. "As you know, the generals are, predictably, scandalised to know that the *People's Desire* propaganda was burnt to coal-black ash. But they are careful not to jump to the conclusion that the event is either anti-junta or anti-foreign powers. They have decided to wait a little to see if this was just a standalone job from some amateur revolutionaries. In light of this, they continue to push ahead with swapping commanders between Rangoon and Mandalay. My boss is deeply upset by the generals' decision. It is now his particular wish to proceed with a second strike."

"How quick would he like it to be done? Tomorrow?" asked Shit-Lone.

"No. He's reasonable. He's OK if it is within a week or two," replied Bo Tin Aung. "He wants something well planned and perfectly executed, which should create such an impact that it will leave an indelible impression on the minds of those old bastards in government."

"I think we'll need a bigger bomb in order for your commander not to be disappointed," said Shit-Lone enthusiastically.

"A bigger bomb goes without saying. My commander will also be pleased to see casualties resulting in death," remarked Bo Tin Aung, in a voice of unimaginable brutality. He turned to me and asked, "Maya, what kind of bomb would you recommend?"

I thought I should have been glad of the resumption of action, but instead I felt shaken and sick when the guys were scheming to perpetuate bloodshed. "I don't know. I have to talk to the old man," I replied uncertainly, "but I'm not sure if he welcomes the idea of killing innocent people along the way."

"He doesn't need to know everything," said Bo Tin Aung. "As far as we're concerned, the father makes the bomb and the son plants it wherever we decide. That's what we are paying them for, isn't it?"

Shit-Lone concurred, "Precisely. The father, who's old and blind, can't make the bomb without the help of his son. I believe Moe Chit would have no qualms about who's going to live or die, as long as he has the money to finance his drug business. By the way, have you a location in mind for the second strike?"

"Of course," answered Bo Tin Aung. "Ever wondered why we are meeting here?"

Shit-Lone looked around and exclaimed, "Are you going to make this cinema a slaughterhouse?! Oh you're a genius!"

Bo Tin Aung gave a smug smile at the praise. "I can't pull this off alone," said he primly. "There's no success without you, and Maya."

His sweet words failed to pacify my disquiet of mind. I felt bombing the cinema was a terrible idea, as in my trade, civilians are supposed to be off-limits. To dissuade him, I said, "This is a crowded place. Where do you expect Moe Chit to plant the bomb? And how is he going to get away afterwards? Shall we consider some other places instead?"

"If you think I'd got my idea from a sudden impulse, then you're wrong," said he. "Remember the other night when Shit-Lone stupidly drove into this area leaving us stranded on a blind street at the back of this cinema?"

Shit-Lone looked embarrassed. He said, "I thought I had already apologised."

"Please don't, because you're to be thanked for helping me find the perfect location for our second strike," said Bo Tin Aung.

"You think this cinema is perfect? How?" asked Shit-Lone.

"Just look ahead, do you see the illuminated signs on the left and right of the stage?" said Bo Tin Aung. "They are the exits that lead straight out of the cinema into the backstreet where we parked briefly the other night. As they are exits, they are also entrances. Moe Chit should conveniently find his way into the cinema and do what he likes."

"That's easier said than done," I argued. "What's he supposed to do once in the cinema? Sit down with the audience and fix the bomb under their seats? But will he have time to do it? Before the movie begins, the auditorium is well lit, like now, and the audience can see what he's up to. After the movie has begun, it will be too dark for things like connecting the wires or setting the timer. He could arouse suspicion, then he'd have little chance of escape."

"Escape? Why?" Bo Tin Aung blurted out. "It is not a problem if he's not going anywhere."

"I don't think I understand you. Is this a joke?" I asked, completely befuddled.

"I was only joking, of course," said Bo Tin Aung casually. "Don't worry, everything will be taken care of. The thing is: I don't need the bomb in the middle of the crowd as I don't intend for large-scale carnage. I only want the bomb to be fixed to the stage, targeting the people in the front rows, whose lives, or deaths if you will, are all I ask for."

I was horrified, as I didn't believe he would be so coldblooded and calculating.

"Moe Chit will get into the cinema from the exit on the backstreet," he continued. "He'll fix the bomb to the side of the stage near the front rows and set the timer for three to five minutes, which would give him plenty of time to leave via the same exit to the backstreet, where he would be taken care of in no time."

"This is brilliant!" said Shit-Lone. "You're just one fucking genius! Let me buy you a drink."

"Yes, why not?" said Bo Tin Aung, standing up.

I lingered in my seat without moving. To my surprise, he said, "If you like the movie so much, you may stay to the end."

His tone was so relaxed as if my unrestricted liberty had never been a problem. But then he quickly added, leaning over to whisper near my ear, "I'm planning the second strike sometime next week. Please go to see the old man after the movie and tell them I need the gadgets by this weekend at the latest. You may also give him an idea of the kind of bombs required to bring the house down... no, I'm just kidding... but you know what I mean."

Now I knew why I was being given the privilege of staying behind. But I couldn't refuse his "good intentions", thinking that, even though I was not totally free, at least I was permitted to roam within the length of my tether.

So I replied, "All right," and stayed to finish watching the entire movie after they had gone.

18

M . A . Y . A .

———∿∿∿———

The movie, which was actually quite entertaining, temporarily took my mind off my tormented thoughts. The performance of the actors, like Lwin Moe and Soe Myat Nander, was first class. The only shortcoming, albeit minor, was that they talked too much throughout. Nonetheless, I had no real complaints. When the dialogue became too long-winded I took a nap. I woke up just in time to see the happy ending: the boys and their girlfriends, estranged from each other due to stark differences in their personalities, had reconciled to become lovers. I thought it was human nature to like happy endings, and I laughed and wept happily, like the rest of the audience. But the mood of joviality wasn't meant to last. When the curtain fell, my heart was again filled with sombre anxiety.

I dawdled behind until the audience was gone and took the side aisle to leave. I came down to the stage, taking a seat in the front row to experience for a moment what it would be like watching a movie while a bomb was ticking nearby towards deadly detonation. I felt nothing but pure horror. I got up, walked underneath the "*EXIT*" sign that was lit up with a pale fluorescent glow above the outgoing passageway. Before reaching the exit, a metal door on my right caught my attention. I held down the handle which turned without resistance. The door opened to reveal a dimly lit room with metal pipes on the walls and coils of heavy wire on the floor. I thought it was only an engine room. Of not much interest, I proceeded to the exit, pushed open the door and came out of the cinema into the backstreet.

Under broad daylight, the backstreet appeared to be exceedingly dirty. The pavement was wet and sloppy with the footprints of moviegoers who had hurried away after the last picture show. Unswept, objects such as old furniture of every kind, rusty pieces of metal and shards of broken glass were scattered all over the place, as if it were some dumping ground in the neighbourhood.

At the back of the cinema there were not only exits but also entries with half-closed doors along the outside wall sprayed with graffiti. One led to what seemed to be a storeroom which was dusty and smelly; the other opened onto a landing with a short flight of stairs to the offices. I was struck by the security of the place, which was almost non-existent, thinking Bo Tin Aung was right that Moe Chit could actually come and go as he pleased.

To my agitation I could almost picture a scenario, so grim and bleak, where the audience didn't see the end coming, didn't stand a chance, and before they were anywhere near the happy ending of that movie, some of them would suddenly be dead. These dark thoughts made me want to retch. I avowed on the spot that I must not let it happen. And my challenge was how to use my power to avert the course of catastrophe and reduce the casualties to a minimum.

On the Circular Train to Danyingon I thought about and pondered all kinds of options. In the end I concluded that I needed to tinker with the construction of the bomb to make it less deadly. Arriving at Danyingon, I found my way to the small village where Siha lived. His house was at the end of a dozen thatched huts on a wooded hillside, with a surrounding low wall and a rusted iron gate. There was no bell for visitors to announce their presence and I only had to push open the gate to enter. I stopped short at the entrance, noticing the old man was lying asleep on an easy chair in the front yard. I thought it imprudent to interfere with his sleep and hastily beat a retreat.

Several minutes later, as I was waiting by a shadowy part of the wall where there was an enormous banyan tree, I was startled by a loud, angry holler from the old man. I went to the gate and saw the old man was waving a stick at a dog that had strayed into the courtyard. I opened the gate and the dog slipped away. I came forward to greet the old man. He was pleased to see me, but apparently had mistaken me for some girl from a family in the village. I went to the kitchen and made some hot water for green tea. After tea, the old man gradually came around to recognising who I actually was and asked me about the revolutionary business. I thanked him for the first bomb and said it had been a success. I also told him the purpose of my visit which was to order another bomb, by specifying that I wanted the bomb to issue hissing sounds and bright sparks before the full blast.

The old man, somewhat puzzled, said, "I don't think I understand why the sounds and sparks. Are they intended as some kind of warning? Are they trying to tell people to flee?"

"Yes, they are," I replied. "There are lives to save."

"But these people are the enemies," he said, "and you don't save lives by throwing a bomb at them, do you?"

He was right to challenge the logic. The thing he didn't know, however, was that I was playing the role of saboteur in a conspiracy where military men were masquerading as revolutionaries to commit an act of violence. I thought I needed to try harder to persuade him. When I was considering how to craft a more convincing narrative, I heard the sound of approaching footsteps outside and turned to see Moe Chit entering the courtyard through the gate. There was another man behind him, to my surprise. It was Shit-Lone, who greeted me and promptly informed me that there was a change of plan.

"Another change of plan on a whim?!" I muttered uncomfortably. "Your friend is pretty fickle when it comes to planning, isn't he?"

He knew I was referring to Bo Tin Aung, and said with an awkward smile, "To be fair, not entirely his fault this time."

"So what's the guy thinking now? Is he going to plant the bomb himself?" I asked bluntly.

Moe Chit, who was listening in, said, "Are we talking about the Big Brother I met the other night? Is he going to handle the bomb this time to prove himself no worse than some fucking chicken shit?"

"No, no, no. You'll handle it, that's official, okay?" said Shit-Lone very solemnly.

"No problem," replied Moe Chit with a resounding drawl.

"Then what's the change?" I asked.

"We're getting a new deadline," said Shit-Lone. "Everything must be accomplished within a couple of days instead of the end of next week."

"What is 'everything' supposed to mean?"

"All other bombs," he answered flatly.

"This is ridiculous," I said. "Are you telling me that you guys have come up with such a brilliant idea while having a drink?"

"No. We had barely touched our drinks when we were suddenly summoned to present ourselves before the commander...I mean the chief..." paused Shit-Lone. He looked discomfited by the presence of Moe Chit, and told him, "Can you get me a glass of water? I'm thirsty."

"No problem," replied Moe Chit fawningly.

After Moe Chit went away, continued Shit-Lone, in a most melodramatic fashion, "When we met the commander in his house, we had the impression that he had lost his mind."

"You mean your commander is mad!?"

"Not exactly mad, only slightly deranged, looking dazed and shell-shocked, his face ghostly, his shoulders drooping," explained Shit-Lone. "In a weak voice he told us he had had a bad dream while having a catnap in the afternoon. In the dream, he was driving down some road; on the car radio a male voice was singing a nameless song. He woke up later and found himself tormented by a pessimistic foreboding. He believed it was because of the song he heard but he had no idea what it was. He sang to us the bits and pieces he still remembered, and asked if we had any clue what it was."

Moe Chit returned with a glass of water. Shit-Lone swallowed it down in one go. When it looked as if he was about to resume his story, he suddenly opened his mouth to sing.

Can't you 'ear their paddles chunkin' from Rangoon to Mandalay?
On the road to Mandalay,
Where the flyin'-fishes play,
An' the dawn comes up like thunder outer China 'crost the Bay!

He paused, glancing around as if waiting for a round of applause.

Moe Chit didn't applaud, he only asked, "What have I been missing here? Are we in a song contest?"

"No. It's a music quiz. You may guess the song if you like," said Shit-Lone.

"This one is easy. It's Frank Sinatra," said Moe Chit.

"Wrong. It's about the title, not the singer. You have two more attempts," said Shit-Lone.

"I don't think I know the title, I'm sorry," said Moe Chit. "Can I phone a friend?"

"No," answered Shit-Lone. "But you can ask the expert."

"Who's the expert?"

"Me," said Shit-Lone haughtily. "If you don't know the title of the song, let me tell you now. It is called '*The Road to Mandalay*', and the singer is Robbie… Robbie Willi…"

"Oh! I always like Robbie," crooned Moe Chit like a fan.

"Damn it. Haven't I told you the singer is beside the point," snapped Shit-Lone irritably.

"Okay, okay. Tell me what the point is?" asked Moe Shit.

"The point is…" Shit-Lone stuttered somewhat, "… the point is as soon as I told my chief the name of the song, he immediately flew into a rage. He kicked me in the ass and cursed me for telling him something so horrible. He believed his dream to be a bad omen and feared that a catastrophe was coming."

Moe Chit, evidently perplexed, said, "It's only Robbie. I don't get why your chief should be so upset."

"Haven't I told you it is not about Robbie?" cried Shit-Lone with a remonstrating sigh. "In fact, I don't even expect you to understand, because it is Maya I have been talking to all this time, not you."

I, of course, understood. The commander wanted to stay put in Rangoon, and the dream of going to Mandalay had made him paranoid. And I said, "So the guy now wishes to proceed with utmost urgency."

"Exactly," answered Shit-Lone, "like a clearance sale, everything must go before the end of the week."

"This is absurd," I said. "I know it's the cinema you guys target next. But what about the last bomb?"

"The traffic lights!" Moe Chit stepped in with the information.

I frowned, wondering how Moe Chit had known it.

"I told Moe Chit when I went to find him in downtown," explained Shit-Lone, and winked me with one eye as he continued, "You should not be surprised in the least that traffic lights is chosen for a target."

I returned the wink, remembering Bo Tin Aung to always get pissed off by the clatter of vehicles screeching to a stop before the traffic lights at the junction outside his apartment.

Moe Chit took the opportunity to share his enthusiasm in the matter. "I like the idea of taking down the traffic lights; just imagine all the cars stranded by the ensuing traffic jams!"

"Don't be silly. We're not talking just traffic jams, but chaos and mayhem," remarked Shit-Lone, his eyes twinkling with a malicious glow. "In the explosion, the traffic lights will be uprooted and dismantled, cars crash and burst into flames, pedestrians made to run for their lives, and the streets will be strewn with dead bodies…"

"This is insane!" I cried.

"Yes, insane but necessary," said Shit-Lone. "In the next day's newspapers, the headline would read something like this: 'Huge bomb brought traffic from Rangoon to Naypyidaw to a standstill. A thousand people have perished…'"

"It's almost epic," said Moe Chit. "But I don't think you can kill a thousand with just one bomb. Do you mean you are to order more bombs from us?"

"No, one large bomb will suffice. Perhaps I can be a little charitable by lowering the death toll to, say, a hundred, instead of a thousand," said Shit-Lone. "Still, with just a hundred dead, I would be very proud to declare: Mission Accomplished!"

Moe Chit, getting teary-eyed, said in a trembling voice, "You're a hero, you're the champion!"

"No, no, no, that's not all," said Shit-Lone. "There's more to come, which is even better."

"You mean there's still something more than...mission accomplished?" asked Moe-Chit.

"Of course. Immediately after mission accomplished..." paused Shit-Lone, and resumed, by deliberately speaking slowly to keep Moe Chit in suspense, "...is the time...that...we are laughing...all the way... to the...BANK!" before he burst out a most satisfying laughter.

Moe Chit's eyes turned blood red in addition to being watery. He said, "I envy you. I just hope it's not too late to hop on the bandwagon of the revolution, which some say pays rich dividends."

Shit-Lone surveyed Moe Chit's face for a while with a half-funny, half-deadly gaze. At length he said, "No, it's never too late. Hey man, this is your revolution too! Don't forget you are the one to drop a bomb into a crowd tomorrow and cause some injury. That makes you a hero too. You'll be remembered for the stupid shit you've done for democracy."

"I don't wish to be remembered," replied Moe Chit modestly. "I only wish I could, like you, laugh all the way to the bank too."

"It will come, it will come," cackled Shit-Lone with a cunning laugh, "as long as you can deliver me bombs of a power equivalent to that of Hiroshima."

"No worries. I understand what you mean," said Moe Chit. "I'll tell my dad to start working on the bombs immediately, with maximum harm and injury guaranteed."

"Moe Chit, you're a good comrade, one of the best," said Shit-Lone in a tone of exaggerated satisfaction as if everything about the bombs was almost a done deal.

I raised a shout of protest. "You guys hang on just one second," I said. "Before you guys came, I was in the middle of talking to Siha regarding the design of the bomb…"

I stopped short, pausing in mid-sentence, when I noticed the old man had fallen asleep while we talked and was snoring in his chair.

Moe Chit said, somewhat apologetically, "Nowadays my dad sleeps a lot during the day, but at night he is as energetic as a young man. Don't worry. Whatever instructions you gave him, he'd remember. You want bombs that kill without mercy, you've got it. You guys won't be disappointed."

"Good, very good," praised Shit-Lone. "In order not to waste another minute of your time, I guess we'd better head off now."

I didn't want to go just yet, as this would be my last chance to influence the construction of the bomb for the purpose of making it less deadly. But I needed a pretext to stay in the presence of Shit-Lone. At that moment, the old man woke up with a start. Looking languid from sleep, he slurred some words that didn't make sense.

Moe Chit said, "My dad needs time to become fully awake. Prior to that, you can't discuss anything with him. But that's okay. Trust me, I can handle it all right. If you're going now, goodbye."

Suddenly the old man stood up, and after looking around at nothing in particular for a while, mumbled, "I'll go for a piss."

Moe Chit hurriedly said, "Don't rush yourself, or you'll fall on your head again." He took his father by the arm, leading him toward the gate.

Shit-Lone said, "We should also be heading back. Let's walk you out."

I lingered in my seat without moving for a long minute, wondering how I could possibly remain behind. Shit-Lone hailed me from outside the gate, "C'mon, we're catching the seven o'clock train."

I rose to my feet with the utmost reluctance. As I slowly walked out, I felt I had to make one last attempt to rescue the situation. I decided to speak to the old man, no matter what, by reminding him of our previous conversation about a certain buzz and spark, and offered to stay behind to help with the bombs.

But the moment I stepped out of the house, I found I was caught in a rather awkward position and quickly needed a place to hide my face. The old man, standing in front of the low wall with his longyi gathered up at the waist, was in the midst of relieving himself.

I went behind the enormous tree and waited there. Shit-Lone came to find me. "The lion-man is tending after his business by proceeding in fits and starts; it looks like he'd take hours to finish," he said. "Shall we just go? I can cover you as you only have to keep to my right-hand side."

Knowing I was at my wits' end I reluctantly accepted his suggestion. So I departed, with an intense wave of unspeakable sadness, as at this point, the conspiracy, for all its evil intents and diabolical purposes, appeared to be unalterable and unstoppable.

On our way to the station, the sky was turning the colour of charcoal. It felt kind of tragic that the day seemed to be practically surrendering without resistance to the darkness of night. My heart was heavy and tormented with pain. I felt sorry for the innocent people who might be maimed and killed in the cinema; I felt awful too that I could not help them and I was to blame for their wretchedness. Upon arriving at the station, the pain went from bad to worse. I had a stomach cramp and puked violently on the tracks. As usual, the Circular Train was late again.

19

M.A.Y.A.

THE SECOND BOMB, AS IT HAPPENED

I had a night of bad sleep, tossing from one nightmare to another. I went to bed thinking there was going to be a massacre over the next twenty-four hours. I dreamt of the cinema on fire, people stamping on each other, women and children crying. In one of those nightmares I tried to work on the bomb by reconnecting the wires, and the bomb exploded in my hands. I must have screamed out senselessly. Bo Tin Aung woke me up and asked me what was disturbing me. I said it was nothing and went back to sleep. He held my hand in his, showing a level of care and intimacy which had become rare lately. But there was no comfort, and the weird dreams returned as soon as my head hit the pillow. Without the slightest idea how it ever came about, in the dreamscape I was being chased through the woods. I ran and ran before I was captured. I found myself strapped to a chair, my pants pulled down to the knees. Someone I didn't know said, "Brace yourself, baby. I'm going to marry you, and this is going to be some rough ride!" I was crushed and battered in spite of my hard struggle. Then I was rescued, mercifully, by a ray of sunlight that fell through the window blinds, and woke up in a cold sweat.

The wall clock struck half past two in the afternoon. It was very quiet in the apartment. I wondered a little if Bo Tin Aung had locked me inside when he went out. But it didn't really matter when I was not going anywhere. I was staying regardless, because there were lives to save. It was frustrating as I still hadn't figured out how to do it. Besides I was a little unsure of myself when I kept experiencing mild fatigue for no obvious reason. With a sick stomach, I went to the bathroom and vomited up some water. I took a shower, scrubbing my skin rigorously with a brush as if to rub off the imaginary dirt from my nightmares. When I came out of the bathroom, feeling better, I heard the sound of footsteps and keys jangling outside the main door. I had no doubt it was Bo Tin Aung returning from work. And there he was, appearing on the landing as the door opened. He was in full military uniform, with keys in one hand and a large padlock in the other.

He said as soon as he closed the door behind him, "We're meeting Shit-Lone at Zawgyi Café before we go to Mingala Cinema for some serious business."

"Good. I quite like the coffee there," I replied.

He scanned my face, where a few strands of wet hair hung down over my eyes, and my naked body with only a flimsy white towel folded above my breasts for a while. I thought he would jump at the opportunity.

I was wrong. He just said, "Shall I give you twenty minutes to get dressed and all that?"

"That'll be fine," I replied, a little surprised at what was stopping him. I wondered if my body, which had put on weight recently and looked rounder, was no longer attractive enough to turn him on physically.

He took a can of beer from the refrigerator, popped it open and drank mouthfuls from it while peering through the window blind at the street outside. The noises of cars screeching to a stop at the traffic lights made him groan irritably.

"You just wait. I'm going to tear you down in pieces!" he cursed in a strangled voice like a wounded animal.

"That'll be tomorrow or the day after tomorrow?" I asked.

He ignored my question, giving the leather belt that tightened around his belly a tug, and belched forth a stream of gas from his stomach.

I was a little curious about his outfit, and said, "Are you not changing into something less formal?"

"No. I'm still on duty. There's a special operation," he said, without much expression on his face.

"You can't be serious. A special operation... this afternoon?" I wailed. "Does it mean you're not going to... the cinema?"

"Something has come up unexpectedly. Can't help it, you know," he said vaguely. "I'll have to trust you guys for the performance if I can't make it back in time."

"Yeah. There's Shit-Lone who you can trust entirely," I returned, somewhat sarcastically.

"Shit-Lone of course, and you too," he said, as if to make me feel better.

"There's also Moe Chit, right?" I retorted, just to provoke him because I was not pleased that he would be absent from the operation.

"Moe Chit is central to our success. How could I forget him?" he said, with a dash of seriousness.

A little surprised by his tone I wondered if he genuinely meant it and chose not to comment. He might have found my silence akin to a protest, and said, "Please don't sulk. I'll be around if you guys need me."

I didn't understand how he could be on a special operation and still be around to assist at the same time. I thought what he said was crap, only to appease me. Without another word, I retreated to the bedroom to get dressed.

We ate our late lunch at Zawgyi Café, the same restaurant on the side of Bogyoke Aung San Market where I was first introduced to Shit-Lone and learned something about the conspiracy of terrorising Rangoon with a spree of bombs. Having little appetite, I ordered a salad bowl and coffee. At 4.30pm Bo Tin Aung announced he was leaving after having finished his plate of mixed beef and pork. I looked at him with a large question mark on my face because Shit-Lone hadn't turned up yet.

"He should be here any minute," he said. "I have given him clear instructions about what to do in my absence. There's nothing to worry about, okay?"

Then he left, and I remained, watching anxiously, from the outdoor patio of the café, the ceaseless flow of people streaming from all directions on a busy afternoon in Rangoon.

At 5.30pm, Shit-Lone arrived in his ugly Mazda. I told him Bo Tin Aung was busy and had gone already.

"Never mind," he said, totally unsurprised; he didn't explain why he was late either. Instead, he hastened me to go, saying we were a little pressed for time as we were meeting Moe Chit in ten to fifteen minutes outside Mahabandoola Park.

At 5.45pm, Moe Chit duly arrived. He climbed into the car with a parcel under his arm to sit beside me in the back. Shit-Lone muttered a "hi" without turning his head, and drove off as soon the door was shut.

"Are we all here?" asked Moe Chit.

He sounded nervous and I was struck by the paleness of his flat face and the deep anxiety in his eyes. He placed the parcel on his lap, his hands shaking slightly.

"You look miserable," I told him. "Are you all right?"

"I'm feeling extremely unwell today," he replied.

"Don't tell me you're going to drop dead in my car," said Shit-Lone chuckling. "You must not die before we get to the cinema."

"You're a cruel man!" said Moe Chit. "For the sake of mercy, can you slow down a bit?"

"What's the problem with you? We're in a hurry," snapped Shit-Lone.

"I don't see Big Brother among us. That's my problem," said Moe Chit. "Where is he?"

"The guy is busy, fucking busy," replied Shit-Lone, exchanging a quick glance with me in the rear mirror, and kept driving at top speed.

"Then who's calling the shots in his absence?" pursued Moe Chit.

"Does it matter?" said Shit-Lone. "Now you have Maya and me, the usual team. Is there anything you don't know, whether it's about the time or the place?"

"No, not at all," answered Moe Chit. "I only want to know why the guy isn't here, and who's calling the shots instead?"

"No one, you stupid fuck!" Shit-Lone began to curse. "After I've dropped you off, you only have to haul your ass into the cinema and bring the house down. When things are that simple and straightforward, you don't need someone to call the shots."

Moe Chit was quiet, as if intimidated, but not for long as he broke the silence by asking, "If you don't mind, can you tell me who exactly the mysterious guy is?"

"Your question came out of nowhere," said Shit-Lone. "Can you stop talking while I'm driving?"

"Answer me, you dickhead, or I'll quit," demanded Moe Chit in exasperation.

Shit-Lone must have begun to smell something weird about Moe Chit today, without knowing exactly what it was. However, there was one thing he was pretty sure of, which was that the guy must not be allowed to quit or there would be no operation. He slowed down the car a bit (he had to as we were near the cinema and the street was busy), and said gently, "Okay. Let's talk if you insist. But tell me first, what do you think of me: a mere friend or a close friend?"

"Hmm… a close friend, of course," answered Moe Chit hesitatingly.

"Good. As your close friend, I've no reason not to tell you what you want to know, right?" said Shit-Lone. "But the thing is: it is a long story, and we don't have the luxury of time to tell it in its entirety as we are up against an unalterable deadline…"

"You can be brief…" suggested Moe Chit.

"That I can't," stressed Shit-Lone.

"What do you mean you can't?"

"Because I will only tell you everything in fullness or you'd get the wrong idea, which is dangerous," explained Shit-Lone, adding quickly after a slight pause, "As a close friend of yours, what I'm going to do is treat you by taking you downtown and sharing with you some really juicy gossip over a good drink. How about that?"

Moe Chit was tempted. "Sounds good. Let's do it."

"I certainly will… but not before we have got down to the cinema and finished what we have set ourselves to do first," said Shit-Lone. Before Moe Chit had time to respond, Shit-Lone abruptly changed the subject. "By the way, have you brought all the bombs with you?"

"No. We don't need another bomb until tomorrow. Why?"

"Why? Big Brother wants them all in one place today, that's why!" grumbled Shit-Lone audibly. "How dare you want to know everything about Big Brother when you can't get the smallest thing right at his request?"

"I'm sorry. It's my dad who stopped me from taking both bombs, as a matter of safety and precaution," pleaded Moe Chit. "But we can go and pick it up later before we go downtown for our drinks."

"That'll be too late," mumbled Shit-Lone, without explaining why. He pulled the car to a stop before a red light. The cinema was now only a block away. And he went on, "We're almost there. Let's really concentrate ourselves on what to do next. In a moment I'm going to drop you off in front of the lobby. You'll go to the backstreet and sneak into the cinema via the nearest exit. The rest, which I don't have to repeat, is bloody simple. Afterwards… well, afterwards if you ever emerge from the cinema again, you'll find my car waiting on the main street. Got it?"

Moe Chit stared ahead out of the window, murmuring uncertainly, "The main street? Is it on my left when I leave the cinema?"

Shit-Lone shrugged, and said, "Tell me what the time is on your watch?"

"It's six o' clock," replied Moe Chit.

"Perfect. 6.30pm is the target time," said Shit-Lone. "That means you have exactly thirty minutes to find your way into the cinema and plant the bomb. By the way, is it the watermelon in your parcel?"

"It's not a watermelon. We don't use the same disguise for concealment every time," answered Moe Chit. "This is a birthday cake. Guess what? Today is my birthday."

"You must be kidding!" cried Shit-Lone.

"Why should I lie about my birthday? I've just turned thirty today," said Moe Chit seriously. "It's great to be thirty, some people say, as one can expect amazing things to happen…"

"Don't believe those people," Shit-Lone interrupted him. "Green light now. No more talking, unless you want to say goodbye."

Glancing at the cinema which was looming large into view, Moe Chit said, in a tone that was almost sad, "Yeah, time to say goodbye."

The car wheezed to a stop in front of the cinema. "Hurry up. This is a not a parking area," urged Shit-Lone impatiently.

Moe Chit picked up the parcel and exited the car. "See you guys later." He waved us goodbye, his face weary and nervous.

"I bet you will!" chuckled Shit-Lone, driving off immediately.

My heart sank as the car sped away. It seemed my chance of averting disaster was diminishing rapidly. I told myself I must act now, or never. The car slowed down to a stop before the traffic lights at a busy junction. Out of the window I could still catch glimpses of Moe Chit shuffling in and out of a multitude of people. Walking with his head dropping on his chest, he looked depressed and lifeless.

"There's something fearfully wrong with Moe Chit. Don't you think?" I said to Shit-Lone,

He took a quick glance at the pedestrians, and answered coldly, "He's damned. That's what it is."

"I think he needs help," I said firmly.

He disagreed, only quietly with a face of indifference mingled with a spice of contempt. He kept his eyes staring at the traffic lights ahead and mumbled, "Why has it taken so long for the lights to turn?"

"I fear that he'd put the operation at risk in his kind of state," I said. "I might have to back him up if necessary."

"Don't be stupid," said Shit-Lone, without taking me seriously.

I knew what I was talking about and I did not need his approval. Without another word, I opened the door and hopped out of the car.

"What do you think you're doing, you silly girl?" shrieked Shit-Lone after me. "Come back to the car!"

I didn't care what he said and slammed the door behind me with all my might. Cars on the road were moving again at the green light, and I quickly jumped onto the pavement and hid myself behind a tree. As Shit-Lone hesitated in the car, his ugly Mazda blocked one lane and the vehicles behind started to blare their horns. The traffic congestion caught the attention of a policeman on patrol, who waved angrily at the Mazda to get moving. Shit-Lone, who must have realised that he could not abandon the car to run after me, drove off reluctantly. Watching the ugly Mazda disappear in the tide of traffic, I was delighted to have got away successfully. Now my challenge was to find Moe Chit and do something to avert the carnage.

I hurried down the road to the rear of the cinema. As soon as I turned the corner, I saw from a distance a man sitting silent and self-absorbed on a heap of bricks by the low wall. It was Moe Chit, whose face was depressed and gloomy; he was murmuring to himself as if he were praying fervently. Deep in thought, he was unaware of my approach until I stood next to him and gave him a tap on the shoulder.

"Maya! What are you doing here?" he cried out, startled.

"I caught a glimpse of you from afar and came over to say hello," I said. "Are you okay?"

"No. I feel terrible!" he said; he was stating the obvious from the look of his ashen face and frightened eyes.

"It's a bad time to feel terrible," I said. "Everybody is watching you."

"You mean I'm being watched?" he said, glancing around nervously.

"No!" I hastened to clarify. "I mean you've got something important to do. There are people like Shit-Lone, as well as the other guy you call Big Brother, who must be concerned how you're getting on with your job."

"Tell me, what do you know about Big Brother?" he suddenly asked, his voice tight and serious.

I remembered how he had pestered Shit-Lone about Big Brother earlier in the car. I wondered why he should make a fuss of it when he should be concentrating on the job in hand. I said, "It baffles me why it's such a matter of urgency to you. It's not an appropriate time to talk about these things."

He rolled his eyes rapidly, like a scared animal, and said, "Because I just saw Big Brother outside Bogyoke Aung San Market an hour ago."

"Are you sure?" I was shocked.

"Not a hundred percent. Only someone startlingly familiar at a glance," he explained. "It was when I was having my lunch at a food stall inside the market, I raised my eyes from my plate of curry rice and pork without meaning to look at anything in particular, and saw the guy cross the street from the side of Zawgyi Café."

"Describe him," I said, keeping a calm face.

"There was a certain insolent swagger about the way he walked, strutting in his green soldier's uniform down the street and parting the crowd around him without ceremony…"

"A soldier's uniform? You mean you saw a Tatmadaw? What's the big deal when Tatmadaw are ubiquitous in Rangoon?" I said dismissively.

"That's true," he said. "I also rejected the idea that I had met the Tatmadaw man before. But the thing was, as soon as I returned to my plate of curry rice and pork, I had a vision, an awful vision perhaps. It'd suddenly and inexplicably become clear to me to whom that familiar face belongs. It's the Big Brother!"

I thought I was beginning to believe he had seen Bo Tin Aung leaving Zawgyi Café after lunch with me.

And he went on: "I immediately broke off from my lunch to follow him. He was alert, always looking over his shoulder. I was careful to keep a safe distance. Some streets later, he stopped under a lamppost. A jeep came. He jumped on board and was gone. Although I had never risked myself by getting too close, I thought I had had a good look at him. I am 99.9 if not a hundred percent sure that the guy is Big Brother!"

I was silent, wondering what it meant when Bo Tin Aung's true identity was blown.

"I couldn't have been more terrified," he continued in a quivering voice. "Isn't it spooky that the Tatmadaw is behind everything in this country, including terrorism? I was completely flabbergasted. And who am I, as someone who has taken direct orders from a Tatmadaw officer, to bomb the cinema? A loyal supporter of Tatmadaw, or some perfect idiot?"

I still didn't know what to say. I told myself to keep a serene face when I continued weighing the pros and cons of denying my knowledge of Big Brother. That, however, had just the opposite effect, when Moe Chit suddenly cried in a gasping voice, "Maya, how come you don't look surprised at all?"

"No, I was just thinking…" I murmured.

After staring me straight in the face with suspicious eyes for a while, he said, "Now I get it! You people have always known it! That was why Shit-Lone revealed nothing in the car when I asked him. And you too. I remember the first time I met you at Danyingon Station, Shit-Lone introduced you as the fiancée of his partner. That's Big Brother! Am I right or am I wrong?"

He was absolutely right, and Shit-Lone was to blame for his big mouth. But what now, when Moe Chit was waiting with his jaws agape for my explanation? After a quick calculation, I reckoned a flat denial would only make things worse. I thought, perhaps with a story of half-truth, I could possibly turn things around.

"No, you're not wrong. Big Brother is a Tatmadaw," I said, adding immediately, "but he's a good Tatmadaw."

"A good Tatmadaw? What's that?" he asked, as if he had never heard of such a thing.

"There are good guys in the ranks of the Tatmadaw, laying low and waiting for the opportunity to topple the regime government. Big Brother is one of them. Otherwise what do you think he's doing by dropping bombs around Rangoon?" I argued.

"You mean he is a Tatmadaw who's also a revolutionary, or a revolutionary who's also a Tatmadaw?!" he said, slightly amused.

"That's right. Now you know the secret. Are you feeling better now?" I asked.

"Perhaps. You know, it gave me the creeps when I caught the guy outside Bogyoke Aung San Market. I felt there was some sort of intrigue going on, and I began to fear for my life," he said, and resumed, after a short silence, "Does it mean that I should be less afraid of the guy who was such a brute?"

I remembered Bo Tin Aung had treated him like dirt during their first meeting. I said, "Big Brother can be quite rude sometimes, but he's actually a terribly good Tatmadaw."

"Not sure about that. A good Tatmadaw perhaps, but only a so-so revolutionary," he pondered.

"What makes you say that?"

"You know my order from Shit-Lone is to kill people in the cinema. Would a revolutionary sanction such killings?"

I was impressed. This guy was not so stupid after all. "It is, of course, wrong," I stressed. "No revolutionary would approve that kind of killing whatsoever the circumstances!"

He looked at me, wide-eyed and perplexed. "Are you going to tell me something that I don't know?"

It was time to take my plan another step forward, I thought. "Exactly, that's why I'm here… Big Brother sent me," I said, pausing to do a bit of juggling in my mind for my story to make perfect sense before continuing: "It is like this: Big Brother has never entirely agreed with Shit-Lone, yet he doesn't want to oppose him openly because they've been good friends since they were kids. Big Brother has, however, hinted to me that I should find the opportunity to warn you to be careful about hurting innocent people with indiscriminate violence. If possible, kill no one and hurt nobody whatever you do with the bomb."

"That is very considerate," he drawled.

"Indeed," I concurred.

When I was secretly glad that he seemed to have bought my story without question, he suddenly caught me somewhat off-guard by asking, "That being the case, mightn't he as well cancel the bomb?"

He had exposed an obvious flaw in my story, and I was momentarily mute. Without knowing what was going through his mind, I tested him, "Cancel the bomb... is that what you want?"

To my amazement, his reply was loud and clear: "Of course not!"

"Why?"

"Because the bomb is my lifeline," he stated emphatically. "I've got paid for the bombs. I'm running a drug business in Rangoon. I need the money, desperately. Although it scared me to death when I saw Big Brother outside Bogyoke Aung San Market, I have still come and brought the birthday cake along, not because it's my birthday, but for the simple fact that if there's no bomb there'd be no money. For the reward, I'll do whatever it takes, even if it means risking my own life. So please don't tell me Big Brother wants to cancel the bomb."

"No, he never intends such a thing," I told him truthfully, in the meantime finding him somewhat beyond redemption by adhering to his bad habits.

"Nice to hear that." He heaved a sigh of relief. Picking up the parcel from the floor, he said, "I can't wait to finish with this. But now you've come with a new briefing: kill no one and hurt nobody in the process. Is this at all possible?"

I didn't have an answer. I was thinking perhaps I could redo the wiring of the bomb to make it less deadly, but the deadline was only ten to fifteen minutes away and I didn't have enough time for that sort of reworking.

As I was wracking my brains, Moe Chit suddenly said, "Mind you, it's a very powerful bomb and it is meant to kill a lot of people... unless we don't put it in the auditorium."

I looked at him almost with huge admiration. This guy was, after all, not completely incorrigible.

"Good thinking," I said. Remembering the engine room which I had accidentally stumbled upon during my last visit to the cinema, I thought if we put the bomb there we could still cause some reasonable damage to the cinema but without the loss of lives. I told Moe Chit my idea.

"That'll be great," he said. "I think Big Brother will be pleased by a bomb that causes little harm to innocent people."

"That's for sure. But shall I remind you..." I said, as I was already thinking how to explain to Bo Tin Aung why the bomb had failed to kill, "...that you must keep this conversation between ourselves. As you know, Big Brother would deny everything in order not to upset Shit-Lone."

"I know, I know," he said, with a clever smile. "You're Big Brother's fiancée. You call the shots, okay?"

I smiled back, admitting nothing, and said simply, "Let's go. I'll show you where the engine room is."

We started for the cinema, walking side by side like a couple having a leisurely stroll. Pausing outside the exit, I quietly took in my surroundings. The backstreet was getting dark as the sun set behind the buildings. The gaggle of people in the area seemed preoccupied with what they were doing in their idle hours. As no one was apparently paying attention to us, we quietly slipped into the cinema through the pair of swinging doors at the exit.

Once inside we pushed forward, quietly squeezing our bodies along the wall. Midway down the corridor, I found the engine room with the metal door. It was at this moment, Lwin Moe, a leading character in the movie, cracked a joke. It must have been the funniest joke in the whole movie as the audience went crazy, laughing uproariously. I took the opportunity to hold down the handle to enter. But to my bewilderment the door stood fast against all pressures, as if it were locked from inside. I tried harder, but it still resisted to yield.

"The room is locked," I said, disgustedly.

"What shall we do now?" Moe Chit whispered behind me. "Shall we put the bomb back on the stage as planned?"

"Definitely not," I said resolutely, appalled by the guy who just wanted to finish the job at his convenience and the rest was no concern of his. "You can put the bomb anywhere inside the cinema as long as it's away from the auditorium."

"Then put it at the exit. That will save us time getting away afterwards." He made it sound as if it was only a joke.

But although a joke, it struck me as not a bad idea after all, as the exit was situated at the farthest point from the auditorium inside the cinema. "Let's do it," I said.

"You sure?" he asked, incredulous.

"Absolutely."

We returned to the exit and found a spot on the floor in the corner just behind the door. Moe Chit opened his parcel, taking out a toy birthday cake with a large candle in the middle.

"Have I told you it's my 30th birthday?" he grinned clownishly.

"Happy birthday," I said. "But will you hurry up, time is running out…"

He plucked out the candle from the middle of the cake. The birthday cake fell apart, revealing the bomb inside. With the use of duct tape, he fixed the bomb firmly in place to the corner of the wall.

"Now I'm going to set the time for the final blast," he said, glancing at his watch. "The time is 6.25pm…"

"That's to say, five minutes," I said.

"Great. If Big Brother is here, he should be very pleased with how exact we have kept the timing," he said. After he was done with the setup, he put the toy birthday cake back into the parcel bag, tied the ribbon at the mouth and stood to go.

"You still have to switch on the initiation device," I reminded him.

Embarrassed, he knelt down again to press a button on the back of the bomb. The clock on the device instantly started ticking as the five-minute countdown began.

"Thanks." He stood up, holding out his hand. "You're a great partner."

"Same here." I shook his hand, and said, "Good job. Let's get out of here."

He turned to go, as if in a hurry. "I'm meeting a dealer at Central Station at seven," he said, pushing open the door with enthusiastic haste.

As the door widened to a crack, the backstreet came into view. My perspective was rather limited. But in spite of the little I saw, I couldn't be more astonished. I pulled Moe Chit back and asked, "Did you notice?"

"What?" he muttered, staring at the door that swung back to close automatically.

"When we entered the cinema there was a little crowd out there, but the backstreet is now kind of deserted," I said, feeling an uncomfortable sense of apprehension.

"It's a street; people come and go all the time," he argued.

"Well, like it or not, something's rather fishy out there," I said. "My instinct is never wrong."

"What's that? A woman's instinct?" he sneered. He pushed open the door a crack, peering out with squinting eyes for several seconds, and announced with a suppressed laugh, "No. You're wrong. I thought I saw a guy at the corner near the main street. It must be Shit-Lone who has come to pick me up. Let's go."

I didn't move, as my mind was still filled with an ominous disquiet. But he couldn't wait to get out. I plucked at his sleeve, trying to stop him. He broke loose, burst out of the door and strode away, thrusting out his hands and shouting at the same time, "Shit-Lone! Shit-Lone!"

I was appalled. *What's he thinking by making all that noise? Has he forgotten he has just planted a bomb in the cinema?*

With a touch of exasperation I stepped out of the exit after him. Once in the open I immediately found that I should have followed my instinct rather than the stupid guy, who had stopped well short of the main street where Shit-Lone was supposed to be waiting.

But Shit-Lone was nowhere to be seen. Instead, a dozen men in dark green soldier fatigues had emerged from a passageway by the opposite building, staring fiercely across the street at Moe Chit who was standing rooted to the spot as if frozen with fear. At the sound of a roaring yell from the officer-in-charge, the soldiers took a step forward, their leather boots crunching sharply on the ground beneath.

Moe Chit, who had suddenly recovered from the initial immobilising shock, beat a retreat. He didn't turn to run; he merely walked backwards without taking his eyes off the soldiers. To my perplexity, the soldiers, though seemingly poised to strike any moment, stood still, as if awaiting a command.

I thought we had walked into an ambush. Noticing that no soldiers had been deployed on the dead-end side of the street where there was a low brick wall, I called out to Moe Chit when he drew near, "Let's go to the wall!"

He stole a backward glance at me. To be pretty clear about the direction, I pointed to my right, and repeated, "The wall! To the wall!"

Without a moment to waste, I turned on my heels to run. After a few yards sprinting down the pavement, I was suddenly aware that Moe Chit had not come after me. I swirled around and saw that he had slipped and dropped to the floor outside the exit. To my surprise, the soldiers could easily have got him but they did not try; they were only watching from a distance with high alert.

I thought if Moe Chit could get back on his feet he could still flee. And I yelled to encourage him, "Pull yourself together. Get up and get to the wall now!"

But before I had said all I wanted to say, I felt myself being grabbed from behind. There was a hand on my mouth, and everything I said had got muddled up horribly. Another hand wrapped around my neck, choking me so that I could hardly breathe. I lost the strength to fight back, and was roughly dragged across the pavement into the building through a door next to the exit of the cinema.

Once inside, my assailant shut the door with a back kick of his leg. He forced me to sit down on the floor. In a hushed voice he said, "Will you stay quiet if I let go?"

I nodded, and he released me from his claws. I didn't howl or scream because it wasn't going to help. Moreover, it was also because I had found the man's voice curiously familiar. I turned round and at once recognised the guy in spite of the dimmed interior.

"What the hell is this about?" I blurted out furiously.

"Didn't I tell you I'd be around if necessary?" said the guy who was none other than Bo Tin Aung. "I'm here to save you."

He opened the door a crack, took a peep at the backstreet and sighed, "I'm afraid your friend will not be so lucky."

I stood up to look outside. Moe Chit had already climbed to his feet; but the soldiers had also closed in, surrounding him in a semi-circle, blocking his path to the wall.

"Are the soldiers your men?" I asked Bo Tin Aung.

"Yes they are," he said. "As a matter of fact, they're acting on a piece of intelligence that there is a plot to bomb the cinema…"

"A piece of intelligence?! This is absurd," I cried out in protest.

"Will you keep your voice down?" he said, continuing: "After I left you at Zawgyi Café, I came here and have been working on the upper floor office of the cinema which has been turned by the military into a temporary command post. Shit-Lone called me urgently to say that you are concerned about Moe Chit's strange behaviour and have gone after him. I don't blame you because you don't know there's been a change of plan. I've been waiting here to get you out of trouble."

"Always a change of plan!" I groaned bitterly. "So what do you want? To arrest Moe Chit?"

"I always want to arrest that son-of-a-bitch," he uttered in disdain.

"But why? You yourself are the mastermind behind the plot," I said.

"Of course, I know, we know, my commander especially. It's my commander who has ordered the arrest so that he can deal better with the pressure from the top guys," he said.

Outside on the street there seemed to be a momentary impasse when neither side had made an evident move: the soldiers did nothing more than watch cautiously from a comfortable distance, whereas Moe Chit, who could not have retreated any further, was standing with his back against the door of the exit. Suddenly I was seized with great dread, and said to Bo Tin Aung, "If you want to arrest him, do it now!"

"I can't. So far he has done nothing calling for an immediate arrest," he replied.

"Then what are you waiting for?"

"What a silly question," he said, glancing at his watch. "As a matter of fact, I'm waiting for the crime… to occur…"

He did not finish speaking, because precisely at the instant he said "occur" came the sound of a loud explosion, causing the four walls around us to shake.

A strong wave of hot air carrying a suffocating smell of powder rushed into the building through the door gap and hit us. We both cried out something senseless as we stumbled and fell. In that almost involuntary burst I heard myself mutter "Shit!" I was thinking about what might have happened to Moe Chit and it wasn't a pretty thought. Bo Tin Aung spit out a loud "Damn!" He quickly sprang back to his feet, poked his head out of the door, and cried in a cold, listless tone, "What the fuck is this?!"

I staggered to my feet, but could not get a proper view of the street veiled behind a thick screen of black smoke. As my visibility improved with the smoke partially cleared, I began to see the structure at the exit had been severely damaged by the explosion – its door was missing and a section of the adjacent wall had been shattered. Some soldiers had fallen to the ground and were being helped by those who were still standing.

I couldn't quite locate the whereabouts of Moe Chit initially. He was not seen outside the exit; it seemed as if he had made good his escape moments before impact. But then I saw something which caused my heart to ache. At about ten feet from the exit there was the body of a man lying crumpled across the pavement and the street gutter. I immediately recognised it was Moe Chit as the man was still holding a white plastic bag in his hand. He must have been blown away and dumped in the street gutter by the explosion. A soldier approached and gave him a kick in the head. He didn't move as if he felt no pain. The soldier kicked again, and again. There was not a sign of life from him as his body remained still and motionless. I could tell he was dead, and I wept. When the soldier was not over with the kicking, I begged Bo Tin Aung to intervene.

"What's the difference now? The son-of-a-bitch is dead," he said cruelly. But upon my repeated pleading, he took a step out of the door and shouted across the street to order the soldier to stop.

A dark ferret-like man in a light green longyi emerged furtively from the ruined exit of the cinema. It was Shit-Lone. As soon as he spotted Moe Chit lying in the gutter, he rushed over and started slapping his face as if trying to wake him up. When Moe Chit failed to respond, Shit-Lone slapped harder until Bo Tin Aung intervened again.

"Don't waste time on a goner," Bo Tin Aung boomed across the street from our elevated perch.

Shit-Lone came over to join us. He saw me inside the door and greeted me: "I'm glad that you're safe."

"Thanks," I muttered.

"Do you have anything to report?" asked Bo Tin Aung.

"What do you want to hear first? The damage or casualty?" said Shit-Lone.

"All at once, okay?" Bo Tin Aung uttered impatiently.

"Fine. First the damage. I have done a check inside the house. It was no good. Everything was in the right place, not even a chair had been overturned. It seemed the bomb had been put in the wrong place, which was at quite some distance from the auditorium. As a result, the only damage is limited to everything you see from here, including the exit and part of the adjoining wall," he said in a depressed voice. "As far as casualty is concerned, unfortunately there's only Moe Chit. If you like, you can add the soldiers wounded by the flying debris as well as those men and women in the audience who have suffered minor injuries during the evacuation."

Bo Tin Aung cried in disgust, "What has he done? What the fuck has he done?"

"You mean Moe Chit?" Shit-Lone said. "He's dead. Perhaps only Maya can explain."

Bo Tin Aung turned to me, with an uneasy twitching of his eyebrows.

I knew I would sooner or later be called upon to explain for a bomb that had failed to deliver the sort of carnage they had in mind. Only I didn't know it had come this quick. I said, stuttering between sobs, "What do you want to hear? Are you guys still not satisfied that Moe Chit is dead?"

Bo Tin Aung made not a sound, his face grave like a tombstone. Shit-Lone said with a glance at the curious crowd gathered in the distance near the main road, "We're sorry that Moe Chit is dead. But if you look at the people over there, do you think some of them should have, for better or worse, joined him too? Can you explain why it wasn't so?"

His coldblooded words made me tremble all over. But as I looked over Bo Tin Aung's shoulder to the crowd of people, I saw several cinema ushers among them, and it was then I knew how I could talk myself out of trouble.

I said, "I don't know what I could have done better when I found Moe Chit's behaviour strange and out of sorts. His confidence was low, and I supported him by going in the cinema with him. But then the plan of you guys had one major flaw, which had not taken into account the presence of ushers…"

"What ushers?" asked Bo Tin Aung with a frown.

"The cinema ushers," I said. "Inside the cinema there was an usher idling under the wall near the stage, watching the movie and laughing with the rest of the audience. To facilitate Moe Chit I had to lure him away. I approached the guy and told him I felt very sick. He appeared to be helpful and kind; he lent me an arm and walked me out of the auditorium. Once in the lobby I said I was feeling much better and told him that I could take a small rest myself before rejoining my family inside the cinema. The usher left me and went out to the street for a smoke. I re-entered the cinema and found Moe Chit already waiting for me at the exit. He said nothing; he looked perfectly fine and I had the impression that he had done everything accordingly to your instruction..."

"My instruction? What was my instruction?" grumbled Shit-Lone loudly. "I've told him to kill everyone in the cinema!"

Bo Tin Aung said nothing. His expression had however become less severe as if he had found my version of the event believable.

I went on boldly, "I don't know what your complaints are here. You asked for a bomb, you got the bomb. You need some dead bodies, now you've got at least one. Are you guys still not satisfied?"

"Honestly speaking we're utterly dissatisfied, because the commander is paying 10,000 kyat for every corpse," moaned Shit-Lone. "Dead bodies aside, we had always intended Moe Chit to go to prison instead of the morgue."

Bo Tin Aung hastened to explain. "We know Moe Chit was involved in drug trafficking, and it was my duty to put him away. There was no better time to do it than after he had delivered all the bombs. It is quite disappointing that he has left the last bomb in Danyingon. What a gigantic mistake! But now he is dead, I'm sorry, and he's forgiven."

He sounded mournful and genuinely sad. I was a little touched by his humane behaviour which was a stark contrast to Shit-Lone's heartlessness.

"Maya, thanks for filling in the details. You have done a good job, no complaints here," continued Bo Tin Aung, his voice still sorrowful. "My thoughts are with the family. I think you should go down to Danyingon and inform Siha of the news immediately."

"You mean now?" I asked. "What am I supposed to say to him?"

"Tell him there was an accident and offer our condolences," he said.

"Siha will be devastated. He's old and crippled; how is he supposed to carry on living without his son?" I sobbed.

After a moment's pondering, Bo Tin Aung rummaged in his uniform, took out some money and said, "Give this to the poor man to cover his more urgent needs. Promise him more to come to compensate for his loss."

"It's very charitable of you," I said. Touched by his generosity, I thought the soul of Moe Chit should be consoled to know that Big Brother was, after all, a good Tatmadaw. "If you think I should go to see Siha at once with the money, I guess I'd better be off now as it's getting dark."

At this time, a truck appeared on the driveway outside. The team of arriving policemen started pushing back bystanders and cordoning off the crime scene with coloured tape.

I said to Bo Tin Aung, "I can't get to the main street with all these people and the police."

"You leave by that wall at the end of the street, it's more convenient," remarked Bo Tin Aung. "But even if you go to the main street, they're not going to arrest you even though they saw you with Moe Chit not long ago."

"Why?"

"I told them you are the informant, so that's all right," he said, with an air of cool insolence.

"I would never do anything like that!" I shrieked.

"Well, you're one now," he pronounced dryly.

A black van had arrived with some workers in white overalls. They put the body of Moe Chit in a plastic bag for conveyance to the morgue. That was the last I saw of him.

Bo Tin Aung took me by the hand and led me outside. We pushed past a bunch of policemen to walk down the pavement to the wall at the end of the street. I stepped over a layer of bricks, landing on the other side of the wall. As I was about to turn to go, he suddenly said, "I hope you still have not forgotten your role in this."

"My role? What's that?" I asked.

"The bomb."

"What about the bomb?"

"You go to Danyingon and bring back the third and last bomb," he said. "After the second bomb, which is an obvious failure, everything now hinges on the success of the last bomb. Shit-Lone said he has specifically asked for both the second and last bomb to be available at the same time. How that son-of-a-bitch...I mean how Moe Chit should have disobeyed such an important instruction by having left it behind. Anyway, Siha should have it ready for pick-up, and you..."

"But how can I raise the subject to Siha in his bereaved condition?" I interrupted him scornfully.

"Don't be sentimental. Bereaved or not is not the issue, urgency is the issue," he said. "Now Moe Chit is dead, the police will turn up sooner or later at Danyingon for an investigation once the identity of the bloke is uncovered. I want no traces left behind which could lead back to us. I'll find time to deal with that after I have finished my work here..."

Still furious, I was not really listening, which I would later regret.

And he went on calmly and coldly, "It is therefore critically important that you go to Danyingon now to procure the bomb at once. If you think the old man is a problem, then say nothing about the death of his son. Just ask him for the bomb, get it and get out immediately."

I had never heard anything more coldblooded and cruel. I stood stunned and horrified at the frightful evidence of what was actually behind this man's supposed kindness and generosity. Seething with indignation, I hurriedly took off, afraid he'd see the outrage on my face.

"See you around," he called out after me warmly.

I walked on as if I hadn't heard him. Moving ahead, I saw in the corner of my eye something very wrong with this man. His presence – tall, heavy, dark and ominous – had left me sick and shaken. There was also something more vicious than mere callousness in his unctuous tone, and I couldn't quite discern what poison was hidden within. My thoughts were in total disarray. I sped away, as far as my feet would carry me.

Upon arriving at Central Station, sitting in the carriage waiting for the train to begin its journey, I kept thinking how I was supposed to break the news to the old man, and how he would take the blow at his age. I didn't know if I was capable of consoling him. Or should I, as Bo Tin Aung suggested, just grab the bomb and run?

20

M.A.Y.A.

I told Siha Moe Chit was dead as soon as I entered the village house.

He barely reacted. He just said, "Ask me how I feel? I don't feel *anything*."

With a disconsolate shrug of his shoulders, he broke off in a sort of soliloquy. "There's no pain. None at all. He's only a son by name; no blood relation. I picked him up in Shan at a poppy farm some twenty years ago. He was only nine or ten, just a child. Not handsome or lovely, only a bit impish and unusual-looking; he had these really small black eyes in a small face with a sickly colour from his addiction. When I met him, he'd just got beaten up for stealing opium for his own enjoyment. Blood and dirt were all over his face, but no tears.

"The farm's headman made me an offer. 'He's an orphaned child of the war, roaming the jungle and taking refuge with the farmers. Make him your own if you like. Take him away now or you won't see him the next time you pass through; he'll be long dead, for obvious reasons.'

"I had never imagined having a son. My own son? It sounds kind of unrealistic for a man like me – I mean, I was in my mid-forties, too busy fighting the junta my whole life to ever get married. I hesitated; but the boy, excited and eager, begged me to adopt him. So I took him with me and made him a kind of son.

"To be honest, I never expected somebody like him to live very long. As a product of our terrible times – wars, upheavals, a little calamity here and there, a wretched government and revolutions – he was prone to get caught up in it all, the conflicts and clashes, destined to die young when his luck ran out. Like now. So there's nothing to mourn, really. Anyway, for his departure, I wish him well and smooth sailing to a better place…"

It was almost like a funeral speech – so much so that I wondered if he would start chanting next. But he only said, after a long silence, "I think we need a drink."

He staggered to the cupboard on the other side of the dining room, took two glasses from the upper shelf, placed them carefully on a tray, and began filling them with wine. I heard him mutter a curse, probably having spilled the liquid. He stood quietly before the cupboard for a while, back to me and head sinking so low that it appeared lost below his neck. From the rise and fall of his shoulders, I could tell he was weeping. He said he felt no pain for the death of his nominal son, but now he was weeping, uncontrollably. I didn't know what to say to console him. As a matter of fact, I wanted to cry, too. And I cried in silence.

After that he recovered, turning towards me with eyes welling up, his face tearful. Wiping his nose, he said, in a slightly embarrassed voice, "I've never cried in my whole life. Now I'm crying shamelessly for the bastard!"

He returned to the long table where I sat and handed me a glass filled to the brim with wine.

I hesitated about drinking. "I'm not sure if it is appropriate…"

"What's so inappropriate? Don't think we're drinking for the dead. No. I'm done with the bastard," he said. "I just need a drink, that's all. If you want something formal, let me propose a toast: To the revolution!"

You can't refuse a toast proposal like that, I thought. I raised the glass to my lips and sipped politely. The old man emptied his glass in one draught, refilled it to the top, and mused, "Even if you won't say it outright, it's the junta that killed my boy, right?"

He was not wrong. I nodded.

After a lengthy pause, he said, with surprising defiance in his voice, "We can't win fighting the junta. But we must go on fighting the junta. We will go on fighting the junta." He swallowed down his wine with a painful expression as if it was poison. Touched by his unwavering determination at a time of deep sorrow, I took to my wine almost with awe and reverence.

With that the emptied glasses were refilled and the refilled glasses emptied, without the old man having to propose toast after toast. It was enough that Moe Chit was dead and the business of revolution unfinished. The wine tasted bitter; but the bitterness suited my mood, giving me curious comfort. Before I was drunk, I seized the chance to ask the old man about the bomb.

"It's in the shed at the back of the house, by the wall," he mumbled. "You can find anything there, from spare parts to ingredients enough for a dozen bombs. If you're not in a hurry, stay for another drink with a poor old man."

Unfortunately, I was in a hurry. Bo Tin Aung's advice still rang loud in my ears: "Get the bomb and get out immediately." But on second thought, I chose to stay, knowing the agony of bereavements. I had lost my mother to the junta's atrocities and understood how it felt. I couldn't refuse the old man when he needed a companion as a merciful relief from his pain. So I remained, listening to his laments. On and off, he wept, and I wept with him. He drank, and I drank with him. And before I knew it, I was drunk and fell asleep.

Then, without knowing how long I had nodded off, I woke up to a stabbing pain in my belly. Night had descended. In darkness, I heard the sound of the old man's snoring. I needed to relieve myself, but had no idea where the toilet was. There was no hope of asking the old man, who slumbered drunken on the floor. I crept outside through a door with a broken frame at the back of the house.

The backyard was an oblong, overgrown patch of garden planted with a few melon vines and some feeble vegetables. But there was no house resembling a toilet cubicle. The air was hot and humid. The sky was overcast, and rain seemed to be in the offing.

I crossed the yard to the other end where there was a clump of trees. Behind the thick foliage there was a structure of half-wood and half-metal. I opened the door and smelt a strong but familiar smell of chemicals. Then I realised it was not some toilet, but instead the shed where explosives and their ingredients were stored.

Now my belly was burning with pain akin to menstrual cramps. With a huge effort I rushed to the back of the shed and squatted down behind some trees for urgent relief. I didn't pee or poo; instead I discharged something that felt hot and thick and watery. Could this be my lagging period that had finally arrived? I seriously doubted it.

Normally my period would cause only the release of a fair amount of blood, not profuse like gallons. If it wasn't my belated period, then what could it be? My periods, though not always regular, were never a cause for concern as I hadn't been fooling around. But should I be concerned now after months living with Bo Tin Aung? Staring at the blood that looked like purplish-red strawberry jam under my legs, I began to seriously wonder if I might have been pregnant. At the same time, I wondered also what it would mean for me to be pregnant at only sixteen.

Lost in the abyss of my idle reverie, I was suddenly startled by a loud noise coming from the main house. I peeped out from the corner of the shed and saw light flashes flickering behind the dark windows.

"Where's the switch? It's supposed to be on the wall. Oh, got it!" Someone spoke loudly and wrathfully.

Moments later the interior of the house was lit up. Immediately thereafter sharp voices of men, shouting and swearing, and violent noises of a scuffle, erupted. Above all the stir and din I heard the fearful yells and awful groans of the old man, sounding desperate in a state of helplessness, like the long wailing howl of a dying wolf. Before I had any idea what was happening, the house went dark again in a snap, and all the disturbing noises subsided that instant.

A little later, I heard the sound of a door opening and footsteps entering the backyard. I quickly hid round the corner of the shed and held my breath. The steps stopped approaching, as if whoever was in the garden had paused to appraise the surroundings. After a moment or two, someone cleared his throat and asked in a husky voice, "Did you use a knife to cut him down?"

"No," answered a second voice with a sneer. "There's no need. He's old and weak, no more than a fly; and you don't use a cannon to kill a fly. Why?"

"Because I keep smelling a whiff of blood in the air."

His partner drew in the air several times in audible sniffs before he replied, "My nose tells me nothing of the sort. It must be the weather. So hot and humid, feeling kind of clammy and damp. I guess rain will come anytime soon."

Just as soon as they struck up the conversation, I was relieved to know the men were no strangers, and whose voices were well known to me. The one who said he smelt blood (probably the blood I discharged) was Bo Tin Aung. The other man was, of course, none other than Bo Tin Aung's loyal sidekick, Shit-Lone. I thought a little about whether I should reveal myself, but decided against it, as I didn't want them to catch me squatting over a pool of blood in a state of undress. Besides I was also somewhat dumbfounded to hear Shit-Lone hint at having done something brutal and vicious to the old man. The fact that they had turned up at the place at this hour also puzzled me profoundly.

"You sure it's only the dank air? Not blood?" asked Bo Tin Aung.

"I don't blame you for being bloodthirsty," chortled Shit-Lone. "Now after the father and son have been conveniently dispatched, who is next? Maya?"

It was odd to hear my name as part of the question. But the answer was odder still when Bo Tin Aung replied, in a completely cold and unfeeling voice, "I fear it will be her turn."

I was in shock.

"Are you serious?" asked Shit-Lone.

There was no reply.

"How long has she been on board? Three months?" asked Shit-Lone again.

"Four months, three weeks, and two days," answered Bo Tin Aung.

"You're meticulous. I guess you keep a record of every girl…" Shit-Lone stopped short as if he didn't want to embarrass his friend, but then continued, still somewhat teasingly, "Getting tired of her already after such a short time?"

"Yes… and no," mused Bo Tin Aung. "You know it was only physical in the beginning…"

"You mean rape?"

"Fuck you. I was actually a little in love with her…" said Bo Tin Aung softly.

"You mean with her well-shaped, desirable little body?"

"That too," said Bo Tin Aung, a little peevishly. "I did ask her to marry me."

"That's your old trick!"

"No. At one time I was pretty serious with this fanciful idea of family and children," said Bo Tin Aung.

"That's only natural as you've a responsibility as the only son in your family," said Shit-Lone. "What stopped you?"

"Something has been constantly nagging me ever since I picked her up on Dala beach…"

"You mean ever since she was kidnapped…" Shit-Lone contradicted him again, as someone who couldn't keep his opinions to himself.

Bo Tin Aung must have had enough of the taunts, and cried scornfully, "Hey. Stop being such a prick! Your running commentary is absolutely unnecessary."

"Sorry," mumbled Shit-Lone.

"Where was I?" asked Bo Tin Aung as if somewhat lost.

Shit-Lone reminded his friend, "You said you'd marry her," and added, in his habitual tone of banter, "but you're only playing with her and it's time to cut her loose…"

Bo Tin Aung hastened to explain. "That's not what I said. The thing is: I never trust her, as I always suspect that she is connected to the *Tatmadaw Dei* bombing."

"You mean she's a terrorist?" said Shit-Lone. "Then what's the matter with you, thinking to marry a terrorist?"

"The first time I said I wanted to marry her, it was partly from my heart and partly a slip of the tongue," said Bo Tin Aung. "Later when I proposed to her with an imitation gold ring, I was thinking only to use marriage as a tool."

"Just as a tool?"

"Yeah. When my commander had this idea of throwing a few bombs around Rangoon, I immediately thought of how I could use Maya, a suspected terrorist with experiences in explosives, as a perfect candidate for the job," said Bo Tin Aung. "You know she'd do anything if I pledged to marry her."

"Of course you were never serious about marrying her. Why then did you take the trouble of bringing her to meet the monks at Shwedagon?" asked Shit-Lone.

"She once said it was her wish to have a wedding ceremony at Shwedagon to be officiated by a high monk," answered Bo Tin Aung. "To gain her complete trust, I had to make things look as real as it gets, by arranging for a monk to talk to her regarding the ceremony."

"And what did the monk say?"

"She was advised not to rush the matter, as I understood."

"As you understood? What does that mean?"

"I wasn't with her at the discussion. I didn't even know the monk who interviewed her, as I was not welcome to sit in with her. But knowing no monks would think it OK for a sixteen-year-old to marry somebody twice her age, I was sure a wedding ceremony was out of the question, at least not in the immediate present."

"You're such a smartass," praised Shit-Lone with a hollow laugh. "Was she disappointed?"

"She was, of course, upset, but it wasn't too bad. I coaxed her like a pet and she was quickly happy again," said Bo Tin Aung.

"I still remembered the afternoon we met at Zawgyi Café where I, at your instruction, disclosed to her the plan to terrorise Rangoon with a spree of bombs," said Shit-Lone. "I'm amazed that she still agreed to work on the bombs after she was told there was no wedding ceremony. How did you accomplish that?"

"I told her that we should make some money now and marry later when there is this chance of becoming filthy rich…" explained Bo Tin Aung.

"And she was persuaded…?"

"It appeared so. But I sensed also that she'd have jumped at the opportunity even without my kind words," said Bo Tin Aung. "She was bored after months of confinement in my apartment. All she wanted was some fresh air, and to be free…"

"But she's never free. You have people monitor her every move," observed Shit-Lone creepily.

"That's not necessary. I don't have to monitor her every move. I've got her uncle," said Bo Tin Aung. "She knows she can't run away or her uncle will be dead."

"Her uncle?"

"Yeah. You know we have arrested a guy named Kloh. It's her uncle," said Bo Tin Aung. "He's now kept in the Insein Prison Hospital for tuberculosis."

"You sure her uncle is guilty?"

"As guilty as sin, except that we can't prove it," said Bo Tin Aung resentfully.

"And Maya?"

"For the connection to her uncle she's, of course, guilty as well," answered Bo Tin Aung decidedly.

"I admire your logic," said Shit-Lone dryly; he didn't sound like he was trying to be ironic. "Then what are you going to do now? Kill her… after you make love to her for the last time tonight?"

"Make love to her for the last time? I like the idea," mused Bo Tin Aung. "And kill her? Yes of course. It's only a matter of *modus operandi*. Well, we'll know exactly what to do after we have disposed of the last bomb."

"I feel sorry for Maya. I always liked her…" said Shit-Lone, with a rare melancholy in his voice.

"You know it's a sin to covet your neighbour's wife," muttered Bo Tin Aung uneasily.

"That's not what I meant. She sometimes reminds me of my little sister, beautiful and wilful, who died very young, before her fourteenth birthday, in a traffic accident," sighed Shit-Lone.

"I'm sorry," said Bo Tin Aung.

"Give her a clean death if you must, I entreat you," said Shit-Lone. "Don't make her suffer too much. I feel it's a bit cruel and notoriously insane to waste the life of a pretty girl like her."

"Cruel? Notorious? Insane? Pretty? That's purely from your point of view," snorted Bo Tin Aung.

I shuddered at the emotional indifference in his tone, which was astonishing. His revelation, of his false love and the idea to destroy me, stunned me like a bolt from the sky. For months I had been living in a world of self-deception, by concealing things which were awful and abhorrent with the palpable semblance of outward love and tenderness, as a necessity to survival. I figured it was now the time to wake up for good.

Bo Tin Aung suddenly asked, somewhat out of the blue, "Hey, what's over there behind the trees? A hut?"

"It's the shed, where bombs are manufactured," replied Shit-Lone. "I once had Moe Chit take me to see what's inside. I had only a half-glimpse, for as soon as Moe Chit opened the door, there was this strong odour that smelt like the urine of my dead grandmother. It sickened me so much that I at once turned and ran."

"I don't think it's urine. I guess it may be ammonia or nitric acid. You fool!" Bo Tin Aung chided.

"Whatever," said Shit-Lone. "If you can stand the abominable smell, go take a look. I'll wait for you here."

Shit-Lone's suggestion almost freaked me out. I thought I would probably meet the worst fate imaginable if Bo Tin Aung found me at the shed. I turned around to look at the high fence behind me, and wondered how fast I could vanish before the man, who had only moments ago laid bare his intention of killing me at the next opportunity, was anywhere near.

As I was making all sorts of calculations, I was, however, somewhat puzzled not to hear the noise of boots crunching the dead leaves in the field if Bo Tin Aung had decided to come over to the shed. It was very quiet out there. So I decided to stay put, and not make a move before I had a clear hint of what my enemy was up to.

As I huddled waiting, I felt my forehead dappled with drops of moisture. I thought I must be perspiring heavily under the great stress. The sweat began dripping down my brows; my eyes grew misty, my cheeks wet. It made me feel very uncomfortable. In the oppressive silence I didn't dare do anything for fear of causing a noise that might betray my presence. It must be the most agonising silence I had ever experienced. And then, after what felt like a very long time, the dead air was broken by a great uproar. It was Bo Tin Aung who exclaimed, as if he was hugely amazed, "What the fuck did you just say? Rain? It's here, you clever dick!"

Alas! Almost at once I realised the drops of moisture on my face were not exactly my sweat but fine particles of drizzle floating in the air, like subtle harbingers preceding the arrival of a long-anticipated rain.

Scarcely had Bo Tin Aung's voice trailed off, than a torrential downpour tumbled from the sky which had become as dark as night. The rickety shed next to me shook in the wind and rain, the beating rainfall drumming noisily on its tin roof. I had little shelter from the nearby trees, which were standing helplessly like weeds trailing in the waves. I was soaked through in the drenching rain, but I kept very still, in dread of being discovered.

Bo Tin Aung was heard to speak again. "I don't mind taking a peep if there's a covered walkway from here to the shed…" but quickly added, "No, no, forget it. I'd rather go home now than be anywhere else. I worry about Maya and the bomb she's supposed to be carrying with her right now. I hope she won't have gone astray for whatever reason. Tomorrow is going to be a big day, and nothing must go wrong again. We'll get out of here as soon as the rain stops."

At the sound of the opening and shutting of the door, the guys withdrew into the main house.

I remained cowering at the back of the shed, quiet and shivering in the rain, which went on more or less continuously for some time, until it eventually petered out. Then, without the need to strain my ears, I began to hear footsteps marching out of the main house, followed by the creaking sound of the iron-wrought gate at the front yard and the querulous voices of the guys laughing and babbling as they hit the road back to town. It was at once a huge relief, but only mentally. Physically, for all the time I was made to squat under the tree, I experienced a sort of paralysis of my limbs as if I were in the process of being transformed into a gravestone by the cruel rain. But was the rain to blame for all I was made to endure? Of course not. I thought I'd have been sorrier if it were not for its perfect timing, and so I was thankful.

The sky slowly cleared after the rain. A yellowish round moon emerged from the clouds, shining a bright light on the backyard where small pools of rainwater glistened like crystals. As I lay on the grass, awaiting the paralysis to pass, I found a bug or something like a beetle, which must have been caught off-guard by the rain, struggling on the surface of a puddle nearby. I picked it out of the water and dumped it on the grass. It was motionless and I wondered if it had drowned.

As my circulation began to improve, I was eventually able to stand straight. I took off my clothes and washed my body with water streaming down the sloping eaves of the shed. Then I suddenly remembered what was of more urgent concern, and I quickly got dressed and made a desperate dash for the main house.

At the front porch, I stumbled upon the body of the old man, which felt stiff and cold. It was dark and I couldn't see things very clearly. It took me some time before I found the power box at the corner of a side wall. I hit it and hit it again but no light came forth. I sighed, noting that Rangoon, as well as the whole country, was infamous for its intermittent energy supply. I was, however, mortified by the unfairness of the situation. How lucky it was for Bo Tin Aung and Shit-Lone to have the use of electricity at a time when they needed it, and how unfortunate it was for the old man to have been fully exposed and left to the mercy of his slayers.

After some fumbling around I managed to find a pocket flashlight in a drawer. Under its light, I checked the body of the old man and found that he had been strangled to death. His eyes bulged from the sockets, his tongue stuck out with vomit around his mouth, and his head had collapsed to one side as if Shit-Lone had completely broken his neck.

Seized by extreme anger and sadness, I broke down and cried. I suffered terribly from a sense of guilt, thinking I was to blame for the fate of the old man. Had I listened and listened hard by paying more attention to the words of Bo Tin Aung, when, outside the cinema, he said glaring over his shoulder at the dead body of Moe Chit, "I want no traces left behind which could lead back to us. I'll find time to deal with that after I have finished my work here," I should have guessed what that signified.

Now the father and son were both dead within a matter of hours. I was particularly pained by the fact that I was present on both occasions, almost as if my folly and ignorance had got them killed. I thought if I were to redeem my guilt, the only way was to make the culprits pay for the deaths. But as I bent my mind towards revenge on behalf of the father and son, I realised the task was near impossible because I myself had also become a target on the murderers' hit list. In a moment of hopelessness I sat slumped beside the dead body of the old man and cried bitterly.

Later, after I had grown weary of hearing my own sobbing, I staggered to the back garden to get some fresh air and to clear my mind. Near the small puddle of water, I was amazed to find the beetle which I thought had drowned was still alive. It was, however, not going anywhere because it was trapped in an embarrassing upturned position. Sticking out its hairy legs from its abdomen and kicking back and forth, it strived to restore some normality to its body. All efforts seemed to be in vain. I was in a fatalistic mood, and I whispered to the poor little thing, "Hey, you're just as hopeless as me."

Nevertheless the beetle was not to be discouraged; it kept working at what appeared to be a thankless task. Then something incredible occurred. Without me knowing what it had actually done or just by being sufficiently stubborn, the beetle succeeded in tipping the balance in its favour. It rolled to one side, sitting on its stomach. After another stationery moment to complete whatever internal procedures it would undertake for the takeoff, it spread its brown wings, slowly ascended and soared away into the air, bathed in bright moonlight.

"You've done it! Dude!" I cheered after the beetle, which flew away from the backyard, past the shed and vanished into the dark bushes. I was curiously thrilled by its triumph over a seemingly hopeless situation through sheer persistence. The experience was both awe inspiring and uplifting. I thought I could not have been better encouraged at a time when I was down and out, weak and forsaken. The heroism of the humble creature had heartened me to grapple with my circumstances. I was able to see that there was something more than just a crazy feat of resilience on the part of the beetle. In fact, it didn't just labour away blindly in the hope of a miracle. Instead, it knew once it had overcome the initial obstacle, it had a pair of wings as its weaponry to rely on for the ultimate escape. Standing in front of the shed, I began to realise that the odds were not overwhelmingly against me, because I had my weapon too. It was the bomb sitting inside the shed.

As I went on to discover, there was a mixed assortment of bombs, mostly incomplete, inside the shed. At the far corner I found the device the old man had prepared for the last mission. It was similar in design to the second bomb, but more powerful for the purpose of upending traffic lights on the roadside. I studied the device to gauge if it was any good in what I was hoping to accomplish. Consequently I decided that I'd need to reconfigure the trigger mechanism in order to be in control of when and where to push the final button. There was no lack of tools in the shed, and thanks to the pocket flashlight and its illumination, I was able to carry out the work with considerable finesse. The bomb was rebuilt and refuelled, and a magnetic trigger mechanism with pressure points at the base for the choice of time delays to be activated by contact with an iron rod of several inches long, was installed.

While I was conducting a final check on the bomb, I began to ponder how I was supposed to proceed from this point onwards. The key, as it appeared, was to gain access to Bo Tin Aung by returning to his apartment as if nothing had happened. To do that, I would have to come up with a damned good excuse to explain the lateness of the hour. *What excuse would that be…?*

If he had no problem readmitting me to his apartment, the rest would be relatively straightforward. I'd only have to sit and wait to see how the finale played out and deal my hand as appropriate. *But how was I to decide what was appropriate…?*

Last but not least I must not underestimate all the uncertainties involved. Given the unpredictability of Bo Tin Aung's character, I'd definitely need some sort of parachute for my own protection should things for no reason go awfully awry. *And what sort of parachute, to be exact…?*

The thinking, difficult in the extreme, began to tire me when I was getting nowhere. I nodded off momentarily. But I didn't close my eyes for too long. I had another attack of cramp in my belly which woke me up, and it was at that very instant I seemed to find inspiration in the most unlikely corner. The cramp and spasm of pain reminded me that I might be pregnant. I confess I had once found the idea horrible, even disgusting; but in my odd circumstances, not anymore. Almost like the missing piece of a jigsaw puzzle, my suspected pregnancy suddenly seemed to fit perfectly in the bigger picture.

This was based on my knowledge of a tender side of Bo Tin Aung who had a weakness for children. His face would unfailingly light up with a ridiculous glow whenever he encountered lovely babies. The fact that he was still childless at thirty made him feel remorseful and incomplete; at the time he proposed to marry me, he had specifically asked me to give him a child. It was therefore something I thought I could exploit. I'd tell him I was pregnant, loud and clear, although I didn't know if he could be persuaded with something I myself was not completely sure about. But it didn't matter, did it? If I said I was pregnant, who was going to challenge me? Even he only half believed what I said; I seriously doubt if he had the heart and mind to hurt me or imprison both mother and child should the situation get out of control.

Resolved to have revenge for the death of Siha and Moe Chit at any cost, I told myself: *Let's face it, pregnant or not, the hour of reckoning is upon us.*

Time was running really late. With great haste, I put the bomb in my backpack and carried it over my shoulder for all its weight. I headed to the station, just in time to catch the last train. In the empty carriage, I leaned my head against the window and closed my eyes to relax.

The train pulled in at Pan Hlaing Station. Coming on board were two nurses in white uniform and an old Indian man with an avuncular expression whom I guessed was a doctor. They struck up a conversation as soon as the train resumed its journey. I didn't quite catch everything they said, except one of the nurses, who had a loud voice, lamented she had had an extremely busy day as a result of several traffic accidents. The others concurred sympathetically. The name of a hospital, Pan Hlaing, was mentioned in passing. Suddenly I felt what I had just heard was more than I could have wished for. Their conversations had supplied me with some useful details such as their professions and the name of the hospital, which greatly helped me to assemble a credible story for use to explain my absence for the past few hours.

Outside the window there was a perfect round moon hanging in a cloudless sky, its light a bright yellowish colour. The breeze that swept into the carriage felt soft and cool. The air smelled of sweet flowers of the season, occasionally mixed with that of waste by the trackside. I had the feeling that the outlook could not have been more propitious. I felt peaceful and calm, as though untroubled and unaffected by the bleakness of the mission I had to fulfil. The beautiful moonlight, the cloudless sky, the pleasant smell in the wind, everything about the journey gave me a kind of peculiar serenity. It seemed as if nothing could go wrong.

21

M.A.Y.A.

―――∿∿∿―――

On arriving at the terminal, I alighted from the train onto a deserted platform. I walked out of the station to the street outside, crossing to the opposite side to turn into a broad boulevard that led straight to the night market half a mile away. By the time I had reached the night market, it was closing down and people were leaving. I stopped by a food stall, bought a piece of banana cake, and it was when I was taking a bite I became aware that I was being followed. I didn't have to look over my shoulder to see. I simply knew how to pick out stealthy, circumspect behaviour from people in the crowd – someone who turns the corner when you turn the corner, someone who slows down or speeds up when you do. Composed, I swallowed down the cake in a few quick bites, and continued on my way out of the market via the southern access.

Beyond the night market was a property development site, abandoned and left to waste after the investors had disappeared during the economic downturn. Children played football there in the day and people in the neighbourhood used it as a shortcut to get to work. I entered the site, keeping my eyes open for signs of danger, but got through to the end and emerged at the other side without incident.

After further twists and turns through an endless maze of disorderly houses and sordid lanes, I was on the street where Bo Tin Aung lived. The night was far advanced and the traffic was at a standstill, which enabled me to walk in the middle of the street, keeping a safe distance from the wet, dirty pavement as well as from the hidden corners with concealed pitfalls.

Before long, the building I was returning to was within sight. Glancing up, I saw the dusty grey façade of the building with its many windows, some open and some closed, with or without lights. When I cast my eyes upon the pair of windows covered with an iron grating, which belonged to Bo Tin Aung's apartment on the fifth floor, I was surprised to see no light from inside. It simply meant Bo Tin Aung was not at home, and I began to suspect he was the man who had been following me all along.

But I was far from being certain, and when I was near the building I started to run. Immediately I heard footsteps racing from behind. As I tried to squeeze through the space between cars parked in front of the building, I felt someone grab me by the neck. I was violently pulled back, my body bumping into what felt to be a man's chest strong as steel. In fear I screamed.

"You shut the fuck up, will you?!" said the guy in an angry and threatening voice, covering my mouth with his hand. "Why do you have to run? You're home!"

I was gagged and couldn't speak. He removed his hand, and I said, "I panicked suddenly, not knowing it was my husband who's been following me all this time…" I put special emphasis on the word "husband" for a degree of intimacy which I thought might be useful.

Bo Tin Aung said, much relaxed in tone, "You scared the shit out of me vanishing for well over some five hours. You'd better be good with your excuses."

"I'll tell you everything; you decide if it's good," I said. "Prior to that, shall I warn you that you're pressing with all your weight on the bomb inside my backpack?"

He took a step back and said, almost cheerfully, "You've got the bomb with you! That makes me glad."

I handed him the backpack. "Yours now. Check it out for yourself."

He stared at the backpack without accepting it, and asked uncertainly, "Will it explode in my hands?"

"Of course not!" I said. I found his hesitancy extremely undesirable in the situation. I felt I needed to prove to him that it was "safe" to play with the device if he could be persuaded to be more personally involved, which was critical for the success of my plan. So I said, "Come with me. Let me show you."

I led him to a quiet corner and asked him to kneel down with me. I took out the bomb from the backpack and said, "Still remember Moe Chit, who once remarked that bombs made by Siha are toys that any brainless dumbass age three and above can handle without a problem?"

The mention of Moe Chit made him frown uneasily.

"It's just a toy. It won't blast off in my hands just like that. Why?" I said, and added, after a moment of suspense, "Because you don't have an initiation device."

"Where's the device?" he asked.

I took out a metal rod from a side pocket of the backpack and said, "This is it. To activate, you only have to stick it inside the bomb like you insert a pencil into a sharpener."

To make it completely clear to him, I brought his attention to a hole on the screwed top of the bomb. With a degree of exaggeration, I shook the rod as though it was a syringe before sticking it into flesh. "You push the stick through this hole to the end, and when you hear a click, it means you've set the bomb to detonate after twenty minutes," I said reassuringly.

He stood in tense silence, eyeing closely the movement of the rod. I pushed the rod inside, pausing halfway, and pulled it out immediately. I said, "You've got the idea? Or would you like to see it go all the way to hell itself?"

"That'd be fine," he said, his voice still intense. "I've got it. It's not very complicated."

"No. It's as simple as ABC," I said.

I was relieved that he had not demanded a full demonstration, because the thing he didn't know was that I'd actually set the time-delay to zero instead of twenty minutes. Had I pushed the rod to the very end, it would have blasted off instantaneously, killing both of us. I knew I was playing with fire, but I thought it worth the risk. Because this was how I had equipped myself returning to the apartment, considered to be the world's most dangerous place. Should I have found myself trapped in a hopeless situation where my life was at stake, I would strike without a moment's hesitation for mutual annihilation. Still, it depended how things played out at the end of the day. I thought I could always reset the trigger mechanism to some other durations, for example, five to ten minutes, should a change of circumstance require it.

With an abstract nod, he said, "I think Shit-Lone will have no trouble setting it up tomorrow."

I was alarmed. He struck me as still not too keen to be personally involved. I felt perhaps a little provocation was necessary and I said, as if completely out of the blue, "Now Moe Chit is dead. No one would remember how he challenged you to handle the last bomb to prove you weren't chicken shit. Actually you can leave the bomb to Shit-Lone if you're afraid."

His face contorted in an ugly expression of intense loathing as though his big, silly ego were under serious attack. He cried in disdain, "Me afraid? Nonsense."

I replaced the bomb and the initiation device in the backpack and said, proffering the package up to his face, "No nonsense? Then all yours now."

"It's no big deal," he said and took the backpack with a grunt, and remarked, if somewhat surprised, "This thing seems quite heavy."

I said, "The bomb weighs at least ten pounds, just imagine how I have carried it all the way from Danyingon."

But there was no sympathy. He quickly tossed the backpack back into my arms, and said, "We're going to the site together tomorrow. Why don't you hang onto it for now?"

This guy wasn't to be fooled easily, I thought. I was a bit frustrated after all that I had said and done to entice him to take the bait without success. Hugging the backpack, I wondered gloomily if my plan for revenge, which had taken me a long time to concoct, was nothing more than the combination of a certain simplicity of thought and the unbridled optimism of youth.

Suddenly he said, "You know what? Because of your disappearance, a police warrant will be issued after midnight for a citywide, door-to-door search for you or your dead body."

The emphasis he placed on the word "dead" made me feel a bit unnerved. He made it sound as if I had lost my value after I had brought back the bomb, and he could now get rid of me on a whim if he wished.

"Am I under arrest because I've come back late after picking up the bomb at Danyingon at your instruction?" I questioned him.

"Don't worry. Now you're back and no one is going to arrest you. But you'd be interested to know many a citizen in Rangoon would be kept awake through the night if I hadn't spotted you at the night market and thereof cancelled the warrant," he said. "Now tell me: what kept you so late?"

"I'm this late because something has happened to me," I said quietly.

"Should I be worried?" he asked.

"I don't know. Perhaps you should hold your judgment before you've heard every word I say," I said.

"Okay. I'm listening," he said. But he quickly changed his mind. "Why don't you tell me later?"

"Why?"

In a lighthearted tone he said, "Just look at us – two people standing in the dark like some homeless living on the street, who are in fact residents of an apartment on the fifth floor of this building. If you don't mind, shall we go back to our cosy little nest first? After all, you're still living with me, aren't you? You'll still sleep with me, won't you?"

He grabbed me by the shoulders and steered me through the entrance gate as if I were a piece of luggage. Once inside the building and as we ascended the stairs, he kissed the back of my neck, whispering, in a voice grown grossly carnal, "There is always something delicious about your smell, almost like a strange perfume oozing from every one of your open and shut orifices…"

We entered the apartment, and I told him to get off me. His hold on me, rigid and ironclad, was starting to hurt. He ignored me as if he hadn't heard. It was only after we had crossed the narrow corridor to reach the living room that he finally decided it was safe to release me from his control.

I placed the backpack in a corner, and sat down on a chair next to a low table where there was a crystal vase with a bunch of flowers.

"No. Don't sit down," he said in a coarse voice.

"Why? What's the problem with you…?" I mumbled, noticing his face twitching unnaturally.

I slowly rose to my feet, and he ordered me to go and stand by the window. When I hesitated, he gave me a shove so hard that I almost fell. When he repeated his order in a heavy voice like a threat, I reluctantly obeyed.

I stared out of the window to the quiet street below, wondering what was on his mind. On the street there was a man and woman waiting on the pavement. A taxi drew up. They squeezed into the back. The taxi drove off; its taillights blinked like the eyes of a cat in the dark. It was at this moment that Bo Tin Aung appeared in the reflection on the windowpane. I feared he was going to rape me knowing that it was our last night. But no, not yet. He stepped aside to take out a bottle of wine and drank directly from it. While he was drinking, his eyes seemed to jump from place to place – sometimes they were fixed on the flowers, sometimes they stayed on my body.

I turned towards him and asked if I could start telling him my story. He said nothing, and kept drinking and gazing at the flowers. It didn't take him long to finish the whole bottle. I began to sense what was coming. There was always a noticeable pattern beginning with alcohol and ending in sex and violence. Sometimes he'd choose sex before violence; at other times it was sex after violence, depending on his mood and the atmosphere.

He picked out a twig from the vase, whipping it up and down forcibly, causing the tiny petals to fly all over the place. It seemed that he was warming up for a preliminary appetiser of violence before the full course of sex.

"What are you doing?" I asked. "Can you please listen to me first?"

Instead of a reply, he took a step forward and hit me with the twig. Once, twice, thrice. I yelled, dropping on the floor with pain. When he was about to hit me again, I shouted at him, "Go on if it pleases you to torture me for being late. But you should know that you are not only hitting your fiancée or wife, you might as well be hitting the mother of your child!"

The effect of my words on him was almost instantaneous. He forcibly held back his arm mid-whiplash. "What the fuck did you say? What mother… what child?" he mumbled, somewhat incoherently.

"Just listen and I hope you like what I'm going to tell you," I said.

After a moment of pondering, he put down the twig and said, hovering above me, "OK. I'm listening."

"It's a long story," I said. "Shall we both sit down first?"

He helped me to my feet and eased my body into the chair. "Never mind the long version of the story, just tell me the bit about the child," he said. He looked concerned. Some real concern that didn't appear to be fake.

"You must hear my story in full, as I want no further misunderstanding between us," I insisted.

He wasn't a man of tolerance, but he had to agree, reluctantly, that beating me was for the moment not an option.

I began. "You told me to go to Danyingon to pick up the bomb. Siha, the old man, asked me to stay for dinner. I declined his kind offer, remembering that you told me to go there and get out immediately. Besides, I was also not feeling well. So I left and…"

"Was there rain on your way back?" he suddenly interjected.

"Rain? No. Why?" I asked back, assuming complete innocence.

"Nothing. It was in the weather report. Perhaps it was only a localised rain," he said. "Now, the child, what about the child?!"

"Have patience," I went on. "I took the Circular Train home. As I said earlier, I was not feeling well and my condition got worse on the train. I was feeling dizzy, and I felt nauseous as well. Arriving at Pan Hlaing Road Station, I found I couldn't possibly hold myself together any longer. I got off, and threw up violently in the public toilet. To my dismay, it was not just an upset stomach, because when I relieved myself, I found blood in my discharge too. I felt tired and weak. All I wanted was to lie down and sleep. As I made my way out of the public toilet, I collapsed on the floor. Some women in the toilet carried me over to a bench in the station and let me rest there. There was an old lady, who said she was a former nurse and suggested I see a doctor. She was very kind. She went as far as to fetch me a taxi and asked the driver to take me to a nearby hospital while she had a train to catch…"

He screwed up his eyes thoughtfully. I paused, in case he had something to ask. But he said nothing and I resumed.

"Once in the hospital I was laid on a bed and told to wait for the doctor. After an hour the doctor still hadn't appeared. I thought I'd better go when I was feeling better after a short rest. I was also afraid that you'd worry about me. But the nurse said my turn would soon come and told me to wait. I therefore stayed, which I still regret, because it took another forty-five minutes before the doctor finally showed up. He was a white-haired Indian man in his sixties. He apologised for the delay because the casualty ward was running riot with several traffic accidents. He asked me about my complaints while taking my temperature and blood pressure. 'I think I can guess what your problem is,' he said confidently. With the assistance of the nurse, he checked my belly and looked between my legs with some special equipment. Finally, he told me in a firm and matter-of-fact voice, 'Young lady, I think you're pregnant.'"

"What? You're pregnant?! That's why you said mother and child!" cried Bo Tin Aung ecstatically. "I think you should have stayed in the hospital. Do you know you could have endangered the precious species in your womb by running around like that?"

"I'm sorry. I didn't think about it," I said. "I was in a great hurry to come home to tell you the news. The doctor said it was okay if I wanted to leave, just to be careful."

"This is absolutely fucking good news, isn't it?!" he said. He sank onto his knees, like someone who was about to propose. But he had already proposed; it was only the actual wedding which was unfulfilled. He buried his head in my lap, and whispered fervently, "Hi there, my little guy. Do you hear me?" Glancing up at me, he said, "Thank you. You've made me complete."

His look of gratitude and the display of fatherly love deeply touched me.

I wept, with unexplained happiness. It amazed me that my pregnancy had turned out to be something much more profound and poignant, almost blissful, than a pure story. Within its own truth, there was a child waiting to be born; and there were his parents: a man and a woman facing each other with tears rolling down their cheeks. I felt my heart was melting like snow under the sun, and I was losing focus on the purpose of my return. While I still remembered I had come back with a plan, I began to wonder if there were other ways to resolve our differences peacefully, when killing each other never seemed the perfect solution. In the consideration, perhaps I should, before anything else, reset the time-delay from zero to something less deadly if there was the opportunity.

"Is it a boy?" he asked.

"I don't know. I think it is a bit early to tell," I replied.

He shot me a sceptical look. "You're the mother and you should have a feeling about that," he said sternly. "So what do you think?"

I knew what he wanted to hear, and I said, "A son, obviously."

"Of course it's a son, because there have been no daughters in my family for the last three generations," he said.

"You happy now?" I asked.

"Happiness doesn't begin to describe my feeling right now," he said. "It's just crazy that you have not only come back with a bomb, but also brought me a son! This is insane!" He seemed to be genuinely enthused by the good news, and suggested, "Shall we celebrate, perhaps with a sumptuous meal at some first-class restaurant?"

I told him I didn't think it was a good idea. "It has been a long day. I'm very tired, just to think of what I have gone through. I want to rest now if you don't mind."

He nodded benignly with perfect understanding. When he was not vicious or violent, he could be quite tender and considerate. He carried me into the bedroom, helped me to change into my nightie, and covered my body with a light blanket after seeing that I had comfortably lain my head on the pillow. He kissed me goodnight, switched off the light and left.

I closed my eyes with a little sigh of relief, thinking how fortunate it was that I had stumbled on this thing called pregnancy, which had not only kept me alive but also amazed me with undreamt happiness.

Suddenly I was startled by his footsteps outside the room. He opened the door, popped his head in, and asked, "There are a number of hospitals in the area of Pan Hlaing, for example, the Sakura, the Siloam, the Central Women's Hospital, the Bahosi, and there is also the Academy Hospital… which one did you go?"

Without a better reply, I honestly told him I didn't know. "It was nighttime, the street was dark; the hospital nondescript as I was quickly carted inside as soon as the taxi arrived at the front door…"

"I would think it was the Pan Hlaing Hospital which is only a short distance from the station," he tried with a guess.

"Maybe," I said. "Everything was such a blur. I might have seen a name but didn't recognise it. The truth is, I was very sick then. It is also true that I'm extremely exhausted right now. Can we discuss this after I have had some sleep?"

He gave up, and said, "Never mind. Goodnight," and he was gone.

I didn't know why he should bother about the hospital I went to. But I just couldn't care less what he was thinking right now. I might have told a thousand lies, but I had also said one important truth, clearly and in complete honesty, which was: I was wrung out and dog-tired. For the moment nothing was more important than getting some sleep. I therefore, without taking the trouble of tormenting myself with further anxieties, pulled the blanket over my head and fell asleep immediately.

22

M.A.Y.A.

—◆◆◆—

I slept a very long time as if I never wanted to wake up again. Dreadfully fatigued, I was oblivious to the arrival of a new day, which seemed none of my business, as I had no obligation to rejoin the waking world against my wishes. Or so I thought, forgetting it is only the privilege of the dead to sleep forever. At last I woke up, but not naturally. I was stirred from my lethargic slumber by Bo Tin Aung returning from work.

"What time is it?" I asked drowsily.

"You mean you don't know?" he said in a shocked voice. "Good afternoon."

"Are you sure?"

"No. I should have said 'Good evening'," he said. "It's almost five o'clock in the afternoon. Get up now and get dressed. Shit-Lone will be here at six. He's going to join us for dinner before we set out to give the city one final test on its state of law and order. C'mon, get moving, you lazy girl!"

Slowly waking up, I began to remember my secret and the story I shared with him, and I said, "No. I'm not lazy. I'm just tired. Have I told you I'm pregnant?"

"How can I forget?" he said. "Now get up. We have work to do."

"Work? What work?" I mumbled, eyeing him, still clad in a dark green uniform. "You're the Tatmadaw; you go to work, not me."

"I have been working like a stupid ox the whole day," he said. "Since nine in the morning, I have had three meetings, presided over two committees on terrorism and corruption, partaken in three operations and made five arrests. That's not all. You know what? I've even managed to make a visit to the Pan Hlaing Hospital…"

I sat bolt upright, fully awake. "The Pan Hlaing Hospital? Why?"

"Last night you told me there was this hospital guy, an Indian doctor in his sixties, who said you were pregnant. I wanted to talk to him," he answered.

"What for?"

"To confirm a few facts," he said, blinking his eyes.

"Like what?"

"Like… prenatal care," he answered.

"Prenatal care? What's that?"

"It's among some of the things you should do or not do for the health of the baby… if you're pregnant," he explained.

I was wide-eyed. "If I'm pregnant? You mean you don't believe me?"

"I don't know what to believe now, because I can't find the doctor of your description, or the record of your visit last night to the hospital," he said with a stern face.

I told myself this was not funny. It looked as if there was a crack in my story, which appeared to be in danger of falling apart. Under his unrelenting gaze, I felt the rush of blood turning my face red hot with nervousness. I craved for some private space and time to sort out my thoughts so that I could justify a few otherwise unjustifiable facts in my invented story. I said, "I don't know what you're talking about. I'll be back in a moment."

I climbed off the bed. He grabbed my arm and asked, "Where are you going?"

"I'm going for a pee, okay?"

He released me, and said, "You go ahead. I have something to show you later."

Sitting on the toilet seat in the bathroom, I was so tense that I couldn't pee and I took the time to recompose myself after the scare he gave me.

There was a knock at the door. Before I answered, he had already barged into the bathroom because my mind was so preoccupied that I forgot to bolt the door.

"Excuse me?" I asked, incredulous.

"Have you peed?" He looked down at my legs.

"No. But that is none of your business, is it?" I said.

"You're wrong. I have some real business with your pee," he replied. "I'm going to conduct a test with your urine."

"Test? What test?!" I raised my voice in exasperation.

"The pregnancy test, of course," he said, taking out some kind of kit from the chest pocket of his uniform. He placed the kit on the edge of the washbasin and turned on the tap to wash his hands.

"I don't understand…" I stuttered. "You're to carry out some test after you went to the hospital and didn't find the doctor there?"

"Well, I probably went to the wrong hospital, but I'm glad I went there after all," he said. "You know why?"

"Tell me," I said, warily.

"I was very fortunate to have met a very helpful nurse in the hospital," he said. "The nurse, a middle-aged lady called Ma Feng, having learned that I wanted to find out about the case of my wife who was treated for complaints surrounding her pregnancy last night, asked me to fill out a form with the basic information before she went away to look up the records. Thirty minutes later she returned with nothing of the sort. I was disappointed, obviously. I began to suspect I had gone to the wrong hospital. I thanked her and took my leave. But Ma Feng, in her eagerness to help a senior Tatmadaw like me, asked a rather odd question, 'Are you sure your wife is pregnant?' Upset by the question, I replied, 'I don't know. You tell me.' I was only being sarcastic. But Ma Feng was serious. She took a glance at the form and said, 'Your wife… is very young. In my experience, girls at sixteen tend to think they are pregnant every time they miss their periods.' I told her my wife got the opinion from a certain Indian doctor. She shook her head and said, 'I'm sorry there's no such doctor in this hospital.'

Well, to keep the story short, as a way to help clarify the matter, she gave me this kit and told me to go home and perform the pregnancy test, with a reminder that 'If she's really pregnant, bring her back and I'll tell you guys everything about prenatal care'."

He opened the kit to take out a test tube.

"Is it really necessary?" I said, my voice quavering.

"You're only sixteen. The nurse is right that you can have made a mistake," he said.

"What if it is a mistake?" I returned hastily, with draining confidence, as if I wasn't sure about my pregnancy anymore.

He replied, after a moment of hesitation, "That's OK, although it's not to say I'm not disappointed."

He tried to sound nonchalant, like it was no big deal; it was so fake that I knew it was just not okay. He said, "Well, in the unfortunate circumstances of a mistake, we'd carry on our business as we've planned. We'd go and take down the traffic lights, and we'd probably kill somebody in the process…"

A cold shiver ran down my back. I knew what he meant by "in the process" which would most certainly involve hours of non-stop torture and rape before cutting me into pieces.

"In any case we shall find out very soon one way or the other, right?" he said, kneeling down to take off the pair of white panties round my knees. "I think you need to separate your legs wider."

He removed the foil wrapper and squinted to study what was written on the tube. I had always disliked injections and needles, and I asked him, "How deep are you going to penetrate me with this thing?"

He said, with a hollow laugh, "It's not like that. There's no penetration. I'll only place the tube next to your lips down there, OK? Now sit tight and don't pee until I tell you."

He was still laughing and his hand was shaking when he lowered the tube into the toilet bowl. I sat frozen in apprehension, fearing a disaster was about to occur. Suddenly he shrieked and cursed loudly, "Fucking shit! I've dropped the damned thing in the water!"

I shifted my body to one side to look down into the toilet bowl. The tube was floating like a rudderless boat in a pool of water. With welcome relief I thought it might be the end of the horrible test. But pitifully, it was too soon to think I was lucky.

He checked inside the kit and after a moment of fumbling, fished out another test tube. He said, "I don't know why these things have to come in a pair. The pharmaceutical people must know how to exploit users' clumsiness for profits."

To repeat the procedure, he removed the tin foil wrapper and the cap and ordered me to open my legs. I didn't notice that I had crossed my legs again. I must have done it unconsciously out of fear and objection to the test. At his command, I separated my legs a fraction, slowly and reluctantly.

He waited and waited, then suddenly said, "This is the only test tube left. We can't lose it again. Let's try this."

Putting down the tube, he knelt before me and asked me to put my arms round his neck.

I hesitated, wondering if he suddenly wanted to have sex with me. At his prompt, I did as I was told. Then he started to lift my body by grasping me firmly around waist. He was a muscular man whereas I was petite. With ease he picked me up and carried me over to the washbasin. He told me not to sit, but squat, and I squatted astride the washbasin facing him.

Peering with a lecherous eye at my body, he said, "You're beyond gorgeous! I don't think we have tried this position before." He seemed to have become intensely interested in the idea of sex as I noticed his hand moving over his crotch area as if about to unbutton his trousers.

In my position, which was awkward and vulnerable in equal measure, I could do nothing but submit to his whimsicality should he attempt to force himself upon me. I had, however, also observed that there might be a certain advantage in submission. I thought I could probably find the opportunity to sabotage the test by offering myself to his beastliness, and I said, "Very well, if you want to fuck me now, then forget about the test."

I opened my legs so wide that his eyes turned red hot. At the same time I moved a hand surreptitiously to the test tube that was sitting to my left and quietly brushed it off the edge of the washbasin. I thought he wouldn't even notice it when his mind was fully occupied with sex. But I was horribly wrong, as it appeared that he was not to be seduced.

"Are you fucking serious?" he roared, throwing himself on his knees in a desperate attempt to rescue the tube.

To my dismay the tube had failed to follow the good example of its predecessor by falling straight into the toilet bowl; instead it had bounced off the edge of the bowl and landed somewhere under the enamel water tank.

While he was groping under the water tank for the lost tube, I, despite the setback, had quickly come up with a fresh idea to subvert the test when I thought I still had one last weapon: my urine. In my guesstimate, there would be no test if I had little or no urine to offer. Therefore, upon seeing the guy still kneeling on all fours in search of the tube, I took the opportunity to eject. In an attempt to empty out the fluid in the shortest possible time I squeezed my belly with all the pressure I could possibly summon. And as my urine forcibly gushed forth, it flew over the washbasin and hit him on the head, wetting his hair.

"What the fuck is wrong with you!" he railed maniacally. "Haven't I told you not to pee? Stop it now!"

"It was getting so urgent that I lost control, sorry." I murmured an apology.

I said it was urgent and I honestly meant it, because I had been retaining a great amount of water since last night. I said I'd lost control; I wasn't lying either, because once it had started it was beyond my power to slow or stop the flow. I could only watch helplessly at the rise of something akin to a plentiful spring that gushed out of a cleft covered with tiny maidenhair ferns, tumbling in a natural fall over the rusty wall of the washbasin and whirling like a circle in a spiral on an ever spinning reel before disappearing through a tiny sinkhole at the bottom.

With secret glee, I figured this should spell the end of the test. Yet I had again been overhasty to think the battle was won. His ability to respond to the situation with great alacrity astounded me. In less than no time he had found the tube, picked it up, and stuck it under my legs when my pee, to my chagrin, was still running in small cascades.

"Now piss away as much as you like," he grunted. Turning to glance at his watch he began to count audibly. At the end of about five seconds, he pulled the tube out from the stream of urine, which was now weakening to drips and drops.

"You don't seem very cooperative," he said in a dark, reproachful voice.

"I confess I was a bit confused. I thought you were playing a sex game with me using the test tube," I muttered in weak defence.

With his stare fixated on the tube, he said, "In three minutes, it is going to say something about you, and me, and us. It'd better be good." Without a backward glance he marched out of the bathroom, and kept repeating, almost like some weird chant of a death threat, "It'd better be good, it'd better be good…"

I climbed off the washbasin. The exercise had exhausted me. My head was swirling. My back, where it had stuck against the tap, ached with pain, and my knees wobbled terribly. I sat down on the toilet seat and took time to recover.

The door of the bathroom was left ajar. Bo Tin Aung, facing in my direction, was standing in the centre of the living room before the low table and gazing anxiously at the bunch of flowers in the crystal vase. From time to time he turned to look at the walled clock, apparently waiting for the three minutes to pass. His face was hard and serious with a deep frown. The light of a late afternoon sun meandered into the living room through the iron grating at the window, making the place feel like a jail. But he was no prisoner; he was instead only the jailer or executioner waiting to carry out the sentence.

With a gesture of impatience he picked up the tube and checked it as if reading the temperature on a thermometer. But the reading had no appreciable effect on his stern expression. Either the result on display was not what he expected, or it was inconclusive. After another glance at the clock, he decided to wait a while longer. It was when he raised his head after he had returned the tube to the table that his eyes found me watching him from the bathroom. I hastened to shift my body behind the door before our eyes locked. It was at this moment I felt a stabbing pain in my belly and found that I was depositing in the bowl something hot and thick and watery. Without even having to look into the bowl, I knew there was blood the colour of strawberry jam. The symptoms, similar to what I experienced yesterday, seemed to reaffirm the belief that I was pregnant. I felt greatly relieved. I told myself that I should not be afraid of the test result, as I believed the verdict, which would soon come, should work favourably in all my hopes and schemes.

A short while later, there came the first sign of a possible outcome from the living room.

It was the noises he made, like a dog that barked and whined. It was difficult to tell from the queer noises, which were half-elated and half-petulant, whether he was happy or angry. All I could surmise was that the long wait was over and the result was here. I was a little nervous, but also optimistic when I thought I had something invaluable in my womb for my protection. I reckoned I might as well go to him in the living room so that he could share the news, believed to be good, with me. I wiped myself clean, rose to my feet, and put on my jeans and T-shirt. As I was about to step out, I was horrified to hear a sudden wave of sounds in the living room, of furniture toppling and glass shattering. I was dumbstruck and froze on the spot. The sounds were unmistakably of that of someone who had overturned the table and hurled the crystal vase to the floor, breaking it into clattering fragments. And who was that someone except Bo Tin Aung who could now be heard swearing at the top of his voice as though he was mental!

My heart sank. I began to see all was not well.

Why was he so mad? Had he found something wrong in the result, something he didn't like, or even a lie? Before I had a clue what was troubling him, I heard the rattle of glass as if he was messing with the bits and pieces of broken vase on the floor. I was intrigued. I ventured a peek through the door, and saw, with dread, that he was just rising to his feet, his hand wielding a large piece of glass. He took a step forward to the window, and held the glass up against the outside light as if he was appreciating the luminosity along its sharp blade. Suddenly he burst out laughing, his hand waving the piece of glass like it was a dagger. I tensed up, with a sense of doom. The signs couldn't be clearer, I thought. Notwithstanding how much I believed my abdomen pain and the strawberry jam to be a sign of a certain fact and truth, it was obvious that he had seen something completely the opposite in the result of the pregnancy test. And he was going to kill me because I had lied.

Realising I could no longer count on the protection I thought I once possessed, I quickly closed the bathroom door and bolted it securely as my first defence to the imminent danger. Immediately I could sense his approach when the heavy sounds of his military boots were heard tramping across on the wooden floor. As if it was not enough to ruffle my troubled mind already full of catastrophic possibilities, I also heard his continual and uproarious laughter as if he was happy despite his mind being filled with murderous intentions.

He halted outside the bathroom and rapped loudly at the door with his knuckles.

"What do you want?" I asked.

"Let me in," he said. "I've got something to show you."

"Go away. I'm busy," I said.

"What are you busy at right now?"

"I have offloaded a ton of blood in my poop, and I haven't finished," I said.

"Really? Can I see?"

"There's nothing to see. It's horrible," I said.

"No, I'm concerned. Has someone told you that you're pregnant?" he said.

It sounded to me like he was ridiculing me. "No, not now. Please go away," I pleaded.

"Let me in, okay?" He turned the doorknob and tried to push the door open.

"Will you just go away?" I cried.

He found the door locked and started kicking it. I cried and begged him to leave me alone. He wouldn't listen and continued attacking the door. The situation was desperate. I was so terrified that I raised my voice to a long string of screams on the off chance that there would be someone outside our apartment who could hear me and come to my rescue.

"Stop it! The neighbours will hear us," he said irascibly.

If so, they are to be thanked, I thought, and carried on screaming.

"You crazy girl!" he groaned. "Now you've drawn people's attention to the apartment."

I didn't believe him. But I was curious, and stopped screaming to listen. It was then that I heard, to my disbelief, the sound of the doorbell buzzing long and short in the abrupt silence.

"Can you keep quiet while I answer the door?" said Bo Tin Aung.

"Fine," I muttered in reply. I was, however, determined to start screaming again as soon as the door was open.

"Who's this?" Bo Tin Aung called out in a ferocious voice.

There was no answer.

"Go away and mind your own fucking business!" he threatened with a snarl.

There was still no answer. But the stranger had remained, as it appeared, when suddenly a man coughed, so violently as if he were in the final stage of tuberculosis.

"You joker, is that you?" asked Bo Tin Aung. It seemed to be someone he knew.

After another moment of delay, the coughing stopped, and the man outside said, "It's me."

The voice, kind of clownish, was no stranger at all, and to my dismay no saviour either. It was Shit-Lone. He was asked to arrive at the apartment by six o'clock for the operation to begin.

"Come in." Bo Tin Aung opened the door and said, "You're late again."

When Shit-Lone entered the apartment, he was still coughing, but stopped short as if he had seen something horrible. "What's that in your hand? A knife? You don't mean you've already killed…" he stammered.

"Hold your tongue, will you?" said Bo Tin Aung. "No one is dead."

"You mean not yet?" said Shit-Lone. "But why the sharp glass?"

"It's laughable," returned Bo Tin Aung casually. "I accidentally dropped the vase to the floor, and found among the debris this piece of glass almost in the perfect shape of a five-pointed star."

I didn't know what to believe with what I heard. But it was Shit-Lone who clarified for me by saying, "I'm sorry. I don't have your imagination. It is just a knife to me, and a very sharp one at that, which I don't find laughable at all."

"Well, if not laughable, then I've just had a good laugh all to myself," said Bo Tin Aung. "You know a five-pointed star is a good omen."

Always a contrarian, Shit-Lone said, "This shit a good omen?! Don't talk to me like I am a sixteen-year-old. Tell Maya."

"That's what I was just trying to do," said Bo Tin Aung.

"Where's Maya?" asked Shit-Lone.

"She's in the bathroom," answered Bo Tin Aung, "not feeling very comfortable."

"Hi Maya!" Shit-Lone greeted me from outside: "We're going to dinner now. You coming?"

"Hi!" I said. "You go ahead. I'm having some trouble with my… stomach."

Shit-Lone lowered his voice and asked, "What's wrong with her?"

"Well, it's complicated," replied Bo Tin Aung. "Let's go to the living room."

They adjourned to the living room and started talking. From a distance I couldn't quite catch what they said. But I could guess, and believed that Bo Tin Aung must be bragging that the good omen and the five-pointed star were only a bunch of bollocks; and he was angry because I had lied and how much he wanted me dead. Although their conversation was no more intelligible from the living room than bees buzzing in the air, I was able to catch a word or two and occasionally a complete sentence when one of them, mostly Shit-Lone, had become over-excited.

"Well done!" blurted Shit-Lone, with a smothered burst of unholy mirth. "Congratulations."

I didn't know what that was supposed to mean. I rationalised that the guys might be congratulating each other for all the cash they had received from their commander for the job. Certainly it was about money when Shit-Lone exclaimed, "The Mazda sucks! You know how much it cost me for a full tank of gas? You're so mean!"

"Don't judge me..." retorted Bo Tin Aung; the rest of what he said escaped me.

"All right, all right," said Shit-Lone. And they resumed the discourse in low voices.

After another five minutes, Shit-Lone appeared to have jumped to his feet and groaned loudly, "Why can't we have dinner now instead of later? I'm starving."

Bo Tin Aung said, "Let me check with Maya first."

The unpleasant sound of his heavy boots scraping the floor rose in the air again as he made his way to the bathroom. He knocked at the door and asked, "How are you feeling? Shit-Lone suggests we all go out together for dinner."

"I feel like a piece of shit, OK?" I whimpered. "Give me a break. Can you guys just go ahead to dinner without me?"

After a quiet moment, he walked away. The buzz in the living room resumed. I sensed they were pretty serious this time because Shit-Lone had not blurted out any inappropriate remarks during the whole course of discussion. Then the buzz stopped, and the ensuing silence seemed so thick, as if they had reached a decision which was absolute and unalterable. After a brief interval, I heard the sound of a kind of preparatory bustle, with noises like they were moving furniture around in the living room and sweeping the broken glass to the side. This was very confusing and I was at an utter loss as to what they had embarked upon. As I waited in suspense, my mind was filled with all kinds of dark possibilities. I thought I was coming to the end of my life. But it was too late to regret it now. I might have been naïve enough to think I had the perfect plan and rash enough to take the risk of returning to see it through, but there was nothing to regret for choosing to do what was honourable and right.

Suddenly, echoes of footsteps were heard resounding from the far end of the corridor, almost like a formal announcement that said, "It's time." They were, however, very strange footsteps, sometimes heavy, sometimes light. The light steps appeared to be bouncing in front, whereas the heavy steps, strained along and staggered slightly as if encumbered with something weighty like a sack of flour, or a sandbag, or a bulky rifle of a firing squad. As soon as the footsteps ceased outside the bathroom, there was a brief silence as if they couldn't think of the appropriate thing to say for the occasion. Then Shit-Lone cleared his throat after a small, agitated cough, and said solemnly, "Goodbye, Maya."

Despite my mental preparedness for a certain awful eventuality, his grieving voice still made me quaver with sadness. Before I knew how to react, Bo Tin Aung snapped, "Have I told you to leave her alone? It's time to move."

"Can you at least let me say goodbye," cried Shit-Lone.

"Never knew you were such a pussy," snorted Bo Tin Aung. "Say what you like, but please do it quick."

"Goodbye, Maya, goodbye," Shit-Lone mumbled emotionally.

I refused to respond, thinking, *I know what you guys are up to; your crocodile tears can't fool me.*

After a brief silence, Bo Tin Aung said, "Maya, just say something to make him feel better."

I couldn't believe my ears. Why on earth did I have to make Shit-Lone or anyone else feel better? It wasn't those guys who were going to die but me. That was absurd!

As if to help attach special meaning to the nonsense, Bo Tin Aung added, "He's going to Bagan later this evening. He won't be back till the end of the month."

Now I was getting the picture. Shit-Lone was leaving and Bo Tin Aung to stay behind. Of course, you didn't need two guys just for the torture and slaughter of a girl like me.

"Maya, are you all right?" asked Bo Tin Aung. "Say something so that I know you're okay."

"Goodbye, Maya, goodbye." Shit-Lone sounded like he was in tears.

I remembered Shit-Lone had said that he liked me because I reminded him of his little sister who had died young. Suddenly I felt he was like something of a last hope, and I said, "Goodbye... but I don't want you go."

"But I must, forgive me," uttered Shit-Lone. "Goodbye."

Bo Tin Aung quietly said, "Why don't you wait for me downstairs at the car? Spend a minute or two getting things up and running. Okay?"

There was the sound of the door opening. "Goodness me. This thing is heavy," grumbled Shit-Lone on the way out. Then the sound of the door closing.

Now there was only me and Bo Tin Aung in the apartment. Full of trepidation, I wondered how much longer I would be able to hold him off by locking myself inside the bathroom.

"Maya, I'm worried about you. Can you at least let me put you to sleep before I go?" he said.

Put me to sleep? What a horrible thing to say, I thought.

I said, dejected but also a little defiant, "I don't want to sleep. I just want to sit here until my belly pains are gone."

He became quiet, as if he were making a calculation of the right moment to strike the final blow.

I felt I was on the brink of calamity, realising there was no hope of escape, and I broke down and cried, "Why must you do this to me? Don't be cruel. Can you just leave me alone, please?"

He gasped in exasperation. "Isn't it a bit too early for you to be this impossibly and unreasonably temperamental?!" he said sighing. After a long pause, he continued, with resignation in his voice, "All right, all right. Do what you like. I'm off now."

I don't believe you; like that's gonna happen, I thought.

Yet quite bizarrely, I began to hear the rustle of retreating steps, followed by the sound of a door opening and shutting with a slam. Perplexed, I put my ear to the wall, and heard, with disbelief, the unmistakable rumbling of descending footfall through the stairwell. I listened and listened hard to the echoes until they gradually became remote and indistinct.

I opened the bathroom door a crack, quietly observing the silence flooding in with nervous apprehension. As the silence lingered, I took the courage to fling the door open and ventured to step out of the bathroom. If there was someone waiting in ambush, I'd have been struck dead before I even knew it. But not a rat stirred. I teetered down the corridor, peering into the kitchen and the bedroom along the way until I was standing on the threshold of the living room, which was empty like all other rooms. It was then I was assured that I was all alone in the whole place.

With a sigh of relief, I sat slumped in the chair, feeling tired and weak after being locked up in the bathroom for close to an hour. My muscles ached terribly. A queer, complicated pain kept gnawing in my belly. I tried to relax by taking stock of my situation with half-closed eyes, but dozed off inadvertently. I quickly woke up, startled by a sense of many dangers around me. It was at this moment I began to notice the change in the furnishings in the living room. The chair I was sitting on was supposed to be in the centre of the room near the side wall – now I was sitting under the window where I could glimpse the street below with a mere turn of the head. The low table had also been moved to the side of the chair, but the crystal vase and the bunch of flowers had all disappeared. I remembered having heard earlier the disturbing noises of the table being upturned and the vase crashing to the floor. The strange thing was, however, that I couldn't even find a single fragment of the broken vase on the entire floor, which was immaculate as if it had been swept clean.

As I frowned in perplexity, my eyes were attracted by something on the table with a reflective surface. It was a piece of glass. What made it so special was that it had the shape of a five-pointed star, just as Bo Tin Aung described it. It was the clear evidence that an incident such as of vase shattering had actually occurred. I was, however, left bemused about why on earth Bo Tin Aung had taken the piece of glass as a good omen when I had found it to be nothing but a perfect lethal weapon for all its sharp and knifelike points and edges.

Then there was something more intriguing. On the far side of the table I found the box and the test tube which were initially blocked from view by the piece of five-pointed glass. I picked up the tube and tried to see, as a matter of interest, what it said definitively about my crime. In the middle of the tube there was a small window showing what I believed to be the result of the test. Because of my scant knowledge of these things, I had to read the text printed on the outside of the box for the meaning. As far as the result was concerned, it basically said: "*One pink line in the result window – Not Pregnant. Two pink lines in the result window – Pregnant.*"

Now I knew why I deserved to die, because I saw only one pink line in the small window of the tube.

I felt this was so unfair. It seemed as if I had suffered for nothing for all my morning nausea and drowsiness, in addition to my bleeding and abdominal pains. The idea that I, as a young woman, wasn't even able to interpret the signs of her own body, had really exasperated me. In a moment of resentment I tossed the test tube out of the window, wishing never to lay eyes on it again. As it flew away, it hit the iron grating at the window and bounced back to land on the windowsill and sat blinking in the little patch of late afternoon sunlight. Only then did I see something that made me gasp. I thought I saw in the result window of the tube a second line which I had failed to see before. It wasn't a trick of the light, because after I closed and opened my eyes, the line was still there. It was thin and pale in comparison to the first line, and only now visible to the naked eye because of the few weak beams of sunlight that had found their way through the iron grillwork.

Now I was really curious to find out what the existence of two lines – one solid and the other something of a blur - meant. To solve the enigma, I went back to read the text on the box. Below the line "*Two pink lines in the result window – Pregnant*" there were words in smaller print that read:

One line may be lighter than the other.
Appearance of the results may vary but pregnant all the same.

I was stunned. *Pregnant all the same!* The lines in no uncertain terms confirmed something which I had always believed to be true but had not been entirely sure. Overwhelmed by the justness of the finding, I wept, thinking what a shame that Bo Tin Aung had mistrusted my claim and occupied himself with nonsense such as the pregnancy test!

After only a short moment of triumph, I began to sense something seriously amiss in the situation.

On the basis of common sense Bo Tin Aung should be overjoyed by a result which clearly suggested I was pregnant. But he had behaved weirdly. He had barked and whined like a dog, overturning the table and hurling the vase to the floor. He had held up a fragment of the broken vase to the outside light to appraise it and burst out laughing like some dangerous and murderous mad man. How was I supposed to sort out the contradictions in his behaviour?

I couldn't. Dazzled and confused, I was so frustrated that I began to question if there was anything which might have warped my judgment. I looked back, retracing all the weary thoughts that had passed through my mind. Then I shook my head in bewilderment, as I had suddenly become aware that my interpretation of the reality might not be entirely accurate.

For one, I had not been able to see or hear everything clearly owing to my confinement in the bathroom. Moreover, I was horribly intimidated by the pregnancy test. I had become so paranoid that I had misinterpreted every sight and sound as signs of monstrosity. In other words, my nerves were so tightly strung that I had lost my capacity to distinguish right from wrong, true from false, or reality from pure fantasy.

If so, where had I erred?

Maybe... I had misunderstood Bo Tin Aung. Maybe I was wrong to assume he was utterly unhappy, mad and even murderous, whereas he was in reality only behaving with justifiable excitement that had gone somewhat overboard. Maybe... he hadn't been lying at all but genuinely perceived the piece of broken glass as a good omen. And maybe Shit-Lone's congratulations to Bo Tin Aung was not about some corrupt money but a true delight he had felt for his friend upon hearing the news of my pregnancy. Maybe, too, Shit-Lone had really meant to say goodbye to me as he was leaving for Bagan, which I had wrongly construed as a farewell to someone who was about to be executed.

As I reflected along the same logic, it was incredible to find how everything fitted together almost seamlessly.

Now it wasn't odd to me anymore when Bo Tin Aung said, before he left the apartment, "Isn't it a bit too early for you to be this impossibly and unreasonably temperamental?" because he was already comparing my behaviour to that of a pregnant woman.

And what better proof did I need when I was at this very moment not dead but still alive? Wasn't it obvious that Bo Tin Aung was so pleased with the test result that he had stopped thinking about hurting me? More than that, he had even gone ahead to protect me instead, by having the floor thoroughly swept, leaving no miniscule shard behind in case I might walk into the unlit living room in my bare feet like I had just done. This was very considerate of him and I was incredibly touched.

As I continued probing along a similar vein, it appeared that I was getting one pleasant surprise after another. I, of course, wasn't so naïve as to have forgotten that Bo Tin Aung was a dangerous and sinister man. But that was yesterday, wasn't it? In the changed circumstances, he had impressed me as someone who could be gentle, tender and compassionate, and a really nice sympathetic guy who happened to be the father of my child. Besides, there was something uncanny in the latest revelation. As I sat under the window and daydreamed away, I was filled with a strange happiness I could barely contain. A certain blessedness mysteriously burst out of my heart and made me see, as I gazed into the empty dark space before me, that love and forgiveness could arise in every possible way and manner.

From below, down in the street, came the sound of a car being started. The engine, as it warmed up, grunted like a pig. Amazed, I looked out the window and saw a car pulling out in front of the entrance to the building. It was Shit-Lone's dark blue hearse-like Mazda. I guessed it must have been some five to ten minutes since the guys had left the apartment. I didn't know they were sitting inside the car all this time when I was wracking my brains trying to understand what was going on.

The Mazda sped up, but stopped abruptly after twenty yards in the middle of the road. Someone emerged from the door on the driver's side. It was Shit-Lone, but he quickly jumped back inside the car when he heard the loud honking of another vehicle coming from behind. It was a black van, which managed to swerve aside just in time to avoid crashing into the open door of the Mazda, but it was a close call. The Mazda was obviously at fault, but the black van drove off straightaway without stopping to complain. Perhaps the driver didn't feel it worth the trouble, as there was no accident so nobody was to blame. After all, it was on a quiet street with relatively little traffic where people were free to go about their own business anyway they liked, and behaviours such as reckless driving or jaywalking were simply accepted (and ignored) as commonplace, with little or no connection to one another as long as no casualty was caused as a result.

But somewhat absurdly Shit-Lone seemed to think otherwise. He clearly must have decided that the other party was wrong for having given him a shock with the honker. He jumped out of the Mazda to chase after the black van, but gave up soon after he quickly became exhausted by his heroic feat. He stood gasping for breath, and watched helplessly as the black van raced through the intersection a couple of blocks away, beating the traffic lights by a split second before they changed to red, and fast disappeared on the distant highway.

He stomped back to the Mazda. Still angry, he vented his anger on his car with repeated vigorous kicks at the bumper. Bo Tin Aung got out of the car and Shit-Lone at once stopped acting foolishly. The guys had a chat. Shit-Lone, apparently calm again, raised his arm to look at his watch. Bo Tin Aung checked his watch too, muttered something to Shit-Lone, who stood to attention as if he was taking an order. Then Shit-Lone went to the back of the car, opened the boot, and after a couple of seconds shuffling things around, took out a backpack and passed it to Bo Tin Aung who received it in the cradle of his arms like it were a baby.

I was shocked. With a premonition of disaster, I whipped my head around to take a long look across the living room from wall to wall. To my great disbelief, I discovered that my backpack (which I remembered having left in a corner when I returned to the apartment last night) had disappeared. Then I realised, almost with icy cold certainty, that the guys were all set to take down the traffic lights at the junction with the bomb, now!

I was aghast. I didn't expect Bo Tin Aung, who had always tried to keep a distance from the bomb, to be ready at an instant's notice to get personally involved with the final operation. And the incendiary device on which I, out of sheer goodness of heart, as well as a certain womanish sentimentality, had for a split second last night considered changing the trigger mechanism to something less deadly, but never got the chance, was preset at zero time-delay for instantaneous detonation at mere contact with one of the several pressure points.

I felt so sick that my blood turned cold and my heart was about to stop beating. This was not exactly the contingency for which I had planned. It was almost as if Fate was playing a trick on me, when only a moment ago I was beginning to marvel at the possibility of mercy and forgiveness arising like a divine illumination of hope, the next moment I was already finding myself staring into the most appalling abyss I could ever imagine!

"No!" I hung over the windowsill and screamed hysterically into the street below. The guys were in the car and didn't hear me. Had the window not been mounted with iron grillwork, I'd have gone for a deadly plunge from a five-storey height just to catch their attention and alert them to the danger.

In the late evening the sky dimmed like curtains drawn across a stage, darkening the street below in the bleak, dismal air. The Mazda, its outline becoming fuzzy and faint, sat quietly in the middle of the road like the carcass of a large insect. When I wondered why it wasn't leaving yet, it suddenly dawned on me that there would still be a chance to warn them off if I started running down to the street now.

I jumped to my feet and began to search for my shoes on the floor. Then I heard the sound of an engine clicking and motors revving up. I took a peep outside at the street below. The Mazda was quivering as if it was shaking off a cold. Its lights began to turn on – first the headlights, then the back lights, shedding four short beams of a cheap yellow colour around. Huffing and puffing like a sick old man, it, however, continued to linger. I knew I must hurry up or it would be too late, and I decided to forget about the shoes and dashed straight for the door in bare feet.

With great urgency I rushed through the unlit corridor to the door, grabbed the doorknob, turned it and pushed open the door with only the simple thought of getting out. As the door began to open, I was suddenly seized by a great fear when I remembered that during my whole stay in the apartment Bo Tin Aung had never once left home without locking me inside with a large padlock.

Just as expected, the door opened only a few inches before it stopped going any further as if tethered to a chain outside. With a sense of foredoomed futility, I half-heartedly gave the door another push, almost as a gesture of surrender. To my amazement, the door sprang wide open without resistance. I took a step out, and discovered the door had neither been fastened by a chain nor a padlock. But there were, in reality, a chain and a padlock lying quietly in a corner near the staircase. I was baffled, but only temporarily, as I quickly understood it was because Bo Tin Aung no longer saw me as a captive. Once my pregnancy had been proved beyond doubt he had bestowed me with a trust that was total and unconditional. At last, after four months, three weeks and three days, I was free! I was so emotional that I collapsed on the floor and wept, accusing myself of completely missing the better side of the man for so long in the past. *I must save him!* I thought.

I raced down the flight of stairs to get out to the street, only to find the Mazda had already gone. It might not have left long ago, as I saw a car, similar in size and colour to the Mazda, about fifty yards ahead, turning a bend. Immediately I started running after it.

"Stop! Wait for me! Stop!" I shouted after the car as loud as I could bawl.

Now I was really sorry not to have put on my shoes because the treacherous road surface, rough and deeply rutted by the rain, made it impossible for me to run faster than I wished.

By the time I got round the bend, there was no sight of the car I thought was the Mazda. I gazed up the intersection of roads some blocks away; my eyes took in nothing but one vast space of blinding blaze of traffic lights, bouncing madly in all directions across the evening sky which was sinking rapidly from gloom to deeper gloom. I stood transfixed, feeling a profound sense of awe with the foreboding that something terrible was about to occur.

Then, without any warning whatsoever, a large explosion thundered, making the ground tremble beneath my feet. A cloud of black smoke shot heavenwards, casting a pall over the already darkened sky. To my stupefied astonishment, I saw a car, out of the many cars at the intersection, was on fire.

There was a buzz of excitement around me, with people running in horror and wailing in dismay. It was at this very moment I was suddenly aware, in the midst of a bedlam of horrid noises, of a peculiar sound that seemed to be coming from behind me. As the sound lingered it became a sharp urgent screech. Startled, I turned and saw a small dark-coloured car driving straight towards me. In a short time it had become so close that I could almost see the convulsed face of the driver who was trying desperately to control the car from crashing into me. His mouth was wide open, shouting, "Jump! Jump!"

And I jumped, like a cat, as quick and as agile. Yet it was still a second too late and I was hit. My body was sent somersaulting through the air, and landed moments later in a splash on the pavement.

I thought I was still conscious when I saw the car slither to a halt after having knocked me down. The driver, a white-haired old man, hopped out of the car and rushed over to check on me, shouting, "What's the matter with you standing in the middle of the road? Are you insane?"

I thought he was blaming the accident on me. I didn't want to argue with him. I was full of pain and couldn't quite speak. People began to gather around me. I struggled to get up but someone was holding me to comfort me. It was a lady wearing a white shirt and a red longyi. She said, "Don't move. I'm a nurse and I'm here to help you…"

The old driver asked me again, "Are you okay?"

"Can you keep your mouth shut?" snapped the nurse. "I think you were driving too fast. You're so careless."

"I don't know if I was to blame," the old man tried to explain. "I am at a loss to know what happened. When I came round the bend, I heard the sound of a loud explosion that gave me a big shock. Then I saw this girl standing in front of my car in the middle of the road. I slammed on the brakes and cried out to her to get out of the way. But, after everything is said and done, I still couldn't avoid knocking her down. I'm sorry."

The nurse said, "If you're really sorry, go and get an ambulance…" Then she quickly added, "But you've reminded me, we might not get one anytime soon because of the explosion. If so, how can we help this poor girl now?"

The old man said, in an apologetic tone, "Do you think you can use my car to take her to the hospital?"

The nurse seemed to think it was the only option available and agreed.

With the help of passers-by, I was lifted from the floor and carried into the car. Being moved exacerbated my condition, making me groan with pain. It was a small car and there was not enough room in the back for me to fully stretch out, and I was laid on the seat with my head resting on the lap of the nurse who kept telling me to keep my eyes open.

The car drove off, moving haltingly through the crowd. A swarm of people looked at me through the window with curious interest as if they were looking at a corpse encased in a see-through casket. I was falling in and out of consciousness. At a certain point when I opened my eyes and didn't see the crowd of dark faces, only heavy black smoke billowing in the air, I asked the nurse where we were.

"We've just passed the intersection where there was an explosion," she replied.

Completely awake all of a sudden, I said to the nurse, "Can you help me sit up for a look?"

"Shh, don't speak," she said. "It's just an explosion. What has it to do with you?"

"Everything," I muttered.

Perhaps she didn't hear me. Even if she did, she might think I was only talking gibberish in my stricken state. I cried and begged her. "Would you help me if it were my last wish before I die?"

The nurse said, "Don't be stupid. You're not going to die."

But, as if she was not sure whether I was going to live or die, she changed her mind. With a sigh, she said, "Just one look, if you insist." Then she kindly and very softly propped my head up so that I could peer out through the rear window.

It was night. Sirens wailing in the air. A fire engine had arrived with fire fighters beginning to combat the roaring blaze at the intersection, where a car was burning with the traffic lights toppled on its roof. The white brilliancy of the blaze was dazzling to the eyes. The crowd at the intersection, like lunatics on the loose dancing around a bonfire, obstructed my view with their bodies fluttering like weeds in the wind. I couldn't say for certain that the car in flames was the Mazda. Nevertheless I was sure it was the Mazda I had tried in vain to chase down, because there was something spooky about its appearance, something which was hearse-like despite its body now being a mass of charred, smoking remains in the heat of the crucible. I closed my eyes when I was absolutely exhausted with fatigue and emotion. But with a mighty effort, I opened my eyes again for one last look through the rear window of the departing car at a view which was fast-diminishing like a light at the end of a tunnel. Then I murmured a sad goodbye and closed my eyes permanently.

"Wake up! Stay with me!"

I heard the nurse scream at me. I tried to search for her face but couldn't quite locate it because it was dark. I thought there had been this tiny light at the end of the tunnel, which must have now become extinguished like a candle snuffed out by the wind. There was darkness everywhere, filling up all the space inside and outside the car. I didn't know how a darkness could be this dark; it was darker than darkness itself and not of the night. But it didn't take long for me to figure it out, with a rare clarity which I believe only comes to someone who is dying, that the end was nigh. Knowing it useless to resist what appeared to be my impending doom, I let myself go and passed out into perfect unconsciousness.

2 3

M.A.Y.A.

—⦿—

Someone once told me, with death, your soul is no longer bound to your body – it's liberated and free, leaving your body, which is none of your business anymore, behind to rot. If so, why was I still feeling horribly trapped inside some sort of a cocoon with all this excruciating pain?

"Hello."

A voice entered the cocoon through a crack. There was also a small white light seeping in.

"You're waking up," said the voice. "Now open your eyes."

The cocoon expanded as more light entered until it suddenly burst like a large bubble. I opened my eyes and saw the long face of a middle-aged woman hovering above me.

"Good girl. Now take a moment to focus," she said. "Tell me if you recognise me."

Her voice sounded remotely familiar. She was wearing a white shirt with a red-coloured band in her hair. I guessed she was a nurse, but couldn't quite place her when my memory was blank. I asked, "Where am I?"

"Rangoon General Hospital. I'm the senior nurse, Ma Htat Htat," she replied. "Do you remember nothing of me?"

"…"

"That's fine," she said. "But do you think you can answer a few questions for me?"

I nodded. "I'll try," I said in a weak voice.

"Can you tell me your name?"

"Maya."

"Just Maya?" she said, amused. "That's not enough, but okay for the time being. And how old are you?"

"Sixteen."

"Only sixteen! Just as I thought," she said, shaking her head. "Can you tell me something about your parents?"

I didn't know what to say, and I wasn't pretending in my state of mind.

"That's all right," she said softly. "You're still under the after-effect of anesthesia, which will be completely gone in a few hours. Now as you've woken up, I'll get someone to help you with water and perhaps a little food. I've got something to tell you, but not before your mind is lucid. I'll come back later… to give you more details about your condition. But don't worry. There's nothing too bad except the need to know."

She was gone, and I was left to chew her words of mystery. "The need to know? What is that supposed to mean…?"

As time went on I slowly regained some of my lost memory. By the end of the day I was able to remember I had been involved in a traffic accident, and Ma Htat Htat, who had a long face and a kind voice, was the nurse who had helped me at the scene of the accident.

The nurse said something about anesthetics, which made me worry I might have lost a limb. I reached for my legs, and found them still there to my huge relief, though the left leg was heavily bandaged below the knee. I had the feeling that there was more to the traffic accident, but failed to glean anything more from a pool of jumbled reminiscences as my mind was still affected by the remnants of anesthetic. Then exhaustion settled in and I went back to sleep.

It was in the middle of the night that I woke up with a start. Another scene prior to my accident popped up in my mind with extreme clarity. It was a Mazda burning at the road intersection, with traffic lights toppled on its roof. As if the sequence of events was now triggered, I was able to reconstruct in my mind the recent past and remembered, as a result, that Bo Tin Aung and Shit-Lone had died in the explosion. But curiously, their deaths, dramatic and weird as I recalled, were not a cause for sadness. It was as though I was only looking at things from a long distance in a cold and unemotional manner.

Ma Htat Htat turned up at nine o'clock in the morning. She checked my medical records and told me that I was making good progress. I couldn't wait to ask her, "Is it about my leg that you have something to say to me?"

She pulled up a chair to sit down beside my bed. She said, "Your leg is the least of our concerns. Yes, it was broken. But the X-ray has revealed only a minor fracture which is not as bad as originally feared. Our team of doctors has already fixed it with an operation. The head doctor said it would take around six to eight weeks to heal, and in three months you should be able to walk like a normal person again."

Her account of my injury gave me only minor comfort, and I asked, "If my leg is the least of your concerns, what else must I worry about now?"

She hesitated for a moment as if she didn't know where to begin. She held my hand, and said, "Something unfortunate happened after we operated on your leg. The procedure was considered a success, but two hours later, you were found to be bleeding profusely. It was then we checked and discovered that you were pregnant. We probably would have done something differently should we have known about it before the operation…"

"So what happened?" I pursued.

"You had a miscarriage, and you have lost your baby," she answered, dropping her eyes. "We're terribly sorry."

In the ordinary circumstances, the news should come as tragic and sad. But I was curiously unruffled, and I even remarked, to my own surprise, "That's okay, that's quite okay."

"That's not okay," said Ma Htat Htat uneasily. "In my opinion, it is very unfortunate. I don't think you should suppress your emotions. Let it out, it's good for your health."

I was baffled. "Is there something wrong with my health?" I asked.

"No, no! That's not what I meant," she said, and hastened to clarify, "You should have nothing to worry about. In your case, which has been made complicated by the operation on your leg, a D&C is recommended after you have a miscarriage."

"D&C?"

"Dilation and curettage. It is a surgical procedure performed to stop bleeding and prevent infection, by removing any remaining tissue from the uterus," she explained.

I hoped she could be less technical. "Does it mean I'm all clean after the D&C?" I asked, just to be absolutely clear.

"If by being all clean, you mean that there isn't a teeny tiny bit of the fetal tissue left inside your body, the answer is yes," answered Ma Htat Htat carefully. "I know, of course, this is not entirely consoling…"

"No," I said. "I think this is good news, isn't it?"

The nurse looked at me incomprehensibly and asked, "Are you not sad?"

"Why should I be?" I asked back.

"I don't think I understand you…" she sighed, with a frown. After a thoughtful moment, she said, "Perhaps I should give you time to… get over the unpleasant news. We'll talk again tomorrow."

She must have thought, after she left, that I'd bury myself under the blankets and cry my eyes out. That was, however, not going to happen. On the contrary I seemed obscurely gratified. I was already enjoying huge relief remembering Bo Tin Aung was dead and had stopped being a threat. My joy, if I was permitted to describe my feeling as such, was enhanced by the news of the miscarriage, which had the effect of uplifting my mind and lightening my spirit. What was so great about it was not only had the monster (who I thought I loved when I was not of sound mind) been killed, but its evil seed had also been completely eradicated from my system. I felt elated, almost in perfect bliss knowing my ordeal was at long last over.

Ma Htat Htat was determined to get to the bottom of the affair when she came to see me for a third time, and she started by saying, "I hate to intrude in your privacy, but I think you need help. Perhaps you can tell me something about the father of the child."

"He was a military officer, the Tatmadaw," I replied, with gritted teeth.

Ma Htat Htat stiffened in an instant, and asked, with her face all pursed up, "Was it rape?"

I nodded. Suddenly I became so emotional that I burst into tears.

Her eyes went red. She said, "I could certainly share your pain with a similar experience. I was about thirteen at the time, playing in the woods. Some soldiers who said they had lost their way asked me to guide them through the forest. And I was gang-raped."

Her revelation made me speechless. I was amazed how she could speak with such calmness about a turbulent episode in her past.

Putting on a bitter smile, she added, "Fortunately, as a member of the ethnic minority, I was brought up with a stoical frame of mind. Unembittered, I was able to persuade myself to think of what happened to me as only one of those rites-of-passage moments in the age of persecution. I was actually quite pleased with myself that I was unbroken by the atrocity, or I wouldn't be able to pursue a career as a nurse." She concluded by saying, "It's important that you are strong and don't give up."

"I won't," I said.

"But forgive me if I'm wrong," she said. "On the day of the accident, I wonder if you were trying to kill yourself by standing in the middle of the road."

Now I understood why she was telling me to be strong. "That's not it," I explained. "I stopped short in the middle of the road because there was this explosion at the road intersection. I was then hit from behind by a car. I didn't try to kill myself. It was an accident."

Wearing a perplexed and troubled expression, she said, in a low, almost conspiratorial voice, "Two men died in the explosion. One of them was a military officer, a Tatmadaw. Is there a connection?"

I flinched a bit, and was so nervous that I didn't know what to say, except to ask back, in a shaky voice, "Is that what the newspapers said about the men who died...?"

"No. The incident was not reported in the newspapers. I only learned about it during a morning briefing session where we nurses were told that two men, wounded in an explosion, were certified dead before arrival at our hospital."

I gasped and sobbed. Although I was sure they didn't stand a chance with that kind of bomb, I still felt shocked when the deaths were confirmed.

Ma Htat Htat pressed, in the same low and conspiratorial voice, "Tell me. Is there a connection?"

Still unsure if I could trust her with the disclosure of things which only I knew, I shook my head.

"It doesn't help you by keeping things from me because I'm the only one who can help you now," she said.

"Help me? Why?" I said. "Do you mean I'm in danger?"

"Well, you decide. You just hear me out first," she said. "During the daily briefing I mentioned earlier, a guy who claimed to belong to the Military Intelligence was also present. He confirmed to us the identities of the men who died in the explosion. One was a military officer and the other a city councillor. The guy, as the investigative officer of the accident, asked us to provide information about people who happened to show up at our hospital after the explosion for medical treatment. He wants names, nature of sickness or injuries, and in the case of injuries, the what, when and where. He said he would like to interview the patients immediately once they are identified."

Now I began to realise the gravity of the situation, and I asked, "Where's the guy now? Is he waiting outside to interview me?"

"Don't worry," replied Ma Htat Htat. "The guy doesn't know you are here. In Rangoon General Hospital, we take great pains to protect the privacy of our patients. It is not only a matter of moral respect in our profession, but also because we have a responsibility to protect vulnerable people like women at risk, or minors in crisis situations."

"Does it mean I'm still… safe here?" I asked, apprehensively.

"Only temporarily," she said. "You know those people have planted eyes and ears in the hospital and I don't know how long I can keep them from finding out about you."

"What should I do now? Run?" I blurted out almost without thinking.

"My child, what are you talking about?" the nurse said briskly but kindly. "Why run, if you haven't done anything too outrageous?"

My face went white in an instant. Why had I said something like that? Might it be that Ma Htat Htat had impressed me as somebody who was trustworthy, causing me a slip of tongue? Given the severity of the circumstances, I felt it might be the time to be more forthcoming with her. And I said, "What if I had done something exceptionally outrageous?"

"You choose how much you can tell me," she said. "I only need to know why I should help you as well as how I can help you."

I said, just to begin with, "I was connected to the military officer who died in the explosion."

"Connected?" she said. "In the sense that the military officer who died in the explosion was the same man who raped you?"

I nodded. "Not only was I raped, I was also abducted and locked up in his apartment."

"You're the victim," she said. "Maybe you don't have to run."

"But there's more to it," I continued. "What if I also tell you that I had something to do with the bomb that killed the men in the car explosion?"

She was wide-eyed. "I thought it was only a car explosion. I didn't realise a bomb was involved. And what do you mean you have something to do with the bomb?"

I knew it was no use beating about the bush, and told her, "I'm a specialist in explosives. I can make a variety of bombs if you ask me…"

She cut me short before I could finish. "You mean you have killed them… with a bomb you made?"

"I didn't make the bomb, I only gave it the finishing touches…" I said, trying to be accurate.

"… but you planted the bomb in the car which eventually killed them?"

"No, no, no! That's not true," I cried. "It was the guys who took the bomb with them in the car. As soon as I knew it, I immediately ran after them to try to save them."

"First you wanted to kill them, then you tried to save them?" she said, looking confused. "I think you're directly contradicting yourself, my girl!"

"It's complicated," I sighed. "Listen, please try to understand now I'm not the same person who was raped, abducted and deprived of freedom of movement for a period of several months. I was then, as if possessed, couldn't think straight or clearly. Aside from physical abuses on a daily basis I was also made to become part of a conspiracy. Because of my knowledge in explosives, they involved me in the production of bombs which were the same bombs used in the recent terror attacks in Rangoon…"

She gave out a little gasp, shaking her head incredulously.

"You might think I shouldn't have done those things, but I didn't have a choice. Under the circumstances I would do anything just to survive, even if I had to kill those men," I said. "I did have a little plan to destroy them before they could destroy me. But I changed my mind… after I suspected that I was pregnant."

"You mean you weren't sure that you were pregnant…"

"Just think of it, I'm only sixteen! I don't have people to ask about things like that. I lost my mother to a landmine in Shan when I was only twelve." I broke down and cried. "… and I had never been with a man before I was raped…"

"That's okay, that's okay." She held me in her arms to console me.

I wiped my tears and continued, "I guess it must be something to do with my pregnancy that around that time I took on a different view of the world. And the man who had raped me, tortured me and forcibly confined me to his apartment had turned from an ugly toad into a handsome prince in the process, a good Tatmadaw…"

"Silly girl!" she uttered.

"I know," I said. "On that evening, it was when I suddenly become aware the guys were carrying with them the bomb which contained a deadly feature they knew nothing about, I started a mad pursuit of their car trying to alert them to the danger. But before I could find them I was myself hit by a car from behind."

"I'm sorry," she said.

"Sorry? I don't think that is at all necessary," I said. "Since I woke up from my operation, and thanks to whatever your medical team has done cleaning out my system, I have become, in a sense, sober and sane again. I am no longer the same stupid sentimental cow under the influence of some basic biological instinct…"

"But didn't you at least feel sad for the people who died…?" the nurse asked.

"Of course I did, I'm not that insensitive, as I'm, after all, only human. I felt remorseful and little comfort in what happened," I said. "But please don't get me wrong. It is not my conscience. My conscience is clear. You know why? Those guys… they belong to the vilest scum on earth who are capable of the most horrific crimes imaginable."

"What sort of crimes are you talking about?" she asked.

"Murder, rape, torture, sexual enslavement, you name it!" I said.

She winced slightly. "These are very serious crimes. But speaking from my own experience, I agree with you that these people are more than capable of committing such crimes," she mused, adding, after a pause, "In that regard, I think divine justice has played a hand in the scheme of things. Perhaps it was why the guys could not be saved eventually."

"Why?"

In a solemn and serious voice she said, "Both of us are victims of rape. But ours are not individual cases. We have a military we don't quite recognise, a military which is supposed to protect people who live in their country, but instead they murder them, enslave them and persecute them, transforming their homeland from a haven into a killing field. I have heard tons of stories of how rape, torture and murder have been conducted systematically on a widespread scale on people of different ethnicities, cultures and religions in the country. In the international community, these crimes are called crimes against humanity."

"Crimes... against... humanity?"

"That's right. Merciless, ruthless and cold-blooded crimes like murder, rape, torture, sexual enslavement aimed across a community or communities, they are crimes against humanity," she said. "As such, who could blame you even if you had killed those men? Conversely, even though you failed to save them, you might have in effect saved the lives of many innocent people in the future."

Now I thought I understood. "I told you I'm an explosives specialist. I have been engaged in anti-junta activities. People who don't understand us in the resistance think of us as terrorists. Although I make bombs, I'm not a terrorist," I said. "As you have put it very well, what I do, at best, is aim to save as many lives of innocent people as possible, now and in the future. I can promise you that I'll carry on doing it as long as I'm capable."

She smiled. It was an ambiguous smile, something between merciful and sad.

"You're a very special girl. I'm sorry to have greatly underestimated you from the beginning," she said. "We both are in a sense in the same business of saving the lives of people, but your work takes a lot of guts and courage to accomplish, not to mention the risk to your own life. You have my great admiration. I must help you because our country needs more righteous and fearless people like you."

The next day Ma Htat Htat immediately embarked upon a plan to save me. She changed my records by re-registering me as a new patient. I was also transferred to another ward in order to bury traces that could lead to my existence. But the arrangement was not perfect. For my safety I was switched around the wards a couple of times in a matter of two weeks. At a certain point when Ma Htat Htat had strong reasons to be highly alarmed, I was even placed inside the Intensive Care Ward where visits from outsiders were strictly forbidden.

I knew I was on borrowed time. Ma Htat Hhat, and some doctors and nurses as well, were putting their careers on the line for the sake of me. I knew I had to leave the hospital as soon as possible.

It was always in my knowledge that there was an underground support network formed by ordinary people who were no combatants but instead providers of support like food or safe houses to combatants risking their lives in the field. As soon as I received my first assignment for the resistance, Ahba had described to me in detail the method of contact in times of crisis. I was also reminded of the protocol in an emergency by Uncle Kloh when we worked together on the *Tatmadaw Dei* bombing. After I was kidnapped on Dala beach, I never found the opportunity to get in touch with the network. But now the time had come.

One early morning when the Rangoon sky was dark and heavy, and when most of the city dwellers were yet to wake up from their dreams or be jolted out of nightmares, I was wheeled to the rear entrance of the hospital by Ma Htat Htat and put in a taxi waiting there.

"Where should I tell the driver to take you?" asked Ma Htat Htat.

"I'll tell the driver myself," I replied. "It is better you don't know anything about it. After I'm gone, you should forget me as if I had never existed."

She sighed. "Perhaps you're right. But I'll never forget you, as you will always be in my thoughts and prayers." She kissed me on the cheek and strode away.

The driver, a thin man in his late thirties, said, his eyes following the shadow of Ma Htat Htat, "That nurse is an angel. Last year I had an accident, got hit on the head in the midst of a quarrel and a fight. I lost consciousness, and lay in a coma for seven weeks. It was the darkest time of my life, as after I woke up later, I had completely forgotten my identity and lost all presence of mind. I was, however, lucky to have met the nurse. Under her care, I gradually recovered my health, and most importantly, my shitty memory. I'm so grateful to her that I could never repay her enough. She has asked me to be your driver. It's my honour to serve you. My name is Sam. You can trust me, and please tell me where to take you."

He was speaking so fast that his words were like bullets fired from a machine gun. Ma Htat Htat had told me that the driver was someone I could trust, so long as I remembered he had been a patient in a psychiatric ward for over a year. Bearing that in mind, I told him to take me to the Thiri Mingalar Zay Market. And Sam, as it turned out, appeared to be no less normal than the ordinary people thronging the streets. During the journey he didn't talk much but kept a constant big smile on his emaciated face. So on arriving at the flower market, I decided to entrust him with another task. I asked him to buy me some bananas, then thanked him nicely for his service, paid him and let him go.

At daybreak the market was already running at full steam as evident by the rush of vendors, the movement of vans and lorries, and hordes of buyers and sellers pouring towards the different avenues of ingress. I was overwhelmed and at a loss as to who to look for and where to look in the midst of the bustle and confusion.

With a weary heart and foreboding dread, I leaned heavily on my crutches and trudged my way through the dense crowd into the marketplace. Then I remembered the protocol. I found a corner at the end of a long damp wall and settled down, placing the bananas around me in the shape of little crosses. Some people took me for a beggar and dropped coins in my lap. I thanked them, but money was the last thing I needed right now. As I waited, an hour went by, and nothing worth mentioning occurred except someone paused to talk to me. But he was nobody in particular, he was just being sympathetic.

At five minutes before noon, a little girl came to stand before me with her hands hiding behind her back. I asked her what she wanted. She showed me what she was hiding, which was a bouquet of red, yellow and blue flowers. Astounded, I thought I had seen the first sign of contact. The little girl pointed to a sloped driveway leading to an upper floor where I could see the back of a large, plump woman. The woman slowly turned to face me, and after a furtive glance around the surroundings, she approached me. Squatting before me, she asked, "What do you want?"

I frowned, because this was not the standard protocol. I said, "I beg your pardon?"

She swallowed hard, looking perplexed. She searched in her pocket, found a little piece of crumpled paper, and opened it to read. "Sorry," she said, somewhat embarrassed, "I think I should have asked you: What happened in Rangoon?"

Bingo! This is it! I thought. And I duly replied, "Rangoon is burning," and repeated, "Rangoon is burning."

She smiled in relief. "Now I think I can ask you again: What do you want?"

I motioned her attention to my bandaged leg and the crutches lying on the side. I said, "I have broken my leg. It will take me a month or two to be able to walk again. I'd be grateful to know if there's some such place I can sleep and rest to nurse my injury…"

"That's enough, I understand," she said. She quickly stood up to go and I was dumbfounded by the seeming unhelpfulness. She said she would come back but I never saw her again.

An hour later, it was the little girl who had made the first contact who reappeared instead. There were a man and a woman with her. The man, who was short with cropped hair, introduced himself as Ko Mun, and the woman, younger and with tiny, delicate eyes, as his wife.

Ko Mun said, "Don't worry. You're in good hands. Dr Rice sent us, and we're taking you out of Rangoon."

The protocol, as I understood it, required me to make no comment. I therefore simply kept a blank face. But the couple, who might not have taken the protocol with the same seriousness, found my silence awkward and repeated what they had already said.

I knew a little flexibility was useful in the situation and I said, "Thanks. I know it'll take some time getting there. And I'm with you." I smiled a trusting smile, and they smiled back. Once the connection was firmly established with a special rapport, I knew I was finally on the way to checking out of a city filled with danger and strife.

I WENT INTO HIDING, MY secret refuge being a disused warehouse in the countryside. I lived on a weekly provision of food from a basket passed down into the basement at night, by someone whose face I never saw, nor heard making a sound during my entire stay.

There was no human contact to speak of, which I understood was necessary for the protection and safety of all the people involved. Without newspapers to read nor radio to listen to, I was literally cut off from the outside world. But I was contented, knowing I had come here to rest and remain, after the tumult and turmoil of my days wandering the streets of Rangoon, until I had recuperated my health and strength.

My convalescence was not quite as speedy as I had expected it to be. It dragged on from month to month and I was bored to death by the dull monotony of the idle hours, interrupted only by the nocturnal visits of rats. But as time wore on, the state of my injured leg began to show signs of improvement. A month later I could move around without the help of crutches. Finally, after a hundred days holed up in the warehouse, my recovery was certain and complete. It was also time to rejoin the world I had left behind.

As I finally departed, emerging from the seclusion of my hideaway onto a dirty cow-path, I thought, with an agitated heart at what I saw and felt – the scorching sun, the oppressive heat, the dust and smoke, the blight on tumbling walls and dying trees, and on the blowing wind the awful smell of animal decomposition and human decay – that I was merely returning to the dreariness and ruin of the old world which I had always known.

But I was wrong, as I was soon to discover; the world had undergone some considerable changes during my absence.

The one change that was pretty radical was the arrival of a new government. New, but not a lot different, as some joked, when the old government had only seemed to transform into a different animal but still very much a beast. The rise of a new dynasty had come after the incumbent Prime Minister was removed from his position and placed under house arrest on allegations of corruption. A new cabinet was sworn in. As part of the reshuffle, the former Secretary One moved one notch up the hierarchy to fill the vacant position left by the disgraced Prime Minister, and the former Secretary Two was promoted accordingly to become Secretary One.

In an effort to uproot the power base of the ousted Prime Minister, a government spokesman announced on radio the abolition of the National Intelligence Bureau (NIB) Law because "it did not serve the interests of the general public". In addition, the NIB – a state intelligence apparatus overseeing all aspects of political control of civilians – was disbanded. Following the dissolution of the NIB, three hundred Military Intelligence personnel were arrested, of which forty senior officials were later sentenced to prison terms ranging from twenty to over 150 years.

The general public, initially suspicious of the new government and a trifle sceptical as to its sincerity, was impressed. They wondered if something in the spirit of glasnost in Europe was happening in the country. But that was too much to ask. The junta, instead, in a gesture widely considered as a step toward national reconciliation, had begun releasing prisoners who had been wrongly charged by the NIB and whose detention had been ruled improper. As a result, more than 20,000 prisoners were freed.

Uncle Kloh was among the early batches of the released. Suffering from poor health caused by the inhumane living conditions in prison and inadequate medical care, he didn't make it on the outside very long. He died of lung and heart problems before the end of the year.

With the change in political climate, Ahba had also come out of hiding and returned to Rangoon at the end of the Buddhist Lent. He was wearing a monk's habit and had a shaved head when he showed up at the doorstep. I wondered if he was only dressing the part.

He answered no; he said he felt deep remorse for the people killed in the Mandalay Market explosion, so he became a monk. He also explained that practically, the environment of a monastery had afforded the much-needed shelter and protection to a fugitive.

I asked if he was now a full-time monk.

No, he said; he was still a full-time revolutionary.

His reply made me feel extremely uneasy when I worried that he'd be going away again to hide behind some monastery. To set my mind at ease, he confided in me what Dr Rice told him. According to reliable sources in the government, since the disbanding of NIB, investigations of the Mandalay Marketplace explosion and the Rangoon *Tatmadaw Dei* bombing had been put on hold, not to be reopened, considering some of the military officers who were suspected to be involved were either dead or imprisoned.

So we were safe, I thought, after months enduring fear, torture and separation. Ahba said, wrapping me in his arms, "Let's put aside our troubles, the *Thadingyut* Festival is here."

The *Thadingyut* Festival or the Festival of Light is held at the end of Buddhist Lent on the full moon day of the lunar month of *Thadingyut*. People celebrate the festival, lasting for three public holidays, throughout the country. But I was in no mood to celebrate. I stayed mostly indoors. There were certain parts of the city I wanted to avoid, where there were shopping centres, public buildings and pagodas festooned with lights of many shapes and colours for the celebration. I could not bear the sight of homes lit with paper lanterns and the boisterous outdoor performances when my own family was broken beyond repair with the departure of Ahmay. In my dark mood the *Thadingyut* full moon day was destined to be sad and miserable.

However, something unexpected occurred on the last day of the festival, which swung my mood. My twin sister, Meena, who was supposed to be studying music for a year in Bagan, had returned home to our surprise. Her teacher, the great music maestro, had suffered a sudden devastating stroke and passed away a few days shy of his eightieth birthday; and his death had ironically made it possible for our family reunion. At last I was able to feel less unhappy, almost glad, and celebrated the festival with a sense of distraction from the bereavement in our life and sufferings of the lives of others.

And the world moved on, unstoppably, with the coming and going of people, and events causing shock and surprise with big news headlines. In a sense nothing stays where it is and nothing stands still. But none of it mattered much in a poverty-stricken country and with a military regime which had remained hopelessly the same. The policy of the new government had not translated into anything fruitful, whether it was national reconciliation or political progress in the form of a new constitution and an open and fair election. Had there been a political thaw (as some believed there was) giving the population a glimmer of hope of gradual progress to an end of military dictatorship and return to democracy, it was extremely short-lived. The old NIB might have been disbanded, but the new personnel entrusted with the task of military intelligence saw no reason why they should be doing things any different from the past. People continued to be subject to intimidation, interrogation and arbitrary detention for any act or opinion determined to be an expression of political dissent.

Hence I went back to my line of work.

I had turned seventeen. A year before I had been an unripe green apple; now I had mellowed, maturing from an innocent girl into a young woman through experiences which were both painful and unforgettable. Shortly after our family reunion, I was roaming the streets of Rangoon again, sometimes with Ahba, sometimes on my own, in covert operations that utilised primarily the sound and fury of incendiary devices, as a means to remind the country and its people that we in the resistance would not stop fighting the brutal regime until we had succeeded. Because we had a dream, a shining and unperishable dream of liberty, justice and self-determination, which we firmly believed would become true in some reasonable, if not too distant, future.

END OF BOOK ONE

ABOUT THE AUTHOR

MA'ON SHAN. A full-time human being. A half-serious poet, and a self-important novelist. A Mancunian for his love of the city and the football teams. Currently he lives in Hong Kong.